Praise for Josh Bazell's

Also by Josh Bazell

Beat the Reaper

WILD THING

A NOVEL

JOSH BAZELL

A REAGAN ARTHUR BOOK

LITTLE, BROWN AND COMPANY

NEW YORK BOSTON LONDON

Reagan Arthur Books / Little, Brown and Company
Hachette Book Group
237 Park Avenue, New York, NY 10017
www.hachettebookgroup.com

The publisher is not responsible for websites (or their content) that are not owned by the publisher.

The author is submitting a portion of his proceeds from the book to Partners in Health.

Illustrations by Sam Zanger

Printed in the United States of America

Originally published in hardcover by Reagan Arthur Books / Little, Brown and Company, February 2012
First Reagan Arthur / Little, Brown and Company international mass market edition, March 2012

10 9 8 7 6 5 4 3 2 1

FOR TXELL

The human understanding is not composed of dry light, but is subject to influence from the will and the emotions, a fact that creates fanciful knowledge; man prefers to believe what he wants to be true.
—Francis Bacon, *Aphorisms Concerning the Interpretation of Nature, and the Kingdom of Man*, Dryden translation

But I wanna know for sure.
—Chip Taylor, "Wild Thing"

PROLOGUE

EXHIBIT A

Autumn Semmel feels Benjy Schneke's fingertip trace the top of her thigh, along the lower front hem of her boy shorts toward her pussy. It causes her skin to tighten all the way to her nipples and her pussy to unclench like a fist. She opens her eyes. Says "Stop that shit!"

"Why?" Benjy says.

She nods over her shoulder. "Because Megan and Ryan are right *there*."

Autumn and Benjy are lying on the White Lake side of the spit of land, mostly roots, that separates White Lake from Lake Garner. Megan Gotchnik and Ryan Crisel are out on Lake Garner, behind them.

Benjy says "So? I'm not touching anything that's covered."

"I know what you're doing. You're driving me crazy."

Autumn stands up, stretching down the edges of her bottoms. Looks behind her.

Megan and Ryan are in their canoe, twenty or thirty yards from shore. Megan's legs are over the sides. Ryan's going down on her. Because of the way sound carries over the water, Autumn can hear Megan's panting as if it's right in front of her. It makes Autumn feel dizzy. She turns back to White Lake.

It's like going from one season to another. Lake Garner is a broad oval under the east–west sun. White Lake is at the bottom of a jagged canyon that runs north from Lake Garner's eastern end. The water in White Lake is black, cold, and choppy.

It's magic. Autumn dives in.

She's alert to everything instantly. She can't see, but she can feel her ribcage, her scalp, the tops of her feet. Her arms are slippery against the sides of her breasts, from sunblock or some property of the water. It's like she's ghosting through onyx.

When she's gone a dozen strokes she feels Benjy hit the water behind her. She swims faster, not wanting him to catch up to her and grab her feet. She hates that: it's too scary. As soon as she surfaces for air she turns around.

She can feel the chill breeze on her face. The chop has eaten up her wake. She can't see Benjy at all.

A thrill of dread runs up her right leg and into her stomach at the thought of him coming toward her under water, and she kicks out.

It gives her an idea. She swims in the direction of the western shore. If she can't see Benjy, he can't see her either. So if she's not where he thinks she is, he can't grab her.

It still feels like he's going to, though. She keeps instinctively jerking her legs up, one at a time.

But as the seconds go by, it becomes more and more obvious that Benjy's not going to try to scare her. Then that he's not even in the lake with her, whatever she thought she felt while she was swimming. He's probably gone into the woods along Lake Garner, to watch Megan and Ryan fucking.

It's a bad feeling. Abandonment and dickishness, but also something else: although Autumn loves White Lake, she's not that interested in being in it alone. It's not that kind of place. There's something adult about White Lake.

"Benjy!" she yells. "Benjy!" Her wet hair is cold on her head and the back of her neck.

He doesn't appear.

"Benjy, come on!"

As Autumn starts to breaststroke back toward the south end of the lake, Benjy explodes out of the water in front of her, visible to mid-chest and vomiting a dark rope of blood that slaps her like something from a bucket.

Then he gets yanked back under.

He's gone. The heat of his blood is gone too. It's like Autumn imagined the whole thing.

But Autumn knows she didn't imagine it. That what she's just seen is something terrible and permanent—and which might be about to happen to *her*.

She turns and sprint-swims for the rocky beach at the base of the cliff. Full-out crawl, no breathing allowed. Swim or die.

Something punches into her stomach, and snags there with tremendous weight and pain. As it tears free, she gets an instant head rush and can't feel her hands.

She tries to arch her back to get some air, but she must be turned around or something, because she sucks in water instead.

Then the thing rams into her from behind, clapping shut her rib cage like a book and squirting the life out of her like water from a sponge.

Or at least that's how it was explained to me.

FIRST THEORY: HOAX

1

Caribbean Sea, 100 Miles East of Belize
Thursday, 19 July

"ISHMAEL—CALL ME" is all the Tel-E-Gram says, but I'm busy pulling some poor fucker's teeth out with pliers when it gets slipped under the door, so I don't read it till later.

The guy's a full-on Nhambiquara Indian from the Brazilian Amazon. Beatlemania haircut and everything, though he's in the white uniform of the laundry department.

Of course, *every* department's uniform is white.

I tap his next molar. Say *"¿Seguro?"*

"No."

"¿Verdad?" Like they speak Spanish in Brazil.

"It's fine," he says.

Maybe it is. From what I know about dentistry—which, granted, comes from watching about an hour and a half of procedure videos on YouTube—lidocaine to the posterior superior alveolar nerve will knock out sensation from the third molar in about two-thirds of people. The rest will need another shot, to the middle superior alveolar, or they'll feel everything.

I assume any actual dentist would just go ahead and give both. But that's the kind of thinking that caused me to use up all the lidocaine in the crew clinic in the first place, and almost all the lidocaine I've been able to steal from the passenger clinic. So now I have to tap and ask. And a lot of my patients are too butch, or just too polite, to admit they're not numb.

Well, fuck it. Save the lido for someone too scared to lie.

I twist the molar out as quickly and smoothly as I can. It crumbles into black muck in the pliers anyway. I catch the pieces in my gloved hand just before they hit the guy's uniform.

It occurs to me that I should give another oral hygiene lecture in the warehouse. The last one doesn't seem to have changed anything, but at least there were fewer knife fights down there while I was talking.

I peel my gloves off over the sink. When I look back, there are tears running down the man's face.

Fire Deck 40 is a metal platform between two smoke-stacks, as far as I know the highest part of the ship you can actually stand on. Fuck knows what it has to do with fire.

The sun's setting, wind like a hairdryer. On the horizon

there's a ten-mile-tall wall of clouds running parallel to the ship. Iridescent reds and grays that bulge over each other like intestines.

I hate the fucking ocean. Hate it *physiologically,* it turns out. Being at sea fucks my sleep and makes me jumpy and subject to flashbacks. It's part of what makes the job of junior physician on a cruise ship exactly what I deserve.

Not that I had a choice. If there's another industry that hires this many doctors without giving a shit whether their medical degrees—in my case from the University of Zihuatanejo, under the name "Lionel Azimuth"—are real or just kited off commercially available supporting documents, I've never heard of it. Let alone one that's this poorly infiltrated by the Mafia.*

The hatch in the wall beside one of the smokestacks barks open, and a very black man in a long-sleeved version of the (white) uniform of updeck junior submanagement steps out.

"Dr. Azimuth," he says.

"Mr. Ngunde."†

---

* Like the rest of the world, the mob only became interested in cruise ships after the 1977 premiere of *The Love Boat*—bad timing, since the FBI was then in the middle of an investigation of the International Longshoremen's Association and already had wiretaps and informants in place. By the time the mob got untangled enough to make a move, the cruise industry had outgrown its reach.

† Cruise ships have, on average, crew members from sixty different countries. The cruise lines like to sell this as a happy byproduct of *Let's watch World Cup!* globalism, but in reality the practice dates to a 1981 sit-in by the predominantly Honduran and Jamaican

Mr. Ngunde is staring at me. "Doctor, your shirt is open."

This is true. I have a white undershirt on beneath it, but my white short-sleeved uniform shirt is unbuttoned. It has gold epaulets, so wearing it like this makes me feel like a drunk airline pilot.

"I don't think anyone will mind," I say, looking down over the edge.

From here the ship, which is twice as wide and three times as long as the *Titanic,* is mostly all-white rooftops and telecom equipment, though there are a few pairs of sorry fucks visible whose job it is to watch for pirates. The passenger areas I can see into, like the Nintendo Dome and the rearmost indoor-outdoor pool, are guaranteed to be empty, since all five of the ship's main restaurants started dinner service an hour ago.

Mr. Ngunde doesn't come over to look. It reminds me that he's afraid of heights, and makes me feel guilty for forcing him to come all the way up here to find me. And for taking lightly an infraction that, were he to commit it, would get him fired and dumped at the next port. Apparently I can bowl over a security guard while coming out of a passenger's stateroom, drunk and *dying* to get fired, and get an apology from the security guard. Mr. Ngunde, unless he's driving the Zamboni machine or doing some other

---

crews of two Carnival Lines ships that were docked in Miami. Standard practice now is to not allow any single nationality to make up more than 5 percent of a crew, and to have as many *officers* as possible be of the *same* nationality—ideally one that speaks a language that most crew members don't understand, like Greek.

task that requires it, isn't allowed to be anywhere a passenger could see him. Regardless of what his shirt looks like.

Speaking of the Zamboni machine, I say "How's the arm?"

"Very fine, Doctor."

That seems unlikely. Mr. Ngunde has a large sleeve-hidden burn on his left forearm from trying to add steering fluid to the Zamboni while the engine was hot. I haven't been able to find a tetanus booster on the ship. Nor have I seen enough tetanus in my life to know how concerned this should make me.

"And the diarrhea log?" Mr. Ngunde says.

"Down, actually. Just don't eat the stew."

"Thank you, Doctor. Large number of visits this afternoon?"

"Fair."

"Anything of interest?"

"No."

Mr. Ngunde is asking me whether any of my patients voiced a level of dissatisfaction significant enough for him to report it up toward one of the department chiefs. I don't hold it against him. At some point in the next twenty-four hours, someone higher in submanagement than Mr. Ngunde will casually ask me if Mr. Ngunde has talked to me recently, and if so whether he said anything of interest.

Still, it's a bummer, because it reminds me that I am, in fact, an employee of a cruise line. My job here is showered in privilege: I get my own stateroom, I eat free in most of the restaurants, and—like the senior physician—I have a seat on *Lifeboat One,* the captain's lifeboat.* But

---

* Also known as the *Jewel of the See Ya, Suckaz.*

most of my patients wish they'd never left their shithole slums and villages. They make around seven thousand dollars a year, out of which they have to pay interest on the loans they took to get here, bribes for the supplies they use in their jobs, and wire fees for the remittances they send home so their children, please God, won't have to work on a cruise ship. Whether what I do actually improves their lives or just assists in their exploitation is one for the ages.*

"Please if you will excuse me, Doctor."

"Of course, Mr. Ngunde. Sorry." He's sweating.

When he pulls the hatch shut behind him, I remember the Tel-E-Gram I picked up off the floor of the clinic. Take it out and read it.

"ISHMAEL—CALL ME."

Interesting.

"Ishmael" was my name in the Federal Witness Protection Program, but the only person who ever actually called me that was Professor Marmoset. Who got me into WITSEC in the first place, and then into med school. And later, when I was in trouble, got me out of New York City.

Marmoset's not a talker. He's not even a responder. You hear from Marmoset, it's serious. It could mean

---

* The underlying problem is that cruise lines aren't generally subject to labor laws, human rights laws, environmental laws, or healthcare regulations (or taxes, for that matter), because most of their ships—even the ones that operate solely out of American ports—are registered out of Panama, Bolivia, or Liberia. The last time anyone tried to do anything about this was during the Clinton administration, at which time the situation was judged too entangled with world trade issues to fuck with.

there's a job out there for you. Maybe even one practicing medicine.

Maybe even on dry land.

But without more information, it doesn't bear thinking about. The job I have now is crappy enough without imagining you could be doing something else.

So focus on the sway of the ship. Get nauseated.

You'll find out soon enough.

2

Portland, Oregon
Monday, 13 August

The woman with the Bettie Page bangs and the "DR. LIONEL AZIMUTH" sign at the Portland airport is exactly the one *I* would hire if I were the fourteenth-richest man in America. She looks like a pin-up. A pin-up who can box.

"Not interested," she says as I walk up to her.

"I'm Lionel Azimuth."

"Fuck off."

I don't take it personally. I look like a dick with a fist on the end of it. "I've got a meeting with Rec Bill," I say.*

---

* I don't actually say "Rec Bill." "Rec Bill" is just a nickname I've started using because I keep hearing him referred to as a "reclusive billionaire."

She considers this. "Do you have luggage?"

"Just this."

A second later: "You don't use the wheels?"

"The handle's not long enough."

She looks around, but there's no one else willing to claim to be Azimuth.

"Sorry," she says. "I'm Violet Hurst. Rec Bill's paleontologist."*

)●(

"Why does Rec Bill have his own paleontologist?" I say when we're out of the rain and under the airport garage. It's eight at night.

"I can't tell you. It's confidential."

"Are you cloning dinosaurs, like in *Jurassic Park*?"

"No one's cloning dinosaurs like in *Jurassic Park*. DNA degrades in forty thousand years, even if it's in a mosquito in some amber. The only way we're going to get sixty-million-year-old dinosaur DNA is by reverse-engineering it from currently living descendants. And we'll be eating human flesh in the streets before we have that kind of technology."

"We will? Why?"

"That's where the protein is. Anyway, I'm not a zoological paleontologist. This is me."

We've come to a car. It's an old Saab with rust along the bottom like a waterline. Maybe it is a waterline.

"What kind of paleontologist are you?" I ask her.

"Catastrophic. You might want to just say it."

---

* Violet Hurst obviously doesn't say "Rec Bill" either.

"What?"

"If I work for the fourteenth-richest man in America, how come my car's such a piece of shit?"

I *have* kind of been wondering that. "I don't even own a car," I say.

"Rec Bill doesn't pay much, in case no one's warned you," she says, unlocking the passenger door. "He's worried people will take advantage of him."

"So he does it to them first?"

"He does whatever he thinks will keep him sane. Don't mention the fourteenth-richest thing to him either, by the way. He hates that."

"Because it objectifies him, or because he's only fourteenth?"

"Probably both. Throw it in the back. The trunk doesn't open."

"So how long until we're eating human flesh in the streets?" I say.

"You don't want to know."

We're on the highway. The rain keeps forming a trembling gel on the windshield.

"I think I do."

I want to keep her talking, in any case. I'm not used to casual conversation, even with people who *don't* look like they could steam up their own jungle planet. I'm worried I might say something that resembles my actual thoughts.

"In the U.S.?" she says. "Less than a hundred years. Maybe less than thirty."

"Really? Why?"

She gives me a look like people asking her questions just to watch her talk is something that happens all the time.

Must get frustrating.

"Bottom line," she says, "there's too many people and not enough food. A billion people are already starving, and climate change and oil scarcity will make it a lot worse."

"The issue with oil scarcity being that we won't be able to use trucks and farm equipment?"

"We won't be able grow things in the first place. All modern fertilizers, pesticides, and herbicides are made from hydrocarbons."

"And you really think we're about to run out?"

"It doesn't have to be gone," she says. "It just has to be where it costs more energy or money to produce a barrel of oil than you can get from a barrel of oil. We may have already reached that point—it's hard to tell, because energy companies are so heavily subsidized that they can sell gas for less than it costs to make. When you can dump a hundred and seventy million barrels of crude into the Gulf of Mexico and take a write-off on the cleanup, cost-efficiency doesn't really enter into it."

"But won't there eventually be other energy sources?"

"You mean like solar? Or wind, or geothermal? Not too likely. Petroleum is four *billion* years' worth of organisms using radiation from the sun to turn airborne carbon dioxide into carbohydrates. Nothing we can make is going to come close to producing that kind of energy. And even if it did, we wouldn't be able to design batteries efficient enough to store it. That's another thing about oil: it's its own storage and transport medium."

"Safer nuclear?"

"Nuclear's a hoax, even when it *doesn't* leak or explode. No nuclear plant has ever produced as much energy as it costs to build and maintain. All nuclear does is keep France clean while it poisons South America. Which is enough crazy-scientist-lady info for one evening. You talk."

I laugh. "I feel like an idiot," I say. "Here I thought it was all about the climate change."

"That's not really what I meant by 'talk.'" But when I don't respond, she says "And anyway, a lot of it *is* all about the climate change. The oil crash will kill six billion people—at a minimum, because that would take us back to where we were before the Industrial Revolution, and the planet's lost a lot of carrying capacity since then. But climate change will kill everybody else. Climate change will kill everyone on Earth even if we *prevent* the oil crash. We could stop using hydrocarbons right now, and just let the six billion die, and climate change would continue to speed up. We've already pulled the methane trigger."

"Which is what?"

"It's where you heat the Earth to the point where the Arctic methane hydrate shelf starts to melt. Methane's twenty times more powerful as a greenhouse gas than carbon dioxide. Fifty million years ago it turned the sky green. This time it'll do it a lot faster." She looks at me again. "You know, you seem to be strangely enjoying this."

I am. I'm not sure why. The complete destruction of the human race *is* fairly amusing, obviously—particularly if it happens through overpopulation and technology, the only goals humanity has ever taken seriously. But it's just as likely that this woman's suspicions are accurate, and what's making me happy is being near her. With Violet Hurst, what message *isn't* the medium going to kick the shit out of?

Must get lonely, as well as frustrating.

"So when was the point of no return?" I say.

"Forget it. I'm cutting you off."

"But that's what catastrophic paleontologists do? Study the end of the world?"

"The various ends of the world. The specific extinction event that's about to happen is a subspecialty."

"And that's what you do for Rec Bill?"

"What I do for Rec Bill is confidential. And no."

"Can you at least tell me what he wants to talk to *me* about?"

"Not really."

"Off the record?"

"Sorry," she says. "He wants to tell you himself. With Rec Bill, it's all about trust."

She signals toward an exit. "Speaking of which, he wants me to wait around and drive you to your hotel when you guys get done, but I think I'm going to put my foot down on this one. I clearly love catastrophic paleontology enough to bore the hell out of strange men with it, but even *I* have to go get drunk afterward and pretend I've never heard of it. Just tell Rec Bill to call you a cab. And keep the receipt."

3

The twelfth floor of the main building of Rec Bill's office park seems to be one enormous room, dark except for a spotlight over the receptionist's desk and another one over the waiting area. The waiting area's floor-to-ceiling windows have channels cut into them that guide the rainwater into tree shapes. The noise from them is making it hard for me to pick out sounds from the dark rest of the floor.

About twenty yards in, an entire office in a glass cube lights up. It looks like a diorama in a natural history museum. There's even a man getting up from the desk.

For a moment I think he's been sitting in the dark, waiting for the light to go on, but then I realize that's too stupid: it's just that the cube has gone from opaque to transparent. Liquid crystal in the glass or something.

As the man comes out of the office and walks toward me, more spotlights come on to light his path. He's late forties, with a gym body and a ponytail. Blazer, untucked shirt, designer jeans, wedge-toe loafers: the full douchebag tuxedo, though I decide to suspend judgment when I see his face. It's been lined by something that looks a lot like pain. Incised by it, more like.

At the moment, though, he's smiling. "What do you think?" he says to me. "Real or fake?"

I have no idea what he's talking about. Between the light-up office and Calamity Jane back in the car, I wonder if he's trying to hypnotize me with weirdness, like Milton Erickson was supposedly able to do. Then I notice he's looking at an oil painting on a freestanding white wall beside me.

It's a city-under-starry-night kind of thing in the style of van Gogh. In fact it's signed *"Vincent."*

"I don't know," I say.

"Guess."

"Can I touch it?"

"Go ahead."

I put my palm on the chunky paint. "It's fake."

"How can you tell?"

"You let me touch it."

"Fair point," he says. "Although it cost almost as much as the original."

He keeps frowning at it, so eventually I say "Why?"

"It was done by a computer. The idea was to use MRI to figure out the order and content of the brushstrokes. But next to the original it looks like shit. One of my materials guys thinks it's because the original has too many false starts and corrections."

"Next time you should copy someone who could paint."

"Ha," the man says. "I'm Rec Bill."*

"Lionel Azimuth."

"I know. Come into my office."

"I think I'm going to show you the DVD first," he says. He's behind his glass desk. The only things on it are a small pink-and-gold ashtray with a facedown business card in it and a white padded envelope that's been cut open rather than torn.

"Get you something to drink?" he says.

"No, thanks." If Rec Bill wants my fingerprints, he can send someone to the fucking ship.

If he does.

I don't know what he wants, because I don't know who he thinks I am. Professor Marmoset would never have told him the truth about me, but I assume anyone this rich would have run a background check.† And Lionel Azimuth barely has a background.

"What has Dr. Hurst told you?" he says.

"Nothing."

"Good. I want to see how you react to this."

---

* Etc.

† Rec Bill's wealth, as I understand it, comes from a piece of "underware" he bought for ten thousand dollars from a classmate in high school and then licensed to every computer operating system ever made. It allows computers to calculate time in binary as opposed to in the 60/60/24/7 system.

Rec Bill swipes and taps some not-obviously-marked spots on his desk, and a part of one wall lights up as a monitor.

Something else he does dims the lights.

The video starts silently. For a while it's just photographs, mostly sepia and black-and-white, run together with the "Ken Burns" feature of somebody's editing software. Woods and lakes. Native Americans posing in suede. Some bearded men in flannel outside a mine entrance. In sudden Koda-chrome, so that it looks like the 1970s, a family in a canoe. Then back to black-and-white for more woods and lakes.

Eventually something artful happens: there's a color shot of a rock wall at the edge of a lake, apparently taken from the water. Then a closer shot from the same perspec-tive, and an even closer one. At which point you can see that the rock has a primitive-looking drawing on it.

It's a moose face-to-face with a much larger animal that's curving up from below it, like a serpent or a giant seahorse. The creature has horns and a snout. The moose's lower jaw hangs open in comical surprise. A bunch of smaller animals lie around looking dead, on their backs with their feet in the air.

The image freezes. An amateurishly boomy male announcer voice with a hiss behind it says *"The knowl-edge that a mysterious creature exists in the waters of White Lake has been known for centuries. Numerous Native American tribes, including the Chippewa and oth-ers of the Anishinaabe peoples, tell legends of the Crea-ture that recede to the depths of time. Mysterious disappearances of dogs, livestock, and other animals have been recorded for four hundred years or more.*

"And what of the present? Many residents of the modern-day town of Ford, the nearest town to White Lake, say they have actually seen the monster. Several say they have observed it on multiple occasions."

There's some handheld modern video of a bunch of people with their backs to the outside of a convenience store. A voice, maybe the announcer's but weak in the open air, says "Who here has seen the monster?"

Everybody in the group raises their hands. "Twice," one woman says.

The video abruptly switches to a teenage girl in a hiking outfit and wraparound sunglasses, walking away as the camera pursues her along the front of some woods. It's a bit like a slasher movie.

The voice says "Young lady, have you seen a monster in White Lake?"

"Please don't videotape me," she says.

"Just yes or no."

"Yes, okay?"

The screen goes black as the voice returns to announcer-style. *"Some have managed to photograph it."*

There's a multicolor jag, and the image turns into what seems to be handheld video of an old television playing a videotape. The television's screen bulges outward, so a lot of what's going on is obscured by glare. You can barely read the pixelated text along the bottom: *"THE DR. McQUILLEN TAPE."* Whoever's doing the filming zooms in on the upper-right corner of the television screen, and the image turns into almost pure grain. But just as you're starting to wonder whether there's a store out there that exists only to rent shitty, ancient video equipment to people making hoax movies, you realize you're watching a duck floating on some water.

Then the water explodes, and the duck is gone.

It gives me a hitch in my chest. The ferocity and speed of the attack, along with the thrash out of calm water, remind me of a shark.

I don't like sharks. I haven't since I spent a bad night in an aquarium eleven years ago.

A voice on the video says "Hold on a sec," and the image on the television freezes, then rewinds in fast motion, then stops and starts to play again frame by frame.

Now I'm sweating.

The duck. The water. Something rising out of the water, dark but hidden by the splashing, then blotting out the duck entirely. The something gone, and the duck with it, no way to tell what it was.

There's a flash, and suddenly Rec Bill and I are watching relatively high-quality modern video again, this time of a bleak-faced old man standing in front of a pier.

The announcer voice, with its hiss, comes back long enough to say *"Some even say they have tangled with it."*

"Happened some years ago," the old man says.

Then he just stands there looking forlorn.

Someone off camera asks him a question you can't quite hear.

"Oh, I can remember it," he says. "I can remember it like it was yesterday."

"Okay," Rec Bill says to me. "Check it out. This is where it gets interesting."

EXHIBIT B

Lake Garner, Minnesota
19 Years Ago*

It's nine a.m.—late to get a line down, like Charlie Brisson gives a fuck. He's not out on this bullshit lake in the middle of the fucking woods to fish. He's here to get shit-faced and forget that his wife is fucking his fucking shift manager.

The shitfaced part is working, at least. Brisson woke up half out of his tent, frozen, his face bit to shit by mosquitoes. But what he woke up picturing was Lisa getting cornholed by Robin.

He's *still* picturing it. There aren't exactly a lot of distractions around here. Maybe Brisson should have thought

---

* **How I know this:** Video sent to Rec Bill, subsequent investigation.

about that before he came out to the woods. Maybe he shouldn't be such a fucking, fucking idiot.

He just can't accept it. It's like some new Lisa has taken the place of the one Brisson loved. Good Lisa would never have done this to him.

Brisson knows that's bullshit, and Good Lisa never existed in the first place, but *fuck*—he just misses her so much.

The sobs break out of him in a *Heh-heh-heh* pattern.

He leans forward so the sun will stop fucking him in the eyes, his legs out in front of him on the bottom of the canoe. Drooping farther and farther forward until suddenly it feels like he's spinning and he jerks upright, almost tipping the boat.

After that he tries to pay attention to the line. Like that helps. The line just sits there. The whole lake's laughing at him. It's as empty as Brisson's motherfucking life.

Heh-heh-heh.

Fuck crappie. Fuck fucking walleye. After Brisson found out Lisa was fucking Robin, Lisa swore to him they never fucked in the section office of the mine while Brisson was down-shaft.

Of *course* they fucked in the section office of the mine while Brisson was down-shaft. Why not? No safer place. Brisson stuck twenty-eight stories underground, no way back to the surface except by calling the fucking *section office* for the elevator.

Sorry to fucking *interrupt you!*

Brisson cries away. Covers his itching, spasming face with his hands.

Which after a while strikes him as interesting, because it means he's no longer holding his fishing rod.

He looks around for it. Scorch scorch scorch from the reflected sunlight, and another hit of vertigo.

The rod's not in the boat. It's not floating, either, at least not nearby. Brisson can't remember whether it's the kind that's meant to float. Or whether he's got a spare back at the campsite.

He has a panicked moment where he thinks he might have lost the oar, too, but then he finds it by his feet, thank you, Jesus. Yanks it loose to row for shore, where fuck it—fuck all of it—he can start drinking again.

ɔ◖(

Back at the campsite, though, Brisson is confused.

No fucking way did he drink all that beer. Brisson only drinks beer as a chaser. Other than when his wife turns out to be an evil lying whore, he's not that much of a drinker in the first place. And he's still got plenty of Jim Beam.

There are a few surprise empties lying around—he's not claiming to *remember* last night, just to be able to reconstruct it from available evidence—but nowhere near so many cans as to indicate that he drank all the beer. And no way bears took it. Brisson has personally seen a bear drink beer from a bottle two-handed, but he knows they don't like aluminum.

Brisson kicks through his tent and the rest of his shit, then goes back to check the canoe. Like there's going to be a couple of six-packs in it that he somehow didn't notice while he was fishing.

There aren't, but the view from there reminds him of what he did with the rest of the beer.

He put it in White Lake.

꒛◖꒱

Not like White Lake is really its own lake. It's a dogleg
off Lake Garner, separated by a spit of land that doesn't
even reach all the way across.

But neither is it the *same* lake. Brisson's never seen fog
on Lake Garner, for example, whereas White Lake seems
to have it more often than not.* And though Brisson's
never heard of a kid or even a dog drowning in Lake Garner, White Lake is some kind of death trap. White Lake is
where Jim Lascadis's six-year-old died, that poor motherfucker. Meaning Lascadis. Poor motherfucker of a kid,
though, also. Jesus.

Lake Garner's nice and White Lake's a hellhole.

Except to store beer.

꒛◖꒱

Brisson slip-slides down the White Lake side of the spit of
land. The spit's made mostly of roots, as if the scraggly-ass
birch trees along its spine have eaten away all the dirt. The
roots are slimy—cold, sharp, and rotten smelling.

But Brisson's got to do it. It looks like he tied a bungee
cord to the trunk of one of the trees and then tied the beer
to the other end of the cord. But for some reason the bungee now runs taut from the tree trunk to the water—something's snagged down there. He should be careful the

---

* Hence "White Lake," maybe.

six-pack or whatever it is doesn't get shot at his face like a rubber band as it comes free.

Fuck, though, the water is cold when his feet reach it. Brisson's in his tighty-whiteys, which are now soaked and muddy, and probably torn, but he has no interest in taking them off. The idea of being entirely naked on this wall of thorny roots is frightening.

He sits and plunges his legs in up to the knees, then pulls them out again. The water's so cold that he can feel the individual rivulets of it heading toward his groin.

Fuck that. He stands back up. Turns to face the wall and takes hold of the bungee cord like a rappelling line. So what if he gets clobbered by beer in the back of the head? Maybe it'll kill him. Won't be the worst thing that's happened to him this week.

Brisson backs slowly into the water. The roots above the waterline were slimy, but the ones underneath are *mossy* and slimy. Standing on them is like balancing on rolling pins, particularly now that his feet are numb. In fact, before he's taken half a dozen steps, Brisson's feet fly out behind him and he flops, face-first, onto the spiny wall.

He bounces off from the pain. Retracts into a sideways fetal position, which feels like it does some more damage but at least gets his legs out of the freezing water.

His teeth are chattering. He looks down at his chest and stomach, expecting to see them gushing blood in a dozen places. But all he sees is mud and a few bright and leaky spots of opaque red. He tries to wipe away the mud to look at them, but this just ends up making a kind of blood/dirt paste. He gets a horrified premonition that he's punctured his balls, and checks.

Intact. Like *that* matters.

But he's alive, and now he has an idea. He climbs back up the roots like a ladder. Tries to untie the bungee, and when he can't, goes back to his campsite and finds his Gerber knife. Cuts the bungee at the tree trunk and walks it halfway back down the slope to give it slack.

It works. Three six-packs, the bungee woven through the plastic rings that hold them together, bob to the surface. Hauling them up causes three or four cans to flip loose and either fall back into the lake or slip down between the roots, but there's not much Brisson's willing to do about *that* except say "fuck" a bunch of times. As soon as he's got the survivors in hand he pops one open and drinks from it. Figures this time he can use the Jim Beam for a chaser.

Then he's sitting on the spine of the spit of land, leaning back against the tree, left leg on the White Lake side, right leg—significantly warmer, since it's in the sun—on the Lake Garner side. Wishing he'd thought to get the Jim Beam before he sat down. Or brought it when he got the knife.

Where is the knife? He doesn't really know or care. He wants to nap.

He

꒰ ◕ ꒱

Brisson wakes up with a strong urge to twitch his left leg. Breathes in air that's pure hot rotten fish, and chokes. Looks down.

His left leg, to mid-thigh, is in the mouth of a gigantic black snake stretching out of White Lake.

The snake's rocky head is shaped like a piece of pie, with its eyes on the sides of the wedge like on an eagle's. The pupils are vertical slits.

The snake's teeth don't look like snake teeth, though. They're serrated triangles, with just their tips pressing into his flesh.

Right then and there Brisson pretty much loses his mind. He thrashes, and the snake hisses and bites down, snapping bone. Brisson's body tries to throw itself down the other side of the spit, into Lake Garner and away from White Lake.

The snake doesn't let him go. It raises its body partly out of the water to gain leverage.

It's no snake. It's got *shoulders*.

Whatever the fuck it is, it slowly moves its head side to side, scissoring its teeth through what's left of Brisson's leg. Already blacking out, Brisson falls backward toward Lake Garner.

Which is essentially all he remembers until he wakes up in the hospital.

But fuck: he sure as hell remembers that much. Remembers it *clearly*.

And if you don't believe him, he's got something to show you.

4

The video pans down the front of the old man's pants. His left leg is tied off in a stump. The video ends.

Rec Bill turns the lights back on.

"What do you think?" Rec Bill says after a moment.

My entire fucking skin is crawling with sharkiness. Bullshit though this guy's story clearly is, it was brilliantly told. That old man wasn't acting. Nobody can act that well. And if he was lying, which is the only other option, he's perfect at it. He's a full-on psychopath.

"About what?" I say.

"Wait. Read this," Rec Bill says. He slides the padded envelope across to me.

I pull it off the table with my palm so it won't be so

obvious that my hands are shaking. Turn it over in my lap. There's no postmark.

So much for not leaving fingerprints. I pull out a folded piece of paper:

Reginald Trager
CFS Outfitters
15 Rte 6
Ford, MN 57731

July 1st
CONFIDENTIAL.
YOUR COMPLETE CONFIDENTIALITY IS
REQUESTED AND EXPECTED.

Dear Mr. Bill:
  I would like to take this opportunity to invite you may well turn out to be the adventure of a lifetime.
  You may have heard legends of the White Lake Monster. If not, please find enclosed a preliminary version of a soon to be completed documentary on that subject (enclosed).
  On Saturday, the 15th of September, I will personally be leading an expedition to search for and observe the Monster. So certain am I from recent events that this expedition will be a success that I am offering to provide all reasonable costs of transportation to Ford, as well as on-site outfitting, guidance, and lodging including one night at the CFS Lodge and an estimated four to twelve nights in the field, at no cost to you unless the Monster is found and determined as below (see below) to be a

<u>previously unidentified, unnaturally large marine animal similar to that of the legend.</u>

If the Monster is in fact spotted in accordance with the below agreement, you will be charged the amount of one million dollars U.S.D. ($1,000,000) for yourself and an additional one million dollars U.S.D. ($1,000,000) for anyone you choose to bring with you, the full amount to be paid into an escrow account immediately prior to the expedition setting out.

To ensure fair agreement on whether the Monster has or has not been seen to a degree fulfilling the conditions requiring payment, I am pleased to say that a very high ranking Member of the U.S. Federal Government has agreed to serve as Referee. Out of respect for the privacy of this individual, his or her identity will be divulged only upon his or her arrival at the CFS Lodge on the evening before the Party is to set out, eg Friday the 14th of September. (This person is <u>not</u> the Congressman who forwarded you this letter.) At that time you will be free to accept this individual as Referee or not, and to put funds into the escrow account at that time, or else to leave at no cost to you guaranteed. However, I am 100% confident you will approve of this person as Referee.

Because the Monster is a limited natural resource belonging to the town of Ford, we will require that you bring no photographic or video equipment along on the trip, including no cell phones with camera functions etc. Also, as White Lake is in an undisclosed location (it is part of

*another Lake and is not on most maps) we require
that you bring no direction finding equipment,
including any form of GPS (Global Positioning
System). For the safety of the Monster and the party
participants, no weapons will be allowed. The
Monster is not believed to be dangerous to large
groups, but the guides will carry sufficient arms to
defend the party in the event of an attack. However,
as the Monster is presumed to be a unpredictable
and possibly aggressive wild animal, guests will be
required to sign a waiver indemnifying the
organizers of the trip against any injury or loss of
life. If any of these rules are broken, subject to the
opinion of the Referee, the person breaking the
rules shall forfeit all funds in escrow.*

*To ensure the private and respectful nature of the
viewing, the Party will be limited to no more than six
(8) Guests, on a first come first serve basis, and all
recipients of this letter are asked to keep its contents
confidential so that those who do embark on this
journey are able to do so safely and successfully.*

*In the event that you do in fact become one of
the Guests, I look forward to making your
acquaintance.*

> *Sincerely,
> Reginald Trager
> CEO, CFS Outfitters & Lodge*

The signature at the bottom says "Reggie" instead of
Reginald.

"So," Rec Bill says. "Any chance it's real?"

He seems serious.

"Are you serious?" I say.

"Yes. I am."

I mean, the video *did* get to me a bit. But I have shark issues.

"Is this why you have a paleontologist?"

"No," he says. "This has nothing to do with that."

"Then why do you have a paleontologist?"

"That's proprietary."

Whatever. "No. There is no chance this is real. If you're not bullshitting me, then someone's bullshitting you. Or trying to scam you. Or kidnap you."

Rec Bill smiles. "Reggie Trager checks out clean. No criminal record."

"Everyone has to start somewhere."

"And even if he *is* running some kind of scam, that doesn't prove the creature doesn't exist."

"It doesn't need to. The creature does not exist."

"How can you be sure of that?"

Fair question.

The real answer is that, like for most scientists, lake monsters, ghosts, superpowers, and UFOs are part of what got me interested in science in the first place. So my heart's been broken for that shit for years. You get old enough, you make your choice: you accept what science actually is and decide to do it anyway, or you go find something that lets you keep the illusions you have left. It's a cold hard world, love, and these are cold hard times.*

---

* Although I did see a UFO once. I was rotating through the Yucca Indian reservation during med school and one night I was lying on my back on top of a mesa you weren't supposed to go on because it

What I say to Rec Bill is "A million reasons. If there's a creature, what's it eating? And don't give me that bullshit about dogs and livestock—how's it getting livestock if it lives in a lake? And where are the bones of these livestock? Where are the bones of the creature's ancestors, for that matter? If there have been sightings, how come they're not on YouTube? Why can't you see the creature on Google Earth?"

Rec Bill keeps smiling.

"What?" I ask him.

"The Boundary Waters have two point five million acres of lake-land that you're not allowed to take a motorboat into or even fly a plane over. Most of that has partial tree cover. There are animals all over it that a large predator could eat without anyone noticing. The area's been protected since 1910 or something—a friend of Teddy Roosevelt's went there on vacation and liked it.* And on

---

was sacred, and I saw something classically saucer shaped race upward across the stars. I rolled over to follow it, and as the angle changed I realized it was just a low-flying bird with white wings and a white bar across its chest. I'm still disappointed.

* This turns out to be a simplification. General Christopher C. Andrews did go there in 1902, and did argue the case for preserving the Boundary Waters to Teddy Roosevelt. However, the closing off of large portions to motorboats and airplanes didn't happen until decades later. It was still being debated in 1949, for example, when people opposed to the ban (because they owned or worked for deeply placed hunting lodges that could only be reached by boat or plane) bombed the house of an outspoken guide and environmentalist who thought—correctly, it turned out—that a ban would increase rather than diminish the area's appeal as a tourist destination.

top of all that it's surrounded by a national forest, a national park, and a Canadian provincial park, and it's contiguous with Lake Superior."

"Then it doesn't matter how big or protected it is," I say. "Any place contiguous with Lake Superior has had fur trappers all over it. If they had found a monster there, they would have made a felt hat out of it."

"Maybe the monster wasn't there at that time. Or wasn't awake. Maybe it hid out. People have been all over the surface of Loch Ness, and we still don't know what's down *there*."

"Of course we do. Every inch of Loch Ness has been mapped by sonar."

"Not the tunnels and caves in the walls."

"Those are a myth. The walls of Loch Ness are sheer basalt, and the bottom's flat. We know how many golf balls are on it.* You should ask your paleontologist about these things. If she's not too busy doing whatever it is she does for you."

He ignores that. "So what about the old man in the video?"

I'd like to stop thinking about that guy now. "I admit he tells a good story. That doesn't mean he can survive getting his leg bitten off with no one around to tourniquet it."

"Maybe he tourniqueted it himself. We know he had a bungee cord."

"He *says* he had one. Maybe he did use it as a tourniquet. And maybe his leg got crushed so hard that his popliteal and femoral arteries fused shut. But neither of those things is likely. Most untrained people who try to tourniquet a limb

---

* 100,000.

don't manage to cut off the arterial flow—they just cut off the venous return near the surface, which makes things worse. Most people who are *sober*." I look around for a clock. Don't see one. "I can't believe we're having this conversation."

"Are we? You don't seem very open to alternative viewpoints."

"I'm not."

"In fact, you seem angry."

Good point. I *am* fucking angry.

Irrationality annoys the shit out of me always, but to get it from *Rec Bill?* A guy way too rich to be this stupid on a regular basis, but who, when he *does* choose to get all whimsical, somehow calls *me?* Knowing that I, like everyone else, will drop everything to meet him because I think I might get a *job* out of this bullshit?

Which, really, is the problem. This isn't Rec Bill's fault. He's not the delusional one in this scenario.

"Look," I say. "How long have you been in remission?"

It startles him. "Professor Marmoset told you that?"

"No. He never would."

"How did you find out?"

"I'm a doctor.* Stomach or colon?"

"Colon," Rec Bill says. "Stage III-C. Six years out."

---

* I've also seen the back of his neck, which has the remnants of *acanthosis nigricans,* a skin condition that for unclear reasons correlates with abdominal cancers. Clearly I should have just told him this, both for ethical reasons and because it might have saved a lot of trouble later, but apparently I'm too much of an angry dick. And besides, I'd already given away the thing with the painting.

"So you've beaten the odds."

"So far." He knocks on the glass of the desk.

"But you've also realized that everyone eventually dies. Unless it turns out there's some kind of magic in the world."

A flash of imperiousness crosses his face. "I wouldn't put it that way."

"Are you in the Singularity Movement?"

"Yes."

"Exactly."

"What do you mean, 'Exactly'?"*

I say "Testing the edges of reality is nothing to be embarrassed about. But bullshit like the White Lake Monster isn't the way to do it. The physical world has rules, and physical objects in it tend to obey those rules. The only things that don't are emotions and experiences. You want magic, you should try meditating. Or starting a children's hospital."

"You don't think that's a bit condescending?"

"Like I say, I'm a doctor. If you want to see a rare living creature, go look at a polar bear. Or date someone from Stockholm."

"I did my junior year in Stockholm."

"Then try North Dakota. But if you want my advice, here it is: do not do this stupid thing."

---

* The Singularity Movement is a bunch of wealthy computer people who believe that when computers become sentient it will be possible to interest them in extending the life spans of wealthy computer people. It's something you get involved in when you don't have any problems left that are real. Or at least that are fixable.

He sits back, smiling. "I'm not planning to. I'm going to send someone else. If it's real, I'll go along on the next trip."

"That's not going to work. Anyone stupid enough to take that job is stupid enough to get fooled by whatever this scam turns out to be."

Rec Bill points at me. "Okay. See, *that* is where I think you're wrong. And Professor Marmoset was right. You're perfect for this."

"Me?" I say. "To go on your dumbass expedition?"

"Yes."

"You're claiming Professor Marmoset recommended *me* for something this stupid?"

"I didn't tell him the details," Rec Bill says. "I just asked him for someone smart enough to evaluate what seemed like a potentially compelling scientific mystery but tough enough to deal with it if it turned out to be a criminal enterprise."

"What do you mean, 'deal with it'?"

If this is the part where Rec Bill tells me he's looking for someone willing to punish whoever's behind this once it turns out to be bullshit, it's also the part where I tell him to fuck off. Which would be unfortunate from the perspective of making sure he pays for my cab back to the airport, but would at least get me out of his office.

"Keep people from getting hurt," he says.

Fuck. He got that one right.

"Listen," he says. "I just want you to go on this expedition for me. Find out if it's real."

"It isn't. And any further effort you put into it is going to lead to disappointment, or worse. Thanks for considering me."

"I know it's unlikely. It's erring on the side of credulity. And if you go and decide the whole thing is a hoax, I'll accept that. In the meantime, what's the harm?"

"You mean besides my wasting my time? I'm not sure, but I guarantee you there will be some. Six people at a million dollars apiece—or eight people, or whatever it is—is a lot of money, believe it or not. And whoever's behind this has some reason to think they're going to get it."

"What about the independent referee?"

"The independent referee doesn't mean shit. You think you can't buy someone—what was it, 'high up in federal government'?—for part of six million dollars? You can buy those people by having their deck weatherproofed. How much do you think they paid your congressman to forward the letter?"

"Five hundred dollars," Rec Bill says. "I checked. But if the referee doesn't turn out to be a whole lot more impressive than my congressman, we'll just back out."

"I'm guessing it's more complicated than that. Why are they demanding that you not bring guns or communication equipment?"

Rec Bill throws his hands up. "Because they're criminals who are trying to rip me off, and I'm an idiot for even considering the possibility that they're not. I understand that. What I need to know is how much you're going to charge me to go to Minnesota and check it out."

I don't know what to say.

I try "More than you would be willing to pay."

"How would you know?"

"All right. Eighty-five thousand dollars."

"Eighty-five *thousand?*"

"Yes."

I've chosen this number randomly, but it does fit certain criteria. One is that if I ever figure out a way to get the Sicilian and Russian mafias off my ass, it will almost certainly be expensive.* Another is that I've been hearing for weeks—and not just from Violet Hurst—how cheap Rec Bill is, so I know he'll never go for it.

Just to make sure, I say "And that's not a negotiation. That's take it or leave it. And it doesn't include expenses. Which could double it."

Rec Bill looks horrified. "How could you possibly spend eighty-five thousand dollars on expenses?"

"I haven't figured that out yet."

"This is to go *camping*. For a *week*."

---

* The issue is that David Locano, a former lawyer for the Sicilians and Russians, has a deal with both mobs where they keep trying to find me and kill me, and he keeps refusing to testify against them—even though that means he rots in supermax at the Florence Federal Correctional Complex in Colorado. I put him there, but that's not why he wants me dead so badly. He thinks I killed his fuckhead son. Which I did, three years ago, and would happily do again.

It's kind of a détente, because if the Russians or Sicilians ever *do* manage to find me and kill me, Locano will no longer have any reason to keep his mouth shut. Whereas if they stop seriously trying, and Locano finds out about it, he'll turn state's just to be able to get out and come after me on his own.

The obvious solution, it seems to me, is for someone to get off their mafia asses and have Locano whacked in prison. But it's possible the Feds have realized this, too, and have him too well protected. If that's true, and *I* were the Sicilians and Russians, I would probably try to take me alive to retain a bargaining position. Then again, Locano's son tried that once, which is how this whole mess got started.

"Even if it was," I say, "it would be a week of trying to save you a million dollars you don't need to gamble in the first place. And it would require ongoing coverage on my ship, after which I might or might not get my job back.* If you can't afford it, get some of your Singularity Movement people to chip in. If they haven't already."

Rec Bill mutters something I can't quite hear. I ask him to repeat it.

"I said *fine*," he says, looking ill. "Eighty-five thousand. Plus another eighty-five thousand for expenses that have legitimate receipts."

"What?" I say.

"You need me to say it again?"

"You're joking."

"No."

"Fuck."

He still looks queasy. "You and me both."

I don't feel so good myself.

"Fuck," I say again. "Well at least you're not sending Violet Hurst."

Rec Bill looks surprised. "I am sending Violet Hurst. I'm worried about her. That's why *you're* going."

---

* This is probably wishful thinking on my part.

SECOND THEORY:
MURDER

5

"Do you think we're going to fuck?" Violet says. "I'm not offering. I'm just asking your opinion."

I'm driving. "Are you drunk?"

Over the tops of her sunglasses: "No, I'm not, thank you, Doctor."

Maybe she isn't. Right after we passed Duluth, which turns out to be a bunch of freeway exchanges between new-looking paper factories, every one of them pumping smog as big and opaque as clouds out its stacks, we stopped at a Dairy Queen for lunch. Violet got two beers from the gas station next door, and when I didn't want one she drank both of them. But that was an hour ago.

Maybe there's just someone who talks like this. That'd be cool.

"Yeah, probably," I say.

"How dare you. Why?"

"We don't know each other, we'll be in a strange place for a few days. There's nothing sexier you can say to someone than 'You'll never see me again after next week.'"

"You know that from working on cruise ships?"

"I'm pretty sure I knew it before."

"From your years as a man-whore?"

"We prefer 'drifter.'"

"Hot. Not as hot as 'You'll never see me again after next week,' but hot."

"You don't think it's true?"

"I think there's a U-shaped curve. Some people, you meet them, you want to fuck them for their fancy mysterious shit, then you *don't* want to fuck them cause you're sick of them, then you do again. Because you actually know them."

"Must be nice."

"I'm not saying *my* experience supports that. My experience supports the gradual recognition that whoever I'm dating is a complete asshole. But still."

This is precisely the kind of topic I should be avoiding. I'm not about to tell Violet Hurst any real thing about myself, so why should I ask *her* questions? But women who look like Wonder Woman and say drunk shit to me in a car aren't something I've spent all that much time around.

Maybe I should drive more.

"Something recent?" I say.

"More recently than that, actually," she says.

"Ongoing?"

Or have a talk show.

"I don't even know. It's the usual male thing: extreme interest, sudden bolting. Which gets old after a while. Okay, now you just think I'm a slut, cause I'm being all flirty and I have a semi-boyfriend."

"Now you just think I'm judgmental."

She turns to me. "You're slightly smarter than you look."

"It's a U-shaped curve. After five minutes I start seeming stupid again."*

"Ha. Well I'm not a slut. Not in a bad way, anyway. I'm just slow to acknowledge the obvious and admit that my semi-boyfriend is a non-boyfriend."

Yes, but I'm smart enough to stop. Or jealous enough that some dipshit out there has a chance that I and most other people on Earth—on the run or not—will never have, and doesn't even appreciate it.

I'll never know.

"I'm not sure. Depends what's on the radio," I say.

"You know, you're funnier when you don't talk."

I laugh.

"Laughing counts. Anyway, how's *your* love life?"

See? You should never say anything to anyone.

"It isn't."

"Since when?"

"A long time."

"Why?"

"I thought the idea was to stay mysterious."

"Mysterious and creepily avoidant: not the same thing."

---

* Like most people raised on American movies, I have poor access to my emotions but can banter like a motherfucker.

"Hey, at least I'm not on a secret paleontological mission for Rec Bill."

"Other than this one."

"Good point."

"Thank you. What did you do before you worked on cruise ships?"

"Went to medical school. Shit like that."

"In Mexico. I Googled you. Why there?"

"Didn't get accepted in the U.S. Still wanted to go."

"You were a bad kid?"

"Bad everything."

"How was it?"

"Fine."

She sighs. "It's kind of like pulling teeth, talking to you."

"I do that sometimes. On cruise ships."

"Really?"

"It's part of the job."

Nothing derails a conversation like medical grotesquerie.

"Where are *you* from?" I say.

"Don't change the subject."

"What subject?"

"You."

But we both know I've worn her out. It's something I'm good at.

"Holy shit," Violet says.

We're on the main drag of Ford, a couple of hours later. Not the same highway exit as CFS Outfitters and Lodge, which we're due to check into tomorrow—the exit before that. Ford proper.

Ford proper looks like someone's used it to test-market the Apocalypse. Everything—the houses, the VFW hall, the strip malls, the low brick office buildings—is boarded up, broken down, or grown over. The only people we see are a few crypt-lichs in down vests and baseball hats, who drop their cigarettes and lurch off in different directions when they see us coming.

I have the same prejudices about rural Americans that most urban Americans do,* but this place is nothing anyone chose. When we pass a guy in his twenties on a bicycle, it seems like a brash piece of athleticism until I notice the two-liter Pepsi bottle bouncing off the top of his rear tire and realize he's single-batching meth.

"This is horrible," Violet says.

"I thought you were from Kansas."

"Fuck you. I'm from Lawrence. It's not like this at all."

"I was about to be impressed."

"Get over it. But this place shouldn't be like this either. Bob Dylan's from around here."

"A long time ago."†

---

* That they're deluded racists who will vote their rights away to any plutocrat willing to name-drop Jesus. Just as conservatives blame poor people for not being wealthy, progressives blame them for not being educated.

† I listened to some early Bob Dylan a few months after having this conversation, and it seemed full of ambivalence about being from Minnesota. For example, "Bob Dylan's Blues," from *The Freewheelin' Bob Dylan,* has a spoken introduction that sounds like something Sarah Palin would say: "Unlike most of the songs nowadays are bein' written uptown in Tin Pan Alley—that's where

"And they elected Al Franken, sort of."

"And Michele Bachmann."

"*These* people didn't have anything to do with Michele Bachmann. Her district's way south of here."

The convenience store with gas pumps out front is open, at least. I recognize it from the documentary that got sent to Rec Bill. It still has an optical-orange Budweiser poster of an elk in some crosshairs in the window. And two blocks farther up I can see a diner called Debbie's that has a car in front of it.

I turn into the lot. Maybe Debbie's is open too.

Cat bells go off when Violet and I open the door, the glass of which has been partly broken out and re-backed with plywood. There's no one in the dining room. But the fluorescents are on, and there's an "OPEN" sign in the window.

"Hello?" Violet says.

At the other end of the room, a blond woman in a white T-shirt comes partly out of the kitchen. Forty-five the hard way.

"What can I do for you?"

"Uh... are you serving food?" Violet says.

The woman stares at us well past long enough for it to

---

most of the folk songs come from nowadays—this, this is a song, this wasn't written up there. This was written somewhere down in the United States." But when *The Freewheelin' Bob Dylan* came out, Dylan had been living within walking distance of Tin Pan Alley for two years.

be weird. "This *is* a restaurant, Sugar. Sit where you like. I'll be out in a minute. Menus are on the table."

Violet and I take a booth at the front. We've spent so much time side by side that it's startling to look her in the eyes.

"What?" she says. "Do I have something on my face?"

"No."

She checks her reflection in the mirror anyway. To stop looking at her I take one of the menus. It's sticky, like it's been sprayed with atomized syrup.

From the kitchen, we hear something metal bang something else. Then a woman, possibly the same one, shouting *"LEARN TO FLIP THE GODDAMN SIGN."*

"Huh," Violet says. "Do you think maybe we should leave?"

"We probably should. I wouldn't mind giving it a minute, though."

Her eyes go wide, all playful and excited. "You mean as part of the *investigation?*"

The door from the kitchen bangs open harder than you'd think the glass of its porthole would stand—which, maybe, is what happened to the front door—and the woman stalks back to our table like she's ready to slap us.

"You kids made up your minds?" she says.

"Are you sure you're open?" Violet says.

"That's what the sign says."

"Right, but we can—"

The woman smiles grimly. "What are you having, Sweetie?"

"French toast, please," Violet says.

"A hamburger and a chocolate milkshake," I say.

"We don't do milkshakes," the woman says.

"What are you, five?" Violet says to me. To the waitress she says "Do you do beer?"

"Pabst and Michelob Light. We may be out of Pabst."

"Two Michelob Lights, then."

"You still want that burger?"

"Sure, thanks," I say.

"Hey, are you Debbie?" Violet says.

"Can't no one help who they are."

On her way back to the kitchen, she stops at a horizontal freezer along the wall. Takes out a cellophaned pack of prefab French toast. Violet doesn't see it happen.

It's interesting. I've been in restaurants this hostile before, but most of them have been in Brooklyn south of 65th Street, or Queens east of Cross Bay Boulevard, and have existed for purposes other than serving food.* This place isn't necessarily that—I'm sure the world is full of restaurants that come by their shittiness honestly—but it's strange.

"Check it out," Violet says.

I follow her eyes to a sign on the wall: "KEEP COMPLAINING. IF THE LIGHTS GO OUT, I'LL KNOW WHERE TO AIM."

Violet says "What the fuck is wrong with this place?"

---

* Zagat's on a Greek place I used to go to in Ozone Park: "You'll 'shop for guns stolen from luggage at JFK' at this 'intimate' 'bazaar for sociopaths,' but you may want to 'Bring your own food from the chicken place next door' and 'Borrow your neighbor's Purell.'"

EXHIBIT C

Debbie's Diner
Ford, Minnesota
*Still Thursday, 13 September**

Slamming back into the kitchen, Debbie Schneke wonders if you are for *fucking* serious. First Dylan and Matt fuck up the run to Winnipeg—come back *lit up,* they're on so much fucking meth—then JD forgets to flip the "OPEN" sign, and two goddamn *cops* come into the restaurant.

---

* How I know this: Information for this exhibit, as well as for Exhibit J, comes from personal interviews and from testimony and surveillance transcripts included in the unsealed (public) redaction of *Final Report of the Grand Jury in Re The People of the State of Minnesota, Plaintiff, v. Schneke et al., Defendants* (*CJ 69-C-CASP-7076*).

Just as she's got three thousand tabs of pseudoephedrine ground up, washed, and mixed with brake cleaner in an Erlenmeyer flask on the counter.

The whole fucking kitchen's a disaster. What's the special today—Frankenstein? And she's supposed to cook a fucking *hamburger* for a *cop?*

Debbie goes to the screen door that leads out back. Through the mesh she can see a bunch of the Boys sitting on crates and trash cans and shit, but she knows they can't see her. If they could, they wouldn't be lounging around like monkeys.

"FUCK YOU!" she screams, sending some of them scrambling.

Debbie doesn't even know if it's safe to turn on the gas for the grill. She doesn't think the mash has reached the stage yet where it plus propane turns into that shit they gassed people with in World War I,* but how the hell is she supposed to know for sure?

Her decision: the gas stays off. Fuck the cop. She'll microwave his hamburger. If he even *is* a cop. Him and that lady look like FBI or DEA or something. They're too sexy for regular cops. Debbie wonders how long they've been fucking each other, and whether their spouses know.

Oh, and—Oh, no way. No fucking WAY. Even if she microwaves the burger, how is she going to cook the fucking BUN? Or the French toast for the lady-cop? God DAMN it!

Debbie goes beyond herself with fury. Yanks open the door of the walk-in refrigerator: Matt Wogum and Dylan Arntz, both bound and gagged with duct tape, blue and

---

* It has reached that stage.

sluggish looking from the cold. Not even shivering anymore. One *more* thing she has to worry about.

"God DAMN you!" she screams, and slams the door. This is all their fucking fault. She can't believe she ever trusted them.

What would be *enough* for these goddamn kids? She already feeds them, fucks them, and buys them cable. What else do they need? Debbie to jam an Xbox up her cunt, so they can multitask?

And all she ever asks of them is to be one slightly *fucking* bit cool—and DON'T SNORT THE MOTHER-FUCKING PRODUCT.

Matt Wogum she'd known was hopeless. Even though he'd done the Winnipeg run with Greg Bierner a dozen times, he'd claimed he never noticed Greg was using. For that alone Debbie would have had him killed along with Greg, only then there'd have been nobody alive who had made the trip. At the time it seemed smarter to keep Matt around.

Wrong, what else is new. Dylan, the best one she had, the most trustworthy—the one who sometimes still goes to high school, who Debbie gives handjobs to because he's too shy to come in her mouth—goes on *one* fucking trip with Matt Wogum and comes home too fucked up to blink right. Him and Matt Wogum telling some bullshit story—which, now that Debbie thinks about it, is probably true—about how *Wajid,* the fucking Yemeni kid, hadn't been able to get the pills from the warehouse of his cousins' pharmacy on time because the cousins were getting suspicious, but wasn't willing to let Matt and Dylan wait at his apartment because he was holding a goddamn *religious meeting* there.

That's the problem with the goddamn Yemenis. They're only in it to send money to Hezbollah or whatever. It's not their money, so it's not their problem. They don't act like professionals.

And of course Matt and Dylan then had to go to some *bar* to hang out, where *naturally* a couple of Canada Skanks asked them if they had any cocaine. And Matt said yes because he had some fucking *meth* on him, then made Dylan snort some too so the skanks wouldn't think it was some kind of date rape drug.

Which, to be fair, Matt probably *had* to do. Debbie sure as hell wouldn't accept a suspicious white powder from someone who looked like Matt Wogum—and Debbie *makes* suspicious white powders.

But *whatever* happened up there in Canada, Debbie now has no one to send to buy more pills. The mashed-up three thousand are the last of it—unless she lets Dylan live, the idea of which makes her feel sick. But what's the alternative? Deal with the fucking *Sinaloans?*

The thought makes her want to scream and then repeatedly slam her hand in the oven door.

Debbie *hates* the fucking Sinaloans. Always sending some gold-tooth midget wetback around, all *"Joo is workin for us now, lady."* Wanting her to sell finished product up from Mexico at one quarter the profit she gets from cooking it on her own.

So far she's gotten away with kicking them the fuck out. But if the Sinaloans ever get their shit together and stop killing each other, they could be a goddamn nightmare. They all work in the meat-processing plant in Saint James as cover, so they're good with knives. Just out of nervousness, Debbie's had to buy a bunch of new guns for the Boys.

And now she has to *hope* one of those dwarfy fuckers comes back? And brings product with him, so at least she'll have something to sell?

Debbie rips a handful of tinfoil off the roll and caps the beaker of mash with it, puts the whole thing in the fridge. Fuck else is she supposed to do with it?

Starts the electric toast belt that runs through the top chamber of the oven. Turns on the propane. Thinks to the potential mustard gas, *Oh, you just do me the favor.*

At least with the mash out of the open air she can smoke. Debbie's been smoking too much lately, thanks for reminding her, but right now it feels like the only usable air in the room is on the other side of a lit cigarette.

As she inhales her first puff she puts the bun and the French toast on the belt, and the hamburger in the microwave. Screw that pig, even if the propane's on. Then punches the door to the back parking lot open.

The Boys, now arranged on the low back wall and a couple of cars, fall silent. They look sulky and afraid.

"Soon as the cops are gone, take Dylan Arntz out of here and beat holy hell out of him," she says. "Matt Wogum I haven't decided on yet."

The older ones, the ones who matter—probably the rest of them too—will know what this means.

Regarding Dylan, it means he gets one more chance.

Regarding Matt, it means someone better goddamn start digging a hole.

6

Debbie, assuming that *is* her name, puts our plates down. Mine has a burger on it, Violet's the previously frozen French toast. Otherwise both plates are blank.

Garnish: the life crutch you never appreciate till it's gone.

The burger looks good, though. Or at least the bun's toasted, which gets you halfway there on its own. "What else for you guys now?" Debbie says.

Violet says "Can you tell us anything about White Lake?"

Debbie turns outraged so fast it's like a split-second werewolf movie.

"What? Motherfucking WHAT?"

"Uh . . ." Violet says.

"WHAT did you just say? You people come in here pretending to be *cops,* and—what *are* you, anyway? Goddamn *reporters?*"

"No," Violet says. "We're scientists."

"Sure you goddamn are. And you just *happen* to come in here, asking who I am, asking about the goddamn White Lake Monster—"

I'm out of my bench seat by then, but I stop. "Did you say—"

"I didn't say *shit.* And I sure as hell didn't say it to you people."

"But—"

"You two just get the hell out of my restaurant. *Get.*"

"Can I just—"

She picks up my plate and smashes it to bits on the table. "GET THE FUCK OUT OF MY RESTAURANT!"

By the time the burger parts hit the floor I've got Violet out of her own seat and am scanning it in case she's left a purse. She hasn't. Violet Hurst, alone among women wearing cargo pants, actually uses the pockets.

At the door I turn back for one more try. "Can—"

"You want a monster? Go find Reggie Trager!" Debbie yells, winging the other plate at my head.

I get the door shut just as the plate bursts against the plywood.

"Jesus *fuck,*" Violet says as we back toward our rental. The car's a chunky station wagon from a division of GM that I thought went out of business five years ago. "What the fuck was that about?"

"Lady doesn't like scientists," I say.

"No shit. It's too bad: the French toast looked good."

"It was frozen."

"Really? That bitch! How do you know?"

"I saw her take it out of the freezer."

Violet stops with her hand on the handle of the passenger door. "Were you going to tell me that?"

"I thought you would enjoy it more if I didn't."

"That's some kind of joke, right?"

Luckily, just then there's a noise from behind the restaurant like someone knocking a bunch of garbage cans over while they or someone else shouts in pain.

I slide the keys to Violet over the roof. "Start the car and stay here."

"Fuck *that*."

"Do it. If I'm not back in three minutes, call the cops."

ɔ ⌒⌒(

Out back there are a dozen or so teenage boys stomping the shit out of what looks like another teenage boy, though it's hard to tell because they're packed around him pretty tightly and his face has blood all over it. Not a lot of technique happening, but the enthusiasm's good.

I ignore the attackers and let the blood pull me through to where I'm kneeling over the kid on the ground and shielding him. He's unconscious but breathing. Laceration over one eye you can see bone through. A bunch of less serious cuts on his face and scalp. His skin is strangely cool.

His eyelids start to flutter. "Don't move," I say.

He scrambles onto his back. Touches his face and sees the blood on his hand. "Aw, shit!"

So much for a C-spine check. While he's distracted, I pick a gory canine tooth off the asphalt and put it in my jacket pocket. "Stop moving. Tell me if this hurts."

"It hurts!"

"Wait till I start."

"Hey!" someone shouts. "Mister!"

I look up. Despite my ignoring them, the other teenage boys don't seem to have vanished.

They're a weird range of ages. Thirteen and child-like to about seventeen and shaggy. Different species from each other, practically, though they all have on the same outfit: oversize coat and baggy jeans, both so covered in brand names they look like downtown Los Angeles in *Blade Runner.* At least these kids seem healthier than the born-to-be-wired lardtards I usually see dodging their grandparents on the cruise ship. Like they spend a lot of time outdoors, even if it's just to kick someone's ass.

On the other hand, a lot of them are now pointing guns at me.

Mostly shotguns and hunting rifles, but—particularly among the older kids—some expensive-looking handguns as well. The kid who seems oldest, in the center, has a Colt Commander that's as shiny as a disco ball.

"Yeah, you," this kid says. "Mister *Dumbass.*"

I have no idea what to do.

Nonviolent crowd control is the hardest part of the martial arts. You can't spend your nights just heart-punching the heavy bag in the officers' gym and expect to stay good at it. You have to practice your joint locks and your leg sweeps and so on—something I can't really say I've been doing, at least not to the level where I feel confident

I can defuse ten close-together firearms without someone getting hurt.

And it *is* kind of important to me that no one get hurt here. Does not Sensei Dragonfire tell us, "Control rather than hurt, hurt rather than maim, maim rather than kill, kill rather than be killed"? Ought not I, of all people, to take that admonition personally? And did I not inject myself into this conflict in order to *keep* a child from being injured?

I decide to bluff it out. "That's *Doctor* Dumbass to you," I say, standing up with the injured kid in my arms.

The kid with the Commander blocks my way. "I thought you had to have brains to be a doctor."

I step around him. "That's a common misperception."

"It's none of your business!" he whines.

"You've made it my business."

I'm almost past him—and by extension, I'm guessing, past the rest of them too—when he steps in front of me again, this time jamming the Colt into the left side of my neck.

It's a very stupid move. The thing it causes to rise up in me doesn't give a *fuck* that everyone around me is a child, or that so many of them have guns. The thing wants me to throw the kid in my arms to one side, pull *this* kid's gun past my head, step on his left foot while kicking his right knee out sideways, then palm-strike his throat and hold on. So that when I stomp his chest and he goes backward, both his gun and his larynx come off in my hands. Take it up with Sensei Dragonfire later.

The thing scares me more than the gun. Particularly since Colt Commanders are single-action, and this kid's neglected to pull the hammer. I shrug past him, causing him to jump out of the way of the feet of the kid I'm carrying.

When I'm almost to the edge of the building, Violet Hurst appears from the other side. Holding her cell phone up and yelling "Nobody move, you fucking cocksuckers! I've got the cops on the phone *right now.*"

"You get *reception* here?" one of the kids behind me asks. He sounds genuinely astonished.

I hear the kid with the Commander say "Fuck!" as he tries to pull the trigger on us. Then I bowl into Violet, taking us and the kid in my arms back around the corner just as gunfire tears open the plaster, showering it all over our backs.

Violet's a badass about it. She lands on her feet, turned around and already running. We pass Debbie, who's standing in front of the plywood door, one hand shading her eyes, and screaming "Don't shoot the fucking restaurant, you assholes!"

"Give me the keys," I say to Violet.

"They're in the ignition."

Like I say: badass. I throw the kid in the back and start the car with the gas so flat we jump the curb in front of the parking space before we fishtail out of the lot.

Sport-driving always reminds me of Adam Locano, who was my best friend from the time I was fifteen until I was twenty-four—the ages at which a man does most of his sport-driving, unless he goes on to be a professional racer or a dipshit. Adam and I were *already* dipshits. We both worshipped his father, whose advice on cars was to treat them like women: steal them, strip them, dump them when they get too hot, don't overly rely on them. I'm sure he had other cheap metaphors I'm forgetting.*

Not that the rental's all that sporty. I've still got the gas pedal all the way down, and the automatic transmission keeps trying out new gears and then realizing they suck and going back to try gears it unsuccessfully tried earlier. I pull the emergency brake through the first right turn, and it doesn't affect things at all.

Just before the second right I see a pickup truck enter the rearview. Rifle barrels like bristles.

At the third right turn Violet says "Where are we going?"

I've just turned us away from the highway and back toward Debbie's. "Shake these fuckers off."

At Debbie's I cut diagonally through the lot, heading out again on the street I took three minutes ago.

In the rearview, I see the pickup truck wrench to a stop in front of the plywood door. Now that they know we're willing to come back to their home base—for whatever reason—they'll have to stay and defend it. Or at the very least split up.

"Hey," I say to the kid in the back. "You awake?"

"Yeah."

"Where's the nearest hospital?"

"I don't need to go to the hospital."

"That wasn't the question. Where is it?"

---

* I stuck around these people, by choice, literally until they started trying to kill me. It's something I like to think about whenever I feel that some shitty thing that's just happened to me is anything other than justified.

"Ely. But my doctor's right near here."

"Forget it. Unless he's got a CT scanner in his office, he's just going to send you to a hospital anyway."

"He does have a CT scanner in his office."

"Not too likely."

"Dude, I know what a CT scanner is," the kid says. "It takes a bunch of X-rays in a row. Like cross-sections. My half-brother got a million of them."

"Why?"

"He had a brain tumor."

"And he got scanned *here?*"

"Yeah."

I think about it. Ely, where Violet and I are supposed to spend tonight in a hotel, is half an hour farther up Route 53.

"Fine," I say. "Where's your doctor?"

The kid sits up enough to see out the windshield. "Turn left right now."

"Hold on to something," I say. "And give me some lead time." I try the emergency brake again through the turn. It still doesn't do anything.

"Go as far as you can, then turn right," the kid says. "It'll be a dead end."

"In front of that big brick building?"

"Yeah."

"We also need to call the police," Violet says.

"Aw, come on, lady!" the kid says.

My sentiments exactly. "You don't want us to?" I say to the kid.

"No fucking way."

I sigh. "Fine."

"What?" Violet says.

"I think we should respect the kid's wishes. Besides, we don't really know what would have happened if I hadn't butted in."

"They would have beaten him to death."

"Nah. It looked like they were pretty much finishing up." I catch the kid looking suspiciously at me in the rearview.

"They tried to shoot us," Violet says.

"Shoot *near* us. What *is* that building?"

"It's the old mine factory," the kid says.

I don't know what that means. It's impressive, though: red brick and iron, left for the weeds.

"What's your name?" I say.

"Dylan."

"Dylan, what day of the week is it?"

"Fuck should I know?"

"It's Thursday. Remember that. I'm going to ask you again in a few minutes. Okay?"

"Okay."

"Got any medical conditions?"

"Yeah. I just got the shit kicked out of me."

"Other than that."

"No."

"You really don't think we should call the police?" Violet says to me.

"Dylan? What do you think?"

"Seriously: no fucking way. They'd just make things worse."

I look at Violet and shrug. Ask Dylan if he takes any medications.

"No."

Even from up front I can smell the ammonia evaporating

out of the blood that's all over him. May explain his aversion to cops.

I say "You know, where I come from, the people on meth beat up the people *not* on meth, not the other way around."

"Maybe I should move there."

"Maybe you should. How much are you using?"

"I'm not 'using.' I've done meth twice. Once last night and once a couple of hours ago."

"Is that why those guys were kicking the shit out of you?"

"I'm not a mind reader, dude."

"I'll take that as a yes. Got any allergies?"

"Yeah. To people kicking the shit out of me."

"You know, I'm beginning to see why that happens."

"Lionel!" Violet says. "Dylan, I'm Violet, and this is Lionel. I still think you should consider going to the police."

"Your name is *Lionel?*" the kid says to me.

"What about it?"

"Nothing."

"Okay, then. Turn here or go straight?"

"Straight." Past a row of aluminum-sided houses with various amounts of sky-blue tarping on their roofs. Not the first such row we've seen.

"Dylan, what's up with Debbie the waitress?" I say.

"How should I know?"

"And what does she have against Reggie Trager?"

"I don't know who that is."

"You're going to pull *that* shit?"

"Hey, I didn't ask you to rescue me."

"You're right. We should drop you back off."

"Lionel!" Violet says. "I think he means well," she says to Dylan.

The ground along the road to our left falls off steeply. I can see water flashing up at us through the trees. "Is that White Lake?" I ask.

"Are you kidding?" Dylan says.

"No. Is it funny?"

"That's not White Lake. It's Ford Lake. I take it you people aren't from around here."

"No, we're not."

Dylan says "The road is gonna curve to the right, but we're taking the soft left out of it."

"The first one?" I say.

"Yeah."

I take it. It puts us into a cul-de-sac that follows the line of the water. The houses on the shore side are huge. The ones on the inland side are smaller and higher up so they can see the lake.

It's obviously the expensive part of town. Most of the houses look just as derelict as they do everywhere else in Ford, but there are three in a row on the lake side that still have well-maintained lawns and trees and no broken windows. One even has an American flag on a pole over the doorway.

"It's the green one," Dylan says.

I park on the street in front of the house. Pointed the wrong way along the sidewalk, but ours is the only car I see. Maybe some of the garages have others, or maybe there's just no one around.

"Dude, I can walk," Dylan says when I try to help him out of the car.

"How do you know?"

"Watch and learn." He winces and limps all the way to the porch at the side of the house, then up the steps.

The porch has two doors, one of which is steel-plated and has a plaque on it: "MARK McQUILLEN, MD." I ring the bell.

I've heard the name somewhere before, but Violet figures it out before I do. Whispers *"The Dr. McQuillen Tape."*

Right. The thing eating the duck on Rec Bill's DVD. Even now it gives me the creeps.

We hear footsteps, and the lock being undone on the other side of the door.

"Lionel," Dylan says.

"What?"

"It's Thursday."

7

Ford, Minnesota
Still Thursday, 13 September

"Dylan Arntz," Dr. McQuillen says in the open doorway. "What have you been doing to yourself?"

He's a tall old man with narrow shoulders and excellent posture, and he holds his head back at an angle like he's looking down through bifocals. Maybe he wears them sometimes. "Never mind, I can smell it. Come in and be careful. No need to get blood on the walls."

As he watches Dylan's gait for signs of neurological damage, he takes a lab coat off a hook and pulls it over his cardigan. His hands are enormous. "What happened?" he says to Violet and me without turning to us.

"He got beaten up by some other kids behind a restaurant," Violet says.

"Debbie's," McQuillen says.

"You know the place."

"It's the only restaurant in Ford that's still open. Though I suppose the bar might serve food." To Dylan he says "Go into the examining room, young man. There are gowns under the table."

"He told us you have a CT machine," I say.

McQuillen looks at us for the first time. "Who are you?"

"Lionel Azimuth. I'm a physician. This is my coworker, Violet Hurst."

"Also a physician?"

"No," Violet says.

"Nurse?"

"No," she says.

"That's too bad. We could use one around here. You're not a drug rep, I hope?"

"No. I'm a paleontologist."

"At least that's more useful than a drug rep."

Violet laughs. "I'll be sure to tell my parents."

"I like that," Dr. McQuillen says. To me he says "I do have a CT machine. It's a single-slice GE that I bought used, with a grant from the state that I have since paid back. Thank you for bringing Dylan in. Good night."

I hold Dylan's tooth out to him as a peace offering. "Is it all right if we stay?"

McQuillen takes it and shrugs. "*I'd* want to. Although I'm afraid your lovely 'coworker' is going to have to remain in the waiting room."

ᕁ ● ● (

"Follow my finger with your eyes, please, Dylan." Dr. McQuillen drops his penlight into the pocket of his white coat and takes out a tuning fork, rapping it on the table as he brings it up. "Hear this?"

"Yes."

"Louder when I do this?" He presses the handle to Dylan's forehead, then moves the head back to near Dylan's ear. "Or this?"

"That," Dylan says.

Dylan's in his underwear and a gown that's open down the back. Swinging his feet off the edge of the table he looks like a child who's somehow gotten himself into a boxing match, with McQuillen and me as his cornermen. I'm using wet gauze and scissors to untangle the blood clots on the back of his scalp.

"Can you see that spot over there? Focus on it," McQuillen says. "What's fourteen times fourteen?"

"Uh—"

McQuillen pulls Dylan's broken nose away from his face, twists it, and lets it snap back into place.

"Ag, fuck!" Dylan says. While his mouth is still open, McQuillen slots his tooth back into his jaw, which he then holds shut.*

Dylan hums in pain.

"Stay closed now for a few minutes. Let it set." McQuillen puts the earpieces of his stethoscope in. "Shh. I need to be able to hear." He runs the stethoscope across Dylan's back, then listens to Dylan's chest and

---

* Factors believed to increase the success rate of tooth reinsertions: minimal time outside the mouth, transport of the tooth in an appropriate medium (ideally cold milk, next best the patient's saliva), and minimal trauma to the root while cleaning the dirt off of it.

abdomen while using his other hand to feel for liver and spleen abnormalities. Turns the head of the stethoscope side-on to use as a reflex hammer up and down Dylan's arms and legs.

It's fun to watch. It's the kind of routine that makes you wonder if you'll ever be that expert at anything.

McQuillen prods Dylan's spine and kidneys. "You're going to need stitches in two or three places, and you're going to need to stay here so we can watch you. Otherwise, you've gotten very lucky." He pinches one of Dylan's triceps,* causing Dylan to squeal.

"What about the CT scan?" I say.

"What about it?" McQuillen says.

"Are you going to give him one?"

"I see no reason to. His jaw is intact, as are both zygomas—at least to an extent that would rule out surgical intervention. There's no evidence of a LeFort or a suborbital. We've checked him for anosmia. He's not visibly leaking CSF, which means he's unlikely to require brain surgery. And as for hematomas, this one has a pretty hard head." To Dylan he says "What hurts most right now?"

"My nose," Dylan says through his teeth.

"See? We'll need to check for renal injury, but I have a perfectly good microscope. There are a lot of things you can tell about a patient without irradiating him, you know. In the nineteenth century, gynecologists operated blind."

---

* The singular of "triceps" is "triceps," because "triceps" means "three heads," referring to how the muscle splits at one end into oh, shit, I drifted off there. "Biceps" and "quadriceps" are similar.

"I think the standard of care may have changed since then."

McQuillen smiles. "Nobody likes a smart-ass, Doctor."

"That's right, Lionel," Dylan says.

"As for you," McQuillen says, "keep smoking meth. You won't be a smart-ass for long. First you'll be stupid. Then you'll be dead."

"I'm not smoking it."

"You will be. Then you'll be injecting it. I'll give you some clean hypodermics before you go. No need for you to get hep C while you're killing yourself with methamphetamine. I'm seventy-eight. I would appreciate it if you outlived me."

Dylan rolls his eyes.

"What about C-spine injury?" I say.

"Not worried about it," McQuillen says, in a condensation of a much longer discussion we then have.

"You're at least going to do plain films."

"I'd be treating you instead of the patient. Were you never in a scrap like this when you were young?"

"Not exactly."

"That doesn't surprise me. People barely act like physical beings now. Do you know what percentage of severe head injuries will cause a subarachnoid?"

"No."

"Five to ten. *Severe* head injuries. And a fast-moving subdural will show signs in the next two hours. A slow-moving one isn't going to show up on CT yet anyway."

"And what if he *does* get symptomatic while he's here? What are you going to do, drill a hole in his head?"

"Yes, actually," he says. "Don't worry, Dylan. It's not going to happen. Doctor, you don't worry either. If there's one benefit to practicing medicine in these parts, it's that you don't tend to get sued."

I go around to look Dylan in the face. "Dylan, Dr. McQuillen thinks it's all right for you to stay here. My advice is to come with me to the emergency room in Ely."

Dylan, still clenching his teeth, says "I think you've made that clear, dude."

"Good, then," McQuillen says. "Mr. Arntz, having been one my patients since approximately nine months before his birth, has chosen for now to remain one." To Dylan he says "All this being predicated on your willingness to stay here for observation, of course. Do you think you can go two hours without doing meth?"

"I only did meth once," Dylan says.

"What happened to twice?" I ask him.

"Thanks a lot, Lionel," Dylan says. "I'm gonna need a cigarette, though."

"You won't get that either," McQuillen says. "Deal or no deal?"

"Deal," Dylan says.

To me Dr. McQuillen says "Would you care to sew him up while I do the urinalysis? I'm guessing microscopy wasn't a large part of your medical school curriculum."

He's guessing right. "Sure."

"Dylan, you know where the bathroom is. Sample cups are in the medicine cabinet."

"Where's the drill?" I say. "In case we need it while you're gone."

"Second drawer down. It's a Black and Decker. Kidding, Dylan! *Although it is,*" he whispers to me as he walks past.

"Dude, he schooled you," Dylan says, still without opening his mouth. I'm sewing his forehead closed, holding the skin together with tweezers.

"Say that again when we're drilling through your skull."

"You are one weird-ass doctor, man."

"Uh huh." So weird-ass I'm about to grill him for information. Before I have time to think about how sleazy that is, I say "So if that lake we passed wasn't White Lake, where is White Lake?"

"It's not near here."

"I thought Ford was the closest town to it."

"It is. But White Lake's out in the Boundary Waters."

"Out in the Boundary Waters where?"

"Way out. Few days, at least. Pends how fast you can paddle."

"And what's the deal with it?"

"What do you mean?"

"Violet and I are thinking of going there."

"Don't."

"Why not?"

"It sucks."

"Sucks how?"

I possibly say this with a bit too much interest. He goes quiet.

"Dylan?"

"I don't know. Forget I said anything."

"You didn't say anything."

He fidgets, forcing me to stop sewing.

"What?" I say.

"Dude, if you're some kind of cop, could we wait on the stitches till the real doctor gets back?"

"I'm not a cop."

"Come on, dude. I don't know anything about that shit."

"What shit?"

"The people who got killed. That's what you want me to say, right?"

"The people who got *killed?* What the fuck are you talking about?"

"You brought it up."

"Not people getting killed."

I back away to look him in the face, but he avoids my eyes.

"I didn't know them. They were older'n me," he says.

"What happened?"

"Oh, come on, man. I don't know."

"What *might* have happened?"

"They got eaten. Okay?"

"They got *eaten?*"

"It's this thing creatures do with their teeth."

"Thank you for that. What did they get eaten *by?*"

But before he can tell me—or avoid telling me—McQuillen interrupts us from the doorway. "Doctor. If you're not in the middle of a suture, I'd like a word with you alone."

 ⟩⟨⟨⟨

From his tone I'm worried McQuillen has found something in Dylan's urine. But once we're in the examining room across the hall—it's empty, not even a table—it turns out he's just furious. "Doctor, if you're going to behave like a moron, I would appreciate your not doing it in front of my patients."

I'm relieved and embarrassed at the same time.

"You were asking Dylan about a monster in White Lake," he says.

"Kind of, yeah."

"Why?"

"I heard there was one. Now Dylan says there is."

"Heard there was one from whom?"

"A guy named Reggie Trager."

"Under what circumstances?"

I see no point to lying about it. "He sent a DVD about it to the man who hired me to come find out if the monster was real."

McQuillen sags against the doorframe. "Oh, Christ. Not this again."

"What do you mean?"

"And this time it's *Reggie Trager* who's publicizing it?"

"He's running a tour for rich people who want to see the monster. What do you mean, 'Not this again'? It's happened before?"

McQuillen squints and stretches the skin of his face all around in a gesture of frustration. "Some people tried to organize a monster hoax in Ford a couple of years ago. Not a tour, as far as I know, just a rumor that a monster existed. They picked White Lake because it's hard to get to and it isn't on maps. The one smart thing about that plan."

"What was the point?"

"Ford's a mining town. In 2006, Norville Rogers Ford

the Ninth or whatever he was sold the mine so he could buy real estate in North Florida. The company that bought it from him shut it right down—their only interest in it was as a hedge in case high-hematite iron ever got expensive again. Which it won't. The Chinese can strain ore out of dirt now. They're not about to pay people in Minnesota to dig it out pure.

"All Ford has left is its position on the edge of the Boundary Waters. You can't build waterfront anymore— Reggie's place is grandfathered in—but you could probably convert the permit of the iron plant. And even if you couldn't, there's plenty of available space. Tourism is the only hope this town has. Some people thought that was worth lying for."

"And Reggie was one of them?"

"I never heard that he was, although most of the town was involved in some way or another. I can tell you I never heard anything about Reggie leading a tour to White Lake. *That* I would have remembered. I've never even seen that boy in a canoe."

"So what happened? Why didn't the hoax take off?"

"A lot of fools put a lot of effort into trying to make sure that it did. But right before they were going to unveil their monster to the world, a couple of teenagers got killed out at White Lake in a boating accident. I don't know if people saw it as some kind of divine punishment or they just felt it would be in particularly bad taste to launch a monster hoax right then, but the result was that people came to their senses, and the project was shelved."

"Reggie's got an unfinished documentary about the monster. There's something called 'The Dr. McQuillen Tape' —"

He shakes his head. "Of course there is. If you've seen it, you may have noticed that it's of a pike eating a loon. Not a particularly big pike either. I did take that videotape. I certainly never gave those idiots permission to use it, though, let alone for them to drag my name through any of this."

"There's also a man—"

"—who claims his leg was bitten off by the monster. Yes, I've seen that part as well. The documentary was being made for the hoax two years ago. Reggie probably hasn't added to it at all."

"So...what about that guy?"

"With the leg? If you believe his story, I suggest you write it up for the *New England Journal of Medicine*. I'm fairly certain it would be a first."

"Do you know him?"

"If I did, and he was a patient, I wouldn't gossip about him. But I will say this: I have never treated anyone for a bite wound from a lake monster. Now perhaps I can ask *you* a question. What the hell does someone who calls himself a man of science think he's doing going on a tour to see a mythical being? Never mind that: I can see you have no good answer. What the hell are you doing encouraging Dylan Arntz's fantasies about what happened to his friends out there two years ago?"

Like I have a good answer to that either.

McQuillen says "I would appreciate it if you refrained. I have a telephone that I do sometimes answer. If you have other ludicrous questions, please hesitate to call me. If you find you can't resist, I'll try my best to answer them. In the meantime, I'll walk you out. I can finish up with Mr. Arntz alone."

"Dylan, the visiting doctor is leaving," Dr. McQuillen says as he ushers me past the examining room.

"Bye, dude," Dylan says with his jaw clenched.

"Take care of yourself, Dylan," I say. To McQuillen, I say "How's his urine?"

"Undefiled."

We get to the waiting room and both stop.

Except for a lamp on the reception desk, all the lights are out.

Violet's gone.

EXHIBIT D

Ford, Minnesota
Slightly earlier on Thursday, 13 September*

Violet gets bored of hanging out in McQuillen's waiting room, reading *Time* from six months ago and *Field & Stream* from who gives a shit. It's not that she doesn't sympathize with hunters: she understands people's need to pretend the world's still full of resource-intensive animals they can party-kill out of fucked-up rage, just like she understands people's need to reenact the Civil War because they don't like the way *that* turned out. The problem is that the two groups overlap so heavily.

Violet's pretty sure she remembers seeing a bar a ways down Rogers Avenue from Debbie's Diner. McQuillen definitely mentioned one. And she's pretty sure she can

---

* **How I know this:** Violet Hurst, various easily made conjectures.

take a more direct route than Azimuth did driving here.
Cut out some distance and avoid the restaurant at the
same time. No reason not to walk.

She uses the yellowing prescription pad on the receptionist's desk to write Azimuth a note, which she leaves
under the car keys. Turns the desk lamp on and the room
light off so he won't miss it.

꘏꘎꘎꘍

It's gotten dark out, sliver moon over the lake but everything inland mostly blackness with occasional streetlights. The chill and the smell of woodsmoke remind
her of Halloweens back in Lawrence. She can see her
breath.

She figures it's about fifty degrees Fahrenheit.
Which—the Fahrenheit part—pisses her off. Violet will
never be able to instinctively judge temperatures in Cel-
sius. She wasn't raised to. And being raised without the
metric system is like being raised with a harness on your
brain.

In metric, one milliliter of water occupies one cubic
centimeter, weighs one gram, and requires one calorie of
energy to heat up by one degree centigrade—which is 1 percent of the difference between its freezing point and its
boiling point. An amount of hydrogen weighing the same
amount has exactly one mole of atoms in it.

Whereas in the American system, the answer to "How
much energy does it take to boil a room-temperature gal-
lon of water?" is "Go fuck yourself," because you can't
directly relate any of those quantities.

Violet decides that while her watch face is still glowing,

she should calculate the temperature using cricket noises. Because the equation she knows for that—like most equations she knows—is in metric.

By cricket it's ten degrees centigrade out. Which by conversion is fifty degrees Fahrenheit.

It gets her off the porch. Whatever's out there is better than thinking about *this* bullshit.

Whatever's out there is pretty damn eerie, though.

Past the three-blocks-long fancy district, the number of streetlights drops off sharply. Most of the houses don't have lights on either, and a lot of the ones that do have papered-over windows for no reason Violet can guess. The small boats in some of the driveways are mummified in blue tarps and chains, with the chains spiked to cement blocks. Everything she passes has a "FOR SALE" sign on it.

For a while she can hear what sounds like a Tom Petty album playing somewhere ahead of her, but the source, when she reaches it, turns out to be the open front door of a house with all its lights off. Later, what seem at first to be red flares on the horizon resolve into the cigarette tips of a ring of people standing in the middle of the street, talking in murmurs.

No reason for them *not* to be in the middle of the street, Violet supposes. There aren't sidewalks here, just loud gravel shoulders, and she has yet to see a car.

Still, she circles the smokers without alerting them, half expecting them to put their faces into the air and start sniffing for her.

The bar turns out to be four blocks past Debbie's. It's called Sherry's—raising the possibility, Violet supposes, that if she goes inside, a woman named Sherry will come after her with an ax. Worth the risk.

Inside, it's a deep, narrow space of dark wood and Christmas lights, with only four stools and two people: the bartender and, on the left-most stool, one customer.

Both are males in their early thirties or so, which in Portland would make them hipster man-boys, but here means they're grown men in practical haircuts who look like they've been through some shit. The bartender in particular has the electrocuted expression Violet associates with people who have been through rehab. The guy on the stool has the sloping back and lowered shoulders of a bear. They're both big, and neither of them is leering.

Violet likes the big guys. The little ones always want to resent-fuck her. It may explain why Dr. Lionel Azimuth, with the forearms and the laugh like a garbage disposal, makes her want to take her bra off.

Or maybe nothing explains that.

She takes the right-most stool. Says "Got any interesting beer?"

"All beer is at least mildly interesting," the guy on the other stool says.

Violet couldn't agree more. Beer is the perfect population-overshoot scenario: you put a bunch of organisms into an enclosed space with more carbohydrates than they've ever seen before, then watch as they kill themselves off with their own waste products, in this case carbon dioxide and alcohol. Then you drink it.

"You mean like a hefeweizen or something?" the bartender says.

"Maybe not a hefeweizen per se."

"I was just using that as an example." He pokes through the refrigerator under the bar. "Doesn't look too good. If you're not from around here, you might find Grain Star interesting."

The guy on the stool raises his bottle. Cool retro label.

"Sounds good."

"Grain Star it is," the bartender says.

"But what makes you think I'm not from around here?"

Both men laugh. "Saw this place in the Michelin guide, huh?"

"Yeah," Violet says. "It was under 'Bars in Ford that are actually open.'"

The bartender spins two St. Pauli Girl coasters onto the bar and puts a pint glass on one and a bottle on the other.* The bottle steams water vapor when he opens it. "I don't have St. Pauli Girl either," the bartender says. "The coasters were here when I bought the place. I'm still going through them."

"Then we should use them up," Violet says. "One more for the bartender, please."

"Thank you, but I'm a Diet Coke guy, myself." The bartender raises his glass to show her, and Violet and the

---

* "Pint glass": 470 ml in the U.S., 570 ml in the U.K. (Britain's not on the metric system either, which is why the pickup line "Funny how it's 'Gonna give you every inch of my love' even though Britain's on the metric system" doesn't work as well there.) So Violet may be onto something.

guy on the left-most stool lean to clink it with their bottles. Violet's liking this place more and more.

"Not bad," she says after she's swallowed. Not good, particularly, either. Grain Star is sweet, thin, and metallic, though she supposes it's unusual enough that you could form an attachment to it if you did something fun while you were drinking it.

Doesn't seem too likely. Not unless Dr. Azimuth shows up and takes her to their hotel wanting to pull her hair from behind.

Violet didn't just think that. She belches. Says "Fuck's the matter with this place?"

The bartender and the guy on the stool trade glances. "There's a couple good bars in Soudan you could check out," the bartender says.

"I'm not talking about the bar," Violet says. "The bar's great. I'm talking about the town."

"Oh, that," the bartender says.

"Right. Ford," the guy on the stool says.

"Yeah," Violet says. "Ford."

The guy on the stool says "Personally, I blame the mayor."

"Most people do," the bartender says.

"Why? What's wrong with him?"

"He's something of a dickhead," the guy on the stool says.

"Who hangs out with even bigger dickheads," the bartender says.

"Who he makes look good by comparison."

"He also inspires a lot of resentment."

"Or so he likes to think."

"What do you mean?" Violet says.

"We're just fucking with you," the guy on the stool says. He nods toward the bartender. "He's the mayor."

"And *he* owns the Speed Mart and the liquor store. Congratulations: you've just met the second- and third-biggest employers in Ford."

"Nice to meet you. Who's the first?"

"CFS. By a long shot."

"Debbie employs more people than you or I do," the guy on the stool says. "Unless by 'employs' you mean 'pays them with money.' "

"Hey now," the bartender says.

"You mean Debbie the psychopathic waitress?"

"You've met Debbie," the guy on the stool says.

"Yeah. What's her fucking problem?"

As he's about to answer, the bartender says to Violet, "You wouldn't happen to be an officer of the law, would you?"

"No."

"No offense. It's just that you look like someone from a TV show."

"Oh, start. But no: I'm not an officer of the law. Either in reality or on a TV show."

She watches them try to figure out how to politely ask her what she *does* do. "I'm a paleontologist."

The guy on the stool turns to her. "Like in *Jurassic Park*?"

"Exactly like that."

Although the only part of the *Jurassic Park* movie Violet now considers realistic is how everybody calls the male PhD "Dr. Grant" and the female PhD "Ellie," she doesn't mind the association. Both the book and the movie were instrumental in her choice of career. And they've turned paleontology into a job that everybody thinks, at least, they can relate to.

"I call bullshit," the bartender says.

"I'll show you my badge," Violet says.

"Really?"

"Yeah. There's a badge for being a paleontologist. What's wrong with Debbie?"

The two men look at each other. "Well...she's had it rough," the bartender says.

"That's true," the guy on the stool says.

"What happened?"

"She lost a kid a couple of years ago," the bartender says.

"Shit," Violet says.

"Which maybe isn't an excuse for flipping out, but maybe it is."

"Could well be," the guy on the stool agrees.

"There were some kids behind her restaurant," Violet says.

The bartender shakes his head. "The Boys just work for her. None of them is her son. She just had the one, Benjy."

"What happened to him?"

The two men trade glances again.

"What?" Violet says.

The guy on the stool shrugs. "That's...not all that clear."

"What do you mean?"

After a moment, the bartender says "Benjy and his girlfriend got killed skinny-dipping in a place called White Lake."

Violet almost chokes on beer.

"You've heard of it?" the bartender says.

"Yeah. How did they get killed?"

"Police ended up deciding they got cut up by a boat propeller."

"But you don't think that's what happened?"

"It's what the police decided."

Violet studies them. "You guys are fucking with me again. You're trying to make me think it was the monster."

They stare at her.

"You've heard about William?" the guy on the stool says.

"William?"

"William, the White Lake Monster."

"Okay," Violet says. "First off, now I *know* you're fucking with me. I've heard there's a monster. I've never heard it was called William. Or that it killed people."

Which means they *have* to be fucking with her. If there had been deaths at White Lake, Reggie Trager's letter would have mentioned them, as advertising.

She pushes her empty beer bottle toward the bartender. "Second off, I need another one of these."

"If you're opening the fridge anyway," the guy on the stool says.

"You people are so full of shit," Violet says.

"Well," the bartender says, digging through the refrigerator, "yes and no."

Len unrolls a T-shirt on top of the bar. Len is the bartender. The guy on the stool is Brian. They all traded names before Len went back to the storeroom for the shirt.

It has a cartoon of a lake monster on it. Kind of an apatosaurus-plesiosaur mix, but with a smile and one raised eyebrow. Text underneath the creature says "Ford, Minnesota." A speech bubble next to its head says *"I'm a BILLiever!"*

"You can keep it," Len says. "I've got tons of these pieces of shit. I should use *them* for coasters. Just don't wear it around Ford or you'll start a riot."

"Why?"

"People around here think that somehow agreeing to do the hoax caused all those people to die."

"What do you mean, 'all those people'?"

There's a pause. "There were, uh, two other people who died too," Brian O' the Stool says.

"At White Lake?"

"Oh, no," Len says. Like *that's* ridiculous. "Chris Jr. and Father Podominick got shot. Around here."

"So what does that have to do with it? *I* almost got shot around here today. Ford's a dangerous place, Mr. Mayor."

"I'll relay your concerns to my chief of police."

"Seriously: what does that have to do with White Lake?"

Brian says "The two guys who got shot—Chris Jr. and Father Podominick—were kind of the ones who had the idea for the hoax in the first place. And they got shot only five days after the kids died."

Violet says "A *priest* had the idea for the hoax?"

Maybe there *is* a reason Reggie Trager chose to not get into this squalid shit. Four dead bodies, and anything at all having to do with a priest, and it starts to get creepy.

"Also, Chris Jr. was Autumn Semmel's father."

"Wait. What?"

Violet's a bit drunk. That's the joke about Violet Hurst: she's a lightweight. Partly because of the antidepressants, which even if they don't do shit else for her are worth it for that reason. She suspects, though, that right now she'd be confused even if she were sober.

Brian says "Autumn and Benjy died, and right after that Father Podominick and Autumn's father got shot. So it did kind of seem like there might be a connection."

"Yeah. I can see why it would."

"You have to understand, though," Len says, "the whole thing started out as a *joke*. I mean, look at the T-shirt." He's got a beer in his hand where the glass of Diet Coke used to be. Violet didn't see the change.

"But the two guys who got shot," she says. "If Debbie thought they were responsible for the hoax, and that her son somehow died because of the hoax, then why doesn't everyone just assume Debbie shot them? Or had her Boys do it?"

Brian taps the side of his nose. Len, seeing it, says "Hey—come on. That's just hearsay."

"Doesn't mean it isn't true," Brian says.

"Doesn't mean it is."

"Is it?" Violet says.

Len doesn't answer.

Brian says "Don't ask me. I've been shamed into silence."

"I don't think it is," Len says finally. "She definitely didn't have the Boys do it. She didn't have them yet when it happened. And it's kind of hard for me, at least, to picture Debbie doing something like that by herself. Plus, the person she *really* blames for the hoax is Reggie Trager. And as far as I know she's never tried to kill *him*."

"Why Reggie Trager?"

"Who knows? I'm sure he was involved—the whole *town* was involved. But I didn't see him at any of the meetings, and I went to most of them. That's another thing: nobody's ever tried to kill *me* either."

"I'm already dead inside," Brian says.

"And," Len says, "maybe Father Podominick and Chris Jr. getting shot didn't have anything to do with Autumn and Benjy dying after all. Maybe someone mistook them for deer. Nobody knows, cause nobody knows who did it. Meanwhile everybody feels all guilty. Like it was our fault the monster turned out to be real."

Violet replays that last bit in her head. "You're saying the monster is *real?*"

Both men seem suddenly interested in the wood of the bar.

"Oh, come on. I'm not going to quote you."

"Whatever happened to Benjy and Autumn," Brian says quietly, "it wasn't a boat propeller."

"How do you know?"

"There were two other kids out there with them. Good kids, who everybody knew. They said there was no motorboat out there. That it was something else."

"I'm listening."

"They didn't fully see it."

"So what did they think it was? What do *you guys* think it was?"

"There's a few different theories," Len says, still not looking at her.

"I'm listening."

"Look, a lot of it sounds pretty crazy."

"Understood."

"You know...like dinosaurs. Or—" He looks up at her. "Hey, is that why *you're* here?"

"Only partly," Violet says. "What are some of the other theories?"

"Well...something from space. Or this thing that the Ojibwe call a *Wendigo*. People have been seeing *that* thing forever."

"What is it?"

"Some kind of Bigfoot-type thing."

Brian says "*I* think—is it okay if I tell her what I think?"

Len says "Don't be a dickwad."

"I think it came out of the mine. You're not going to believe this, but after the mine closed, the government sent a bunch of scientists down there to check it out. I'm not making this up: they were here in town. They came into the store a couple times. I think they were trying to trap it, but they couldn't, and they ended up just pissing it off. Or waking it up. I'm not saying it wasn't originally from space, or isn't a dinosaur or a Wendigo or whatever. But I think before it moved to White Lake it was down in that mine for a long, long time. Maybe since before there were warm-blooded creatures up here for it to eat."

When the door at the back of the bar bangs open, everyone jumps.

It's Dr. Lionel Azimuth, coming down the aisle of the bar like a bowling ball. Scaring the shit out of Brian and Len even further.

Violet stands to meet him. "Hello, darling!"

She puts her arm through Azimuth's and—swear to God, an accident—stumbles into him. It's like stumbling into a telephone pole.

"We were just talking," she says. "These people know about William."

"Uh huh. Time to go home, *dear*."

Violet leans close. Exhales wetly into his ear as she says "William the *White Lake Monster*." Causing him to stiffen up, unclear whether from the information or her lips brushing his skin.

Brian and Len still look nervous. "Don't mind him," Violet says to them. "He's a big square. He's a *doctor*. He just doesn't approve of my drinking."

"You two know about the White Lake Monster?" Azimuth says to them. "About the hoax?"

"Uh…" Len says. Azimuth follows his eyes to the T-shirt on the bar.

Violet, wanting to spare Brian and Len having to go through it again, says "I'll tell you about it in the car."

"She's not driving, right?" Len says.

"No," Violet says, "she's not. She walked here."

Azimuth says "Okay. But one thing. What's the name of the guy in the documentary who says he got his leg bitten off?"

Len and Brian look at each other.

"Charlie Brisson," Len says.

"Thanks," Azimuth says. "How much do we owe you?"

"It's on me," Len says. To Violet, he says "Just don't forget your shirt."

Ely, Minnesota
Still Thursday, 13 September

I carry Violet into the Ely Lakeside Hotel like I'm looking for some train tracks to tie her to. It reminds me how much you have to weigh to look like a bombshell.*

Back in Ford I made her tell me everything she'd learned from those dipshits in the bar before I would start the engine—I was afraid she wouldn't remember it all when she woke up. Telling me involved a lot of her putting

---

* Although as someone who, in strictly medical capacities, has hauled my share of corpses around, it never ceases to amaze me how much easier it is to move someone who's sleeping but alive— and therefore still balancing—than someone who's actually dead. Moving a dead body is like moving a futon.

her hand on my thigh for emphasis, and my having an erection that felt like part of the car.

The teenage girl who checks us into the hotel says "Looks like *someone's* having fun." I can only hope she's referring to Violet being drunk, and not to my having access to her unconscious body.

I put Violet to bed, dressed, in one of the rooms, and go down to the hotel bar. It has a porch overlooking some lake. I get a Grain Star of my own and take it outside to look at the water. Beyond it, dark as a jungle, is the Boundary Waters.

Eventually the bartender comes out and leans against the railing next to me. Blond and thirty-five, with a sun-aged smile that I like. "Do you mind if I smoke?" she says.

I think about that. Cigarettes are so fucking awful for you that they make your urine carcinogenic and your brain unable to regulate how much oxygen it gets, and as a doctor I probably have a responsibility to say something along those lines. But I have no idea what. Preventative medicine's hard to bill for, so the only research on how to change human behavior through communication gets done by the advertising industry.

"Only for your sake," I end up saying, thinking I need to formulate something better. "Am I keeping you up?"

She lights and does the slow exhale. "Not yet."

Nice.

I get along with bartenders. There are plenty of women to sleep with on a cruise ship—it's called a *cruise* ship, for fuck's sake—but if you're into superficiality, bartenders are special. Not to belabor it, but they do spend most of their time being sociable behind a barrier.

I should go home with this woman and tell Violet about it in the morning. Better yet, take her to my room and project as much noise as possible through the wall. Kill any chance with Violet I might have.

Since Magdalena Niemerover's death because of me eleven years ago, I've observed the following rule: if a woman gets so close to me that she cares what my birthday is, I never talk to her again. It keeps me from endangering anyone, and has other benefits as well, since half the time *I* don't remember when Lionel Azimuth's birthday is supposed to be. And the last thing anyone needs is to try to throw me a surprise party.

Violet and I haven't reached that point yet. But my lies are piling up fast—commission, omission, whatever. If it's not too late for us to have stranger sex now, it will be soon. And if I'm going to have sex with her on the premise that she actually knows something about me, I might as well go do it now, while she's passed out.

I should end the possibility. I'm too weak to, though.

"I won't take up much more of your time," I say to the bartender. "My wife and I have to get going in the morning."

If anything, the bartender looks relieved. Now we can have something even *shallower* than a sexual relationship.

"Where to?"

"We're just tourists," I say. Which, it occurs to me, is true. Here in civilization—even civilization with a view of not-civilization—Ford and its discontents seem a million miles off. "Anything we should see?"

"You planning on going canoeing?"

"Probably."

A werewolf howl rips out of the Boundary Waters, full force from across the lake.

The bartender sees my face and laughs. "It's just a loon," she says, making me wonder how many of northern Minnesota's mysteries are going to turn out to be just a loon. "Don't get your hopes up."

9

"I don't really remember the details," the librarian says, picking up the phone, "but I know who does. Hold on a sec."

Violet, in her sunglasses, is listing against the counter. I woke her up early and dragged her to a place here in Ely that, I shit you not, was called the Chocolate Moose.

Ely is not like Ford. Its central avenue looks like something from a ski town, all souvenir shops and organic grocery stores. Two blocks over there's an intersection with a granite WPA office building on each corner, one of which has the public library in it.

So far, the library hasn't been much help. We've read back issues of Ely's two weekly newspapers on the library's computers, but they're both strangely circumspect when it comes to Ford. I don't know if they consider Ford too far away to be interesting or whether what happens there just isn't a good fit with the weddings, high school football games, and letters to the editor that make up the rest of the papers' material. But Ford hardly gets mentioned.

We *have* managed to confirm that the four deaths there actually happened—Autumn Semmel's and Benjy Schneke's as the result of "a boating accident" at the end of June two years ago, Chris Semmel Jr.'s and Father Nathan Podominick's in "a possible hunting accident" five days later.

And, interestingly, we've learned that the University of Minnesota was at one point considering building its High Energy Physics Lab at the bottom of the closed Ford Mine. Which might explain the visiting scientists, although U Minn seems to have come to its senses and put the lab at the bottom of the Soudan Mine instead.

Past that, it for some reason seemed like a good idea to ask the librarian.

"Carol?" she says now into the phone. "It's Barbara. Is the sheriff in? I've got some people here who want to know about White Lake."

"That's really not necessary," I say quickly.

The librarian covers the mouthpiece. "Don't worry, they're not busy."

"No, really—"

She's not listening to me, though. She's nodding and saying "Uh huh, uh huh" to whoever's on the phone. She covers the mouthpiece again. "Carol says to come on over. What are your names?"

"Violet Hurst and Lionel Azimuth," Violet says.

"Their names are Violet Hurst and Lionel Azimuth," the librarian says. "I'm sending them across right now."

"And Reggie *Trager* is running this tour?" Sheriff Albin says.

Albin's early thirties, with a small, knobby head and a slow way of talking, possibly due to the industrial-grade bullshit-detection software he seems to be running. Naturally, he's done nothing since Carol sat us down in front of his desk except grill the shit out of us. And write down our names.

"That doesn't seem like something Reggie would do?" I ask, even though I've been trying to stay quiet enough that Albin doesn't feel the need to look me up after we leave.

He barely shrugs. "Who's your employer?"

"We're not allowed to say," Violet says, with the fearlessness of the just. "It's a large private philanthropy."

For all I know that's true, although I'm pretty sure the check *I* got was from a company with "Technologies" in its name.

Albin weighs Violet's nonresponse and decides to let it go. "Has any money changed hands between your employer and Reggie Trager?"

"No. At least not yet," Violet says.

You can practically see Albin wondering if what Reggie's doing is indictable in advance, under RICO, and if so whether Albin has a responsibility to take it to the DA. Not a lot of thanks in that, I'm guessing.

"And has he stated specifically what kind of animal it is that you would be expected to find at White Lake?"

"No," Violet says.

"Although your employer sent a paleontologist."

"I'm the only life sciences researcher he has on personal staff," Violet says. "I think that has more to do with why I'm here."

Albin looks at me.

"I don't do research," I say. Which is true.

Then at his notes. "And the letter was on CFS stationery. How long is this 'tour' supposed to last?"

"Six to twelve days," Violet says.

"Six to twelve *days?*"

"What's wrong with that?"

"It's just a long time to take people who aren't canoers on a canoeing trip."

"I think we'll be on land for most of that time," Violet says.

"Reggie said that?"

"No..."

"Then I would question that assumption. Do you know where White Lake is?"

"No," Violet says.

Albin gets up and goes to a gun cabinet that turns out to have maps in it instead of shotguns. Cute. He takes one out and unrolls it on his desk.

It's a Fisher elevation map. Yellow land, tarp-blue water. I used to use them in my former line of work.

On this one, though, there's blue all over the place, like the holes in a sponge.

"This is Lake Garner," he says, pointing to an elongated blue horizontal oval. "And this is White Lake."

White Lake looks like a lightning bolt touching down at Lake Garner's northeastern end. Together the two lakes look like a musical note with a jagged vertical stem.

"White Lake looks so narrow," Violet says.

"That's because Lake Garner is fairly big," Albin says. "White Lake is about a hundred yards across where it touches Lake Garner, and it gets wider as it goes north." Albin points to the southwest corner of the map. "Meanwhile, Ford is three maps that way."

"How long a trip is that usually?" Violet says.

"Could take two days, could take a week," Albin says. "Depends which portages you use."

" 'Portages'?"

"Por*tahg*es," he says, changing the pronunciation so that instead of rhyming with "cordage" it rhymes with *"fromage."* "Same thing. Just American versus French-Canadian."

"I don't—" Violet says. She looks at me.

"No idea," I say.

Sheriff Albin lets his head drop in a moment of exasperation. "Okay. I'm going to have to teach you about portages. They're the key to the whole Boundary Waters."

EXHIBIT E

Ill-Star Lake, Dakota*
Saturday, 2 April, AD 1076†

Two Persons really gets his back into it now that he can
hear the beat of an airborne ax whirling toward him from
behind. But still his mind stays weirdly clear. Thinking,
*You couldn't really throw a large ax from the canoe I'm
in. It would just tip over.* Unlike from the Dakota‡ warboat chasing him.

The warboat, with its crew of six hard-rowing Dakota
face-eaters, is the trunk of a single enormous red pine.
Hollowing it out has to have taken months of work by a

---

* Now Boot Lake, Minnesota.

† **How I know this:** Sheriff Marc Albin, Lake County Sheriff's
Department.

‡ Known to Whitey as the Teton branch of the Sioux.

large group of people—Two Persons has had that job himself, though not, thank Gods, in years. Meanwhile, the canoe Two Persons is test-driving is so light and fragile that with each oar-stroke it digs its nose deep into the waterline, then shudders as it bobs free. Something else to report back to Knowledgeable Raccoon. If, of course, Two Persons survives the next few minutes.

The ax, spinning horizontally—*Why?* he thinks. *Just to show me that your giant fucking canoe is so stable you can throw things from it sideways?*—passes just to the left of Two Persons' ducked head, then curves to the right before it contacts the water. It skips once and heavily goes under. A moment later Two Persons is past the spot where it went down. It does move along, Knowledgeable Raccoon's new all-bark, carryable, one-man canoe.

Still, fuck Knowledgeable Raccoon, if for no other reason than the off chance that he's the one who told the chief that Two Persons has been skimming the grouse take. For Two Persons to receive the virtual death sentence of trying out Knowledgeable Raccoon's new boat just for stealing a few fucking grouse is ridiculous. Two Persons has screwed three of the chief's daughters and two of his wives. But there you have it.

Or maybe this assignment *does* have to do with the daughters and wives. Two Persons flinches as the shadow of something overhead crosses his face, and a falling ax head, spun to stay vertical, nicks cleanly through the bottom of the canoe right in front of him.

You know, that could be a problem, "Knowledgeable."

The canoe immediately starts shipping water, but less so than Two Persons would have thought. Or maybe he actually has it flying now, his flailing arms turning the paddle into a wing.

The canoe scrapes rock. Showtime: he hasn't let himself believe he was this close to shore. He jumps out and lifts the front end like Knowledgeable taught him to, rolling the whole thing over so he can duck under it and run.

Looking back, he gets a glimpse of Death itself. The Dakota warship is turning sideways, either so everyone in it can jump out and chase Two Persons onto land or so they can all hurl projectiles at him at once.

Two Persons, figuring he's about to find out, reminds himself that the sense he now has of his back being protected by the bark canoe is pure illusion. He lifts it high above his head and exits the water, dancing up a couple of boulders to reach the woods between Ill-Star Lake and Lake Waste-of-Time,* no problem. Because now the canoe really is up in the air—and it doesn't weigh *anything*.

Still, visibility's not the greatest, and if he snags the tip of the canoe on a branch, or drives it into the ground, it's *Goodbye, face*. Most of what he can see is the underbrush at his feet, which explodes into fleeing animal life with every step he takes. Two Persons has never made this much noise in his life. Among mammals alone he identifies a fisher, a martin, an ermine, and a wolverine.

An ax ricochets off his right side, knocking him sideways and almost down but just missing him with its edge. Apparently the Dakota have joined him on land.

But through the branches ahead he can see water again.

Then he's there: Lake Waste-of-Time. His instinct is to throw the canoe out onto the water, so you know what?

---

* Now known as Corners Lake. What, are you going there?

That's what he does. And it lands more or less upright, stabilizing quickly once it starts to take on water again through the gash in the bottom.

Two Persons splashes out to where it's drifting, but uses Knowledgeable Raccoon's recommended means of getting in, since he can't afford to fuck this up: hands on either side, first foot down in the center, other foot drawn in beside it. Now he's ready to row, and just in time: he can hear the Dakota crashing out of the trees.

Looking around him, Two Persons realizes he no longer has the paddle. He can't remember putting it down, but clearly he didn't have it with him when he crossed between the lakes, because he was carrying the canoe with both hands.

Fuck!

He throws himself onto his stomach and starts rowing by hand. He can only reach one side at a time. Water has never felt thinner. The boat seems to move in a circle.

He starts alternating sides more regularly. The shore behind him leaves his peripheral vision. The water turns deep. Even so, he can't understand why the Dakota haven't caught him and killed him until he looks back and sees them still standing on the shore a full sixty furlongs behind him.

Staring at the canoe. And talking in low, serious voices.

While on the *far* shore—the one that marks the border between the Dakota and Ojibwe* lands—Two Persons can now see his own platoon gathered. Including Knowledgeable Raccoon, who goes from frowning with concen-

---

* Known to Whitey as the Chippewa.

tration to howling in triumph like a wolf while giving the Dakota the "fuck you" sign.

Fuck you is right, Two Persons thinks, rolling over in the water at the bottom of the canoe, exhausted.

Fuck all of you.

10

"Carrying a canoe from one lake to another is called portaging," Sheriff Albin says. "The path you use to do it is called a portage."

"Huh," I say.

I haven't really been listening to him. His story sounded like bullshit—particularly the part about the Dakota eating people's faces—and was reminding me of this cologne that mob guys used to wear called Canoe. Maybe they still do.

It also made me wonder why Sheriff Albin's spending so much time on us. It's one thing to try to get information about a potential crime being committed by Reggie Trager. It's another to get out maps and take us back to Olde Indian Times.

"Portages are tricky, is the thing," he goes on. "They grow over, the shoreline changes, you're not allowed to put up signs or score trees to mark them. Even if they're still where your map says they are, they can be hard to spot from the water. And just because it's a portage that you can get a forty-five-pound Kevlar tripper over doesn't mean you're going to be able to move a two-hundred-and-twenty-pound, four-person aluminum touring boat and all your gear through it. The trail could go straight up a cliff. It could just be too long.

"So if you're going lake to lake to lake, there might be a dozen different paths you could choose from, depending on what you need to portage and who's going to be doing the portaging. Getting the right route from point A to point B is like opening a combination lock."

Jesus. Enough already.

"What do you think happened to Benjy Schneke and Autumn Semmel?" Violet says, making me want to fuck her even more than usual.

Albin's face darkens. "Is Reggie Trager using *that* to sell his tour?"

"No, he isn't. We heard about it in Ford, then looked it up in the library."

"You're sure about that?"

"Yes."

It calms him down a bit.

"What *do* you think happened?" I say. I'd rather Albin get suspicious and look me up than go back to boring me to death.

"It wasn't within my jurisdiction."

"You don't cover Ford?"

"We do in most cases. Ford's not in Lake County, but

they contract with us for services—we send them a bill, they don't pay it, we patrol there anyhow. Saves us trouble in the long run. But out in the actual Boundary Waters it's usually Parks and Recreation, and homicides anywhere in the state except the Twin Cities go to the Minnesota Bureau of Criminal Apprehension, down in Bemidji."

"So you didn't take the call."

As far as I can tell, there is no reason at all for him to respond to that.

"I did take the call."

"And you talked to the other two kids who were there?"

"Numerous times. Both families have since moved, incidentally. Don't go looking for them."

"We won't. Did you see the bodies?"

Violet gives me a sharp look. Albin *still* doesn't get mad.

"Yes, I did."

At which point I begin to understand what's going on.

Albin *has* to believe there's a 90 percent chance that Violet and I are con artists, morons, or both. But it can't be every day that people claiming to be a paleontologist and a physician walk into his office and express interest in a case that supposedly involves a human-eating lake monster. And which, two years later, still hasn't been solved.

"What do you think happened?" I say, for what feels like the fifth time.

"The MBCA report called it a motorboat accident."

"I thought motorboats were illegal in the Boundary Waters."

"They are, but that doesn't mean people don't bring them in. A lot of the lakes around the edges of the Boundary Waters are half in and half out, and it's legal to use motorboats on the half that's out, so things get pretty porous. A couple of weeks ago, when it was warmer, people were waterskiing on Ford Lake. Which is legal on the third of the lake that's closest to civilization."

I try to picture anyone from Ford waterskiing. I actually went waterskiing once myself, in the early nineties, with David Locano and his son. The three of us—no worthwhile human being in the group—with our own powerboat and stretch of pristine, previously drinkable water, all for a dumb rush lasting three minutes at a time. If that doesn't make you feel like Pharaoh, nothing will.

Violet says "But how would anybody get a motorboat as far in as White Lake, after what you've just told us about portaging?"

"There are portages in the Boundary Waters for motorboats. Those are illegal too—they have been for decades. But there are a lot of them still out there. Dredged, usually. Sometimes with rails. Parks and Rec will pull rails if they find them, but it's a big area out there, patrolled mostly by aircraft."

"Was there a motorboat found at White Lake?" she says.

"No. The two kids who were nearby when Autumn and Benjy died said the four of them went out in two canoes, one of which the survivors used to get back to Ford. There was no way to prove that, though. There *was* a canoe from CFS still out there when I got there, but if the kids were using a stolen or borrowed motorboat, they might have towed a canoe just to paddle around in once they got there."

"CFS *Lodge?*" I say.

"Outfitters and Lodge, yes," Albin says.

"Which Reggie Trager *owns?*"

"Yes, although at the time Autumn's father owned it. Reggie inherited it when Autumn's father died."

"Wait a minute," I say. "Chris Semmel Jr. owned CFS?"

Albin squints, like he's reviewing whether he should share this information.

"Right," he says.

"And after Autumn and Chris Jr. died, five days apart, Reggie Trager inherited it?"

"Correct. Chris Jr.'s wife could have kept it, but she wasn't from around here, and for obvious reasons didn't want to stay. Back when Chris Sr. left it to Chris Jr. in the first place, he said that if none of the Semmels was willing or able to stick around and run it, Reggie Trager should get the chance."

Yet another reason for Trager not to have mentioned any of this in his invitation. "Was Trager charged with the murders of Chris Jr. and Father Podominick?" I say.

"No."

"Why not?"

"There was no evidence he committed them, and three people willing to say he couldn't have because he was with them at the moment the shots were fired. Even the motive wasn't as exciting as it seems. Reggie gives something like eighty-five percent of the profits from CFS to Chris Jr.'s widow."

"Out of the goodness of his heart or because he has to?"

"It was the deal in the will. In terms of money, Reggie probably makes around the same amount he did before, only now he has to run the whole place on his own."

"Maybe they were about to fire him."

"No one ever told me that they were. Chris Jr.'s widow included, who is no fan of Reggie Trager."

"What does *she* have against him?"

"She thinks he's guilty."

"On what basis?"

"None that would interest a jury."

"Or you, from the sound of it."

"Obviously I prefer not to charge people with crimes they can't be convicted of. But if you're asking me whether I think Reggie did it, the answer's no. I wouldn't say I know him well, and I'm certainly aware that most people are capable of most things if they're pushed to it, but with Reggie I just never saw the push."

"So who did you think did it?"

He shakes his head. "I have no idea. Chris Jr. and Father Podominick were comfortably off, in a town of people who were a lot less comfortably off, but neither one of them seems to have had real enemies. Or even people who would have benefited from their deaths."

"Do you think the person who killed Chris Jr. and Father Podominick also killed Autumn and Benjy?"

Albin gives it a couple of chair-rocks, looking at me.

"No. I do not."

"Why not?"

"Not exactly a similar MO. Murder with a hunting rifle I can at least understand. And whoever shot Chris Jr. and Father Podominick was good enough at that to do it without leaving evidence. What happened to Autumn and Benjy seemed like something else entirely."

"Was White Lake searched for a portage that someone could have gotten a motorboat through?" Violet asks.

"Yes, and I didn't find one. I also didn't find one in

Lake Garner, but that's a lot bigger and harder to scout. So maybe there was one and I missed it."

It's a nice question, but I don't think Violet's headed where Albin is. "Can we see Autumn and Benjy's autopsy reports?" I say.

"No. I don't believe that's legal."

I don't know if it is or isn't.* I try "Is there anything you need to tell us to keep us out of danger?"

I don't know what oaths to protect people sheriffs here or anywhere else are required to take, but I assume there are some. And maybe they allow, or even require, Albin to cough up information it would otherwise be illegal or unethical to share.

At least, I *think* that's what he's been getting at.

"Ideally, walk away now," he says. "I look at this, I see a lot of downside and essentially zero upside. If you do insist on going through with it, don't give Reggie Trager the benefit of the doubt just because I don't think he's guilty. I'm not a grand jury. Don't go anywhere in Ford except CFS—the town's too dangerous. And keep me posted on absolutely everything that happens. Which I don't mean as an option. I'll give you my direct line and my e-mail address. If I decide at any point that you've withheld information that even *might* be useful

---

* I still don't know. Autopsy privacy laws vary by state and are complicated by the fact that the federal Health Insurance Portability and Accountability Act (HIPAA) of 1996 protects in perpetuity the privacy of any medical conditions the patient had while alive. Which, it seems to me, would include whatever it was the patient died of. Wasn't every victim of a fatal bow-hunting accident once just some geek with an arrow sticking out of him?

to a criminal investigation, I will make certain you become sorry to have done that. Do we understand each other?"

We nod. Violet says "Yes sir."

"And one last thing. When you get out to White Lake—don't go in the water."

11

"That guy totally thinks Aquabigfoot is real," Violet says.

"I agree." We're back on U.S. 53, headed to Ford to check into the CFS Lodge. She's driving. "So do we need to discuss it?"

"What?" she says. "That the sheriff of Lake County thinks the monster is real, or that the monster might actually *be* real?"

"The sheriff part."

"Whew. For a second I was worried you were getting all spandrelly on me."*

---

* This is evolutionary biology talk, but it's interesting.

There are two great schools of junk science in evolutionary biology. One is people claiming to know the specific environmental

"You got the wrong guy."

"Although I *would* like to know why somebody as unstupid-seeming as Sheriff Albin thinks it's possible."

"Yeah," I say. "Exactly."

---

pressures that led to the development of complex zoological phenomena, like when psychology textbooks say that people hate mimes because striped shirts set off our ancestral fear of tigers. Although that happens to be true. The other is people claiming that complex zoological phenomena can arise without *any* environmental pressures. Like when biologists call something a "spandrel."

Technically, a spandrel is an evolutionary side effect—a trait that comes about not because it raises the likelihood that an organism will reproduce its genome, but as the result of the development of a different trait that *does* raise that likelihood. Ronald Pies calls a spandrel "a kind of genetic hitchhiker that does nothing to improve the ride." It's not that spandrels aren't real, because they probably are, the classic example being nipples on men— which serve no known evolutionary purpose, so may only exist because nipples are beneficial on women, and get formed at such an early stage of fetal development that it's easier to just hand them out to everyone. (The same argument used to be made about orgasms in women. I am but the messenger.) Usually, though, identifying any specific trait as a spandrel just means you've been too lazy to work out the real reason it evolved. (Or that you're up to something worse. The history of people trying to judge human traits as either contributory or not to some idea of evolutionary "progress" is horrible, with individuals judged to have "decadent" or "degenerate" traits inevitably labeled as parasites—"a kind of…hitchhiker that does nothing to improve the ride." Things that have been labeled as evolutionarily useless even though they clearly aren't include grandparents, gay people, and the appendix.)

CFS Outfitters and Lodge isn't just *on* the highway exit that's one past greater (so to speak) Ford—it *is* the highway exit. You curve under a giant CFS billboard into the parking lot of the store, which is a three-story A-frame with posters for shit like North Face all over its glass front and back. From there you follow the signs to a road that runs from the far corner of the lot down to the lodge.

The start of the road's blocked off by traffic cones, but a tall, thin, early-twenties kid in a bush hat but sunburned anyway comes over to your car with a clipboard. "Ki help you folks?" he says, after Violet rolls down the window.

"We're here for the tour Reggie Trager is running."

"Get your names, please?"

"Violet Hurst and Lionel Azimuth."

The kid checks for us on his clipboard, which seems strange for someone expecting only six or eight people. Then again, maybe clipboards are like guns, and people who carry them start wanting to use them.

"Doctor. Doctor," the kid says. "I'm Davey Sugar. I'll be one of the guides on your trip. Welcome to CFS."

The appeal of spandrels, I believe, is that if things can exist that have a looser-than-usual relationship with cause and effect, then maybe things can exist that have *no* relationship with cause and effect. Which would mean they were outside reality, and therefore magic. Terms like *sub*lime, *super*natural, *para*normal, *epi*phenomenal, etc. do their best to make this sound legitimate. But objects outside reality can't be studied. And objects mistakenly *thought* to be outside reality, then shown to actually be within it, instantly become as boring as everything else. By definition, the Beyond stays out of reach.

He looks so earnest, and so unlike someone involved in a sordid fake-monster tour, that I feel compelled to make sure we're all talking about the same thing. I lean over Violet to say "What do you think? Is the White Lake Monster real?"

The kid smiles broadly as he backs up to move the cones. "I'd have to say I'm agnostic about it. Be pretty great, though, wouldn't it?"

꙳ **∩∩** ꙳

The road crests the hill, and suddenly we can see all of Ford Lake below, light flashing off it like a chain-link fence made of sun. Even the brick hulk of the old Ford Mine—with, presumably, Dr. McQuillen's house hidden in the bend beyond it—looks good.

The lodge itself is idyllic: a dozen lakeside cabins painted the yellow of Smurfette's hair, on turf that looks as lush as moss. Beside it an inlet with an "E" shape of floating docks, tarp-covered boats parallel-parked along the docks' edges.

In the rutted and tree-shaded dirt parking area next to the marina are three pickup trucks, including one with a contractor's cage over its bed, a couple of injured-looking compact cars, and one big, black, perfectly shiny SUV with Minnesota license plates.

We leave our shit in the car in case we have to flee.

꙳ **∩∩** ꙳

Two guys in polo shirts and painter's pants are coming around the registration cabin when we reach it. We know it's the registration cabin because it's got a line of sunflowers along its back wall and a wooden sign above them that says "CAMP FAWN SEE—*Registration*" in log font, or whatever you call it when the letters are burned into wood. One of the two guys is white and in his sixties, with white hair and rimless glasses. The other one's Hispanic, in his thirties, with a mustache.

"Evening," the white guy says.

"Are either of you Reggie Trager?" Violet says.

"Hell no." He turns and yells "Reggie! Customers!" Then he and the other guy head toward the pickup truck with the contractor's frame.

Violet and I continue to the front of the cabin, which faces the lake. On the lawn there's a man talking on what used to be called a cordless phone, and also drinking a beer and steering his crotch away from a large black Labrador that's jumping at it.

He holds up a hand to acknowledge us while he says "No, listen, Trish, I gotta run. I know. I'm sorry. You too. You too. Okay. I'll call you later." He's got a slight southern accent: Arkansas or Alabama, or some other state I can't actually recognize the accent from.

The man's boyish, with muscular legs and dark hair in a thick buzz cut, but he's wearing corduroy shorts smaller than anyone under sixty would be caught dead in. They show off a long, rubbery burn scar down the outside of his left leg. He smiles at us lopsidedly as he turns off the phone. "Sorry. My mother."

The dog, seeming to notice us for the first time, springs at us. Throws itself sideways against Violet's legs, then against mine, where it stops and leans on me, thumping its heavy tail.

"Bark," the man says to it. It doesn't bark. To us he says "Dr. Hurst and Dr. Azimuth?"

"Right," Violet says.

"I'm Reggie Trager."

"Nice to meet you," Violet says. "Can we pet your dog?"

Interesting opener. Not that the dog isn't cute.

"She's not mine, but go ahead," Reggie says. "Take her home with you. Her name's Bark Simpson."

"Oh: *Bark,*" Violet says, causing the dog to hurl itself off my legs and back onto hers.

Just as well. Reggie's coming in for the handshake.

Up close, he's not quite the same person. The left side of his face is a fishnet of scars. Not burns, like on his leg, but fine lacerations, like from shrapnel or spraying glass. The reason his smile is lopsided is that the left side of his face is paralyzed. His left eye stares wider than his right, almost fully round.

The weird thing, though, is that it's not a bad effect. The paralysis gives his face a slight cartoonishness that goes well with how young he looks. It kind of works.

"You met Del and Miguel?" he says.

At their names, the dog abruptly stands and looks bereft. Turns around a couple times, then gallops off toward the parking lot.

Reggie shakes his head. "She just realized that Del left. Bark! Don't go on the highway!"

"They the two guys who got in the truck?" I say.

"Yeah."

"We didn't actually meet them. Who are they?"

"We all work together. They're sort of the Tattoos to my Mr. Roarke, if that means anything to people your age." He winks at me with his nonstaring eye. "Come on in. I'll introduce you to some of your fellow guests."

12

In the registration cabin, though, there are just four Asian guys, and the two who are standing—tracksuits, sunglasses, coming up on their toes when they see me—are obviously bodyguards.

The other two, on opposite couches, are harder to figure. One is punk-chic, with chunky-cool glasses and a sleek suit over an expensive-looking western shirt. Early forties, hair dyed brown, reading a guidebook. The other is about the same age but fat and sprawling, with the wet lips, coarse features, and bad shave of the mentally disabled or whatever they're being called these days. Jeans and a T-shirt that says "NOW IS COLA ONLY." He's playing a video game on a cell phone.

The stylish one stands when he sees us, causing his bodyguards to move closer to his sides.

Reggie introduces us. His name is Wayne Teng. The slob's his brother, Stuart. The bodyguards are allegedly both named Lee.

"Sorry," Teng says. "My brother and our associates do not speak English."

"But you do," Violet says.

"Very poorly."

"It doesn't seem like it."

"Thank you. You are medical doctors?"

"He is. I'm a paleontologist."

"Like in *Jurassic Park*?"

"More or less."

Teng translates for his brother and bodyguards. I recognize the words *Jurassic Park*. Even the brother looks up.

I follow Reggie over to the registration desk. "Is this it? The whole group?" Assuming Teng's bringing his bodyguards, it puts us at six.

Reggie pulls out some forms. "Not really sure. We've got five more RSVPs in the affirmative."

"Won't that be too many?"

"The only real limit is what you guys are willing to accept. But I'll worry about that when it happens. I'm sure *someone* will come to their senses."

"Why? Is the monster fake?"

He winks at me. "Shit, I hope not." Puts two keys on the desk. "Cabin Ten."

"Both of us?"

"What do you mean?"

"We were supposed to be in separate cabins."

"You were? Shit. Let me think." He chews a nail. "Problem is, we got a lot of people coming in with the referee."

"Who's the referee?"

"I'm not allowed to say till he or she physically gets here."

"Which is when?"

"Few hours. Let's see: Del's already bunking with Miguel...." He looks up at me, half his face wincing. "The room you're in now, you can separate the beds, if that helps."

"It's fine," Violet says, coming up behind me. "For one night, I think Dr. Azimuth can handle it."

Cabin Ten is nice enough, but the air's a bit moldy and filled with sexual tension, so Violet and I decide to go to Omen Lake, where the rock paintings are.

Davey, the kid with the clipboard, sets us up with a canoe. Green Kevlar, looking like canvas that's been shellacked. Light as shit: it's got a yoke like a toilet seat across its middle bench that you're supposed to put your head through so you carry the canoe upside down on your shoulders, but if you don't want to do that—because you can't really see anything that way, or because anybody who wants to can break your neck—you can just carry it above your head with your hands.

Violet teaches me some strokes, and after you get your mind out of the gutter we make our first portage halfway up the west side of Ford Lake. Cross a couple more lakes and we're there.

Omen Lake: not that ominous. It's dumbbell shaped, with orange-red cliffs facing each other across the narrow part, where the pictograms are. The water's so clear you can see boulders on the bottom, and the leaves on the trees are already turning colors that, relative to green, absorb less infrared light.* We're the only ones there.

Violet takes us right to the base of the cliff. Then stands in the boat and grabs hold of the rock.

"Push out from the left to keep us steady," she says.

"What are you doing?"

She swings out onto the cliff face before I can get my oar in place. The canoe spins away from the wall. By the time I get it under control, she's ten feet off the water.

"You can rock climb," I say.

"All paleontologists can rock climb. And this is a nice rock. It's probably four billion years old."

I lie back to watch her do it. It's not the worst view in the world.

So when the lake *does* suddenly turn ominous, it feels like a trap's been sprung. One minute: sun, and Violet from behind and below. The next: water that smells like salty rot and pumps malice off its surface like sound from the face of a speaker. The previously minor splashes and drumming against the membrane of the canoe now feeling like the exploratory peckings of hungry underwater animals.

I search for something that's changed: a cloud across

---

* Namely yellow, orange, and red respectively. The presumed benefit being that leaves that reflect more (and absorb less) IR are less likely to catch fire as they dry out. Still, see the footnote on pages 124–26.

the sun or a new vein of cold water that I can feel through the Kevlar. But there's nothing. Just invisible darkness, and the fact that I'm sweating all over, and gone.

What I tell my patients with PTSD—of whom, in the desperate world of cruise ship labor, I have many—is that the panic attacks are currently thought to be of physical rather than psychological origin. The reminder of whatever shitty thing happened to you communicates directly with the most primitive centers of your nervous system, which from their own strange memories cue the physiological changes before you even know you're afraid. The panic comes in reaction to the sweating palms and the shortness of breath, not the other way around.

Knowing this is supposed to make people feel better, or at least less responsible for their craziness. It may even be true. But out on Omen Lake, with my vision dimming and my sides wet with sweat, terrified of a freshwater lake that's been photographed and visited a million times, it doesn't do me much good. The only thing I can focus on besides fear is raw anger.

Eleven *years?*

All this because of some ugly things I saw in a shark tank *eleven years ago?*

Magdalena died the next day. Most of me died with her. But guess what? Freaking out all the time doesn't seem to be bringing her back.

Was signing up for a twelve-day canoe trip a particularly good idea? Survey says no.

How bout working on a cruise ship?

Still: *For fuck's sake. Get over it.*

"Lionel!"

The spookiness evaporates like it doesn't want to be

seen with me. Violet's come back down the rock face. The canoe has drifted ten feet away. I use something called a J-stroke to get it back to the rock.

Once she's seated, Violet stays twisted around, looking at me. "Are you okay?"

"Yeah, sure."

"You don't look okay. What happened?"

"Nothing. I'm fine. How were the paintings?"

"About what we expected."

We didn't expect much. Books describing the paintings in English go back at least to 1768, and both carbon dating and the Ojibwe say the paintings are twice that age. Which doesn't *entirely* rule out a hoax—the Ojibwe could have painted them in 1767, using two-hundred-year-old fish oil—but does make Reggie Trager unlikely to have been involved.

Violet's still staring at me. "Are you sure there isn't something you want to tell me?"

"No," I say, pushing off the wall with the end of my oar to get us going.

Which at least is true.

ɔ♙♙(

Back at the lodge, there are a couple of nice pieces of distraction. First, Del—the guy who works with or for Reggie or whatever—meets us at the dock to tell us Reggie wants us to join the rest of the group in the registration cabin for an announcement. Second, when we get to the registration cabin, in addition to Wayne Teng's party and what looks like every employee of the lodge, there are five new guests. One of whom, Tyson Grody, is famous.

Grody has to be in his mid-twenties by now. He's a singer-dancer thing who came out of a boy band. Pop songs you hear in a cab en route to some expat bar and think are sung by an actual middle-aged black man. Women on cruise ships always have him on their fuck mixes.

In person Grody's tiny, bug-eyed, smiling, and twitchy, but at least he's got a pair of actual black men with him. They're enormous. When they first see the Teng brothers' bodyguards, there's a four-way sunglass stare-off that makes you hope for some Super Street Fighter IV action later on.

The two other new guests are a grim-faced couple in their late fifties. His and hers Rolexes, hair and skin the color of their safari outfits. Same pushed-out lower lips.

"People, I've got some bad news," Reggie says from the front.

When everyone's quiet, he says "The ref's not here, and won't be until tomorrow afternoon. So we won't be leaving tomorrow morning. We could leave as soon as the ref gets here, but there wouldn't be much point, since we'd still get to White Lake a full day late. We'd only end up spending an extra night in the field. So I'm going to delay the start of the trip by a whole day and leave Sunday morning instead.

"If that's a problem, and any of the guests can't stay, I understand. If any of the guests *do* choose to stay, we can go into the field for one day less than we were planning and still get back here on schedule. Or we can stay in the field for the full length of time and get back a day later. Whichever you decide. Obviously, your extra night at the lodge will be free of charge, along with any activities we can interest you in while we're here. Fishing, canoeing—whatever you want. And whether you come with us or not, I hope you'll join me and Del and Miguel and some of the guides for dinner." He looks at a clock on the wall. "Which should be right after this."

"Can you at least tell us who the referee is?" Violet says.

Reggie shakes his head. "You know, I just asked that question and was told it has to remain secret, even with the delay. Legally and personally, I have to respect that. Again, I apologize."

He looks tired, and maybe disappointed, but not particularly anxious. I wonder if there ever *was* a specific referee. Someone Reggie thought he could rely on but then got fucked by. Or whether all along it's been a gamble, with offers out to anyone even possibly sucker enough, or greedy enough, to accept whatever Reggie's offering. Which, after all, is for a single corrupt act in the privacy of the woods.

If it's a gamble, I can see where Reggie might want to let it ride for one last night.

"We're still interested in the trip," Wayne Teng says.

Tyson Grody says "We're cool to wait too."

"We'll consider it," the grim safari guy says.

Reggie looks at Violet and me. "We'll have to check with our boss," Violet says.

"Thank you," Reggie says. "Thank you all." He looks genuinely touched, though it could just be that his frozen-open eye has a tendency to run.

14

"Here's what *I* want to know," says Fick, the grim-looking safari guy. To Violet, though she's eating and pretending not to notice. "Why does evolution have to contradict the Bible?"

Reggie's guys Del and Miguel, at our end of the table, perk up. Earlier, Fick described himself as "a businessman," and his wife, "Mrs. Fick," as "a homemaker," and Miguel said "That's cool—Del and I make homes too." Del and Violet and I laughed. Even Mrs. Fick smiled. Fick not so much.

Also not smiling was the bodyguard of the Teng brothers who's seated with us—either because he doesn't understand English, like Teng said, or because he's pretending he doesn't—and Clipboard Davey, our earnest young guide.

Davey has turned out to have an equally willowy and sun-desiccated wife who's also working as a guide for Reggie's tour, one Jane. Right now Jane is at the end of the other table, sitting next to Tyson Grody, and Davey looks worried.

I'd be worried too. I wouldn't call Grody attractive, exactly, but he's got the energy of a mongoose, and the shamelessness. When Violet and I met him, he introduced his bodyguards to us, swear to God, as "M'blackberries." Neither of them seemed offended by it, or by Grody in general.

"Miss," Fick says. *"Miss."*

"You're talking to me?" Violet eventually says.

"Sure am."

"Can you pass the corn?" she says to Miguel.

Exactly what I was thinking. I haven't had creamed corn since I was a kid. Particularly with the burnt part mashed into it, it's awesome.

Miguel pushes it over. Fick says "Why *does* evolution have to contradict the Bible?"

Violet pours. "I don't know. Does it?"

"Not in my opinion."

"Okay."

"But I would say that where a lot of people who believe in the Bible respect scientists, not too many scientists respect people who believe in the Bible. Why is that?"

"I have no idea," Violet says.

"Do *you* believe in the Bible?"

She looks at him. "You're asking me about my religious beliefs?"

"Why, are you an atheist? Most scientists are, in my experience."*

———————
* Mine too.

"I don't know that I believe anyone's actually an atheist," Violet says. "Everybody believes in *something* irrational, even if it's just that they'd be happier if they had a nicer car." She turns to me. "Don't start on my car. Jump in any time, but don't start on my car."

"You think believing in the Bible is irrational?" Fick says.

Violet looks around. Del and Miguel both nod, egging her on. I just eat, but I'm impressed. I never argue with people whose opinions I don't care about.

Violet sighs. "Believing that it's the word of God?" she says. "I don't know. What's the evidence for it?"

"More people believe it than don't."

"So reality is subject to democracy?"

"No, but unless there's evidence to the contrary, the wisdom of the crowd is a good place to start."

"There *is* evidence to the contrary. The Bible says humans were created the same week as the planet. Jesus says the world's going to end within his audience's lifetime. You can try to semantically twist those things so they don't contradict your hypothesis, but that's not rationality. It's just faith."

"I wasn't aware that faith was a bad thing."

Violet looks at him. "Did I start this conversation?"

"No."

"Good. I never said faith was a bad thing. It's just obviously not all that satisfying, or you wouldn't feel the need to try to bully people like me into agreeing with you."

"Oh boy," Del says.

Fick says "Let's keep this respectful, please."

"Why?" Violet says. "Here's what *I* don't understand. When did the definition of religion stop being 'things people should have the right to believe' and become 'ideas other people should be forced to respect, even if they're demonstrably false'? And why doesn't it work both ways? You clearly don't feel a need to respect rationality."

"Maybe I just don't see how believing in evolution is rational. People have been trying to prove evolution since Darwin's time, and it's still just a theory." He looks around, smiling. "Now *that's* what I call faith."

Violet stares at him. "Are you serious?"

"Oh, yes."

"Evolution's a theory in the Pythagorean sense, meaning it's a general rule that applies to numerous real-world cases. Not in the sense that it's never been proved. It gets proved all the time. Every time you get a flu shot you prove evolution." To me, she says "Like I say, jump in any time."

"What is this, trout?" I say.

"I mean about this."

"I totally agree with you," I say.

"So maybe *you* can answer a question I've got," Fick says to me.

"Probably not."

"Evolution happens because everything's trying to survive, right?"

"Okay."

"But that feeling itself—the will to survive. How did *that* evolve?"

"You got me."

Violet stomps on my foot.

"Dr. Hurst knows, though," I say.

Violet shakes her head as she puts down her fork. "Evolution doesn't require the will to survive. It just requires the *tendency* to survive. If you have a bunch of different molecules, and two of them randomly have a tendency to stick to each other, then you're going to end up with compounds made of those two molecules. And if some of those compounds randomly form in such a way that they tend to stick to other compounds, they're going to form more complicated compounds. And so on till you get to organisms. The will to live might be an advantage for animals that have it, but it's a *product* of evolution, not the cause of it. Sea anemones don't want to survive any more than heroin wants to get injected by a junkie. They both just tend to when the circumstances are right."

"So what about the second law of thermodynamics?" Fick says.

"I was just about to ask that," Miguel says.

"Me too," Del says.

"What about it?"

"Well," Fick says, "you just got done telling us, at length, that it's possible for a bunch of chemicals to randomly assemble into a human being. But the second law of thermodynamics says things tend toward entropy and disorganization, not toward complexity and organization. So does evolution just happen to get an exception to that rule?"

Violet looks disgusted. "The second law of thermodynamics states that *isolated* systems tend toward entropy. The Earth isn't an isolated system. It gets materials and energy from space all the time. It gets a continuous hundred and twenty petawatts of energy from the sun alone,* most of which just dissipates back into space. Evolution doesn't *have* to be entropic, because the solar system it

---

* Apparently this is a large amount of energy.

takes place in—which isn't isolated either—is massively entropic. You just don't understand the physics.

"You know," she says, getting angrier, "I think that may be the problem. You want to believe that anything you don't understand personally is either wrong or not knowable by anyone. You don't understand physics, so physics is wrong. You don't understand biology, so biology is wrong. Anything you yourself can't figure out has to be due to a glowing man with a beard—because *that,* at least, you can picture. And since you're not actually interested in learning anything, 'glowing man with a beard' becomes your explanation for everything. Which I'm then supposed to somehow 'respect.' But what about that is there to respect?"

Fick shows teeth. "Oh, come on, now—"

"Let me ask *you* a question," Violet says.

"Not if—"

"Do you believe in God?"

"Yes," Fick says, suspiciously. "I do."

"Do you believe that God believes in God?"

"You mean does God believe in Himself?"

"No. Does God believe there's a higher God than God."

"No," Fick says. "Of course not."

"Why not?"

"Why would He?"

"Why would you?"

"Because that's what it says in the Bible," Fick says.

"What if God has a book that says there's a higher power than God? Then should He believe it?"

Miguel says "Oh, shit! Time warp."

Del says "Does not compute!"

Miguel says "Lady scientist has blown my mind!"

"If that book was actually written by a higher being, absolutely," Fick says.

"What if there's no evidence for it being written by a higher being, although a lot of people have told God that it is?"

"That's ridiculous," Fick says.

"You're right," Violet says. "It is. But at least you're not accusing God of being stupid enough to use the same reasoning you do."

Miguel makes a whip-cracking sound.

"Is that a regular whip crack, or a pussy-whip crack?" Violet says.

"I don't know. Little of both," Miguel says.

"All right then," Violet says. She and Miguel clink beers.

"I'll thank you to not use that language in front of Mrs. Fick," Fick says.

"What," Violet says, " 'pussy' or 'evolution'?"

"Oh, shizzle," Tyson Grody says from behind us.

Fick stands up. "That's it. We're leaving."

"Don't on my account," Violet says.

"On whose account would you suggest we leave, then?"

There's an uncomfortable pause while people try to figure this out.

"Look," Violet says, "if I offended you, I apologize."

"You did and you should."

"Fine. Let's just agree to not talk about religion. Or science. Christ."

Fick turns to Reggie. "We're going to stay the night in Ely. We may or may not come back tomorrow."

"I hope you do," Reggie says.

"Me too," Violet says blandly.

Fick lets the screen door slam shut behind them.

"Sorry," Violet says to the room.

"He started it," Miguel says.

"Yeah. That's not really an excuse to take a dump on his conceptual framework, though."

"*I* think it is," Del says.

"Thanks, but it's not. If your dog humps your leg, it's understandable. If you hump your dog's leg, it's a problem."

"*Dog* might have a problem," Del says. "*I* don't have a problem."

Miguel says "Del, not everybody wants to hear that, man."

Bark looks up from the floor smiling, like she knows they're talking about her.

"Yeah, like Bark and I have sex," Del says. "Bark and I don't have sex. We make love. There's a difference."

"That's true," Miguel says. "I've seen the videotape."

"You've *paid* to see the videotape."

"Damn," Violet says. "I hope you guys aren't planning on talking that way in front of Mrs. Fick. If Mr. Fick brings her back. I'm sorry, Reggie."

Reggie waves it off. "They'll come back or they won't. Either way, we'll be fine."

"Can *I* ask you a question, Doctor?" Wayne Teng says.

I turn around to face the other table, but of course it's Violet he's talking to, not me.

"Sure," she says.

"Do you believe in luck?"

"Luck?"

"My own life has been very, very lucky. It's hard for me not to see that as some kind of evidence of *something*."

Tyson Grody kisses the back of his own hand. "Hear that."

"Me too," Miguel says.

"If I didn't believe in luck," Violet says, "would I be suggesting we all move on to the casino on the Ojibwe reservation?"

"Be serious," Teng says.

"I am being serious: we should go to the casino on the Ojibwe reservation."

Teng laughs. "Fine. I accept that—for now. And I have space in my car."

"I do too," Grody says.

"You should come," Violet says to me. "I probably won't forgive you for not helping me out with that asshole, but you never know."

"Yeah, sorry about that. I was about to say something that would have totally changed his mind, but I decided not to at the last moment. Anyway, I think I'll stay here."

"Why?"

"I already believe in statistics."

Even on the ship, where the best-looking women are the blackjack dealers, I don't go near casinos. Like a surprising number of other things on cruise ships, casinos are independent concessions, paying a flat rate to the cruise line to use the space. If there's any part of the ship that's going to be mobbed up, it's the casino. And even if it isn't, it's where mobbed-up people are going to want to hang out. Once they're done with the buffet, I mean.

Also, I really shouldn't be spending an evening drinking with Violet Hurst just prior to sharing a cabin with her.

"We're not going there to gamble, SquarePants," she

says. "We're going there to drink. Come on. I'm sure they can TiVo *Judge Judy* for you."

"I have things I need to do."

"Like what?"

"E-mail. Including e-mailing Rec Bill to ask him if he wants us to hang out for the delay."

"Weak. What else?"

"I have to do some reading."

"Bring it with you."

"I can't. It'll blow the mortgage payment. Have a piña colada for me. Charge it to Rec Bill."

"I don't know you well enough for a piña colada."

"A club soda, then."

"You know, your deepening squareness concerns me," Violet says. "I'm tempted to stay here with you."

"That'd be cool," I say, realizing I have no willpower whatsoever.

"Luckily," Violet says, "temptation rolls right off me. And after that bullshit with the fucking Ficks, partial sobriety lacks its usual allure. What?"

"Nothing."

"You think I'm an alcoholic."

"Did I say that?"

"No," she says.

"Did I make some kind of face?"

"No. You had no facial expression at all. Which is fucked up. Who doesn't have a facial expression?"

I stare at her expressionlessly.

"Stop that. You're scaring me. And stop trying to diagnose me."

"If you're worried about the co-pay, we can work that out."

"You know, you should take that act to the Catskills."

"How do you know about the Catskills?"

"I know about a lot of things, my friend. Like that I'm not an alcoholic. Know how I know?"

"Because you're not defensive about it?"

"How dare you. Because I don't have to drink to have a good time."

"Glad to hear it."

"Usually because I'm already drunk. Come with us."

"I can't. Have fun, Dr. Hurst."

She trails a hand down my shoulder as she stands.

"You too, Dr. SquarePants."

15

CFS Lodge, Ford Lake, Minnesota
Friday, 14 September–Saturday, 15 September

The e-mail from Robby, the Australian kid who's covering for me on the ship, is signed "Fuck you very much,
mate," which I take to be good news. At least he's still
engaged.

Cruise ship doctors tend to burn out into either martyrs
or Caligula. I picked Robby because I thought he would
stay down the center of the lane as long as possible before
veering toward martyrdom. Patients get better treatment
from the Peace Corps types than the *Love Boat* ones.

I did my best to leave him detailed instructions—things
like how to argue with the captain to get someone airlifted
when they're having a heart attack and don't have MedE-
vac insurance, how to steal supplies, where to hide those
supplies given that so many crew members use the exam-

ining room of the staff clinic as a fuck pad, and so on.* I told him to watch for groom-on-bride honeymoon violence, since the "security guards" have orders not to interfere with it.† And I told him never to bother the senior physician, Dr. Muñoz, when he's ballroom dancing with the old ladies, because Dr. Muñoz hates that, plus is incompetent. But Robby always has questions even so, about things I forgot to tell him, or that I purposely left out because I didn't want to scare him off.

In the office of the registration cabin, which is where Reggie told me to go to use the Internet, I answer the ones he has now and wish him well as sincerely as I can, given that I essentially lured his ass into the job just so I could flee it. And to do what—go on vacation?

Oh, right: to earn enough money to somehow buy my way out of a mafia vendetta. And come up with a plan for how to do that.

I *have* given it some thought. Mostly about contracting a prison hit on David Locano. But even supposing Locano's not in protective isolation, I'd still need a way to hire someone in prison to kill him. And as far as I know, there isn't one.

In real life, even hitmen who *aren't* in prison are close to impossible to hire privately. Or even contact. No matter what you think of the FBI, and no matter how justified you are in thinking that, they've *got* to be as good at find-

---

* Treating STDs on a cruise ship is mind-blowing. It's like an episode of *Iron Chef* where the special ingredient is genitals.

† The role of the security guards is strictly to observe, in case a lawsuit is filed later for which the cruise line needs friendly witnesses.

ing freelance hitmen as some schmuck who wants his wife whacked is going to be. Every real hitman I've known, or even heard of, in or out of prison, has tried to work for as few people as possible, generally within the same branch of the same mafia. Usually some mafia that now wants me dead.*

The truth is that I have no plan. Nor do I have a plan to invent a plan. And even thinking about it makes me feel lazy and frustrated.

I look around for things to do instead.

I suppose I should toss the office for some kind of evidence of Reggie's guilt in the deaths of the two teenagers and the guys who got shot. Like a diary, or a bag with a meat grinder and a hunting rifle in it.

On the desk there's a single framed picture. Reggie's not even in it. It's of three people on one of the piers of the CFS marina: a couple in their late thirties and a teenage girl who's clearly their daughter. The father and daughter pink-skinned and reddish blond, the mother with dark hair and a tan instead of freckles. All three of them vibrant and smiling.

The girl I've seen before. She's the one in the video who doesn't want to answer the question of whether she's ever seen the monster, but finally says she has.

---

* I know what you're thinking: "Isn't the Aryan Brotherhood— who, sure, want you dead, but only on principle—*famous* for contracting prison hits to outsiders?" Well, yes, and they're also famous for fucking those contracts up. If the AB couldn't kill Walter Johnson in Marion for $500,000 from John Gotti, are they really going to kill David Locano in Florence for $85,000 from me? Plus, come on—sometimes you have to vote with your dollars.

Which would make her father a good candidate for the person offscreen asking questions, and for the narrator of the video, too. Which would explain why the video was never completed.

Because obviously these people are the Semmels. The daughter is Autumn, the father Chris Jr., and the mother whatever Chris Jr.'s wife was called. Or *is* called. Unlike Autumn and Chris Jr., she's presumably still alive.

On a whim, I try to locate her online. I find out her first name from back when she lived in Ford—Christine*— but I can't seem to track her down past that point. In my e-mail to Rec Bill about the ref not showing up, I ask that if he decides to go through with this thing he also get me Christine Semmel's contact information. Not that I can really justify subjecting her to a conversation.

After that I send a quick update to Professor Marmoset. I doubt he'll read it. Getting Professor Marmoset's attention is like getting struck by lightning while being attacked by a bear, only more surprising. But it seems like good form.

Then I get the fuck out of there.

ꝉ ⦿⦿ (

I wake up with Violet bent over me, shouting because I've got her in an arm bar. I let her go.

"Jesus *fuck!*" she says.

"I'm sorry."

---

* Here's how I know Chris Semmel Jr. and Christine Semmel were good parents: they didn't name their only child something with "Chris" in it.

"I was just trying to wake you up. You were screaming."

"I was?"

I try to figure shit out. We're in our cabin, no light except what's coming through the windows. When Violet got back, a while ago, I pretended to be asleep until I heard her snoring. Then I must have fallen asleep, too, because now I'm in my bed, slick with sweat, and she's standing back, holding her arm. In her underwear.

Black cotton. The top's a sports bra. The bottoms as straight across her hips as a censorship mark.

"Are you okay?" I say.

"Yeah, I will be. You were having a nightmare."

"I guess I was."

"What was it about?"

"I don't remember."

It was about the two of us treading water, naked, in a transparent mountain lake, nothing between us and the boulders on the bottom. Until I lowered my head below the surface and saw that the water was actually thick with murk and marine life, including piranha-headed eels swimming toward us from all directions.

I get out of bed. She flinches, then looks embarrassed to have done it, like it's going to hurt my feelings. Jesus.

"How's your arm?" I say.

"Fine."

"Really?"

"Yes."

We stand for a few moments, getting our breath back.

"How was the casino?" I say, to not just be staring at her.

"It was fun. You should have come. Wayne Teng and

his brother played roulette. It was like *Rain Man,* except they lost. And Tyson Grody was really sweet. He posed with all the tourists and the waitresses, even though he didn't gamble or drink. He asked me if I wanted to stay behind and have sex with him and some of the waitresses in one of the hotel rooms."

"Wow," I say. "That *is* sweet."

"Don't be jealous. All right, do."

"Have you heard that guy's music?"

"I like it," Violet says. "I've got a lot of his stuff on my iPod. What?"

"Nothing. Did you ask him why he's here?"

"Yeah. He's an animal rights guy. He wants to make sure William the White Lake Monster doesn't get exploited."

Makes sense. Kid probably grew up in a cage at the foot of his parents' bed, only getting let out for his dance-like-Michael-Jackson classes and boy band auditions. That he'd identify with a threatened rare animal, no matter how much freedom he has now, isn't all that surprising.

Then Violet brushes the hair from her neck, revealing her sternocleidomastoid muscle, and I forget about Grody.

"Did you say something?" she says.

"No."

"Is that an erection?"

I shift to test it. "No. It's just a stuffy."

"Which is what?"

"Penis lodged in underwear at an angle suggesting an erection."

"Really? Can I touch it?"

"No."

"Why not?"

"Because now it's turning into an erection."

Violet's lips part audibly. She slowly drops her arms to her sides, revealing her body in its straining underwear. She looks like a superhero.

She moves her hips. Her pubic bone is just something you have to put your palm on. So I do, and grip her mons, and lift. Put my other hand in the small of her back to pull her toward me.

Our lips and teeth mash, cheekbones like fists, as we kiss.

Out the window, a twig snaps.

As I tackle Violet to the ground, the room lights up above us.

16

There's no explosion, though, or bursting glass. Just a run of light-flashes. I push off the floor and get through the door just as it goes off again.

I get around the cabin in time to see someone disappear into the woods that lead up to the outfitters. In a cabin somewhere to my left, Bark the Dog starts barking. I try to run and sniff my fingers at the same time. Violet's smell gets the hairs on the back of my neck up.

As a flashlight switches on ahead of me and I enter the woods, I suddenly understand why Sheriff Albin is so obsessed with cleared paths. Even though the trees have skinny trunks, like the whole area's been logged, their branches form an airborne web.* Ducking the small, stabby, eye-level branches just makes you more likely to get clotheslined by the chest-high thick ones. It's like oozing at high speed through a filter made of wood. And unlike the lawn, which was as moist and springy as a cake, the ground here feels like rocks and thumbtacks.

It's a bad place to be in your boxer briefs, but it's not doing any favors for the guy I'm chasing either. Even with my thumbs up at my temples so my forearms will protect my face, and never putting all of my weight on one foot, I'm gaining on his flashlight beam.

As soon as I can see his collar, I dive for it. Yank it backward and down, landing him hard on his back.

I shine his flashlight on him.

Overweight guy around forty in an anorak. Winded

---

* **Guest Footnote by Violet Hurst:** Actually, only about half the trees in the Boundary Waters have been logged. The reason the trunks of the trees are so skinny is that the area has a natural "burn cycle" of only 122 years, meaning that if the forest were left alone, every part of it would randomly burn to the ground, mostly from lightning strikes, during a period averaging 122 years. The Dakota and Ojibwe peoples managed to live in the Boundary Waters without changing the length of the burn cycle at all, but Europeans shortened it to 87 years through accidental and intentional fires, and then, with modern fire-fighting techniques, lengthened it to 2,000 years. Predictably (in hindsight), a 2,000-year burn cycle has even worse unintended consequences than an 87-year burn cycle, in the form of things like out-of-control insects and plant diseases. Current thinking is that the original 122-year cycle should be restored, but no one knows how to do it—particularly without aggravating the government-subsidized logging industry that still operates in the unprotected parts of the National Forest. You sniffed your *fingers?*

and squirming from the light. He's got a camera with a gigantic white telescopic lens held tightly to his chest.

"Who are you?" I say.

He breathes in and out a couple of times. "Nobody."

"What's that supposed to mean?"

"I was lost. Get off of me."

Bark comes tearing out of the woods like a disembodied set of eyes and fangs, dark on dark. Hops on the guy's groin with all four feet and joyfully bounces off.

"Who are you?" I say when he recovers slightly. "Don't make me ask you again."

"What's the situation?" Miguel says, coming up behind me. He's in a robe and slippers, holding a 9mm in a two-handed military stance. Through the trees, I can see lights turning on in the cabins.

"Put that away," I say. "This guy was taking pictures through the window."

"Were you yelling before?" Miguel says to me.

"Yeah." Bark starts licking the side of my head.

"Why?"

"Nightmare."

"About what?"

"Don't remember."

Del arrives, in his own robe-and-handgun ensemble. "Who's he?"

"He hasn't said yet," I say.

"He's about to," Miguel says. He jams the 9mm into the guy's temple. "Who are you, motherfucker?"

"Ow, fuck!" the guy says.

I say "I said, put it away."

"Soon as he tells us who he is."

I take Miguel's gun, eject the magazine, rack the chambered bullet out, and toss it into the woods.

"Fuck!" he says, going after it.

"You're both fucking crazy," the guy on the ground says.

"What's going on?" Violet says, reaching us. She's dressed, which makes me realize how sweaty I am, and how cold out it is. Reggie's right behind her in a fleece shirt and his microshorts. There's a lot of shining flashlights in each other's eyes while Bark jumps around deliriously.

"Yo!" one of Tyson Grody's guys yells from down by the lawn. "What's going on up there?"

"It's under control! No guns!" I shout. To Reggie and Violet, I say "This guy was snooping. Taking pictures."

"Of what?" Violet says.

"I don't know."

"Who is he?"

Reggie says "Was there someone screaming?"

Miguel, searching through the brush, says bitterly "It was Dr. Azimuth. He was having a nightmare. Then he threw my gun over here."

One of Wayne Teng's bodyguards is next to Violet, though I don't recall seeing him arrive. No gun, at least.

"All right. Out with it," I say to the guy on the ground.

"Fuck you. Call the police if you want. I wasn't doing anything illegal."

"I'm pretty sure trespassing's illegal," Reggie says.

"This is private property?" the man says. "I need to get a better map of the easements around here. And if anyone touches me again I will sue the shit out of all of you."

"No, you won't," I say, patting down his coat pockets. I

fake a punch to his gut to make him flinch to one side, then pull the wallet from his back pocket.

"You're mugging me!"

"You'll know when I'm mugging you."

In among the crap in the wallet there's a driver's license and a bunch of different business cards, all with the same name, "Michael Bennett." One says "Michael Bennett, Desert Eagle Investigations, Phoenix, Arizona."

"Who are you working for?" I say.

"Bite me. I wouldn't tell you if I knew."

I notice Jane, wife of Davey, coming up through the woods with some of the other lodge staff.

"You don't know who hired you?"

"They used a middleman. It's standard practice."

Del leans down with what is, I realize too late, a drawn combat knife. For a second I think he's going to stab the man, but he just cuts through the strap of his camera. Says "Mind if I take a look at this?"

"Yes—I do. Don't touch that," the man says.

"Is this thing self-stabilized?"

"God damn it, give it back!" He tries to sit up. My hand is still on his collar.

"What's the assignment?" I ask him.

"I'm looking for wildlife—"

"Are these the pictures?" Del says, prying the memory card out. "Watch this."

Pretty much everyone yells "Don't!" as Del pinches the memory card in half and lets it drop.

"Oops," he says.

Then he realizes he's just ruined our chance to find out what the guy was here to photograph.

The guy realizes it too. Stands up, brushes himself off,

and takes the camera from Del's hands. Looks at me and says "Wallet."

I give him his wallet. Del looks mortified.

"Gentlemen, ladies," the photographer says as he turns to go uphill.

"Son, you come back here, your easement's going to be my foot up your ass," Reggie says.

"That's right, motherfucker," Miguel says from over in the brush.

⟩⌒⌒⟨

"Probably wanted pictures of the ref," Reggie says, lighting a joint. He and I are on the porch of his cabin. After the departure of Michael Bennett of the Desert Eagle Agency or whoever he was, and my following him up the hill to get his license plate number, I stopped by Reggie's cabin and asked him if he had a minute.

"Who *is* the ref?" I say.

"In good time." He offers me the joint.

I rarely do drugs anymore, because as I've grown older I've become able to achieve the same states of emotional instability and poor decision-making skills without them, but neither have I quite gotten into the habit of turning them down. I drag deeply, and an artificially cheery assessment of my character and actions sets in almost immediately.

Why don't I do drugs anymore?

"I've got alpha-blockers, too, if you want some," Reggie says. "For the other thing."

"What other thing?" I say on the let-out.

"You know—the nightmares."

I let that lie.

"Were you in the service?" Reggie says.

"No."

"Too bad. They've got some cool things going on with PTSD now at the VA. You know, I could get my doc to talk to you on the phone."

"Reggie," I say to him. "What the fuck are you doing?"

"With what?"

"With any of this. The tour."

He laughs. "Do I look like someone who knows what he's doing?"

"Yeah," I say. "You do. You've got the only viable business in an economic wasteland. You've got friends. You've got enough juice to get someone like Tyson Grody to show up for your crazy-assed monster plan. So why do you *have* a crazy-assed monster plan?"

Reggie tucks the joint into the good side of his mouth to relight it. "I'm not gonna tell you the money doesn't have anything to do with it. I wouldn't mind getting out of here. Move to Cambodia, live on the beach. I've got some personal reasons, too, though."

"Like what?"

"It's something a friend of mine wanted to do."

"You mean Chris Jr.?"

"You've heard of him."

"Yeah," I say. "I heard the monster hoax was his idea. I also heard you killed him."

If it shakes Reggie up, he doesn't show it. "Yeah, well," he says, exhaling. "That's what everybody thinks."

"Did you?"

"No. I loved Chris Jr. He was like a little brother to me—if I could have had a little brother who was that much less fucked up than I was."

"So why do people think you did?"

"It's how I got this place." He gestures out across the water. With the glass lake reflecting a cutting-needle moon, it's spectacular. The air is damp and thick with the sounds of a living environment: frogs or cicadas or something. Pikes fighting loons, for all I know.

"What happened to him?"

"No fucking idea," Reggie says, handing off to me. "I was right here—inside—playing poker with Del and Miguel and another guy, who doesn't work here anymore, and we heard the shots."

"Chris Jr. was shot *here?*"

Reggie points. "Down there. On the pier. Chris Jr. and this other guy, a priest. We didn't find them till the next day, though. We went outside when we heard the shots, but we couldn't see anything, so we figured it was just some jackass shooting off drunk, or night hunting."

So Chris Jr. was shot on the same pier the picture was taken on. With Reggie nearby.

Which means what? I can't really see Del and Miguel risking felony homicide charges to help Reggie fake an alibi. It's possible, but they'd need to really love whatever it is they do for him, or with him, or whatever—or else really love *him*. Most people will think twice about buying into a murder rap, particularly when it's going to give someone they already know is capable of murder a reason to want *them* dead too.

But maybe they didn't know they were doing it. With a decent scope, Reggie could have shot Chris Jr. and Father Podominick from right here at his cabin. Out the bathroom window or something, then hidden the rifle and come back to the game asking what that noise was.

"You have to understand," Reggie says. "Chris Jr. didn't live here. Christine didn't want to, because of school for Autumn and all that, so the whole family lived in Ely. Chris didn't even tell her he was coming out here that night. Said he was going to Sears. He didn't tell *us* either. Christine called here an hour or so after he was shot and asked if Chris had stopped by, but we didn't think he had, so we said no. We still have no idea what he was doing out here. Father Podominick neither."

"Did you notice *anything* that night?"

"Nope. Just the two shots. Police thought they came from out on the lake, or around the shore."

"Did you hear a boat?"

"No, but that doesn't mean anything. Lot of people around here use electric motors, so they can sneak up on the fish. And *everybody's* got a canoe."

"Could someone have shot him from as far away as Ford?"

"I don't know. *I* couldn't have."

Odd thing to say. "Is it possible one of Debbie Schneke's Boys killed Chris Jr.?"

"No. She didn't have those at the time."

"Could she have done it herself?"

"Nah. Not Debbie. She wasn't as bad back then as she is now."

"Not even right after Benjy died?"

Reggie salutes me with the joint as he relights it. "You *have* done your homework, son. But no, I don't think so. Obviously you can't go killing a woman's kid and expect her to be the same afterward. Benjy was a cool kid, too—I knew him because he was dating Autumn. He put up with all *kinds* of shit from us. But Debbie didn't fully lose it till later on, and I think there were other factors involved when she did. I don't really know, though. Her and me'd stopped dating by the time the kids died."

I suddenly feel stoned. "You and Debbie Schneke were *dating?*"

"Oh, yeah. On and off for about six years. Way off, sometimes, but still. She really was a different person back then."

As with every other part of this weirdness, I have no idea what to make of that. "Why didn't you tell the people you wanted to come out here about Benjy and Autumn?" I say. "As a selling point, I mean. Why wasn't it mentioned in the documentary?"

"Fuck, I would never exploit Autumn's death for bullshit like that. I was crazy about that girl. I would have taken a bullet for her. Anyway, the documentary I didn't really have anything to do with."

"Except for sending it out."

"Sure, there's that. But making it was all Chris Jr.'s thing."

"You weren't part of the original hoax?"

"No. I knew about it, I guess, but I got the idea Chris Jr. wanted to do it on his own. Or maybe he just didn't want *me* to be involved. He was thirty-seven or whatever. I'm sixty-two. I'd known his dad since before he was born— I'd been *living* here since Chris Jr. was around fifteen. I figured maybe he wanted a chance to try something all on his own for once."

"And it worked out so well that now you're trying it."

Reggie shakes his head. "Part of why I'm trying it is *because* the whole thing went to hell. Like I say: most of it's about the money. But not all of it. Something or somebody killed Autumn, then somebody shot Chris Jr. If doing this trip brings me face-to-face with whatever or whoever that was, it'll be worth it, money or no money." His eyes are wet. Both of them. "Hey, you want a Dr Pepper?"

"No, thanks."

"I'm gonna have one."

"Go ahead."

When he comes back, I say "Reggie, is there any reason at all to think there's actually a monster in White Lake?"

He looks surprised. "Sure there is. I wouldn't be doing this otherwise."

"Like what?"

"Well. For one thing, Chris Jr. thought there was. I know he did, because right before he died, he bought all this equipment to catch it—giant nets and hooks and stuff. Most of it showed up after he was gone, but it was serious stuff. He was loading up for *something*."

"Okay. Any other reason?"

"Yeah," Reggie says. "I'm not saying there necessarily is one in White Lake. But I have run into one of these fuckers before."

EXHIBIT F, PART 1

Sang Do River, South Vietnam
Monday, 24 July 1967*

Reggie Trager slips on shell casings from a firefight two
days ago as he races to the back rail of the *commandement,*
one hand ripping at the buttons of his pants. He gets them
down just as he gets his ass over the rail and explodes fluid
into the already brown river. On the boat behind him, the
freaky Ruff-Puffs all applaud.†

---

* **How I know this:** Reggie Trager, various supporting documen-
tation.

† I'm not going to get too far into official and unofficial terminology
used by the U.S. Navy in the Vietnam War (according to which, for
example, Rear Admiral Norvell G. Ward was the CHNAVADGRU,
for "Chief, Naval Advisory Group"), even where I've been able to
sort it out. But here are the essentials:

His intestines unclenched for the first time in hours, Reggie breathes deeply, inhaling thick, lead-tasting diesel smoke that makes him feel exactly like he's doing a back flip over the gunwale. He instinctively jumps forward, smacking his face into the back of the wheelhouse. Lets himself slide partly down the wall—his cheek and palms are wet with sweat, even though he's freezing—but not black out.

Reggie feels superfluous enough as it is. On this shitcan alone there are three other people who can do

---

"Ruff-Puffs," or RF/PFs, were the South Vietnamese Regional Forces / Popular Forces, i.e., the guerrillas who fought for the South as a kind of counterpart to the Viet Cong. According to Reggie, they were required to get tattoos saying *"Sat Cong"* on their chests to prove their loyalty—*"Sat Cong"* meaning, depending on the translation, either "Kill communists" or "Boy am I fucked if the North wins this war."

A "shitcan" was an STCAN—a boat made by Services Techniques des Constructions et Armes Navales for the French, then transferred to the Americans when the French fled.

A *"commandement"* was the shitcan that the commanders of a RAG (River Assault Group) rode on.

"Dai-uy" was the South Vietnamese Navy rank equivalent to lieutenant.

And the *Cuu Long Giang*, aka *đông bằng sông Cửu Long* ("Nine Dragon River Delta"), aka "Cool and the Gang," was the Mekong Delta. The Delta is at the southern end of Vietnam but was vitally important to the war because most of South Vietnam's population and rice production were there. Since Vietnam is crescent shaped, the more-or-less-straight "Ho Chi Minh Trail" from Hanoi in the North to the *Cuu Long Giang* in the South cut through Laos and Cambodia, which is the reason the United States gave for bombing those countries.

his job: the lieutenant, the *dai-uy,* and the coxswain. Everybody tries to learn everybody else's job generally, in case there's no one else left alive to do it, but comm and radar get special attention. Nobody wants to get stranded out here. The lieutenant and the *dai-uy,* at least, know more about radio and radar equipment than Reggie does.

Which isn't saying much. Reggie's been in-country for a month. He's been out of high school for seven weeks, having upped voluntarily for reasons that now seem foggy but that he hopes were more than just wanting to live in a war movie. He does recall thinking that joining the Navy rather than the Army, with guaranteed electronics training, would probably land him a job in the radio shack of a five-thousand-man aircraft carrier, calling in artillery strikes with his feet up.

But that's not what the job has turned out to be. The job has turned out to be comm engineer to a South Vietnamese Navy River Assault Group in the fucking *Cuu Long Giang.* Three weeks' basic training at RTC Great Lakes—cut from eight weeks right before Reggie got there—then two days of "localized specialization training" onboard a destroyer docked in Saigon. Then this shit. In which twenty-five of the forty-two American RAG personnel based, like Reggie, at Vinh Long have been killed in action in the last three months.

Or else killed by dysentery. Reggie leans his full weight onto his face so he can wipe his palms dry on his fatigue cutoffs, then pulls himself upright against the back wall of the wheelhouse.

He turns around with his hands still raised and gets a cheer from the Ruff-Puffs in the trailing boat.

Three hours later the Ruff-Puffs are gone, dropped off in the jungle with their ARVN commanders and their solitary U.S. Army accompaniment, a dead-eyed "pacification officer" who didn't say anything to anyone. Reggie's in the wheelhouse, feeling a lot better. Still dizzy but not nearly so cold.

This is the mellow part of the mission, the five-boat flotilla moving along easily, but the whole operation should be pretty simple: they're supposed to go up the river a little ways farther, park, and wait for the Ruff-Puffs to flush the VC toward them. Then use the deck-mounted .30s and .50s to chew the VC up. Reggie has yet to see an op like this go perfectly smoothly, but he's got a good feeling about this one.

Lieutenant Torrent drops down into the wheelhouse, followed by *Dai-uy* Nang.

Reggie has rarely seen them apart. He's even heard they double-teamed the lady reporter from *Life* magazine who went on a sortie with the RAG before Reggie got here, and physically they're close to identical—both barely over five feet tall and weighing nothing, even though the lieutenant is blond and blue eyed and from Oregon, and the *dai-uy* is from the Rung Sat region southeast of Saigon. They both wear Australian bush hats and smoke pipes: the CPO gets them Borkum Riff from somewhere.

"Hot as hell in here," the lieutenant says. "You drinking enough water?"

"Yes sir," Reggie says.

"Good to hear, Sailor. Don't die on me. Get me everybody on the horn. We're doing some recon."

"Yes sir," Reggie says. Thinking *Oh, shit.*

"Recon," to the lieutenant and the *dai-uy,* means going into obscure villages and talking to the people who live there in order to learn the local waterways and seed loyalty. As if either of those things is possible. Reggie's been along on several of these trips, all of them memorable for the sense that the villagers would rather be killing them than talking to them, and were trying hard to figure out how to make the switch.

And none of those earlier trips was this far up the Sang Do. Reggie has no idea how the lieutenant and the *dai-uy* would even have heard about a village around here.

But they're talking to each other in Vietnamese, and smiling, in a way that Reggie, who doesn't understand Vietnamese at all, knows he should worry about. The Vietnamese coxswain joins the conversation. Soon the lieutenant is speaking Vietnamese into Reggie's handset, and the coxswain's turning the wheel into a bend of the river where the shore is only an intermittent mud bank with a marsh on the other side.

The shitcan ahead of them scrambles to reverse course. As it pulls up alongside, Reggie sees the CPO's head appear in the trap above its wheelhouse.

The lieutenant gives Reggie back the handset and jumps to chin himself out of their own trap. Reggie hears him shout above the engines: "We're stopping for recon. We're gonna bank the flotilla and take *your* boat into the jungle."

It's a sensible decision for which Reggie is extremely grateful. The CPO's shitcan has an extra deck gun instead of a radar housing, and radar barely works in the bamboo. It barely works on open water.

Partly out of guilt about not having to go, and partly to misrepresent how healthy he is, Reggie climbs up through the trap to see them off.

He watches the lieutenant and the *dai-uy* pop like monkeys from the deck of the *commandement* to the deck of the CPO's boat. Sees the lieutenant turn around and look right at him and say "Sailor—you coming?"

The CPO says "Lieutenant, I don't think the kid's up to it." He's been watching Reggie from the hatch.

Reggie loves the CPO already—outside of the lieutenant giving him orders, the CPO's the only person in the flotilla who ever speaks to Reggie—but right now Reggie's rapt with admiration. Crouched down on top of the wheelhouse he's got goose bumps again, and the sway of the boat makes him want to throw up.

"Can't get your dick wet without getting your feet wet," the lieutenant says. "What do you say, Sailor?"

The lieutenant's choice of words makes Reggie want to throw up even more. "Sir, I can't leave my equipment behind," he says.

Which is true. Nor can he take it with him. The two VHF radios and the AN/PPS-5B radar set are each categorized as "man portable," but only by some asshole who sells radio equipment. Reggie couldn't haul that shit if he were well.

"So secure it, and let's get moving," the lieutenant says. "You know what I say: 'Know the river, know the locals, know what the fuck you're doing.'"

The lieutenant does say that, fairly often. Reggie, who still feels nauseated but now also strangely weightless and cheery from the attention, says "Yes sir!" and slides back into the wheelhouse.

The vertigo almost knocks him off his feet. Reggie takes

his field jacket off its hook and points to the coxswain and then the trap, miming turning a key in a lock. The coxswain has to resent the shit out of an American teenager telling him to leave his own wheelhouse because he can't be trusted not to loot it, but he just shrugs and climbs out.

Reggie looks around. All of the wheelhouse's windows are open about six inches or so, but they've been that way for at least the last ten coats of paint. Anyone who gets Reggie's equipment out through them is welcome to it.

ᐟ⚫⚫(

Bright green bamboo forms a curtain taller than the wheelhouse all the way around the boat, endlessly parting at the prow to clatter along the bottom as they motor into the marsh, but revealing nothing ahead but more green bamboo. Even the surface of the water is green, with some kind of algae.

Reggie stands on deck, insects hitting his face like tiny meteorites, landing in his eyes, ears, and mouth, making a noise like a million distant chainsaws. Maybe they're panicked to be suddenly out in the open above the deck. Reggie knows that breathing only through his nose like this, harder out than in to try to keep the bugs out of his nostrils, is making him dizzier, but he can't stop doing it. There wasn't room for him in the wheelhouse.

He has no idea what direction they're pointed, or how deep the water is. Last time he looked through the wheelhouse window, no one even seemed to have a map out, though the lieutenant and the *dai-uy* were laughing. He doesn't even know what time it is. For some reason he forgot to wear his watch.

An amount of time Reggie can't begin to judge passes by. Then the bamboo wall ahead of them sizzles with light and parts into sunshine. They've come into a clearing. It feels like they've exited hell.

One end of the clearing has a prehistoric-looking stone building built down into the water. A wooden platform in front of it extends as walkways around two of the clearing's sides. And on the platform itself, half a dozen Vietnamese men in loincloths and T-shirts, thin as storks, stand facing them with poles and machetes.

Here we go again, thinks Reggie.

The engines reverse and then shudder off. Into the weird, sunny-day quiet of no engine noise, the lieutenant and *dai-uy* drop down from the wheelhouse.

One of the men on the platform opposite shouts something at them and waves his pole. The lieutenant and *dai-uy* confer among themselves. Then the *dai-uy* shouts over a response.

The man on the platform yells back. This time, after the *dai-uy* answers, the lieutenant says something. Half the guys on the platform angrily shout back at him, and an argument breaks out that Reggie can't believe is coherent in any language.

Finally one of the guys on the platform starts saying the same thing over and over, and pointing to the side, and everyone else quiets down and looks in that direction. At one end of the walkway around the clearing there's a single aluminum canoe floating, "FOM" stenciled on its hull.*

Apparently that's the only place where it's even mildly

---

* Sorry, one more: "FOM" = *France Outre Mer,* essentially "French but built overseas."

acceptable to tie up a foreign boat. The lieutenant raps on the front window of the wheelhouse, and the engines start up again.

꜀**⚫⚫(**

Reggie, squatting on his heels in the dark hut, tries not to nod off and lose his balance again.

The hut is on pilings. Except for the stone temple near where they landed, every building in the village seems to be on pilings, as do the walkways that connect them through the bamboo. Reggie doesn't know how big the village is, but it has to be bigger than what he's seen, because he has yet to see a woman or child.

The lieutenant, the *dai-uy,* and several of the loincloth guys are crouched around a map with a GI lantern on it, arguing in Vietnamese. The body of one of the loincloth guys is keeping the light from illuminating Reggie's corner.

There's a shooting pain in one of his knees. His other leg is asleep.

He drifts off.

꜀**⚫⚫(**

The lieutenant shakes him awake, and Reggie gets uncertainly to his feet. Everyone else in the hut is already standing.

The mood seems just as hostile and suspicious as before. As they walk back toward the shitcan, Reggie knows that no one will ever explain to him, or even to the CPO, why this is so. Or what, if anything, was accomplished by this particular round of creepiness and boredom.

The trip back to the river's easier, though. The CPO, looking concerned, insists that Reggie ride in the wheelhouse, despite the fact that it's packed and smells like armpit even without him. And the river itself, when they reach it, with its wide sky and relatively empty air, feels like a reprieve. The CPO helps Reggie up onto the rail, and the coxswain helps him down onto the *commandement*.

Reggie takes the opportunity of the lieutenant and the *dai-uy* conversing in the prow to rest for a few moments before he climbs back up the ladder.

He has to lean forward to use the key on the lanyard around his neck, because he's too weak to take it off, but he gets the trap unlocked. Takes a few breaths, heaves it open, and slides inside.

Something punches him hard above one eye and then, with a stabbing pain, in the chest.

EXHIBIT F, PART 2

Sang Do River, South Vietnam
Still Monday, 24 July 1967

Reggie bellows in fear. *That* part isn't like a nightmare, at least: his voice still works. But when he looks down, there's a bright green three-foot-long cobra hanging by one fang from the front of his field jacket. Heavy as an arm.

Reggie's frozen. The snake twists and thrashes like a whip, fanning its hood in and out, but can't disengage its mouth from Reggie's chest. As Reggie stares down in horror, its free fang bubbles with opaque white fluid.

Thirty-one of thirty-three. That's how many of the species of snake indigenous to this region Reggie has heard are poisonous.

He notices someone's hands coming in from the sides of his peripheral vision, but he can't look away from the snake. Even when the hands grab the snake's neck and lop its head off with a Ka-bar.

The snake's body flails all over the room, slapping and spraying Reggie's bare shins. He tries to get out of its way, but he still can't move.

The lieutenant just stands there with the knife and the cobra head, looking at the fangs. White bubble from one, pink from the other.

"Uh oh," the lieutenant says.

⌐◐◑(

Reggie wakes up on the roof of the wheelhouse. Bright sky.

There's something heavy on his chest. It lifts. It's the CPO's head, mouth covered in gore. Reggie screams.

"Hang tight," the CPO says. "I'm sucking the venom out."

The CPO goes back to it. Or doesn't. Reggie can't feel anything specific happening. The whole front of his body is a vibrating ache.

The CPO raises his head and spits. Some of it lands on Reggie's neck. Then, as an afterthought, the CPO leans over the side of the wheelhouse and vomits. All of which is cool with Reggie, as long as he doesn't have to move.

"Hold on," the CPO says, wiping his mouth. "I'll get the antivenin."

He vanishes from sight only to be replaced by the lieutenant, who leans down to stare at Reggie's chest, then stands up again and says "Only way that's survivable is if it didn't go all the way through the chest wall."

"How about some morphine?" the CPO says, somehow already back at Reggie's side. Reggie feels the shot spread through him as a warmth that doesn't stop the pain but walls it off, as if he's fine but has a tray of pain resting on his chest.

"Breathe!" the CPO yells.

Was Reggie not breathing? He breathes.

When the pain is distant enough to allow him to focus, he listens to the lieutenant and the CPO arguing just past his feet.

The lieutenant says "We're leaving him in the village."

"Is there anyone in the village who can take care of him?" the CPO asks.

"Don't leave me in the village," Reggie finds himself saying, though without any actual air passing his lips.

"Are you questioning an order?" the lieutenant says to the CPO.

"No *sir*," the CPO says, with an angry sarcasm Reggie's never heard from him before. "I'm just asking what the point is of bringing him all the way to the village. Why not just dump him in the river?"

The lieutenant glances at Reggie. Sees that Reggie's listening. Crouches down to talk to him.

"Son, we can't take you along on the mission. There's no room for you in any of the wheelhouses, and I can't have you on deck during a firefight. And I can't spare anyone to stay behind with you. You know an E-4 doesn't rate a mission abort."

Reggie wonders if there's a requirement that he respond to any of this.

"You're safer—and we're safer—with you in the village. And we need to get you there fast so we don't miss the ambush. End of discussion, okay?" The lieutenant looks at the CPO. "End of discussion."

The CPO and the coxswain from the CPO's boat swing Reggie out over the water on a cloth stretcher, and on a count of three lower him into the aluminum canoe that's tied up near the village temple. Of course: God forbid Reggie gets off the water at some point before he dies. The CPO pulls the canoe close to the walkway and puts a canteen and a C-ration box alongside Reggie's body. Starts to unroll a mosquito net over him.

Before he covers Reggie's face, the CPO looks around. Says "Shh. Open your mouth. Stick your tongue out."

"What—?"

"Do it quick."

Reggie does. The CPO touches Reggie's tongue with his rough, salty fingertip. When he removes it, something stays behind on Reggie's tongue. He scrapes it off with his front teeth, and it rolls up: paper, like the dots you get from emptying a hole-punch.

Reggie swears that if he lives long enough to use a hole-punch again, he'll try to appreciate it more. Appreciate *all* office supplies.

"Swallow," the CPO says, pouring plastic-tasting water from the canteen into Reggie's still-open mouth. Reggie chokes but gets some down, including the piece of paper. Or at least he can't feel it anymore. The CPO lays the canteen down beside him and pulls the rest of the net over his head.

"What is it?" Reggie tries to say.

"LSD. My wife sent it to me under a postage stamp. I've been afraid to try it, but maybe it'll help with the pain."

Then the CPO pulls the net aside for a moment and reaches into Reggie's shirt for his lariat. "Sorry," he says. "Forgot to grab your keys."

⟩ ∩∩⟨

Reggie wakes up clawing the net off of him, his eyes and throat burning from the DDT it's impregnated with. Tries to lean his head up along the inside of the canoe, but his neck is thick and claylike, and the attempt spikes pain through his chest. His head has gotten clearer, though.

Much clearer. There's some bamboo visible against the sky, and even though it's evening, Reggie can see every pole of it—including the ones that are hidden by the ones in front. He *knows* they're there, because he can deduce them. And what's the difference between that and seeing them with your eyes?

It's like water. Right now, Reggie can't see any. But he sure as hell knows there's some around. And how much of water do you ever see anyway? Just the surface—the least important part, the part it's most willing to share.

Water is letting the canoe rest on it right now. Not pulling the canoe down under, but not spitting it out either. Just being its own thing. Sharing, but staying pure. It's like what Reggie's doing now with the mosquitoes: letting them take their one millionth of him in peace. But what's that chanting?

Reggie focuses. The chanting is real. He can hear it, he means, not just deduce it. It's men. Not a lot of men, but nearby.

A God-awful squealing rips into Reggie's ears like from something being tortured. There's a splash, and the squealing stops but is replaced by a weird kind of snuffling. Then there's a bigger splash, a brief squeal worse than the earlier ones, and the snuffling stops too.

All the while, though, the chanting.

Reggie suddenly feels like a missionary waiting for some natives to put him in their soup, or tie him to a pole and throw spears at him.

There's more squealing. Now Reggie *has* to see.

He shoves himself farther up in the canoe with his feet. The pain from bending his chest almost blacks him out, but something in him suspects this might be the end anyway. Who cares if pain is spreading through him like the rivers of the delta that he's floating on? This isn't some groove poem, dickhead. This is *death* we're talking about.

The boat is rotating now from his efforts. He can see the edge of the stone temple. Then the entryway. Men from the village are seated cross-legged on the platform in front of it. Chanting. The one at the end of the line has a bag. He pulls a piglet out of it. It squeals.

The men pass the writhing piglet down the line. Reggie's canoe rotates as if to follow it. When the piglet reaches the man at the end of the line, he takes it, touches his forehead to it, and throws it out over the water with both hands.

The piglet screams and wheels in the air. Lands hoofs-down and bobs right back to the surface, doggy-paddling and huffing pathetically as it tries to swim for one of the lily pads, as if that could support the piglet's weight.

Then something huge rises up in the water behind the piglet and swallows it whole.

The thing is at least as long as the line of men. It has to be: at the same moment its horrible toothed mouth rises up and engulfs the piglet, a muscular ripple half the length of the platform swells outward from the middle of the water. It causes Reggie's canoe to bob.

The temple rotates out of sight. Reggie can once again see only bamboo and the darkening sky. Inside himself, he's screaming.

Outside too, he realizes.

17

"That's a hell of a story," I say.

"Innit?"

"You had dysentery, you were on morphine and LSD, and you'd been bitten by a cobra."

Reggie shakes his head. "I was on acid and morphine half the time I was in Nam. I had dysentery the *whole* time. And a cobra bite's just not that big of a deal, long as it doesn't kill you outright. What I saw out there was for real."

"Okay," I say. "So what was it?"

To whatever extent I was before, I'm no longer enjoying this conversation. It's reminding me of my own canoe freak-out from earlier, and, worse, it's reminding me of the guy in the video with one leg. Like that guy, Reggie's just told me, with complete conviction, a story that cannot be true.

What is this, a tiny town of psychopaths? Of people who lie so constantly and skillfully they should be in a logic puzzle, or at least running a Fortune 500 company, but have instead elected to participate in a rat's-ass lake monster hoax?* When people go through the kind of shit Reggie's clearly gone through they sometimes turn flat, because nothing they do or say is remotely as charged as what happened to them before. But Reggie doesn't even come across as flat.

"I think it was a water dragon," he says. "It sure as hell wasn't a catfish. Or an Irrawaddy dolphin, unless it was one with huge teeth that ate pigs. Which isn't normally the case: I've checked. It could have been a snakehead, based just on how ugly it was, but if it was, it was bigger than any snakehead on record. I mean, a snakehead that big would just be its own kind of monster anyway."

"What's a water dragon?" I say.

"Something Cambodians believe in."

"But not Vietnamese people?"

"I don't know. Woman who told me about it was in Cambodia."

"And now you think there might be one in White Lake?"

Reggie holds his empty can above his mouth and taps it to dislodge drops. "Fuck, I don't know. Obviously it'd be a

---

* Psychos are at heart just people who think they're smarter than everyone else. If they're wrong it's a debilitating condition, because education and hard work are galling to them, yet being exposed as unexceptional enrages them. The ones who are actually clever, though—as long as they stick to fields that prize social manipulation and high self-esteem over technical skills—can do anything.

hell of a coincidence. Water's a lot colder here, for one thing. Wouldn't shock the hell out of me, though. I'm done being surprised by scary motherfuckers that live in the water."

"So now you want to lead a trip to go find one?"

He lowers the can. "Yeah. The actual leading of the trip is not something I'm looking forward to. Being on the water, I mean. But I have to figure that's what alpha-blockers and marijuana are for."

On a similar theme, I say "And why do you want to move to Cambodia?"

He laughs. "It's not like I'm gonna move into a hut on stilts in a swamp there. They do have land-based real estate. And Cambodia's still pretty free of tourists, long as you stay out of Angkor Wat. You can live on the beach, there's lots of prostitutes…" He glances at me. "I like prostitutes. What can I say? And northern Minnesota is *not* good for prostitutes. It's like going to Mecca for beer-battered pork."

"They make beer-battered pork?" I say. I always forget how hungry marijuana makes me.

"Del does, sometimes. Weather here sucks also. You ever been here in the winter?"

"No."

"It's cold. Like the outside of an airplane. During the summer the mosquitoes are worse than they were in Nam."

"But…isn't Cambodia a little *close* to Nam?"

"Hey, the Vietnamese didn't come over here to kill *us*."

"I suppose that's true."

"Anyway, I figure if Chris Sr. had the guts to buy this place, and Chris *Jr.* had the guts to do whatever the fuck it was he was planning to do with the whole White Lake

Monster thing, the least I can do is get in a canoe for a week and finish what they started. I mean, I do rent the pieces of shit out for a living. Chris Sr. used to ride in canoes sometimes, and he hated boats as much as I do."

"Why?" I say. I'm still thinking about the pork.

"The usual. Vietnam."

"He was there too?"

Reggie looks surprised. "He was my CPO."

"The one who gave you the LSD?"

"Yeah. He saved my ass a million times." He points to the scarred half of his face. "Cluding this one."

Reggie's narrative is starting to feel claustrophobic and paranoid. Or else I am. "What happened?"

"We all got put on swift boats eventually," he says. "One night Chris—that's Chris Sr., obviously—and I were out in one and we had the running lights on so we wouldn't get strafed, and a P4-Phantom strafed the shit out of us because the pilot thought we were an NVA helicopter. I got fuel on me and got lit on fire and all that shit—I didn't even *want* to live. Chris swam me to shore."

"Fuck."

"Yep. Bitch of it is, NVA didn't even use helicopters."

When he falls silent, I say "Were Del and Miguel in the military too?"

"Del was in Nam, but he never got north of a fire base. Might have had to drink a warm beer once or twice. Miguel just likes guns."

"Do *they* believe there's a monster in White Lake?"

"You've met them."

"Right…"

Reggie, eye running, smiles his wicked and goofy half smile. "Those guys'll believe anything."

18

At six a.m. I call Dr. Mark McQuillen from the phone on the desk of the back room of the registration cabin, hoping to impress him and catch him groggy enough to answer questions.

"This is Dr. McQuillen."

"Dr. McQuillen, this is—"

Phoning another doctor this early has thrown me off: I almost say "This is Peter Brown." Someone I stopped pretending to be three years ago.

"It's Lionel Azimuth. I was wondering if I could ask you some questions."

"Not at present. I'm on my way out."

"It's six."

"Then I'm already late. Sunrise is at six-fifty-two, and

I need to be out on Hoist Bay by then. I'd invite you to come with me, but fish can smell horseshit from a mile away."

"That's a good one. How's Dylan?"

"He left here in the peak of health."

"What about Charlie Brisson?" The guy with the leg bitten off.

McQuillen laughs. "Have a good day, Doctor," he says as he hangs up.

Back in the cabin, Violet's asleep on her stomach with one knee fetched up and the sheets pushed down across her thighs. The two-inch stripe of her black cotton underwear is somehow perfectly centered over her pussy. You can crunch the pheromones with your teeth.

I try to get my shit together without waking her, but she turns over as I'm about to leave.

"Where are you going?"

"Back to McQuillen's."

"What time is it?"

"Little past six."

"Will he be awake?"

"I just talked to him on the phone."

It becomes a game after a while, the lying by telling the truth. Like doing crosswords.

"Can I come?"

"Sleep. I'll be back before you wake up. I'll get gas for the Mystery Machine."

She grinds her palms into her eyes. "Don't say that. I hate *Scooby-Doo*."

I should leave.

"Why?" I say.

"The fucking monster always turns out to be fake. It's always just some loser in glow-in-the-dark paint, trying to steal money from a yuppie who doesn't even know the money exists. The only person who ever gets anything out of it is Daphne."

"That's the blond one?"

"Her hair's red. She gets herself kidnapped all the time, because the only way she can come is by being fucked in the ass while she's tied up."

Now I *really* should go.

"How do you know that?"

"Didn't you ever watch that show?"

"I've seen it."

"The blond one is Fred. Daphne's boyfriend."

"So..."

"Daphne's frigid with Fred. She gave him a handjob once and puked. Fred titty-fucks Velma every time they build a monster trap together, then feels guilty about it."

Watching Violet stretch as she says this, her skin matte from the cold, is surreal.

"I thought Velma was gay," I say.

"She just tells Shaggy that so he'll stop hitting on her. She'd rather fuck the dog."

"Interesting. Anyway..."

"Wait. I'm coming with you."

I'm about to tell her not to, but she gets out of bed. As she walks to the bathroom, the twin motions of her pulling her underwear back down over her butt and retucking the sides of her breasts leave me speechless.

I go stand by the bathroom door to try again. "You

know, I would have thought that what you'd *like* about *Scooby-Doo* was that the mystery always had a logical explanation."

"Are you kidding?" she says. "Nobody likes that. It's like that piece-of-shit *Wizard of Oz,* where the wizard turns out to be a fake even though the whole thing's a dream anyway. Who has a dream about a fake wizard?"

"So what's the option—*Twilight,* and *Harry Potter*? Kids growing up knowing more about the physiology of vampires and werewolves than they do about human beings?"

"Wow. Somebody is *grumpy* in the morning."

The toilet flushes, and a minute later she opens the door brushing her teeth. She's got sexy sleep notches beneath her eyes.

"In the first place, Grumpy Grampa, don't be getting on *Twilight,*" she says. "In the second, I'm not sure you want to be holding up *Scooby-Doo* as a physiology textbook. It's about a talking dog."

At McQuillen's I peel the magnetic "GONE FISHIN'" sign off the clinic door before Violet can see it, and make a show of ringing the buzzers on both doors, then knocking. Finally I ask Violet to walk around the house and try to see in through the windows, at which point I slide the polymer lock pick and tension wrench out of the lining of my wallet and spring the deadbolt on the second rake.

I really should have told Violet not to come. Since I didn't, I'll have to either get in and out before she notices or else think of something to tell her when she does.

Depends what's inside, I suppose.

The waiting room's dark, but I know where the desk lamp is. In the closet behind the desk, unmarked boxes: too difficult to search. I move to the hallway.

Most of the clinic I'm already familiar with, like the examining room McQuillen put Dylan in and the one that's empty. A hall closet has janitorial and medical supplies. I open the locked door next to it, but when I go up the carpeted steps I'm suddenly in someone's house. Midway between the dining room and living room, with a nasty *déjà vu* that I've broken in to kill someone. I go back down to the clinic and try the door at the end of the hall. File room.

It's got an armchair with medical journals and a mostly empty bottle of Johnnie Walker Red on it. Next to that a lamp table with a framed photo: McQuillen, maybe forty years younger, standing next to the desk in the reception room. On the desk itself a woman with her legs crossed.

The woman's in every photo in the room. Sometimes alone, sometimes with McQuillen. From the evolution of her eyeglass frames, it looks like she left his life, for all I know life in general, around 1990.

It's a bummer, and along with something I can't quite figure out makes me worry about the old man, but I don't have time to think about it. I check the medications locker, grab a few items I've been wishing I brought with me from the ship, then start on the files. Luckily, of all McQuillen's patients named Brisson, Charlie's chart is the easiest to find. It's the thickest.

Charles Brisson is sixty-four years old. Way too young to look like he did on the video. So young that McQuillen's first note on him is from when Brisson was fourteen.

Reason for first visit: constant thirst and hunger paired with weight loss. McQuillen diagnoses juvenile diabetes and starts him on a drug I don't recognize but was probably zinc-preserved pig insulin. I fan through McQuillen doing a reasonable job of keeping Brisson stable through the usual struggles and crises you get treating diabetic teenagers.

After a while, though, Brisson stops cooperating. Becomes more interested in proving that just because one fucked-up thing happened to you doesn't mean a whole bunch more can't. Particularly if you help them along.

It's like a particularly unfunny flip-book. Alcoholic car wreck in his early twenties. Alcoholic liver enzymes in his late twenties. Bad sugar control the whole time. Leg amputated for diabetic gangrene while he's still in his forties. Five years later, onset of Korsakoff's syndrome.

Fuck should I have thought of that before. In Korsakoff's, people whose memories have been wrecked by thiamine deficiency—usually, in developed countries, from alcoholic malnutrition—start unconsciously creating new memories in real time. Suggest to someone with Korsakoff's that something *may* have happened, and there's a good chance they'll suddenly remember that it did, and give you the details. It should have been the first thing I considered.

I replace the chart. Pull the ones on Autumn Semmel and Benjy Schneke.

Autumn's is two pages long, about a sprained ankle five years ago. Apparently McQuillen wasn't her usual doctor. Which, given that she lived in Ely, makes sense.

Benjy's chart starts with a certificate of live birth eighteen years ago and ends with a note from two years ago that just says "d. MMVA."* Both the birth certificate and the close-out note are signed in McQuillen's distinctive, lost-art handwriting.

Clipped inside the back cover of Benjy's chart is a manila envelope sent to McQuillen from the Minnesota Bureau of Criminal Apprehension in Bemidji. Still sealed.

I try to think of some way of opening it that won't be obvious later, but end up just tearing it across the top.

When I get back to the front room, Violet's in the doorway, leaning in to see without crossing the threshold. "Is he here?" she says.

"No."

"But you went in?"

I pull the door shut behind me and start down the stairs. I don't want to be here anymore. McQuillen coming back because he forgot something is the least of it.

"Door was unlocked," I say. "I was worried about him." True-but-false: it's not just a game. It's an attitude.

"Isn't that still breaking and entering?"

"Not if you don't break anything."

"Are you sure he's not there?"

"I looked around. Maybe I got the time wrong."

As I unlock the car, she notices the manila envelope in my hand. "And you *took* something?"

"Just this. Which he won't miss. He never opened it."

---

* "MMVA" must be some kind of motor vehicle accident— "marine" or "moving" or something. Probably not "moving." What kind of motor vehicle accident doesn't involve something moving?

"What is it?"

"Tell you on the way."

"You can't tell me now? You're freaking me out."

I look over at her. Wonder how much of my lying to her she's actually bought, and how much she's just been too polite to call me on.

Either way, I'm about to distract her.

"They're the autopsy photos of Autumn Semmel and Benjy Schneke."

"What?"

"Yeah."

She blanches. "What do they look like?"

"Like if McQuillen had bothered to open the envelope, he'd be a lot less sure April and Benjy were killed by a boat propeller."

19

"Is there any chance they're shark bites?"

"No," Violet says. She's seated on the floor with her head in her hands and her back to my bed. Behind her, on the mattress, the black-and-white glossies are spread in two hideous rows.

"Are you sure?"

"Yes."

"How do you know?"

"A bunch of reasons."

I don't know what's more embarrassing: the fear or the relief.

"For one thing," she says, "they're bell shaped, like from something bottle-nosed, which as far as I know no shark is. And I've never heard of a shark that could be metabolically active enough in fresh water to attack someone. I don't know any saltwater fish that could do that."

"Salmon don't seem to have a problem with it."

"Salmon molt from fresh water to salt water, once, one way. Which is relatively easy, because they just have to fill their cells with enough junk to stay osmotically attractive to water. When they go back, the fresh water poisons them. It's the final evolutionary stressor before they spawn and die. Anyway, sharks also only have cutting teeth. Like piranhas, or Komodo dragons. Whatever this was had cutting teeth in the molar position but puncturing teeth up front. That's why the front of each bite's all stringy."

"Jesus, that's good to hear."

Violet looks at me. She's taking it pretty well for a first timer, but she looks teary eyed and ill. "How do you figure?"

"I don't like sharks."

"Lionel, whatever this is, it's worse."

"I doubt it. It probably *was* a propeller."

"You said in the car that propeller injuries were short, parallel incisions the same distance apart as the front-to-back depth of the screw. And that parts attached to clothes or hair get shredded."

"Yeah, in *textbooks*."

The bodies in the photos aren't wearing clothes. Bodies in autopsy photos seldom are, but the accompanying report says they were mostly naked when they were recovered. The girl's bottoms were still on. Whether she had long hair isn't clear, since her head is missing.

"You don't understand," Violet says. "I *recognize* this bite pattern."

It stops me. "What do you mean?"

"This bite pattern—it's impossible to miss. I mean, I'm not a zoological paleontologist. I'm not a zoological anything—"

"You seem to be doing okay."

"No offense, but that's because you know even less than I do about this stuff. I'm an amateur. I don't even know where my gaps are."

"Okay."

"But this bite I *know*. Every paleontologist knows it, because it's so unique that it gets used to mark the end of the Cretaceous."

"Which is when?"

"That's the fucking problem. Sixty-five million years ago."

I remind myself that I've essentially just shown this woman stills from a snuff film. I'd put a hand on her shoulder, but I don't have that kind of hands.

"Violet—"

She winces. "I know. I'm a paleontologist. Most of the animals I'm familiar with died out in the K-T extinction."

"Exactly."

"But not all of them."

As gently as possible, I say "I really doubt this is a dinosaur."

"Until 1938, people thought the coelacanth had been extinct since the Cretaceous. Then they started turning up."

"But we don't share a habitat with coelacanths. The only reason we found out they were still around is that we started dragnetting their spawning grounds. Even then, most people who saw one probably thought it was just another fish and forgot about it. You and I are talking about something that supposedly looks like a dinosaur, and hangs out in a national park. And eats people. Where's it been all this time? Frozen?"

She doesn't respond.

"What?" I say.

"That's not completely impossible."

"Of course it is."

"It isn't. I may not be a zoologist, but I know there are frogs that can freeze solid."

"How? Their cells would burst."

"They flood their cells with ultrahigh levels of glucose, then supercool. No active metabolism. Until they wake up, they're just proteins in a block of ice."

"And they can stay that way?" I say. "For sixty-five million years?"

"No. Not for sixty-five million years. Random nucleating events would blow out the cells in that kind of time, and there'd be molecular decay. But this thing doesn't have to have been frozen for sixty-five million years. What if it's only sat out the last couple of centuries? That would explain why there's a painting of it. And there's been a hell of a lot of habitat change in the last two hundred years. In 1780 New York Harbor froze. This summer Minneapolis reached a hundred and twenty-three degrees."

"But just because a handful of amphibians can freeze doesn't mean there are reptiles that can."

"There might be, though. Turtles can pull all kinds of crafty shit to survive at the bottom of lakes that freeze over. They can alter their enzymes. They can stop their hearts and lungs and just breathe through their skins."

"Which means they're still building up lactic acid."

"Unless they're buffering it. There's even a *squirrel* that can supercool."*

"So..."

She avoids my eyes. "So maybe it's like that thing Sherlock Holmes says, where when you eliminate all other options, the one that's left has to be the truth, even if it seems like it can't be."

"Violet, I'm sorry, but that's the dumbest thing Sherlock Holmes ever said. How can you ever know you've eliminated all other options?"

She looks miserable. "Name one."

"I will. This was done by a person."

She looks at me, both hopeful and dubious.

"How could you know that?"

"Because it's *possible* it was done by a person. Which nine times out of ten means that it was. Humans will do any sick shit you can imagine. And if this *was* done by a human, then it could easily have been done by one smart enough to figure out what a dinosaur bite should look like and replicate it. You could probably modify a bear trap to do that."

"But Autumn and Benjy had other people with them when they died."

"Two other teenagers, who weren't even on the same

---

* Don't get your hopes up. The history of human cryogenics is gruesome, particularly if you're a Ted Williams fan. There are cases where children have survived without breathing for up to two hours in very cold water, but these seem to have been due to a combination of simple refrigeration and a circulatory response known as the mammalian diving reflex—which in humans, for unknown reasons, falls off sharply after early childhood.

lake. Everybody involved was probably fucking at the time. Maybe the friends heard noises, or thought the water looked disturbed when they got there. But nobody's told us those kids *saw* anything—including the bodies. No one's told us *anyone* saw the bodies before the police picked them out of the water, which was at least three days later. That's plenty of time to fake a bunch of dinosaur bites."

She stares at me. "Do you think *Reggie's* capable of that?"

"I don't know. But there are plenty of people who are. Don't forget, there were two other murders right here the same week. And no one's suggesting *those* were animal attacks."

"But if the person who shot Chris Jr. and Father Podominick had a gun, and knew how to shoot it, why wouldn't they...I mean, how could they do this? To two children?"

"I don't know. Maybe one person killed the kids, and a different person, thinking Chris Jr. and Father Podominick were responsible, killed *them*."

"You mean someone thought Chris Jr. murdered his own daughter?"

"Who knows? Maybe the shooter wasn't even trying for Chris Jr."

"What do you mean?"

"Nobody even seems to know what Chris Jr. and Father Podominick were doing here that night. So how many people could have known where to find them? And according to Reggie, who granted is not the most reliable source in the world, Father Podominick was shot in the head and Chris Jr. was shot in the chest. So someone with a scope took as much time as necessary to line up the most lethal possible shot on Father Podominick, then had to set up the second shot as quickly as possible, because the second target would have known it was coming. That's why the killer went for the chest shot: it's faster and easier. Maybe the killer never even saw Chris Jr.'s face."

Or clothes.

The whole idea starts to sound dumb to me: who assassinates two people with a scope and doesn't bother to identify both targets?

"Who *are* you?" Violet says.

"What do you mean?" I say.

I know what she means, though. She looks horrified.

A total fucking idiot is who I am.

"Why do you know about shooting people in the head with a scope? Or mutilating people's bodies with—what did you say? A *bear trap?*"

"Violet—"

"Why aren't you afraid when people shoot *guns* at you?" Violet says.

"I was afraid."

"You were *smiling*. And afterward you refused to call the police. Why did you rob McQuillen's office?"

"Oh, come on—"

"Are you even really a doctor?"

Christ. It used to be only my patients asked me that question. Now everybody does.

"Yes. I am."

"Are you also some kind of policeman?"

"No."

"Are you some kind of criminal?"

"No." Not at present.

"Have you ever been in prison?"

"No." Nine months in jail awaiting and standing trial for double homicide, maybe, but prison? Never.

True-but-false: it's not just an attitude. It's a lifestyle.

"Are you who Rec Bill thinks you are?" Violet says.

What a smart fucking question, I almost say to her.

"Yes. I think so."

"What does that mean?"

"Rec Bill asked Baboo Marmoset—do you know who that is?"

"Yes."

"Rec Bill asked him to recommend someone who had a science background but also might be able to protect you if something went wrong."

"To protect *me?*"

"I know: I haven't exactly been doing that job."

"Wait. *Who* wanted to protect me?"

"Rec Bill."

"Rec *Bill* wanted you to protect me?"

"He wanted me to at least be able to if it became necessary."

"Holy shit," she says.

She's forgotten about my criminal tendencies. She's forgotten the pictures of the dead teenagers.

Hard to not see what that means.

I say "Are you and Rec Bill . . ."

"What?" she says, distracted.

"Is Rec Bill the *guy?* The semi-boyfriend?"

It brings her back. "No."

"Then why are you blushing like that?"

She looks away. "Fuck you. I'm not."

"He is!"

"I don't want to discuss it."

"Then we'd better get it over with."

"It's none of your business."

"That you're fucking our mutual boss?"

"What?"

At least now I've got her full attention again.

"Okay," she says. "(A) I'm not fucking him. (B) I'm not fucking you either, so what the fuck business is it of yours? You and I kissed. *Once.*"

"It was the only time I've seen you sober past sundown."

"Up *yours!*" She pushes off the floor. Turns away from me, then away from both the photos *and* me. "That is *bullshit.* And it's presumptuous. Maybe not totally presumptuous, but presumptuous. It's rude as fuck, anyway. And what *is* your fucking problem? Because I'm not really going to believe you if you tell me that it's that you don't sleep with drunk girls."

"Yeah. When *I'm* drunk too."

"Ugh!" Violet says. "Forget I asked. This is so typical. You think Rec Bill wants me, and suddenly you want to *date* me or some bullshit. And I don't even know if he *does* want me. I don't know what the hell *either* of you are thinking. Ever."

"Ever?"

"Rec Bill's not approachable like that. And you don't answer questions."

"Well at least I'm approachable."

"Fuck you. Do *not* try to make me laugh. It's not fun, being around you. You make it *seem* fun, but it isn't. It's scary. Because I don't even know who you are. Seriously: who the fuck are you? And what do you want from me?

Some kind of fling on a business trip? For us to become *friends* without my knowing anything about you? What?"

Damn.

Not wrong or undeserved, but damn. It's amazing how many of the things I've been thinking about her now suddenly seem ridiculous.* And how many of the things I've said to her.

"I don't know," I say.

"Great. Let me know when you decide. In the meantime, do you want the room?"

"No."

"Ugh. Just—ugh. And take your fucking pictures, please."

I guess that means I'm leaving.

---

* Particularly the fantasy I've been having where Violet and I are sitting on chaise lounges on what used to be a ninth-floor balcony but is now a landing on what amounts to a private bay because the waters have risen and the world has ended, and she and I—there's also a parrot around, I might as well say—are playing gin with creased cards and drinking tropical drinks. After which we go inside so I can chase her tan lines across our mysteriously cool sheets.

20

I walk around the marina. Up to the outfitters. Back down to the marina. To the parking lot to stash the envelope of photos in the car. To the woods between the lodge and the main town of Ford.

The woods have had paths blazed through them. Not recently—I have to reverse out of the first couple I try—but on a scale that makes it clear that someone at some time thought it was a good idea for people to be able to move between Ford and CFS on foot. I think I get about halfway before I hear voices ahead of me and stop.

It's Debbie and her Boys, coming toward me. Toward CFS.

The fact that Debbie, who's walking with her hands in fists like she's striding toward a bar fight, is wearing jeans and a fleece vest makes it kind of funny that all the Boys are in camouflage and face paint. But only kind of, because all the Boys have guns.

I run back to the lodge and knock on the door of Cabin Ten.

"Who is it?" Violet says.

"It's me."

"Fuck off."

"I can't. Debbie's on her way here through the woods with her Boys, and I need you to start moving everyone up the hill while I call Sheriff Albin."

There's a pause. "Seriously?"

"Swear to God."

)●●(

"Hi, Debbie," I say when she reaches the spot on the lawn where I'm standing.

"Hell are you doing here?" she says. Her regiment is checking the spaces between the cabins, military-style.

"I've been wondering that myself. Hello, dickhead with a gun."

The oldest-looking Boy, with the Colt Commander, comes toward me pointing it at my face. "You're really looking to get iced, aren't you?"

"If I was, I wouldn't be talking to you. You forgot to pull the hammer again."

He looks at it. Says lamely "It's for safety."

"Then stop pointing it at me."

"Where is everybody?" Debbie says.

"Up the hill, mostly. You and Reggie both got lucky: all Reggie's other guests are out doing tourist shit. You can leave now, before Sheriff Albin gets here, and nobody'll know anything ever happened. But you should do it soon. You know Del and Miguel?"

"Course I know those knuckleheads."

"Then you should know those knuckleheads have guns, and that they're watching us right now with binoculars. I'm guessing they won't take too kindly to your Boys going through their shit." The Boys have started kicking in cabin doors and looking inside.

"I'm not here to steal anything," Debbie says.

"Why *are* you here?"

"Talk to Reggie."

"About what?"

"What's it to you?"

"I didn't come to Minnesota to see a dinosaur, Debbie. I came to figure out what Reggie's pulling."

"Whatever it is, what he's making from it is blood money."

"Which I gather you want a part of."

She moves in front of me. "Watch yourself. He killed my son. I don't have to let him profit from it too."

"Point taken. I heard about your son. I'm sorry."

"Sure you are."

"I am, actually. It's awful. But we don't have to talk about it."

"Gee, thanks."

"What we have to do is figure out how to get you out of here. When Reggie called Albin, Albin was already on Highway Fifty-Three west of Ely."

"How far west?"

"I don't know."

"Why should I even believe you?"

"I'm not sure there's an answer for that."

"And why the hell would you want to help me?"

"I'm a doctor. I'm required to try to help people." Even to me it sounds comical. "And neither you nor these kids needs to go to jail for something this stupid."

I look over at one of her mini-thugs. "What is that, an assault rifle?"

"I'm not leaving till I talk to Reggie."

"Fine. Then stay and talk. But send your Boys home. Or at least send some of them home, with the guns, and get the rest of them to wipe off that dumbass face paint."

Debbie thinks about it. Goes over and talks to the dork with the Colt. He scowls at me as he goes to round everybody up.

Debbie comes back with the corner of her fleece vest lifted to show me her waist holster and the pocket Glock that's in it. "This one I've got a concealed-carry permit for. I do what you say and it doesn't work out, I'm holding you responsible."

"Fair enough." I give it a moment. "Can I ask you a question?"

She looks at me warily.

"What is it that makes you think Reggie was responsible for Benjy's death?"

She laughs darkly. "*You're* here, aren't you? And a lot of other rich people. Reggie's getting just what he always wanted."

"Do you think he shot Chris Jr. and Father Podominick?"

"Want to tell me again how you're not a cop?"

"I'm not."

"Whatever. But yes. I do."

"Why?"

"Same reason."

"So I take it *you* didn't have anything to do with that."

Debbie shakes her head. "You know, I've got no reason to tell you, but I will. I did not shoot Chris Jr. and Father Podominick. I did not order them to be shot or in any other way contribute to their demise."

"You didn't blame Chris Jr. and Father Podominick for planning the monster hoax?"

"Honey, those two couldn't have planned a bowling ball dropping off the roof. I don't know which of them was stupider."

"You think Reggie was manipulating them?"

"That's what he's good at. He's doing it now, to you."

Can't say I'm sure she's wrong.

"Seen Dylan Arntz recently?" I say.

"I don't know who you're talking about."

"Well it goddamn *should* be illegal."

"Well at least for now it isn't," Sheriff Albin says.

"How much is he paying *you*, Boss Hogg?"

"Debbie, I'm not gonna dignify that."

"I'm calling the *real* cops."

"You know, you *do* have the right to remain silent."

I stop listening. They've been at it for half an hour, Sheriff Albin demonstrating his ability to turn any situation immediately boring. Which, now that I think about it, is why people call the cops in the first place.

I hear something: distant helicopter blades.

Reggie, looking worried, comes trotting over from

where he's been making a phone call in front of the registration cabin.

"I've got VIPs coming in," he says.

Sheriff Albin lets a beat go by before he says "All right."

"I've got 'em coming in *now*. Whatever Debbie's doing here, I'll drop all the charges if you can get her out of here."

"Can't say it to my face, child-killer?" Debbie says.

"Debbie, when this is over, I will be happy to discuss anything you want. Just not at this moment."

"What's the rush?" Albin says.

"It's this whole secrecy thing. They're not gonna land the chopper unless everyone down here has signed a confidentiality agreement."

The chopper in question beats into view loud and low over the far end of the lake. It's giant—a Sikorsky Sea King or something. The kind with portholes, like the president uses.

"Why? Who is it?" Sheriff Albin says.

Reggie squirms. "Any chance of you signing a confidentiality agreement?"

"I'm an officer of the law, Reggie."

Seeing Reggie hold his bad hand to the good side of his mouth so he can chew his nails isn't that pleasant. "Sheriff, this is really important. And far as I know, I'm not breaking any laws."

Albin watches the helicopter track around the lake. Finally says "You gonna be here tomorrow? Say at one-thirty p.m.?"

"Yes sir."

"You won't have left by then?"

"No sir."

"I take Debbie home now, you'll be here?"

"Yes sir."

"I'm not going anywhere," Debbie says. "Civil disobedience."

"We're gonna throw your ass out, civil disobedience," says Miguel, who's come over to help.

"Everybody relax," Albin says, so slowly that he makes it happen.

To Reggie he says "Three o'clock I have to be in Soudan. So I'd need to be finished up here by two-thirty. And by 'finished up' I mean I'd need you and I to have sat down and you to have told me everything you have planned for this situation. And convinced me that it's not something I need to worry about."

"Yes sir."

"The way I see it, I'm doing you a pretty big favor by doing it that way. Is that how you see it?"

"Yes sir."

"All right then." Albin opens the passenger door of his cruiser. "Ms. Schneke? Back or front?"

I'm confused.

Where I come from, cops talking about favors and how you need to convince them of shit just means you're supposed to pay them. But I don't get the sense that's what's going on here. As far as I can tell, Albin and Reggie have just made an appointment for tomorrow afternoon.

But if the helicopter means the ref is arriving now, aren't we leaving in the morning? And if we are, and Reggie's planning to blow Albin off, just how desperate *is* Reggie? Albin seems reasonable, but he's the law, and it's stupid to fuck with him.

The helicopter's turning in a wide circle, getting ready to land in the parking lot of the outfitters, so we all start trudg-

ing up to meet it. I try to drift toward Violet on the way, but
she gives me such a go-thither look that I leave her alone.

The rotors take forever to stop turning. You can feel the
dust moving across your scalp and the heat of the jet fuel
coming off the turboshafts.

The parking lot's been emptied and a turnaround of
traffic cones set up by the highway entrance. Guarding
the perimeter are about twenty serious, healthy-looking
young people of the Davey and Jane variety. The rest of
the employees of the outfitters have been sent home.

Eventually the helicopter's gangway folds down. Three
goons get off. Black suits and mirror shades, with curly-
tube earpieces going down the backs of their collars.
They walk what's obviously a rehearsed security grid,
moving their heads robotically and occasionally com-
menting into their wrists. It makes you wonder why Secret
Service agents—or people who want to look like them, or
whatever these guys are—still use curly-tube earpieces.
There's got to be a smaller piece of electronics.

One of them goes over and talks to Reggie. Then into
the wrist. A fourth goon gets off the helicopter and stays
by the steps.

Two kids in their twenties but wearing suits come
down and also stand around. Interns or assistants or
something. After them comes Tom Marvell, the Vegas
stage magician.

I might have recognized Marvell anyway, as the first
black entertainer to permanently headline a casino. But
I also heard an interesting story about him once from a

connection I have in the Justice Department.* When Dominique Strauss-Kahn got arrested in New York in May of 2011 and was looking at seven felony charges, a French law firm supposedly tried to hire Marvell to get Strauss-Kahn out of the country, the best opportunity was being thought to be during Strauss-Kahn's transfer from Rikers Island to house arrest. "Marvell was supposed to turn him into some doves or something," was how I heard it.

Marvell's a smart choice for referee. He may not have anything to do with the federal government like Reggie's letter promised, but he's glamorous enough that people will probably overlook that. In theory he's as qualified to spot a fake as it gets. And the Vegas angle, which I'm guessing is where the bit with the pseudo–Secret Service guys comes in, never hurts.

He just mills around the gangway, though, as more people come down.

First a tall guy in a gray suit with an open-necked shirt, who looks like a model in a watch ad. Odd, but there's no way he's the ref: he looks too bored.

Next comes a girl around fourteen years old, so gangly that an adult that thin would be rushed to a hospital.

Another Secret Service–looking guy gets off the helicopter.

Then Sarah Palin comes down the steps.

---

* It may seem strange that a former criminal who's dropped out of the federal witness protection program still has contacts in the Justice Department. But when I first entered WITSEC someone inside the U.S. Marshals' office tipped off David Locano, who then murdered my girlfriend. And I would dearly like to find out who that person was.

21

Camp Fawn See, Ford Lake, Minnesota
Still Saturday, 15 September

You probably want to know how MILFy she is in person.
Or GILFy, or RILFy or whatever.

She looks fine in person. Smaller than you'd think, and
jowlier. Too much makeup but you knew that. It's strange
to see the back of her head.

All I feel when she gets off the helicopter, though, is
depressed. I knew my time with Violet Hurst was short,
but I didn't think it was *this* short. No way in hell is Rec
Bill going to bet two million dollars on the opinion of
someone who's as famous for being uninformed as Sarah
Palin is. And who, for the record, doesn't have anything
more to do with the federal government than Tom Marvell does.

Regarding the woman herself, I have almost no

curiosity at all—something she gets accused of all the time, but I have an excuse: I'm sick of her shit. God may be present in the company of the righteous, and Zeus in the swans and the rain, but Palin is fucking *everywhere,* and has been for years.*

Although my interest in her does improve a bit when, on the kind of receiving line that forms before dinner to introduce her and her entourage to the guests and employees, she pumps my hand, makes eye contact vacantly, moves on to Del, then notices the tattoo on my right shoulder and halts, staring at it.†

The tattoo is of a winged staff with two snakes twined around it. When I got it, I thought it was the symbol of

---

* When I say I have almost no curiosity about her, I of course exempt the question of how she came to quote Westbrook Pegler in her 2008 speech accepting her nomination as Republican candidate for vice president. (Pegler, a racist so crazy he was expelled from the John Birch Society, wrote among other things that it is "clearly the bounden duty of all intelligent Americans to proclaim and practice bigotry," and—in 1965—that "some white patriot of the Southern tier will spatter [Robert F. Kennedy's] spoonful of brains in public premises before the snow flies.") But since Palin has said that she didn't write the speech, which she gave six days after meeting John McCain for the first time in person (and, according to some sources, as little as forty-eight hours after McCain chose her as his running mate), and since Palin doesn't seem to have quoted or mentioned Pegler on any other occasion, the questions raised by his appearance in her speech—Did she know what she was saying? Did anyone? If they did, what did they mean by it, and what audience did they expect to understand that meaning?—aren't exactly personal.

† What? It was warm out, and my sleeves were tight. No, I was not wearing a tank top.

Asclepius, the god of medicine, but that would have been an unwinged staff with one snake. A staff with wings and two snakes turns out to be the symbol of Hermes, the god who takes people to the underworld.

Palin reaches out and touches it. Says "John. Come look at this."

To me she says "Why do you have this?"

"It was supposed to be the symbol of Asclepius, the god of medicine."

"But it's the symbol of Hermes."

Great. Even people who can't name all three countries in North America know that.

I wonder if Violet's ever noticed it's the wrong symbol. If she did, but didn't tell me because she didn't want to hurt my feelings, I should confront her about it. It might make up for my not telling her the French toast was frozen. Which would at least be something.

"What is it, Sarah?" the tall good-looking guy says, coming over.

"Look at this."

He does, with a California squint. Puts his hands on my shoulders to try and turn me so he can see my other arm.

"I'm Lionel Azimuth," I say.

He smiles with pained condescension. "Sorry. Reverend John 3:16 Hawke."

"Excuse me?"

"That's my name." He moves to the side to be able to see the tattoo on my other shoulder without moving me.

Star of David.

"Ah," he says.

Palin moves around to see. The reverend doesn't get

out of her way, which forces her to awkwardly press up against him. "Oh, my goodness," she says.

"We're close, Sarah. Really close."

He pulls her back and they continue down the line. Violet, like everybody else, is staring. I shrug and try to keep her gaze, but she looks away.

At dinner Palin's oddly hunched over her food, frowning with concentration as she listens to whatever the Reverend John 3:16 Hawke is saying in her ear. Sitting on her other side is the fourteen-year-old girl—a distant relation of Palin's, it turns out, named Sanskrit or something. At present the girl's bright red and silent, possibly in reaction to being across from Tyson Grody.

There's a strange hush over the room. People keep referring to Palin as "the Governor," but in whispers, like they don't want to distract her. The Ficks, who on some instinct stopped by on their way out of town to make sure the ref wasn't someone worth rejoining for, only to discover that she easily was, are beaming now in Palin's vindicating presence.

I say as little as possible, and nothing at all to Tom Marvell, who's at my table. Marvell seems nice enough: earlier, on the lawn, he did a magic trick for Stuart Teng that involved a business card bursting into flames, then repeated it about fifteen times while Stuart cried with laughter and Palin's young relation, mortified, tried not to look like part of Marvell's intended audience. And I'd love to know what his connection to Palin is—where'd they meet, at a Westbrook Pegler convention? But no one who lives in Vegas and is smart enough to be both black and an ongoing success in that mafia theme park is someone I want noticing me.

Violet's over at the grown-ups' table, near Grody. I'm not jealous. It'd be like a Doberman hooking up with a Chihuahua. It's annoying that he gets to talk to her, though.

After dinner, when she and Teng talk about going back to the casino, and the idea spreads to the whole group, I consider going with them just to try for some time with her. Decide not to. I don't need to know any of these people any better. Violet included.

Instead I go back to the office in the registration cabin and do my best not to look at the photo of the Semmel family as I check my e-mail. There's already a reply from Rec Bill to the message I sent him before dinner about the ref turning out to be Palin. Since I know it'll tell me to go home, I leave it for later.

Instead I read the e-mail from Robby, the Australian kid covering for me on the ship. It just says "barfing all over." No capitalization, even.

I ask for details and wish him a speedy recovery if he's the one doing the barfing. Then I open the message from Rec Bill.

"I approve of Palin as the ref. Proceed as planned."

No fucking way.

Grateful as I am to stay out here with Violet, particularly if she starts speaking to me again, I'm astonished. Wasting two million dollars is repellent, no matter how rich you are. At least in the Gilded Age they gilded shit.

Rec Bill comes through on a couple of other points, though. Looks like there really is a Desert Eagle Investigations in Phoenix, Arizona, employing—in fact owned by—a guy named Michael Bennett, who matches the description of the guy who was here. And apparently Christine Semmel, mother of Autumn, now lives in San Diego and has a phone number.

Still wondering why Rec Bill so badly needs the White Lake Monster to exist, I call her.

"Yes?" she says. Her voice is a whisper.

"Ms. Semmel?"

"Yes?"

"My name is Lionel Azimuth. I'm a physician. I'm sort of assisting in an investigation into some possible criminal activity here in Minnesota."

Nothing.

"It's a long story, but I'd be happy to give you the details."

"Is this Reggie?" she says.

"No."

"You're calling from the lodge."

"I am. I'm staying here. But like I say—"

"Has he killed someone else?"

All right, then.

"Someone else other than who?"

After a moment she says *"He killed my husband and my daughter."*

I wait for her to say something else, but she doesn't.

"What makes you think that?"

"I know it."

"Can I ask how?"

Another pause. *"Reggie wanted to pretend there was a monster in White Lake. He killed my daughter to make it look like there really was. Then he killed my husband to take over the lodge."*

"The hoax was Reggie's idea?"

"Of course it was. Chris would never have thought of something like that. He wasn't like that. Not...devious. Father Podominick wasn't either. Reggie put them up to it in secret so people wouldn't be suspicious when he took over. Got them so turned around Chris thought he and Reggie were going to catch the monster and sell it."

Christine Semmel's softly crying now. Nice job, Dr. Azimuth.

"Ms. Semmel, we can stop talking if you'd like."

"It doesn't matter."

She sounds sincere about that, so I say "Then can you tell me about how they were supposed to catch it and sell it?"

"Right after Chris died, all these hooks and nets and things he ordered got delivered to the lodge."

"Reggie told me about that."

"Then I found a list of phone numbers in Chris's handwriting. I called them. The ones who would talk to me all said they were rare-animal dealers. They said they'd never heard of Chris, but I didn't believe them."

"Do you still have the list?"

"I gave it to the police."

"Did you make a copy?"

"No."

Understandable: her family had just been wiped out. But it does mean the police have either investigated that angle or decided not to, and either way there's nothing left to do about it.

"Is there any other—" Evidence, is what I want to say, but I feel that will sound like I don't believe her. "Is there anything else you can tell me?"

There's a pause, just the hiss on the line. I'm about to repeat the question when she says *"Reggie, I know that's you."*

She says it without anger, just with exhaustion and sadness. It's unnerving.

"This isn't Reggie. I promise. If you want, I can call you back later, with a woman."

"I don't care. If you are Reggie, you're going to hell," she says as she hangs up.

22

As I stare at the phone, thinking nothing productive, I hear the door of the cabin open. Lean back to look.

It's one of Palin's Secret Service–type guys. It's been raining heavily for about an hour, and he's got a baseball hat and raincoat on and no sunglasses, making him look like a different person. For a second I want to take him out.

I guess I assumed Palin went to the casino with the others, although it makes sense she wouldn't have if she's trying to keep people from knowing she's in Ford.

"What's up?" I say.

He grunts in a way that sounds like it should be accompanied by a pelvic thrust. I'm not sure why it isn't, since there are just the two of us in here, and who's going to believe me that this guy pelvic thrusted? But he just looks around, including behind the desk and into the office, then says into his wrist, "He's in the registration building. It's clear. Window green, window red. Coming out."

As far as I can tell, both windows are closed and unobstructed.

"What does that mean, 'window green, window red'?" I say.

He leaves.

I wait for a minute or two, but nothing happens, so I get up and go look at the books on the "BORROW ME" shelf. I'd go back to my cabin, but Violet and I haven't discussed that since this afternoon, and I'm not sure whether it *is* my cabin.

I take a more or less random paperback to the couch and lie down to read it. When I'm on the second or third page the door opens, and Sarah Palin and her young relation come in.

"Dr. Lazarus! We heard you might be in here."

"I don't know who from. But it's Azimuth."

She's smiling. As before, it's weird to be near her. Like it probably would be with anyone you've seen mechanically reproduced that many times.

"Can we ask a really big favor of you?" she says.

They're still hovering by the door. I sit up. "Sure."

"Sandisk here needs to get her chemistry homework done. My dad was a science teacher, but I guess I kind of missed out on those genes. So we thought *maybe,* you know, what with you being a *doctor* and all…maybe you could help Sandisk with her homework."

I'm surprised. Both that her father was a science teacher and that she believes in genetics.

Maybe I've misjudged the woman.

"I'm happy to try," I say. "What are you working on?"

The girl stares miserably at the floor. "It's just Chem One. I don't really need help with it."

"Don't need it *yet*," Palin says.

Feeling Sandisk's pain, I say to her "Do you want to sit on the other couch and work, and if you need anything you can let me know?"

"Okay," Sandisk says.

Palin takes the armchair that faces both of us from the side. It's distracting. After a while, when it's obvious Sandisk is doing fine with her binder and her big textbook with colored tabs stuck in it, I pretend to go back to reading, turning pages every now and then for realism.

"You know, I am a real big supporter of Israel," Palin says, causing me to jump.

"Oh?"

"Definitely. Big supporter."

"Huh."*

"Cause you have that tattoo," she says.

"Right," I say. "Why *were* you and the reverend so interested in my tattoos?"

"They just—it seems pretty meaningful when someone gets a symbol like that put on them permanently."

"Like the Star of David, or the Staff of Hermes?"

"Both." She smiles a smile I've seen on her before, although catching it in person is like watching Fox News on

---

* This is what being Jewish has come to, by the way. Everyone you meet either believes the myth that Israel is an apartheid state built on land stolen from the Palestinians and given to European Jews by the U.S. and U.K. to make up for the Holocaust, and wants it destroyed, or believes it but wants Israel to stick around long enough to spark the Zombie Apocalypse. Either way it's unpleasant.

some newly immersive form of technology. It's smug and ironic, but in a way that seems more defensive than anything else. Like if I don't like what she's saying, she was only kidding. It's semi-detached, like a townhouse in Bensonhurst.

"Meaningful in what way?"

Now she's blushing. "Well . . . you know."

"No. Seriously. What?"

"I was hoping maybe I could ask *you* about them."

"Go ahead."

I can see sweat on her hairline. "Am I even making sense?" she says. "Do you even know what I'm talking about?"

"No. I'm sorry, I don't."

Sandisk shakes her head in resignation as she does her homework. Whether it's me or Palin she's exasperated with I don't know.

"Reverend John *thought* you wouldn't," Palin says. "I just wanted to ask you is all. In case you did. I get impatient sometimes. Sorry."

She gets up from the armchair.

"Wait," I say. "It's okay. Tell me what you're talking about."

"I should probably not be saying anything."

"Why? Who *is* Reverend John?"

"He's my pastor."

"What's he doing here?"

"That I *definitely* shouldn't be talking about. Sandisk, honey? You ready?"

"We just got here," Sandisk says.

"You can finish up in the cabin. You can text your friends on the sat-phone."

Sandisk pauses for a moment in blank frustration, then starts to pack up her books and papers.

"You're not going to tell me what's going on?" I say.

Palin hesitates. Waits for a moment when Sandisk is distracted by packing, then bends down quickly. For a second, I think she's going to kiss me.

"Isaiah 27:1," she whispers. She puts a fingertip on my lips and stands back up.

"What about it?" I say. Assuming it's not just someone's name.

"You should look it up."

"You can't just tell me what it says?"

"Sandisk? What does Reverend John always say about telling people what's in the Bible?"

"He's like, 'Go look it up yourself,' " Sandisk says.

"He says any time you can send someone to the actual text is a blessing for you and a blessing for them."

"It sounds more like a way for him to avoid having to memorize scripture, but whatever." Sandisk stands, tottering under her bag. Palin herds her to the door.

"You can't paraphrase?" I say.

"I'd better not," Palin says. "Say good night to Dr. Lazarus."

"Good night," Sandisk says.

They go out, and one of Palin's Secret Service–type guys steps into place to block the doorway after them. Maybe the same one I saw earlier, maybe not.

"Fuck," I say.

Fucking *fine*. I go look it up online:

In that day the LORD with his sore and great and strong sword shall punish leviathan the piercing serpent, even leviathan that crooked serpent; and he shall slay the dragon that is in the sea.

Because shit around here wasn't crazy enough as it was.

꘏ ● ● (

When the party from the casino gets back I go outside toward the lights and the noise. The rain has stopped. It's a little past three in the morning.

I'm done with the book. Liked it: it was old, from when all bestsellers were like X-rated *Dynasty*. At one point the heroine asked the "arbitrageur" bad boy to snort cocaine off her thigh, hoping he'd cut her with the razor.

Down by the water, Palin's talking angrily into her satellite phone, three of her guys walling her off from the rest of us.

Violet comes up to me. "Did you hear from Rec Bill?"

"Yeah. He wants us to stay."

"What?"

"Yeah." I look for some sign that this is good news to her, but maybe she's just too tired. "What's going on? What took you guys so long?"

She shakes her head. "You are not going to believe this shit."

EXHIBIT G

Chippewa River Casino
Eastern Ojibwe Reservation, Minnesota
Sunday, 16 September*

Celia wonders if humidity can shrink your jeans. If it can, she could be in trouble. A mosquito could bite her through these jeans. Pop them like a balloon.

There's a curtain of rainwater falling just a few feet in front of her face, coming off the overhang of the roof. She has to keep her back pressed into the cement block wall to stay dry.

Even so, it's a good spot. The wall's well lit but doesn't have any windows, and this time of year there's no one parked on this side of the casino except employees and people looking for trouble. The lighting makes it a little

---

* **How I know this:** The *Ely Daily Clarion,* various conversations.

too easy for men to see her without her being able to see them, but some guys get turned on by that, or need the low-pressure time to make up their minds.

She hears footsteps. A man coming down the narrow space between the water and the wall. Well dressed, good posture, expensive overcoat. Wingtips. Celia always notices wingtips, because her grandmother once told her they're made to be durable, so men who wear them are cheap. Celia's not sure anyone born after 1940 is aware of that, but still.

"Excuse me. You work here?" the man says. Smiling. Not out here for his car.

"I'm working right now," Celia says.

"I'm glad to hear that."

He stands with his hands at his sides, not too close, like he's trying not to scare her. It makes her back crawl.

Celia remembers Lara, who taught her how to do all this, telling her *If it feels wrong, it is wrong. Get the fuck out of there.*

Like Celia has that luxury.

At least the man's too well dressed to be a cop. An honest one, anyway.

"Why?" she says. "You need some work done?"

"I was thinking about it." He turns to look out into the rain. "Do you have someplace we can go?"

"I got a van right over there. It's clean. It's nice. What kind of work were you thinking about?"

"Oh, I don't know," the man says. "Nothing too weird."

Celia wishes just one of these creeps would say that what he wants *is* too weird. It would probably involve space aliens or something.

The guy says "You know: you blow me, I fuck you

from behind, maybe with a little choking, you call me John, I call you Sarah. You don't act too Indian."

"You're in luck, John. My name *is* Sarah." Celia checks it off on her fingers. "You want me to suck your cock, you want to do me doggy-style, and you want to choke me, and I keep the wigwam talk to myself."

His eyes narrow, not sure if she's making fun of him.

"It's good you know what you like," she says to reassure him. "Are we talking bareback?"

"Yes, on both. How much would you charge for something like that?"

"For double bareback with choking? Two sixty. Non-negotiable. I got a kid."

"Two *sixty?*"

"Up front, baby. Can't take promises outside a casino."

"Fine." The man reaches inside his overcoat.

"Not here. We don't want to get busted."

She turns her back on him and runs to the van, holding her collar up against the rain. She's wearing hooker shoes, and the jeans are ridiculous, but having her back to the man inspires her to move as quickly as possible. At the van she turns around. Says "All right. Show me."

The man leans over to keep his flat European-style wallet dry while he counts, and to keep her from seeing how much is in there. "Two forty?"

"Two sixty."

The bills are crisp and mealy, like they're fresh from an ATM. Celia counts them and fans them up to the light. The rain causes blooms to form on them. She sticks them in her pocket.

"We're good to go," she says. "We've gotta be careful, though. Okay?"

"Fine. Let's do it."

"You know this is illegal, right?"

"Of c—" The man stops himself. "Why would you ask that?" he says.

"You do know this is illegal," she says flatly.

For a moment she thinks the guy's going to hit her. But instead he just turns and runs, splashing through puddles toward the front of the casino.

"Stop! BIA!" she says, pulling her badge and gun out of her jacket pockets. "You're under arrest for soliciting on property patrolled by federal agents!"

He doesn't stop. Whatever. The back door of the van's already open, and Jim and Kiko—both Hispanic, like Celia—played football in college.

She watches them tackle the creep face-first into the asphalt. Sees no reason to go over and help with the arrest.

Jim and Kiko are in Asics and tracksuits. But in *these* shoes and pants?

Negro, *please.*

23

Boundary Waters Canoe Area, Minnesota
Sunday, 16 September–Wednesday, 19 September

We get kind of a late start.

Shortly before four in the morning Palin makes a speech in front of one of the cabins about adversity being whatever and Reverend John would have wanted and it's a trial we've been given and so on. It's actually kind of inspiring, mostly for its assumption that anyone other than Palin gives a fuck whether Reverend John Three-to-Sixteen-for-Soliciting, as Del and Miguel have started calling him, comes with us or not.

Afterward everyone's strangely giddy but not all that psyched about waking up in two hours to go canoeing. So we end up not pushing off onto Ford Lake until around noon—a slim ninety minutes before Reggie's supposed to meet with Sheriff Albin. Someone's problem, not my own.

The flotilla is eleven giant flat-bottomed canoes, with an early-twenties guide at the front and back of each. Where Reggie gets these kids, who all seem to know what they're doing despite being from places like Santa Fe, remains mysterious. We passengers sit two to a boat in the middle, facing each other with our backs against tarped-down piles of camping shit.

Not once in three days do I end up sharing this inter-baggage space with Violet. Del's dog is along with us even though Del and Miguel stayed back at CFS to run the out-fitters, and she and Violet and Palin's young relation Sam-sung form a pack on the first day. Violet and I sleep in the same small tent, so I get to spend six hours every night rock hard and breathing her in, but as we set up the tent for the first time, she says to me "Can we just, maybe, act like professionals?"

"Professional whats?" I say. Because apparently shit comedy is how I respond to stabbing feelings in my chest.*

"I don't know. Professional Hardy Boys?"

Which only makes it worse.

The setups and teardowns are elaborate.† I don't know why I thought going into the woods would require less high-tech equipment than, say, golfing or designing race cars, but I was wrong. And this is a luxury cruise: Reg-gie's guides are cooking three hot meals a day on white gas stoves. Freeze-dried courses out of Mylar bags, maybe, but these days you can get freeze-dried lobster bisque.

---

* If I ever have a heart attack, I'll probably do two hours of material.

† I'm referring to the camping shit, obviously.

The guides, with their sun-blond forearm hair, also do all the portaging. At one point I have to relocate one of their shoulders. The guests aren't even supposed to paddle, although once the guides decide they can trust us to at least not slow the boats down they let us, to fight the boredom.

I'm fine with that. There might be nine other people on this trip whose job it is to pay attention, but without an organized schedule—which not even Palin's guards are on, because it's too hard to sleep in the canoes—having that many eyes just gives you a sense of complacency. Which sets in fast: Palin's guards don't even find the meth camp we pass on the afternoon of the first day. Violet and Samsung and Bark do.

It's small, but it's near the trail, and Palin's guards shouldn't have missed it. Next to a modern octagonal tent there's a wrecked wooden picnic table with one end on a tree stump and an organic chemistry setup across the top. Someone's been bad about washing their glassware. On the other hand, they've managed to string a tarp overhead and get an industrial fan out here. The fan, leaning up against a tree, isn't connected to anything but turns slowly in the wind anyway, Coke Zero bottles tied to its blades.

Inside the tent itself—besides body stench, three sleeping bags, and a whole lot of food wrappers—there's an empty cardboard bullet box marked "7.62 x 39." Like you'd use in an AK-47.

Nothing about this facility says it's been vacated for any other reason than to wait till we're gone. Palin's guards are in favor of breaking all the cooking equipment to encourage the owners to go elsewhere, but my feeling is that we should live and let live, because pissing off a bunch of junkies who might have us in their sights right now seems like kind of a bad idea. Grody's guards are with me on that. It's like a convention for bodyguards, that clearing.

We end up leaving the meth camp intact, possibly because Palin's guards are embarrassed about not finding it in the first place.

The whole incident reminds me of Dylan, and makes me wish I'd tried harder to find out what happened to him before we left Ford.

I'm not saying the trip isn't scenic. Early on the third day a pair of actual otters schools the boat I'm in, corkscrewing to stay on their backs and smiling right at me like a pardon from God. From some of the hills we portage over you can see trees and water to the horizon in every direction. A few of the lakes are big enough to have whitecaps, and being on them in a fog feels like being part of a Viking invasion of Avalon. Here's a campfire under a starry sky. There's a field of flowers. Here's some more fucking rocks and trees.

To be fair, there's probably an aspect to the Boundary Waters you just don't get when you're in a group of forty-four people. There's always a thumb on the lens, so to speak.

Palin seems as interested in avoiding me during the trip as I am in avoiding her, but she also seems to legitimately enjoy being outside, and to be a good sport about the incredibly minor deprivations that do come our way. Tyson Grody too. He bops all over the place.

Just about everybody seems to be in a good mood. People I meet by patching their blisters, like Mrs. Fick, or because we're both pretending to urinate in the woods while setting waypoints on the handheld GPS recorders we're not supposed to have, like Wayne Teng, I often end up sitting with for one or more legs of the trip. Barricaded in by the mounds of luggage, face-to-face with no one else to talk to, you can't help but learn a lot about someone.*

Mrs. Fick tells me a story she keeps saying she shouldn't—with good reason, it turns out—but which I appreciate hearing. One of Palin's guards tells me he and the others wear curly-tube earpieces because the tubes conduct sound from outside, so they don't mute your ear. Then he tells me there's a newer device that attaches *behind* your ear and transmits sound directly through your temporal bone, so it keeps your ear canal from being constantly eczematous from the curly-tube plastic, but it's so expensive only *real* Secret Service guys get to use it. Which these guys aren't. He even tells me the story of how he went from being in one category to being in the other, another thing I'm happy to listen to.

But the story that affects me most—and the one I spend by far the greatest number of hours reviewing later, in the hopes of figuring out what the fuck just happened to us—is the one Wayne Teng tells me on the morning with the otters.

* Unless that someone is me.

EXHIBIT H

Xinjiekou South Street, Beijing University
Beijing
Wednesday, 17 May 1989*

"Wild Thing"—the Troggs version. Teng Wenshu drops it onto turntable one and brings the volume up just as Link Wray bangs to an end. "Wild Thing" is an annoying song to play, because two minutes and thirty-four seconds later you have to play something else, but it seems appropriate. The world has lost its fucking mind.

Teng has today's *People's Daily* open on the mixing board, and unless he's dreaming, it's filled with photos of the protesters in Tiananmen Square. He's looking at a two-page spread of students from the Central Academy

---

* **How I know this:** Conversation with Teng Wenshu (westernized as "Wayne Teng"), various reference books.

raising a forty-foot Goddess of Liberty statue opposite the portrait of Mao at the Jinshui Bridge.

Bracketing the photos—snaking through the entire giant edition—are articles about what an evil dickhead Mao was. The one Teng can see, about the Great Leap Forward, has the phrase "thirty million starved to death."

To Teng, whose parents were theater actors in Beijing before the Cultural Revolution, and lucky-to-be-alive subsistence laborers in a television factory in Xiaoqiang after it, the fact that Mao was an evil dickhead isn't news. Neither is the fact that students in Beijing are protesting, or that the rest of the city is supporting them. Tiananmen Square is six kilometers south of here. His roommates have been going every day.

But for the *People's Daily* to admit shit like this? The *Daily* is the official newspaper of the Communist Party. It's in homes in six hundred and fifty cities in China alone, and probably half that number again around the world. And yesterday you could have read it cover to cover with no idea that the protests—or the past forty years—had ever happened. Or that Mao was anything but a god.

Plus, it's not like the Democracy Movement has somehow taken over the *People's Daily*. This edition is the paper as the Party allowed it to be. Which means the Party thinks it has already lost. Which means it has.

It raises some interesting possibilities.

So far, Teng has stayed the hell away from Tiananmen. It's been one thing for his roommates, whose fathers are all Party members, to go, and to come back raving about the excitement, and the people bringing them food, and the sleeping side by side with girl revolutionaries in silk-scarf tents, talk about Heavenly Gates.* It's been another for Teng to play that game.

The possibility that Teng will someday become a lawyer and a Party member is the only hope his family has. His parents in Xiaoqiang are destroyed. His older brother, having been born while the city's rotting central power plant was still dropping coal ash on the streets like snow, has the intellect of an eight-year-old. Teng, born two and a half years later—and a year and a half after the People's Hydroelectric Plant of Sanjiangyuan came online, when suddenly there were a lot fewer babies in Xiaoqiang who looked like his brother—*owes* them.

And it's not like he hasn't taken risks. For a year now he's spent two hours every morning playing music vaguely evocative of the American civil rights movement on a radio station he rebuilt himself. Granted, the era of the American civil rights movement was also the era of Mao, and Teng tends to play the most inoffensively boring music from then he can find. Also granted, swapping the tubes out of an RCA 1-K Standard Broadcast Transmitter wasn't much of challenge for someone literally born in a communal television factory—provided they were born after the People's Hydroelectric Plant of Sanjiangyuan came online. But people have ended up on some pretty bad lists for less.

And Tiananmen's a classic bust, with an evil past. The place was built by Emperor *Yongle,* for fuck's sake.† Even Deng Xiaoping got arrested there in his student days.

---

* "Tiananmen" meaning "Gates of Heavenly Peace." Laugh it up.

† Yongle's status as an emblem of cruelty in China seems to come in part from his having sentenced historian Fang Xiaoru to "extermination of the ten agnates." An "agnate" is a generation, so sen-

Still, there's an image forming in Teng's mind he can't quite shake.

Teng's radio station, though the size of a large closet and sweltering from the heat of the tubes—more reasons, probably, why the university stopped using it—has two working phone lines. And even if Teng's never done anything with it beyond announcing song titles, there *is* a microphone here: a PB-44A from 1933, heavy as an iron.

He could take to the air. Get news by phone from the Square, or from anywhere else the revolution starts happening. Send it back out with some Doors behind it. Become the voice of the student movement, influencing, if not the odds of victory—it's too late for that—then the shape of whatever comes next.

How risky would that even be? What are the chances there'll be a crackdown *now?* How would one even work? According to the *Daily,* even the Beijing police are now on the side of the students. The Party would have to send in the Army—the *People's* Army. Which would have to fight its way in from the outskirts of the city, while citizens lay on the pavement and turned over buses to stop its tanks and transports.

And to what end? To continue making China, outside four favored cities, into a factory state? To keep the poor

tencing someone to, for example, extermination of the *three* agnates would involve killing them and all their relatives in their generation, their parents' generation, and their children's generation. How, precisely, this would work to the *ten* agnates is unclear, since it can't be easy to execute someone's great-great-great-great-grandfather, and if the condemned leaves four or five generations of offspring then it seems like somebody's not doing their job. But apparently the previous record was nine.

damned and Party members free to do whatever they want, to whomever they want, while setting prices for whatever they want to buy or sell? Who would fight for that?

Plenty of people, he reminds himself. Corruption only bothers the people it holds back. And it doesn't hold back everybody.

Teng forces himself to imagine the consequences if he joined the movement and it *wasn't* successful. If there *was* a crackdown, and the crackdown won.

Let's say he spent the next three weeks here in his studio, constantly relaying information. He'd be hoarse and hallucinating from the heat and lack of sleep by then, but probably also elated. And let's say the Party then sent in the Army—and that the world, for its own corrupt reasons, allowed it to do so. Teng would probably first hear the gunfire through the phone lines, doubting it was real. Then hear it on the streets as he was fleeing.

Teng does his best to picture hiding out at a friend's house in the northwestern suburbs, unsure whether what's keeping him awake despite his exhaustion is that the high school next door is being used to extract confessions, and the screaming goes on all night, or that the reward for him is now a hundred thousand yuan, and the friend isn't that good a friend.

He tries to picture sneaking into a "confession class" for people whose crimes were less serious than his— something that itself could get him shot—just to get his passport stamped so he could buy a train ticket. So he could return home, a complete failure, to his devastated family in Xiaoqiang.

What would happen then? He would be permanently

unemployable, even by the television factory. He'd have to take on black-market technology work, which would require entirely new skills. Most likely computer skills, since doing maintenance on illegal computer networks—another thing that could get you shot—might be the only way to make enough to eat.

Of course, if *that* happened, absurd as it is to think about, and Teng somehow *survived,* it's true he might end up with some skills that were fairly unique. The ability to design and manufacture multi-protocol Internet routers, say. Or, when the state of the art improved some, single-protocol ones.

If things went well, he might even end up with skills so unique that his usefulness—first to local Party members, then to Party members in Beijing, and eventually to China itself—would begin to outweigh his crimes. Who knows? Someday he might be able to operate openly, as the CEO of his own company. Called, say, Industrial Cao Ni Ma. And become so preposterously wealthy that—within twenty-five years of Tiananmen Square—he could turn down a ride to the International Space Station, not because of the money the Russians are asking but because his brother is afraid of heights. Or accept, just as casually, an invitation to hunt lake monsters in Minnesota during the only Year of the Water Dragon that will fall within his and his brother's lifetimes.

In his radio station, with its dusty, fragmenting cotton sound insulation, Teng mocks himself for being timid. None of that is ever going to happen. The *People's Daily* has spoken.

"Wild Thing" is coming to a close. In seconds the arm will skip, done.

Instead of reaching for another single, Teng pulls back the sliders on both turntables. Hefts the microphone over from on top of the Ampliphase cabinet. Clicks the "on" button to test it, and hears it spark in his headphones.

And, just like that, he joins the rebellion.

24

Lake Garner / White Lake
Boundary Waters Canoe Area, Minnesota
Still Wednesday, 19 September

As soon as we land on the northeast shore of Lake Garner I take my pack around the corner of the woods to White Lake. Night's falling fast—it's two hours later than we made camp yesterday and the day before—and I don't want people hassling me. Not even Violet. I don't want to think about what I'm about to do any more than I have to.

Past the spit of land that separates the northeast corner of Lake Garner from the south end of White Lake, I reach the start of the narrow, rocky beach that goes north along White Lake's western shore. Dump my whole pack onto it.

It's already deep grays and shadows here. The wooded ground beside the beach rises steeply as it goes north, leaving White Lake at the bottom of what is essentially a zigzagging granite crevasse. As promised, the place is bleak.

I've just gotten my wetsuit on when Samwise, Palin's young relation, comes around the corner.

"Are you going swimming?" she says, surprised.

"Yeah," I say.

"In White Lake?"

"Yeah."

"Why?"

I steal a line from Violet Hurst: "That's where the monsters are."

She nods, confused. "Have you seen Bark?"

"No. What's wrong?"

"She was on the boat with me and Violet, and when we were about to land she jumped out and ran into the woods, sort of like you did."

"You mean she came around here?"

"No. We think she went straight up the hill."

Which is to say parallel to White Lake, but along the top of the cliff instead of the bottom, where we are. "I wouldn't worry about her," I say. "I'm sure she'll come back. The dog's dumb, but she does seem to like you guys."

Samwise looks worried, though. "Will you keep an eye out for her?"

"Absolutely."

"Thanks."

She leaves, and I pick up my fins and my flashlight.

꙳ ⚇⚇(

The water's cold as shit, and through my diving mask, in the beam of the flashlight, it looks like vegetable soup.

Motionless particulates everywhere. Outside the beam of the flashlight you can't see anything but black.

I should get out of the water and get dressed before Palin's young relation Samwise tells anyone I'm here. I'm already starting to kick at things that are turning out to not be there when I shine my flashlight at my feet. The slasher-movie soundtrack of my breath through the snorkel isn't helping.

But there's something I want to see first. I lift my head out of the water and kick over to the spit of land.

Since Charlie Brisson turned out to be completely unreliable about his leg, I've been wondering how accurately he described the spit. Pretty accurately, I'm surprised to find when I reach it. The spit's just slimy tree roots, with dirt and grass along the top like a buzz cut. With my mask back on I can see that the roots continue to spread out as they go deeper under water, presumably reaching the bottom somewhere below me, or even behind me, farther out into White Lake.

I transfer the flashlight to my left hand and head for the far end of the spit, using my right hand to pull myself across the face of the root wall like it's a horizontal underwater ladder.

Small fish flash silver in the beam of the flashlight, eating at moss so fine it's like green mist. None of them come out past the protective framework of the roots, though. I wonder if it's possible for them to swim all the way through to Lake Garner.

Then the flashlight catches something bright and big ahead of me.

It's a red-orange granite wall. Confused, I draw up and tread water.

I've swum the entire width of White Lake, to the cliff wall on the opposite side. I passed the end of the spit twenty yards back—or what looked like the end of it while I was on land. Beneath the surface, it continues all the way across.

I go back under. There are about six inches of water between the submerged part of the spit and the surface. The spit's just as wide here as it was at the beach.

Meaning that while White Lake and Lake Garner might share the same water, they are, in fact, separate lakes. Not to tiny fish that can swim through the barricade, maybe, but certainly to anything large enough to eat a human. To something like that, being at this end of White Lake would be like being trapped in a wicker bowl.

Spooky. But at least now I can get out of here. As I swim back the way I came, I try to keep the checking of my feet with the flashlight to a minimum.

Even so, I keep doing it, and one time when I do I see a big gray fin glance out of the light, two feet or so from my ankle. Skin that's dull like suede but still slimy-looking.

My mask is gone. My snorkel is gone. My flashlight's gone. I'm just swimming like I'm falling off a building, not even breathing. Trying to decide whether to claw my way over the spit while I'm still at the submerged part or wait for some actual land.

Then I'm on the slope of the spit—the real spit, the above-water part, fins off and gone, running up the ladder of roots, fully aware that if I lose momentum or miss a step I'm going hard into a bunch of spikes. Thrilled to be out of the water anyway. I reach the grass. A tree trunk. Grab it and swing around it to a stop.

Face-to-face with Violet, who's walked out on the spit to find me.

"Lionel—what happened?"

I turn back to the water. Nothing. It's still light enough to see the surface, but there's nothing going on out there that can't be explained by my twenty yards of freaked-out freestyle.

"Did you see it?" I say.

"See what?"

I don't answer her. I'm searching the surface.

"Oh *fuck*," she says.

25

"Knock knock," someone says.

I'm leaning against a tree I don't remember leaning against. Out of my wetsuit, dressed, and supposedly helping search for Bark, but in reality having jumped at the chance to get away from everyone. Particularly Violet, who's mad at me for not telling her I was going in the lake, and because she thinks I'm holding out on her about what I saw.

I tried to explain: just because I saw something doesn't mean it was there.

"How *are* you? I've been looking for you."

Naturally, it's Sarah Palin. Glassy-eyed and feverish, with a smile that flickers on and off. One of her security guards, with his back to us, moves into place down by the shore of Lake Garner.

"I'm fine, thanks."

"I heard you saw it."

"I didn't see anything."

"What was it like? Was it frightening?"

"Like I say—"

"Did it talk?"

I stare at her. Any hope I had that Palin would make me feel sane, at least by comparison, is fading fast. "No. It definitely didn't talk. Why would it?"

"But you faced it."

I almost laugh. "Whatever happened down there, it wasn't me facing something. It was me fleeing from something. Fleeing from nothing, more like."

"Hey, now. Come on. Don't be so hard on yourself. It's *evil*. It's not supposed to feel good."

"Ms. Palin, if there's something you're trying to tell me, you *could* just go ahead and do that."

"Call me Sarah. Or Governor. I'm not that kind of feminist."

"Sarah, then. What are you talking about?"

"You still don't understand?"

"No. I don't."

She chews her lip. "I'm not sure how much Reverend John would have wanted me to tell you."

The guy who can't tell a Fed from a street hooker? I know what I'm about to say is manipulative, but I'm in a bad mood.

"Sarah, maybe there's a *reason* Reverend John isn't with us now."

She nods slowly, turning it over. Finally says "Did you read the passage?"

"The one in Isaiah? Yeah."

"Did you understand it?"

"I'm not sure. Is the idea that there's some kind of sea serpent in White Lake?"

She nods.

"And that whoever wrote Isaiah somehow knew about it?"

"And whoever wrote Revelation. And Genesis. I mean, *your* people know about Genesis."

My people also know about Revelation, because what—we don't go to horror movies? But whatever. "You're talking about Jonah and the whale?" I say.

She looks puzzled. "I'm talking about Genesis."

I guess Jonah's not in that one.

"You know, Adam and Eve?" she says. "The Serpent?"

"You're telling me the White Lake Monster is the snake from the Garden of Eden?"

"No." She looks around. Lowers her voice to a whisper. "I'm saying it's the *Serpent*."

Now, ordinarily I would just roll with this. Validate and back away. But right now I've got a strange need for things to make sense.

"I'm pretty sure 'serpent' and 'snake' mean the same thing," I say.

"Science has *taken* them to mean the same thing. But in the Bible, the Serpent's the Serpent. Then it gives Eve the forbidden fruit, and God turns it *into* a snake. God says 'Go crawl in the dust, now.' Which has to happen *after* Adam and Eve leave the Garden of Eden, because otherwise why is there dust? It's the same with the forbidden fruit: everybody thinks it's an apple, but the *Bible* never says it was an apple. And the Bible *does* talk about apples. It's like how everybody thinks the Bible says there were three wise men—"

"I got it," I say. "So if the Serpent wasn't a snake, what was it?"

"*Exactly*. What was it?"

"I'm asking you."

"I don't know. All we have are clues. Have you ever heard of the Number of the Beast?"

"Six six six?" I say.

I suppose I could physically run away.

"Well it *looks* like six six six."

They say she jogs, though.

"Is it actually nine nine nine?"

Palin laughs and socks me. "*No*. Be serious." She looks around again, then reaches up and twists a green stick off a tree branch, like our Reggie's young guides have just spent four days telling us not to. Uses it to draw three sixes in a descending diagonal row, right to left, with one continuous stroke. It looks like a spiral.

"What's this?" she says.

"A pubic hair?"

"Dr. Lazarus!"

"I don't know. What?"

"What about a strand of DNA?"

I look at it. "Well normally DNA is drawn as two strands, but at that scale it would probably look like one. It's not like it really all hangs out in a line anyway. There's also single-stranded DNA, I suppose—"

She claps her hands together.

"What?"

"You *do* know!" she says. "You may *think* you don't,

but you do!" She mimics me: "*'DNA is usually drawn with two strands. Maybe it's single-stranded DNA.*'" It's not pleasant. "But what if it's just one strand of *double-*stranded DNA?"

"I don't know," I say. "There's one missing?"

"*Exactly.* The one that matches. Do you know what the 'H' stands for in 'Jesus H. Christ'?"

"No."*

"Do you know what 'haploid' means?"

"You mean having only one set of chromosomes?"

"Yes. Like a sperm or an egg."

"Oh," I say. "You're saying Jesus has only one set of chromosomes."

She grabs my arm. "*Yes!* Because he's half Mary and half God. And God doesn't *have* chromosomes. That's why Jesus is the link between the people world and Heaven. And why he had to have a temporary soul for when he was on Earth, which we call the Holy Ghost. *But here's the thing.*"

I wait for it, with a not unpleasant feeling it could be anything. It could be a rubber chicken.

"*Where's the other part of the DNA? The strand that matches this one?*"

"I don't know."

"It's the *opposite* one."

"Okay."

"Who has it?"

"I still don't know."

"The *Other Guy.*"

---

* It's an *eta*, the Greek long "E" sound. "Jesus" is abbreviated "IHS" in the Greek Bible.

"The Other Guy?"

"That's why he's called the *Anti*-Christ. You know who I'm talking about."

"The Devil?"

"The *Serpent*." She points to the spiral she's drawn. "See? Why do you think it looks like that?"

"You mean like a snake?"

"We've almost reached the point where people can re-create themselves by cloning. Which means they'll only *need* one strand of DNA, instead of one from each parent. Which they *think* is going to make them immortal. But it's the wrong immortality, because it means no one gets into the Kingdom of Heaven. Because the Tree of Knowledge isn't *supposed* to be the Tree of Life."

"Cloning?" I say.

"But *we are not going to let that happen*. And you know what? We are *up to it*."

I look at her. The "we" puts kind of a new spin on it.

"Up to what?" I say.

"Killing it."

"Killing a piece of DNA?"

"Killing the *Serpent*."

She stands on her toes, puts her hands on my face, and kisses me. Hard and sexless, like how bar toughs might greet each other in some European country you've never visited.

"Don't be afraid," she says.

When she backs off, she sees something in her peripheral vision and turns.

It's Violet Hurst, staring at us. Palin's security guard behind her all sheepish.

Palin throws her hands up to her cheeks and runs back

toward the camp, trilling "Not what it looks like! Not what it looks like!"

"Don't care! Don't care!" Violet calls after her.

"It's not," I say.

"I could give a shit. Seriously. I was just coming to find you to ask if you'd found Bark. I guess you haven't. Thanks for looking."

26

At three-thirty in the morning I get sick of the sweaty heat of my sleeping bag and decide to get up. Violet's still got her back to me.

Outside in the black-and-white-TV moonlight there's a low-lying fog on the ground of the kind I thought only happened in discos and vampire movies. It's all over the camp and out onto the surface of Lake Garner, exhaled by the warm earth and water. The moon's a sliver again, like it was when Reggie and I were talking on his porch, although I suppose it's facing the other direction now, if that's how the moon works.

I hear soft voices and see a red ember on the far side of the campsite. For fun I sneak past Reggie and one of

Palin's security guys while they discuss why bears are the only animals that are grizzly.

"Tuna fish are the only animals called tuna," the guard says.

"You're right, son," Reggie says. "It's not like there's a tuna bird." For the record, I don't actually see the security guy take a hit off Reggie's joint.

Right before I enter the woods I notice someone else and almost hit the ground, but it's just one of Wayne Teng's bodyguards, watching me without comment.

ꙮ

It starts to lightly rain as I stand at the base of the spit, which extends like an arm into the fog coming off both lakes. I'm not sure what kind of bullshit face-your-fears exercise this is supposed to be, but as long as it doesn't require getting back in the wetsuit I'm okay with it. I can't even see the surface of the water. And if the clouds manage to cover the moon, I won't be able to see anything.

I do hear something, though.

It's a hum. Subtle—not much more than a change of pressure in your ear canals, like when the refrigerator goes on in the apartment next door.

I'm pretty sure that's not what it is, though. I follow the beach north along the edge of the widening ravine that contains White Lake. The beach is narrow and uneven but easy to follow even in the fog: it's got a granite wall next to it.

The hum gets louder as I go. After a while I reach the point where both the cliff wall and the whole ravine angle to the right, revealing a new stretch of water. On it something that has to be a boat: glinting of metal through the drifting mist, and a faint green glow.

I left my binoculars and nightscope back in the tent, of course.

The humming stops. The boat's just drifting.

 ɔ◖◗(

"What are you doing?" Violet says as I'm looking through my pack. "Did you find Bark?"

"Shh. No. There's a boat on White Lake."

"What?" She sits up on her elbows. "Why?"

"I don't know. I couldn't really see it."

"You're going back?"

"Yes."

"Why didn't you wake me up?"

"I did."

"I mean intentionally."

"Because it's probably just another opportunity to get shot at."

Violet starts patting around for her clothing. "I'm coming."

"It's raining."

"Who gives a shit?"

"We have to hurry."

"Fine. I'll take a shower instead of a bath. What's wrong with you?"

Something. I watch her unzip her sleeping bag and, still lying down, pull her jeans up over the gooseflesh of her thighs. They snag for a moment on her mound. She has to pull them free to get them up to her bare stomach.

When I look up at her face, she's watching me watch her. Not judgmentally, but still.

Not a lot you can say to that one.

I unzip the tent flap. It's raining heavily now.

>∩∩(

The boat's a big Zodiac, twenty feet long or so with a fixed pedestal in the center for the steering wheel and metal fishing struts that angle up and out over the sides like construction cranes. Even with the binoculars it's hard to see any more detail than that through the fog. My digital camera, which I also brought, is useless.

"Here," Violet says, handing me the nightscope. The rain's loud enough that we're not worried about talking. "He's still shoveling powder from the bag into the water."

The first thing I do with the scope is sweep the beach behind us. I made Violet hold my hand as we snuck out of camp, so that anyone seeing us would think we were going off to fuck. But as she pointed out, some people wouldn't consider that a deterrent.

In any case, having to talk someone into holding my hand didn't make me feel like a creep and a six-year-old at all.

I use the scope to look out at the lake. Both the downpour and the fog are more opaque under infrared, but I can see that the boat has one fat, heavily treaded tire drawn up in front of it like the figurehead on the prow of a ship, and identical raised tires on both back corners. Next to the front tire is something that looks a lot like a loaded harpoon gun. On the fantail there's a large motor leaned out of the water and a much smaller one with its prop still lowered. That must be the electric one.

"It's amphibious," I say.

"Yeah. Sorry, I thought you could see that through the binoculars. What's he doing?"

"I don't see him."

There's a cloud of glare above the steering structure, possibly from a sonar display, but I don't see the guy until he stands up from where he was hunched between the wheel and what looks like a large built-in ice chest at the rear. He's holding something in one hand like a shot put.

"Now I see him," I say.

"Can you see his face?"

"No. He's on the far side of the boat with his back to us." Also, like Violet and me and probably everybody else who's awake and outdoors right now in Minnesota, he's wearing a hooded anorak. At least we can guess what he's hearing: the drone of raindrops on Goretex.

I sweep the nightscope over the beach again and hand it to Violet.

"Now he's putting something on a big hook that's on a line on that thing that goes over the side," she says after a minute. "I think it's meat."

A few moments later I can hear the winch motor, even above the downpour. It's louder than the electric outboard was.

Violet hands back the scope, and I watch the man straighten up and turn toward us.

Where his face should be, there's a searing spotlight.

"Fuck!" I say, jamming the front end of the scope into my jacket. Too late, though, I know.

"What?"

Without the scope, there's nothing out there but darkness. The light coming off the guy's face is invisible.

"He's wearing active infrared goggles," I say. "The same technology we're using. He can see the light our scope's putting out."

"But can he . . . ?"

"Yeah. He's probably looking at us now." I put the scope back to my eye.

He's staring right at us, face still shining like a lighthouse. Now, though, he's also holding a rifle.

Classic Remington 700, with a big scope and a rainguard. I'm not saying it's the gun used to kill Chris Jr. and Father Podominick, but the two would get along.

So apparently this is the part where we get shot at again. If the rifle has night vision, it's going to be a long fun run back to the woods silhouetted against the bare face of the cliff. It probably makes more sense for us to dive into the lake and try to swim for the boat.

The man doesn't aim the rifle, though. He just holds it low across his body, like he's showing it to me or trying to make up his mind. Then he tosses it into the front of the boat and goes the other direction to tilt the big motor into the water.

"What's he doing?" Violet says.

I give her the scope. "Getting out of here."

In the narrowness of the canyon, the gas engine turns over like a Harley. Deep *blat-blat* noises that continue even as other, higher-pitched noises build on top of them. Then the boat turns hard and retreats back into White Lake, trailing its hook line behind it.

It's gone from sight around the next bend before the

flashlight beams of the people picking their way along the beach reach us.

"What the hell was that?" Reggie says.

"There's a boat on the lake," Violet says.

Its wake is still rippling into our shoes.

27

"Bull*shit*," Violet says.

"Exactly how it happened."

We're in our sleeping bags, lying on our backs. I've just told her about my conversation with Palin.

"She's fucking nuts," Violet says.

"Why? Just because she thinks having one set of chromosomes is the same thing as having single-stranded DNA even though her father was a science teacher?"

"Her father used to wait for seals to come up for air and then shoot them in the head."

"Maybe he thought they were the Antichrist. And how do you know that?"

"How do you know about Westwood Whatever?" she says.

"Westbrook Pegler. He used to be famous."

"And she's famous *now*. And rich. If there's an Antichrist, it's probably her. She's a complete opportunist."

"I think she believes *this,* though."

"She probably does. The problem with the world isn't people who are irrational. It's people who can turn their rationality on and off depending on what's more likely to get them something."

"Maybe, but what's believing in this likely to get her?"

"Besides whatever Reggie's paying her? Don't underestimate the appeal of thinking you're the center of God's attention. Babies have been digging it for years. Fuck. I wish *I* could be like her."

I laugh. "No you don't."

"Sure I do. Being selectively delusional would *rock*. Why do you think I love being drunk?"

"Being drunk wears off."

"That's the problem with it." She sees me looking at her. "I'm serious. I *hate* reality. Everybody does. People love to say 'Beware of Greeks bearing gifts' *now*. But when Laocoön said it during the actual Trojan War, and got ripped apart by snakes, they laughed their fucking asses off. Same with Cassandra."

"That's another Trojan horse thing?"

"Yes."

"So maybe it's just a bad idea to be rational about the Trojan horse."

"And maybe someday I'll figure out why I bother to talk to you."

"It's not like you do, very often."

"Good for me."

She turns away.

"Chicken Little is another one," I finally come up with.

"What happened to *him?*"

"I don't know. But he definitely got referred to as a chicken."*

She rolls, propping up on her elbows. "You know what your problem is?"

"Bring it."

"You don't just make doing dangerous shit look fun, you make being informed look fun. Which is another thing that's not true."

"Thanks."

"It's not a compliment. Good night."

A few minutes after turning away again, though, she says "How was the kiss?"

"I'll never tell. It was fun seeing you jealous, though."

"I wasn't jealous. I have no interest in kissing Sarah Palin. I didn't even before I saw you doing it. It looked frightening."

"It was."

Outside, a bird starts bitching about something or other. It can't be that long before dawn.

Violet says "Just so you know, Rec Bill and I only spent one night together."

"You don't have to tell me about it."

"We didn't even have sex. We mostly stayed up all night talking. We didn't even kiss until after the sun came up."

"I said you *don't* have to tell me about it."

---

* Then eaten by a fox. I looked it up later.

"Fuck you. We were in Tsarabanjina."

"Really? I love Tsarabanjina."

"Are you serious?"

"Of course not. Where the fuck is Tsarabanjina?"

"*Who* were you saying was jealous?"

"You. Where is it?"

"It's part of Madagascar. We were there about six months ago. Rec Bill wanted me to do some rock analysis on a fossil he was thinking of buying."

"The one in the lobby of his building?"

"Well…"

"What?" I say.

"That's not the actual fossil. But—not important."

Not *important?* Small-talk *lifeline,* more like. "What do you mean it's not the actual fossil?"

"The one in the lobby is a cast, like they use in museums."

"They don't use actual fossils in museums?"

"Not to assemble into skeletons. You'd have to drill them, and they'd be too heavy. Real fossils are solid rocks inside other rocks. But will you listen to me, please? It was the most romantic place on earth. We had these balconies overlooking the ocean, and we could see each other from them, so he invited me over. We got drunk and hung out talking."

Great. My postapocalyptic Violet Hurst fantasy has come true. For Rec Bill.

"In the morning we made out a bit, then I went back to my room and fell asleep. And it hasn't happened since."

"Okay," I say. Even neutral sounds bitter, but what am I supposed to do—high-five her?

"Since then I've barely even seen him. We went out for

dinner a few times and it was totally awkward. He invites me to foundation events, but if I go he barely even talks to me."

"Nice."

"Then he texts me when he gets home, and we talk for like two hours."

"By text?"

"Yeah."

"What about? Maybe you should be charging him."

"Okay: mind out of gutter, please."

"I meant for therapy."

"Whatever. We talk about whatever he's thinking about. Articles he's forwarded to me at work. I used to actually read them in case he was sending me some kind of message, but I think he just wants someone to communicate with."

"Are you sure it's him on the other end?"

"You know, you should work with paranoids. You'd be very calming."

"So we've established that he outsources his conversations with you. Is he dating anyone else?"

"Not that he's mentioned. But I don't even feel like I can ask him."

"Which you put up with for *what* reason?"

"Because I don't even know if I *want* a relationship with Rec Bill. That night, there really seemed to be something there. But maybe I imagined it. Maybe I *am* just dazzled by how rich he is."

"Hmm," I say. "You don't strike me as particularly materialistic, but I can see where a man who'll buy a woman a dinosaur might be one to hold on to. Is he a decent human being?"

"I think so."

"Just not to you."

"It's not *that* bad."

"I think it's called 'keeping you hanging.' "

"At least he hasn't fired me. *That's* pretty charitable."

"I don't believe that at all."

Violet reaches past me to get her canteen out of her day pack. Doesn't affect me—I've had a boner since we got back in the tent.

"I'm not saying I suck as a paleontologist," she says. "But the project he's got me on is total crap. Anyone but Rec Bill would have shut it down months ago."

"And it was your idea?"

"No, it was his. But I'm in a better position to judge it than he is."

"Do you lie to him about it?"

"No. I tell him it's fucking ridiculous and he should shut it down."

"So there you go." I add, casually, "What's the project?"

She pauses to let me know she's telling me intentionally and not because of how sly I am. "It's called the Poultroleum Project. The idea is that since Americans kill twenty-two million chickens a day, and chickens are descended from dinosaurs, we should use their bones to make crude oil. No, I'm not kidding."

"Of course you are."

"No. I'm not," she says. "That's it. That's what I do: I run the Poultroleum Project for Rec Bill."

"Is that even possible?"

"Of course not. Oil doesn't come from dinosaurs in the first place—it comes from algae and zooplankton. Which you then have to crush under ultrahigh pressures and temperatures for millions of years in anoxic conditions, using massive amounts of energy."

"Does Rec Bill know that?"

"Of course. I've been telling him since before he hired me."

"Fuck," I say. "He really is in love with you."

"I don't think so."

"So why *doesn't* he fire you?"

"He says he doesn't care whether the project works out or not, because it's worth it to him to have someone in-house who could become the world's foremost expert on petroleum formation."

"Makes sense."

"No, it doesn't. I'm not the right person for that job. Petroleum formation's been the highest-paying subspecialty of geology for a hundred years—it's how we know where to drill. There are ten thousand people out there who are already better at it than I'll ever be. I'm not even interested in it. I think petroleum's done nothing but evil to this planet. To me all technology is a separately evolving parasite on the human race."

"And he's a tech billionaire. Like I say, it must be love."

Violet ignores this. "He also says he likes having researchers who think outside the box, because he's only interested in long shots. Which makes me feel like I'm ripping him off even more. How many major scientific discoveries are the result of someone working on their own, outside of academia?"

"I don't know—penicillin? Relativity?"

"Neither of which involved technology. And both of which were a long time ago. Technology progresses logarithmically—even in the oil world it's past the point where any one person could keep track of it."

She drinks and hands me the canteen. I take it, stupidly touched. "Anyway," she says, "the underlying premise is fucked: net exothermic petroleum synthesis is a perpetual motion machine. And even if you *could* invent a new way to make oil, it would just cause the ecological disaster to happen before the oil-crash disaster, instead of the other way around."

"Maybe he wants somebody with that attitude for the job. *I* would."

"You don't understand. There is no job. I don't do anything. There's nothing to do. I have a ridiculous non-job that probably still exists only because the boss is either hot for me or feels guilty about acting like he was six months ago."

"I thought he was the cheapest man alive."

"I'm not that expensive."

"And if he's only employing you because he's hot for you, he doesn't seem to be doing much about it."

"No he's not, thank you for pointing that out. Anyway, that's not the point."

"What's the point?"

"It's that I shouldn't have freaked out on you for being…whatever you are. A bodyguard-slash-doctor or whatever. It's totally hypocritical of me to act like I'm somehow better than that. Better than you, I mean. I'm *not* better than you, in any way. If anything I'm worse. We both just work for Rec Bill. And what you're doing for him is a lot less shameful than what I'm doing."

"*That's* the point?"

"Yes."

"Violet, you *are* better than I am."

"I'm not."

"You are. Thank you for saying that, but you are. You're just hard on yourself because you think you should be out trying to stop the human race from killing itself, but you haven't figured out how to do that yet."

She looks at me. "Now *you're* kidding, right?"

"No."

"That's like Keanu: so shallow it seems deep."

"Hey, at least it *seems* deep."

"Less and less as I think about it. You may need to recalibrate your character-judgment skills, my friend. All *I* want is to learn to relax and let the world go fuck itself."

"Uh huh."

"Fuck you, 'Uh huh.' And anyway, who are *you* to talk about this kind of shit? You still haven't told me what *your* deal is. What, you were a Navy SEAL? You worked private security in Afghanistan? What?"

It's asinine for me to be as surprised by that question as I am. To cover it up, I stretch like I'm yawning.

"Tell me," she says.

"Nothing like that."

"So...what?"

I turn away from her. "I'll tell you later."

"How bout now?"

"Can't."

"Why?"

"I need you to still be talking to me."

"You're not worried I'm going to stop talking to you because you're so annoyingly evasive?"

I make it trail off: "Now that you mention it."

"And now you're pretending to go to *sleep?*"

"Not pretending. Monster in the morning."

"You've got to be kidding me."

"Sleep well."

"You *know* I'm only going to imagine things that are worse than you could possibly tell me."

"I'll take the risk."

"And the first thing I'm going to imagine is that you *have* no secrets, and just get off on frustrating people."

"Mm."

"Ugh. You are so fucking stubborn." I hear her turn away as well. "Talking to you is like talking to myself."

"I feel that way too."

"That's because you're a narcissist. Good night, Dr. Azimuth."

"Good night, Dr. Hurst."

28

Lake Garner / White Lake
Boundary Waters Canoe Area, Minnesota
Still Thursday, 20 September

Seven-thirty, half an hour after sunrise, and the only thing the sun's done so far is brighten the fog. There's fog all over the place. Even Lake Garner looks like it's inside a cloud. White Lake looks like the Canyon That Time Forgot.

Reggie's handing out coffee, like he's done all four days, I think because he hasn't had enough else to do. His earnest and willowy guides are too efficient. Along with everyone else, he seems skittish about the fact that Bark still hasn't turned up.

"You okay?" I say.

"You mean am I worried about Del's goddamned dog? No. She's probably joined a pack of moose." He shoots a

guilty look, though, over at Violet and Palin's young relation Frodo, who are sitting on a boulder looking desolate.
"I'm fine. Canoe trips and lake monsters aren't really my
thing—weirdos in amphibious boats neither—but at least
we're halfway done with the canoe part. All I need to do
is make it back."

"Reggie, what happened to all the hunting equipment
Chris Jr. ordered that didn't get delivered till after he
died? Like the hooks and stuff?"

He shrugs. "Returned it. Never thought I'd be out here
to use it."

I take two cups of coffee over to Violet and Frodo, but
Frodo's already drinking a hot chocolate, so I keep one
and sit down next to Violet. She leans into me, consciously
or not I can't tell, although when's the last time you unconsciously leaned into someone?* Either way it's nice.

Reggie's guides cook pancakes while we all wait for
the fog to blow over, or burn off or whatever it's supposed
to do. No one talks above a whisper. There's a wet hush in
the campsite that, for an hour, gets broken only by spo-
radic bird calls.

When the hour's up, though, a noise from the direction
of White Lake rips into us like we're inside Godzilla's
throat in THX.

Naturally, everyone goes apeshit, scrambling into a
panicked blur that's for some reason difficult to look at.
Rather than try, I wonder about the timing. Assuming the
noise was set off by a human being—foghorn? laptop
hooked up to a Marshall stack?—then why set it off now?
Why not give us a day or two to poke around White Lake,

---

* Some time you can't consciously remember, I suppose.

for verisimilitude? Or else why not just get it over with last night?

I turn to ask Violet her opinion, but she and Frodo are gone. Not just up from the rock: out of my sight, even though it doesn't feel like enough time has passed for that to have happened. Then again, I'm not sure my brain's working properly. A man with what looks like a rifle case goes by, and it takes me so long to process his face that he's gone before I realize it was Fick. Or that he was running.

Then the entire *concept* of time starts to seem fucked up. Why are memories so low-quality that remembering Violet sitting next to me is worthless compared to experiencing it at the time? I mean, granted, meat is not the ideal recording medium. But meat seems to do all right patching the sensation through in the first place.

Violet, though. I miss that woman. In fact I'm having the strangest feeling about her. Like we've just spent five thousand years as statues on either side of the same ancient Egyptian doorway, wishing we could go inside the pyramid and screw.

Someone yells "Guys, *stop!*" It's Reggie—surprisingly, I can identify *voices* right away. Teng and his guys go by, but without quite seeming three-dimensional. More like they're animated Colorforms stuck onto different layers of glass, the trees behind them like slow-motion fountains. Which I suppose is what they are.

All right, I think. *Enough of this.*

From my jacket pocket I take out a disposable syringe and one of the two vials of Anduril—four doses total—that I stole from Dr. McQuillen's medicine cabinet.

Anduril's an antipsychotic from the sixties. Said to hit

like a hammer but to work, and with fewer metabolic side effects than the shit they give crazy people now. Also said to cold-stop LSD.

It can lock your muscles up, though, which is why you have to take it with an anti-parkinsonian agent. Which I also stole two vials of.

I should have premixed the syringes. Making one up now is taking a seriously long time. I'm not sure why I didn't. Or why I didn't steal all the Anduril McQuillen had. I really need to learn to trust my instincts.

Finally I get a syringe together. Since, at this moment, coordinating an injection into my shoulder seems harder than working in an office for fifty years, I jab the short needle into the top of my thigh through my jeans.

Depressing the plunger causes the needle to spring back up into the syringe. *That's* why I couldn't premix it—self-retracting needle! Amazingly fucking brilliant, modern syringe design is. Like the Unabomber used to say: technology will eventually kill us, but each small instance of it will be charming.*

"Reggie!" I shout as I load up another syringe. "What the *fuck* have you done?"

No one answers.

No one's around.

I can hear voices from White Lake, though.

I lumber around the trees to the spit. Three of the canoes are out on the water, abreast, headed away from

---

* Personally I don't think technology's all that bad. If digital devices really do make children less likely to develop the skills and focus to do things like design more digital devices, how is *that* not a self-limiting problem?

me into the fog. The guides rowing hard, everyone else standing up. Without luggage, three boats are enough for the whole party.

And their guns.

Reggie's shouting "Put down the goddamn firearms!"

I run down the beach until I'm ahead of the canoes. Glare at Reggie as I pass him.

From the front the situation's even worse. Just the *variety* of guns is astonishing. Fick, Mrs. Fick, and Teng have variations on straight-up deer-hunting rifles, although Teng's is stainless steel. Teng's bodyguards have TEC-9s. I didn't think they still *made* TEC-9s. Tyson Grody's bodyguards have various handguns—two each—though Grody is trying to jump and pull their gun arms down. Palin's guards have vicious-looking Skorpion submachine pistols.

Palin herself has a *sword*.

Reggie Trager's following the armada along the beach, coming toward me as he jumps up and down waving, yelling "Stop!"

I don't see Violet anywhere. Or Frodo. I've chosen them and Wayne Teng's brother to receive the other three doses of antipsychotic, Violet because she's Violet, Frodo because she's young, and Teng's brother because he's been through enough shit already. Right now the brother's kneeling in one of the boats, staring ahead with his face slack.

Then one of Teng's bodyguards points and shouts something that *has* to mean "Look! There it is!"

Because look: there it is. Even with the LSD starting to abate.

William the White Lake Monster.

Or, as it resembles from my angle and through the fog, three humps of ribbed black plastic vent hose, twenty inches or so wide, waving cheaply and being made to move across the lake by means you can't see but can guess from the bubbles coming up through the water.

"WAIT," Reggie says. "DON'T—"

"No!" Tyson Grody screams.

Everyone who can opens fire. It's louder than the foghorn, or whatever that was.

The two rear humps go flying off, split open and flailing. Two gloved hands dart up from the water in a surrender motion, then jerk back under when a finger gets shot off.

The tourists and their various paid protectors keep shooting—even the ones in back, who don't have a clear line of fire through the people ahead of them. Grody's yelling and waving his hands in front of the people in his canoe, which is brave as fuck, but he's got enough sense to stay too low to actually stop anyone.

People keep shooting even after a rowboat comes around the bend with Miguel and a couple of other guys standing in it like George Washington, pointing guns back at the tourists. At one point Palin hurls the sword, end over end. Not a bad arm on that woman.

"GOD DAMN IT, MIGUEL," Reggie yells right next to me, just before Miguel and Co. release a single fusillade of bullets. Which, depending on whom you later believe, is aimed either at or above the heads of the people shooting at whoever was working the fake monster.

A silence comes down. Except for the sound of a dog barking: sure enough, Bark is swimming out toward Miguel's boat. Intermittently visible through the fog, she looks a lot more like a lake monster than the tubing did. I don't know why the people in the canoes hold fire.

For a moment, everyone but Grody, who's crouched down weeping, remains standing. Then Wayne Teng bends abruptly at the waist and goes headfirst into the lake, and the counter-roll topples everyone else in his canoe off the other side.

I dive into the water. The cold makes me saner immediately, though at surface level I can barely see through the fog. When I reach Teng, his bodyguards are struggling to keep his face above the water. I consider trying to get him up into one of the canoes, but that would be close to impossible—we'd just capsize another boat. I jerk my thumb toward shore and start to pull Teng with me.

"Call for a MedEvac! Don't let anybody drown!" I yell, like there's someone who's going to listen to this and act on it.

I try to find where Teng's been shot. It isn't difficult: blood's pumping out of his lower left pelvis like a Jacuzzi nozzle, hard enough to break the surface of the lake. If it's coming from the iliac artery, which it probably is, he's got almost no chance. The artery's elastic, and the severed ends you'd have to pull back together are probably retracted into his chest and calf by now.

I push into the wound with one fist, using my other hand to support his weight. As I kick us toward the shore, I try to ignore the fact that when water sluices into Teng's mouth, he doesn't choke or blink his eyes.

Then, when we're about twenty feet from the beach, the real White Lake Monster rips into Teng from behind me, and tears him out of my arms.

THIRD THEORY: MONSTER

29

White Lake / Lake Garner
Boundary Waters Canoe Area, Minnesota
Still Thursday, 20 September

Karl Weick, the organizational psychologist:

> A *cosmology episode* occurs when people suddenly and deeply feel that the universe is no longer a rational, orderly system. What makes such an episode so shattering is that both the sense of what is occurring and the means to rebuild that sense collapse together.... [So that people think] I've never seen this before. I have no idea where I am, and I have no idea who can help me.

I believe Violet Hurst described it as someone taking a dump on your conceptual framework.

The creature that slams past me in White Lake, swiping me with its slimy leather skin as it drives Teng under water and out of sight, then slapping me with something that feels a fuck of a lot like a tail, does exactly that. It turns me inside out, so that now the nightmare is on the outside.

But here's the thing: in nightmares I never break down, because whatever awful thing I'm looking at seems normal. It's only in real life that I wake up screaming and have panic attacks that hit like seizures.

Now that real life *is* the nightmare world, I find myself just calmly treading water. Looking in the direction Teng's body was carried off, thinking, *If that thing wants to eat me, it will. Not much I can do about it.* Or maybe that's the antipsychotic.

"Teng Wenshu! Teng Wenshu!" Teng's bodyguards are calling out. Then, after a while, *"Teng Shusen!"*

Teng's brother answers from over near the beach. Reggie's guides have triumphed again, keeping everyone who ended up in the lake alive and herding them back toward land. We all come onto the rocks together like we're evolving from the sea, water streaming from our heavy clothes.

The cold is sharp. "Hey," I shout. "Reggie gave us all LSD. If anybody didn't drink the coffee, or just doesn't feel fucked up, take charge of whoever you're with. Everybody wet needs to get dry as soon as possible. If anybody's got benzos, now's the time to share them."

Reggie's farther down the beach, helping Miguel's boat land with Del in it, Bark shaking water off her coat. Reggie looks at me and looks away. I'd ask him if I'm right about the coffee, but I wouldn't trust any answer he gave me.

"Who's got a satellite phone?" I say.

"I'm taking care of it," one of Palin's bodyguards yells back, phone to his ear. The canoe he's in is still on its way to the beach. Palin's kneeling in the prow, barfing.

I prepare a shot of Anduril for Teng Shusen, but decide at the last moment to give it to one of his bodyguards instead. Teng Shusen isn't freaking out, just looking around confused, and maybe it's better that someone capable of taking care of him be the one thinking clearly.

The other two canoes reach shore. Violet and Froghat aren't in either of them, and I'm pretty sure they weren't in the one that spilled, so I run back to the campsite calling their names. They're huddled together in the tent I've been sharing with Violet.

LSD in the hot chocolate too. Nice, Reggie.

I inject them both. Go back to the boat with the outboard to check on Del.

Del's got his right hand under his left arm. Not just because he's had a finger shot off, I realize when I pry his arm away, but because a bullet has grazed his left side, opening up Neoprene, skin, and bright yellow fat. Blood runs down the side of his wetsuit in a pink wash. It's a miracle he wasn't shot up worse.

Miguel hands me a towel without my asking for it, then holds it in place for me as I reposition Del to keep both wounds above his heart. "Find some more of these," I say, meaning the towels.

"Fuck off, Bark," Del says, the first words I've heard from him. The dog keeps licking his face as if to wake him up.

When I stand, my muscles are like sand from the Anduril.

"I know," Reggie says, holding his hands up defensively. "You have no fucking idea."

⟩◗◖◖⟨

Sarah Palin doesn't say goodbye. I barely catch sight of her before she leaves. One of her guards puts her in her tent and stands in front of it, while the other two hack at tree limbs with their tactical knives like the druid in Astérix. They basically seem to have gone insane, but ultimately they assemble the branches into a grid held together by plasticuffs, and when Palin's Sikorsky lands on Lake Garner it uses the grid as a ramp to nudge onshore.

Did Palin's bodyguards call for her evacuation before they called the paramedics? All I know is that Palin and her group, which has somehow come to include Grody and *his* group, and even the fucking *Ficks*—like perhaps the Ficks aren't just sour rich people who like clothes from Costco and shooting things, but also host fundraisers in their castle—are gone before the Parks and Rec rescue Seawolf shows up in the sky. Let alone the Piper Cub with Sheriff Albin in it.

I don't try to keep them around. I'm not sure how I would, and anyway I believed them when they said they didn't see anything. It was foggy as hell, and everyone was bananas.

Albin's not too happy about it, though. In fact, he's got an attitude like maybe he, or Violet and I, should have done more, or at least something, to prevent all this from happening.

In movies, cops always put you on the tailgate of an ambulance after shit like this, with blankets and coffee for the crane shot. Albin sends everybody *else* off to various jails and hospitals, but keeps Violet and me—and Bark, who's somehow become our responsibility—around, yelling questions at us between his radio calls to Bemidji. Doesn't get us a plane ride back to Ely for hours, and even then has a deputy meet us at the dock and make sure we check into the Ely Lakeside Hotel so we'll be available later on.

Once the deputy leaves, I bribe the Lakeside's courtesy van driver to take us to CFS so we can pick up our car.

"You don't want to just wait?" Violet says.

"First I want to get Bark back to CFS." Right now the dog's tied up on the putting green, and I know freeing her will soften Violet up.

"What comes after first?"

Maybe it *is* possible to get to know me.

"Supposedly the Ojibwe have known about the thing at White Lake for years," I say. "They've painted it and they have a name for it: the Wendigo. So I want to talk to a fucking Ojibwe."

30

"Let me explain why that's so offensive," Virgil Burton of the North Lakes Ojibwe Tribes says.

We're seated across from him at a low-rise cafeteria table for children in the lunchroom of the community center. I don't recall ever being small enough to fit at a table like this.

"It's not that white people talk about First Nations people being magical," Burton says, "although that *is* kind of moronic when you look at what's happened to us. It's that white people don't *bother* to look at what's happened to us. They'd rather look at the teepees. And the Wendigos."

It's embarrassing as fuck.

"The First Nations had *societies*," Virgil says. "I'm not talking about Robin Hood camps in the wilderness. I'm talking about *civilizations*. Before Columbus got here, one in four people on Earth lived in the so-called New World. Tenochtitlan was the biggest city on Earth. We had books, and governments, and courts of law, and the best armies in existence. When Hernández and de Grijalva attacked the Maya, the Maya kicked their butts. The Aztecs kicked Cortez's butt in 1520. A year after that the Florida killed Ponce de León. Then European smallpox hit, and ninety-five percent of the indigenous population died. Which the Europeans pushed to ninety-seven percent through slavery and extermination.

"After *that,* of course, this place was wide open. Domesticated crops and animals everywhere the Europeans looked. Gold that was already mined. Do you know how much Pizarro's first shipment of stolen gold back to Europe was worth?"

We shake our heads.

"Four times as much as the Bank of England. But *white people,* if you'll excuse the expression, want to romanticize the way the survivors lived *after* that. Like First Nations people *wanted* to be wandering tribes ruled by warlords and living in the woods. We didn't *want* that. That was forced on us by the white man. Those were our *Dark Ages.* But you people would rather talk about shamans, and spirit guides, and the nobility of the simple life. Of course it was the simple life: the whole world had ended."

Changing tack or something, he says "Did you know Hitler had a painting of Geronimo in his bunker?"

"No," Violet says.

"Hitler *loved* the First Nations people. You know what the First Nations people thought of Hitler? They joined the *U.S. Army* to fight him. First Nations got some *history* with the U.S. Army. But Hitler didn't care about that. He just went on loving us. And here's another thing: he had syphilis. He did. You can look it up. He had syphilis and he blamed the Jews for it. There's a whole chapter in *Mein Kampf* called 'Syphilis.'"

"I've read *Mein Kampf*," I say, not realizing how that sounds till it comes out.

"Do you know where syphilis comes from?" Burton says. "That's right. The New World. Like potatoes. And corn. And tomatoes. But did *that* make Hitler hate us? No it didn't. Cause he would have had to look at the facts about us to do that. Which he didn't want to do. He *loved* us, but he didn't want to *see* us.

"And now you folks come here asking about Wendigos. You're both *doctors,* man. Do you ask about educational programs? Do you ask about diabetes rates, and whether anyone's doing anything about *that?* Have you got any idea how many people here are on dialysis? I'll show you the center if you want. *Teenagers* hang out there, cause if they're not on dialysis yet, they will be. We show *movies* in there. We got Netflix. We got ladies coming around helping people do their taxes. People running for tribal council, they *campaign* in the dialysis center. If one in four *white* people had diabetes, there wouldn't *be* diabetes."

"We're sorry to have bothered you," Violet says.

"Don't be sorry," Virgil says. "Just be open-minded. You know what a Wendigo *is?*"

We both shake our heads.

"A Wendigo's a story for children. Children and white people. It's a guy who's starving to death in the winter, so he eats his family. As a punishment, his spirit gets cursed to live in that spot forever. Always hungry. Always trying to kill people so he can eat them, but so weak he has to do it by drowning them. You see where I'm going with this? It's just more *Road Warrior* shit. You've got a people so afraid of starving to death they have to tell their kids not to eat each other. That's all the Wendigo story is: *don't eat each other.* Stay human, no matter how bad things get. Now, what *Europeans* hear is the opposite: First Nations people are magic, and they know how to talk to Bigfoot. But if Bigfoot was real, he would have died of smallpox a long time ago.

"White Lake's a dangerous place. *Anywhere* kids go to party is dangerous—particularly white kids. If there's something going on there, please don't blame it on us."

⟩◖◗◖◗◖

In the car, at the end of a mud turnoff, looking out at a lake we don't know the name off, rain battering the windshield, the whole day seems to fold in on us. Violet starts to cry. If I hadn't been anorgasmic for that shit for years, I probably would too.

"Teng seemed so *nice*," she says.

"Yeah."

"He was nice to his brother."

"Yeah."

"And now he's *dead?* And nobody even knows *why?*"

I try to think of something to say that isn't "Yeah" but can't.

"I feel like I'm going crazy."

"You're not," I say. "Or at least, if you are, I am too. And a lot of other people. We still have some pretty heavy drugs in our system."

"That's not it. It's Teng. And the fact that there's

something living in White Lake. Which goes against everything we know."

Or used to know.

"I don't even feel like I can trust anything back *here,*" Violet says. She turns her wet face to mine. I can smell her tears. Her lips look slick and soft.

It's too much.

"Violet," I say. "There's something I have to tell you."

Her eyes widen and she shakes her head almost imperceptibly. She doesn't want to hear it.

Tough luck, though. For both of us. Among the things that have ceased to make sense in the last eight hours is continuing to lie to Violet Hurst.

"My name isn't Lionel Azimuth," I tell her. "It's Pietro Brnwa. I grew up in New Jersey. I went to medical school in California. Before that I worked as a killer for the Sicilian and Russian mafias."

She just looks at me. Studying my face for some sign that I'm kidding.

"What?" she says.

"I murdered people."

"I don't believe you."

"Even so, it's true. It's the one true thing I've told you."

"You're serious?"

"Yes."

"You were . . . what?"

"A killer. For money. For the Mafia."

"Really?" She just seems puzzled. "Does Rec Bill know?"

A question I deserve. "I don't know. I don't think so."

Then, all at once, it hits her.

"Oh, my fucking *God.*"

She slams out of the car.

I get out on my side. It's pouring. "Violet—come back. I'll drop you off somewhere."

"Stay away from me!"

"Then at least take the car. It's too far to walk."

"Fuck off!"

I back away from the car. "The keys are in the ignition."

She pauses, scared and confused.

"You *killed* people?"

"Yes."

"How many?"

"I don't know. Around twenty."

"You don't *know?*"

"There were some situations where some of them might have lived."

"So you're a serial killer."

"Yes, technically."

"*Technically?* Oh, *fuck.*"

There's stark fear in her eyes, and disgust. But what am I supposed to say? That I've never killed anyone like *her?* That I once went eight whole years as an adult *without* killing anybody? That I'm almost back up to three?

I keep backing away toward the road. Try to get far enough from the car that she can run to it without worrying I'll attack her.

ɔ▲▲▲(

I squelch along the highway till I get to the CFS Outfitters. It takes about an hour and a half.

Now that the rain's letting up, a kid I don't recognize is rebuilding the barrier to the lodge road, this time with sawhorses instead of traffic cones.

"Help you, sir?" he says. He looks at me like not all that many people stop by this place on foot. Or soaking wet.

"I'm Lionel Azimuth. I was on Reggie's tour. Did a woman come through here in the last couple hours?"

"The paleontologist lady?"

"Yeah."

"She's down at the lodge. Are you the doctor?"

"Yes. Did she leave a message for me?"

"Not her. But some Indian guy was looking for you."

"What Indian guy?"

"He came into the outfitters."

"When?"

"Bout an hour ago."

"So where is he now?"

"I don't know. He probably left. I told him you weren't down at the lodge."

"Did he give his name?"

The kid scratches guiltily. "He might have."

"Was it Virgil Burton?"

"I don't remember. I'm sorry."

"What did he look like?"

He shrugs. "Older'n you, I think. He had gray hair, but he didn't look *that* old."

Sounds like Virgil Burton.

"I'm gonna need a ride," I say. "Or to borrow your car."

It's raining hard out of a bright white sky, and the community center is closed and locked. Henry, the kid who drove me here, stays in his Subaru while I look in the community center's windows. I hold up a "one minute" finger to him and jog across a baseball diamond and a small gully to the first house I can see. Clean planks of wood. No one answering the door.

I keep moving. A couple houses down, a woman in her early thirties answers. Around my age, which is weird to see on someone who so clearly has a life.

"Yes?" she says. Suspicious but, thank God, not scared-looking.

"Do you know Virgil Burton?"

"Why do you ask?"

There are tire noises in the driveway behind me. I assume it's Henry, who's been rolling along the street after me at a more or less even pace.

It isn't, though. It's Virgil Burton, getting out of his pickup. When I glance back, the woman is closing the door.

"What's going on, mister?" Virgil says.

"I heard you were looking for me."

"How? From smoke signals?" He sees my face and stops moving toward me. "Look, man, are you all right?" He nods toward Henry, parked along the street. "That your friend?"

"You didn't tell him you were looking for me?"

"No. I promise."

"Sorry. I don't—"

"No need to apologize," he says. "Just get yourself some help. Take care of yourself."

There's nothing more to say. I go and get in the passenger seat of Henry's car.

"Is that the guy you said was looking for me?"

Henry looks surprised.

"No. I didn't say he was First Nations. I said he was Indian. Like from India."

31

Professor Marmoset—whose family, yes, is from Uttar Pradesh, and whose Al Pacino hair does make it kind of hard to guess his age—is on one of the couches in the registration cabin. Legs up, Violet next to him the same way, Bark the Dog between them. Marmoset and Violet loll their heads in my direction when I come in. Violet lolls hers away.

"Ishmael," Professor Marmoset says. "You look like shit."

"I am like shit," I say. The whole cabin smells like Bark's wet fur. "What are you doing here?"

"Rec Bill called me. He heard that Sarah Palin gave the surprise keynote address to the American Association of Chromium Processors in Omaha this morning, and wondered if something had happened that required her to arrange an alibi."

"This *morning?*" Out the window, the sun's just going down.

"Late morning. Pre-lunch. Still, someone's got a pretty good booking agent."

"No shit." I'm almost as impressed by Palin's turn-around as I am by the fact that Rec Bill managed to get Professor Marmoset on the phone.

As if he can read my mind, Professor Marmoset looks at his watch.

"How long are you here for?" I say.

"Not long. I'm on my way to the Mayo. I've got one of Rec Bill's planes at Ely Municipal. I can give you guys a ride to Minneapolis if you want."

"Violet can go. I need to return the car."

He gestures to the armchair. "Then sit. I at least need to hear *your* version of this business."

ɔ ◖◗◗◗◖(

I tell him. He doesn't interrupt much. At the end he says "You know, you can make a *passive* nightscope out of a digital camera."

I just stare at him.

"In case you ever need to."

I say "You can make a passive nightscope out of an active nightscope and a piece of tape."

"For three times the price."

"I'm on an expense account. Any thoughts on the *lake monster?*"

Marmoset yawns. "What's *your* take on it?"

"That there's something fucking down there."

"Okay."

"And if it's mechanical, it's the best piece of engineering I've ever heard of."

"Agreed."

"Which means it's probably not mechanical. Which means it's probably some kind of actual fucking creature."

He frowns. "By 'actual fucking creature,' you mean an animal not generally understood to exist?"

"Yes."

"That seems implausible."

"Of course it seems implausible. It seems fucking insane. But I saw it."

"You saw it?"

"Felt it. Well enough to be able to tell it wasn't anything else."

"So…"

"So I think it's like that thing Sherlock Holmes says. Where anything's possible if there's no other explanation."

Violet looks at me in surprise.

Marmoset says "That's actually the one stupid thing Holmes says. You and I discussed it once on the shuttle to Mercy Hospital. That and how Houdini did the removable-thumb trick for Arthur Conan Doyle and Doyle thought it was actual magic. Anyway, it's wrong: there's always another explanation."

Violet doesn't smile, just keeps looking at me. It's worse.

"And there will be an explanation for this," Marmoset says. "In fact, we even know how we'll get it."

I turn back to him. "We do?"

"Of course. Why was someone so convinced the monster was real that they felt compelled to chase it down in an amphibious boat? At night, in secret? *Reggie* doesn't seem to have believed in the monster. Debbie told you *she* didn't. Dr. Hurst's friends in the bar said they did, but neither of them seems to have enough at stake to feel strongly one way or the other. So what makes the person in the boat so certain? What do they know that we don't?"

"I don't know," I say. "What?"

He raises his palms. "No idea. We don't even have enough information to say for sure whether the person on the boat shot Chris Jr. and Father Podominick. But I think finding that person, or even identifying him, will get us the answers to every question we have."

"You're right," I say. "I'll do it."

Marmoset looks at me sharply. "I didn't mean you literally, Ishmael. I meant the police."

"The police have had two years to deal with this."

"Yes, and I imagine they'll consider it a higher priority now."

"Right. Unless Teng's death gets covered up."

Marmoset looks skeptical. "To protect Palin?"

"Or Tyson Grody," I say. "Or the Ficks, whoever they are—or even Teng, or Teng's company, or his reputation or whatever. Or all of them."

Marmoset wrinkles his nose. "I think that's unlikely. And even if someone *does* manage to keep it quiet, this situation is no longer our responsibility. I wouldn't have gotten you involved in the first place if I'd known there had been actual deaths at White Lake."

"And you're not worried there'll be more?"

"I think we can rely on Parks and Recreation to put up a 'No Swimming' sign."

"What about a 'No Getting Shot with a Hunting Rifle' sign?"

"Ishmael," Marmoset says quietly. "Do you really think your staying here is going to make people *less* likely to get killed?"

Oh, *snappity*.

"The police will find the person with the boat," he says. "There can't be that many companies that *make* amphibious boats, and those companies can't sell that many of them."

I'm not about to let it go, though. "What do you want to bet the boat turns out to have been charged to Chris Jr.? Like the nets and harpoons no one seems to have wanted?"

Marmoset nods. "It's a possibility I've considered."

"I'm going back to White Lake. I'm going to find the guy with the boat and make him tell me what's going on. *Now* is when he'll be there."

"As will the police."

"There may be some cops, but not like there will be once they start dragging the lake. Not to mention what will happen when word *does* get out that Palin was here. The journalists alone will rent every canoe Reggie owns. We know that, and the guy in the boat knows that, so now is when he'll try again. He couldn't even stay away when Reggie's tour was nearby."

"Assuming he or she was aware of that."

"Why wouldn't he have been?" I say. "Everybody else was. You know what I'm saying is right."

"In some respects, but—"

"I'll go alone. There won't be anyone to get hurt."

"Except you, Ishmael. You do count for something,

you know. There are other, more important things you're capable of."

"No," Violet says.

We both look at her.

"Not alone. I'm going with you. Whatever the fuck your name is."

I stare back at her. "Forget it. No way."

"You owe me. We started this together and we'll finish it together. And you're going to answer some fucking questions on the way."

"It's too dangerous."

"Both of us or neither of us."

"You can't stop me."

"And you can't stop *me*," she says. "And I'm a lot better at canoeing than you are."

"But—"

Why would she even *want* to?

I turn from her to Marmoset. "What have you been telling this woman?"

Marmoset shakes his head with an expression I've seen on him a million times before. Dismay without surprise.

"Nothing I don't now regret," he says.

32

Lake Garner / White Lake
Boundary Waters Canoe Area, Minnesota
Saturday, 22 September–Sunday, 23 September

There are a couple of cops—a woman and a man—on chaise lounges on the beach of Lake Garner, both stripped down to their undershirts. At one point she blows him against a tree. Which doesn't make it at all uncomfortable to be waiting with Violet at the other end of the lake.

With the help of maps drawn up by Henry, the trip back has taken less than two days. Our instructions to him: give us the direct route, fuck how hard the portages are. We'll use GPS and a twenty-nine-pound canoe.

And thank the Christ for that. I've just spent two days having a series of exchanges I've spent my entire adult life trying to avoid.

Like:

"Have you ever killed someone just to intimidate someone else?"

"Not that I know of."

"Anyone by accident?"

"No. Well—once someone I took with me on a job killed someone I didn't mean to kill."

"Someone innocent?"

"Underage."

"A kid?"

"Around the same age as Dylan Arntz."

"But not innocent?"

"Like I say: underage."

"What did you do to the guy who killed him?"

"Eventually? Killed *him*."

"Because of that?"

"It didn't help."

"Are there people you're glad you've killed?"

"Glad I killed personally? No. I wish I'd never killed anybody."

"But there are people you killed who you're glad are dead."

"Yes."

"Did you ever kill anyone you didn't know anything about?"

"Yes. I tried not to, but yes. Some people I killed just because David Locano asked me to."

"How many?"

"Give me a minute."

"Would you kill David Locano if you could?"

"That's giving me a minute? Yes."

"Because of Magdalena? And because of your grandparents?"

"Yes."

"Both?"

"Yes."

"Equally?"

"Fuck!"*

Except for the tent Palin was using, which her body-guards took with them, Reggie's campsite is still mostly intact, only now with fluttering crime scene tape around it. When the cops go back to sunbathing, Violet and I discuss the possibility that they're sleeping here, and that we'll have to row past them in the dark and go over the spit at its far end. But exactly at five p.m. the Parks and Rec floatplane glides in to pick them up, using the ramp Palin's bodyguards left in place on the beach.

Violet and I paddle the length of Lake Garner, skirt the tape, and cross the spit. Take the beach as far along White Lake as it goes, then get back on the water.

We try not to talk as we paddle. It's bad enough that the sound of every stroke I screw up comes back at us off the walls of the canyon. And that I'll probably flip out the way I did when we went to Omen Lake to look at the rock paintings. I'm not sure why I haven't flipped out already.

Maybe it's the need to focus. After the second zigzag, we're in geography we haven't seen before, and the cliffs are full of indentations conceivably large enough to hide a boat. Why that should successfully distract me from the idea of an animal conceivably large enough to *eat* a boat, I don't know. But being back on White Lake in clear day-

---

* For longer answers to these questions, see *Beat the Reaper,* by "Josh Bazell," Little, Brown, 2009.

light is somehow easier than it was to have to think about it in advance.

Which is not to say that when we reach the last, and widest, segment of White Lake, where the cliffs are gone and there's forest on three sides, I'm not covered in sweat that has nothing to do with exertion.

Or that when we spot a gap in the shoreline undergrowth that looks large enough to stash our canoe, we don't get ourselves and our boat off the water and into the brush as quickly as fucking possible.

⟩❟❟❟⟨

The sun goes down as fast as it did three days ago.

The moon's bigger, though, and for a couple of hours it's brighter. Then the clouds slide over it, and things turn suddenly *dark*. So dark the branches in front of your face are only slightly purer black than the space around them, and you can hear the lake right in front of you but not see it.

It's an interesting situation. Our senses are jacked from anticipation and the physicality of getting here. And we're invisible, which even the ancients knew is asking for trouble.

Things you could do in that kind of darkness:

Lean against each other for warmth.

Lean toward each other, with your foreheads on each other's shoulders, out of boredom as well as for warmth.

Put your hands between each other's thighs, for even more warmth.

Tackle each other to the ground and fuck like Orpheus and Eurydice, Tarzan and Sheena, and Watson and Holmes all at once, for the kind of warmth that makes it okay to take a while to find your clothes afterward, and leaves your abs trembling and your mouth bruised from having hot wet crotch stubble ground into it.

I'm just saying: those are some things you could do.

)∩∩∩(

Just after midnight we hear something crashing through the trees, then engine noise, then the sound of an amphibious Zodiac flopping onto the lake just across from our position. I put on my new night-vision goggles from CFS and slot their narrow angle of view onto the Zodiac. Its wheels are still rising out of the water as it passes us.

The fucker driving it has his hood up again. But I don't think he knows for sure someone's watching him, because he lights a plastic-wrapped stick of dynamite and tosses it off the rear of the boat without looking around too much.

"Dynamite," I say.

"I see it." Violet's got her own night-vision goggles.

The noise of the explosion still makes us both jump.

The reason you can fish with dynamite, if you're so inclined, is that water isn't compressible, whereas fish are. For a fish, particularly a shallow-water fish, being in the water near an explosion is like being at one end of a Newton's cradle made of wrecking balls. Everything else just transmits the force and stays put. The fish absorbs it, and ruptures. It's the same concept as dropping a depth charge near a submarine.

All that noise makes the time we spent practicing how to silently relaunch the canoe seem a bit silly, but we follow procedure anyway, and as we move into the wake of the Zodiac I take a moment to appreciate how much better our tandem rowing has gotten over the past few days.

Then I take a moment to appreciate how I really should have asked myself a couple of basic questions before getting into this situation. Like whether this guy is or is not using sonar, and if so whether he can pick out a trailing canoe with it.

The Zodiac suddenly leans into a U-turn tight enough to make me conclude that the answers are *yes* and *yes*. Particularly since the guy's now scrambling toward the harpoon gun at the front of his boat.

Violet and I check our canoe sideways to stop its motion. We've taped over the IR lights on our goggles so the guy won't be able to see them, but he seems to be doing fine without them. In any case, the searing light of his own goggles is showing us everything *we* need to see. Like him aiming at us. And firing.

I shout "Hang on!"

I wonder if Kevlar's any good against harpoons.

That's all I have time for.

33

My face punches through the surface, I'm swallowed whole, things get more real than they were a moment ago. When they were already pretty real, just not as real as being in cold black water with something awful living in it and a guy just above the surface with night-vision goggles, a hunting rifle, and dynamite.

Humans, incidentally, are even more compressible than fish.

"Violet!" I yell when I break the surface.

I think the reason I've been thrown so far, and in such a disorienting way, is that the canoe deformed when the harpoon hit it, then snapped partially back into shape, shooting me into space like an arrow from a bow.

"Here!" she says.

I swim toward her fast, head down because it's too dark to see her anyway, my clothes trailing every movement with the wrong rhythm. I'd ditch them, but I don't want to take the time, and I'm still fooling myself that there's something in them I'll be able to use later.

One of Violet's hands swipes my side. I grab onto her and surface. She's mostly invisible, but her eyes and hair glint like the lake.

I say "We go down, hold hands, swim as far as possible, surface, don't speak, do it again till we get to shore. Okay?"

"Yes," she says.

We quickly kiss, if that's the kind of thing you believe we've been doing, and go under. Into the high-pitched silence of the water, which seems to be waiting for either an explosion or a creature that wants to bite our heads off, whichever shows up first.

We swim what feels like a long distance, in as straight a line as we can, then Violet squeezes my hand and we come up gasping. Go down again and this time swim until our hands touch the rocks along the bottom and we know we've reached the shallows. Raise our heads out of the water just in time to hear the rattlesnake hiss of a fuse.

I don't think the dynamite lands all that near us. I don't feel a splash, either when it hits the surface or when it explodes. I just feel the force go through me like something kicking me in the balls, shredding my muscles, and quadrupling my blood pressure at the same time. Then I realize I'm back under water, drowning.

But only for a moment. This is no time to lounge about. Violet and I claw our way onto shore. Then lurch, unable to stand upright, into the pitch-dark woods.

Which are like a birth canal lined with midgets trying to trip us. As we speed-stumble deeper, I keep hammering into things that are either vertical or horizontal, I can't tell which, and hearing Violet do the same. When I reach back to grab her hand, hers or mine is slick with blood.

We seem to go on like this for about an hour, although it's really probably more like ten minutes. Because how long can it take to land an amphibious boat, follow a couple of people who can't see into some woods, and start shooting at them with a hunting rifle?

The first bullet cracks into a tree just ahead of us with the noise of someone hitting a home run. The second smashes close enough to spray moss into my mouth, and splinters into the right side of my face and neck.

Conveniently, Violet and I both trip over things around then, and end up face-to-face.

"This isn't going to work," I say, trying not to spit moss on her. "We have to split up. You go left, I'll keep going straight. If he follows you instead of me, I'll circle back and get behind him."

"I'll do the same if he follows you."

"Don't. It's too dangerous. He'll see you."

"And he won't see you?"

"No. Go."

This time there's no kiss even if you believe that kind of thing *is* going on, maybe out of a shared recognition that I'm back to lying to her. But she does trail a hand down the side of my face that has splinters in it.

Then I'm bashing forward again, peeling off my jacket to leave a trail, patting it down before I drop it for items that might help me kill this fucker. Finding only a digital camera in a Neoprene pouch. If I were Professor Marmoset, I'd be set.

Being someone else entirely, I dedicate thirty seconds of half-concentration to figuring out a way to turn the piece of shit into a night-vision scope. Is there some kind of filter you're supposed to remove? Some submenu of a submenu you're supposed to reprogram? Then I give up on it. Turns out I'm not an electrical engineer.

What I am is someone who's supposedly good at taking out maniacs in the woods. And it's true I'm looking forward to completing the rightward curve I've been trying to make outside this fucker's peripheral vision. As far as I can tell I'm almost back to the spot where I split off from Violet.

Which is why the next rifle shot I hear makes my blood go cold.

It doesn't come from where it should come from. Not if he's following me, and not if he's following Violet. It comes from a completely different direction, and from too far away.

Meaning he *is* following Violet, and I have no idea where the fuck I've been going. Nor do I have any chance of moving fast enough and far enough to keep him from killing her.

I yell "HEY! FUCKER!" Lunge in the direction the gunshot seemed to come from. Get enmeshed in a web of branches. Hear another rifle shot.

It's then that I decide to smash the camera. Not because that might work, but because I can't think of *anything* that might work. Or maybe I should throw the camera instead. Bean that fucker in the head right before he shoots her, pure luck.

As I draw back my arm, though, I realize that neither of those things is what it's time for.

What it's time for is for me to repeat my mantra. Which is:

I am one dumb fucking shithead.

I turn the back of the camera away from me so it won't blast my retinas, cover the front with my palm, and press the "on" button. To my wide-open pupils, the glare from the monitor lights up everything around me.

It's interesting. I'm not even on the ground. For the last little while I've been moving upward through a tangle of branches. I drop back to the dirt through the first hole I see.

After that I'm in motion. I can't see very far ahead, but I can *run*. I can duck around trees I would have otherwise had to find with my face, and can spot dead ends before flailing into them. Eventually I even learn to put the camera on picture display so it doesn't keep automatically retracting the lens and turning off.

I hear a close-by rifle shot and start to move faster. Come around a tree and almost slam into the shooter's back.

I'm shocked that he's moving so slowly. Faster than I was when I couldn't see anything, but barely. He's just ambling along, doing leisurely terminator head sweeps with his night-vision goggles while keeping his rifle still, like he's used to all this and doesn't want to tire himself out.

He hasn't heard me or noticed the light from the camera yet. I'm tempted to just kill him—straight punch to the fifth vertebra, *Nice being chased by ya*—but if Violet's dead I'll want him around to answer for that. And if she's alive she probably has some questions of her own.

I grab the man's rifle away and use my hand with the camera in it to lift his night-vision goggles off and illuminate his face.

"Aw, fuck," I say out loud.

It's Dr. McQuillen.

⸱𐩒𐩒𐩒𐩒(

On the way back to the boat, with Violet in the lead wearing McQuillen's goggles and me at the back still holding the camera, I let McQuillen bang his head on the occasional branch. I'm cold and I'm in pain, and Violet was sheathed in blood when I gave her McQuillen's anorak. I would have given her his shirt, too, but I wasn't sure someone his age would survive the cold, no matter how fit he obviously is.

In case I need to feel worse, I also think about how I went all the way through his office without realizing his CT scanner was missing. Sold, I'm now thinking, to pay for the amphibious boat.

We reach the boat in question.

I say "All right. What's in the water?"

"I don't know."

I don't ask again. Just grab the back of his shirt and wade thigh-deep into the lake with him. Use my teeth to open the knife I took from his coat and cut his shoulder enough to bleed. Plunge him under.

Violet gets the boat's running lights on behind us. It's weird to be able to see normally.

"What is it?" I say when I pull him back up.

"I'll tell you!" he screams. "Get me out of the water!"

I do.

He does.

EXHIBIT I

From: *Editors' Choice,* Science, 12 December 2008, 322: 1718

MARINE BIOLOGY
Carcharhinus? You Don't Even Know Us!

There may be an exception to every rule, but the bull shark, *Carcharhinus leucas,* can claim to be the exception to at least three. Long famous among ichthyologists for its fierce aggressiveness (bull sharks resemble short, wide great whites; the five shark attacks on humans that occurred on the Jersey Shore between July 1 and July 12 of 1916, and inspired the book and film *Jaws,* are now thought to be the work of a single *C. leucas*), it is also the only shark to retain the elasmobranchial ability to not just survive but hunt and thrive in both marine and freshwater environments. *C. leucas* accomplishes this neat trick through an impressive grab-bag of adaptations, including decreased urea production by the liver, diffusion of urea by the gills, the ability to increase its urine output by twenty-fold, and the ability to switch between active and passive transfer of electrolytes, via Na^+, K^+-ATPase, in both the distal tubules and rectal glands. The third unique distinction of *C. leucas* is its range: bull sharks have been found as far north as Massachusetts and as far south as the Cape of Good Hope, in a band that circumnavigates the globe.

Despite being geographically widespread, however, individual bull sharks are sufficiently rare that in the past they've been thought to incorporate over a dozen different species. Specimens from places as diverse as the Ganges, Zambezi, and Mississippi rivers (bull sharks have been found as far up the Mississippi as Illinois) have been subsumed into *C. leucas* only gradually, usually on the basis of anatomical comparison. For example, the Nicaragua Lake shark, or *Carcharhinus nicaraguensis,* was declared *C. leucas* by taxonomical agreement in 1961.

One holdout to this process, because of its particular rarity and presumed population fragility, has been the Vietnamese river shark, *Carcharhinus vietnamensis.* Gordon et al. now use dye-terminator sequencing to compare the genome of *C. vietnamensis* sampled in the wild with that of *C. leucas,* and find that the two are the same. The authors theorize that the Mekong Delta may be the northernmost passage available for bull sharks to cross between the Indian Ocean and the Pacific.

Journ. Exp. Mar. Bio. and Eco. 356, 236 (2008)

34

"A *shark?*" I say. "It's a motherfucking *shark?* You heard Reggie's crackpot story and you put a *shark* in the lake?"

McQuillen spits water. "What do you want? A dragon?"

"No, actually a shark is fucked up enough. It's a shark!" I shout to Violet.

I'm slightly high on how easy it's being for me to think and say "shark." Later on I'll figure out why and get depressed,* but at the moment it just seems cool.

---

* I think it's just this: the sharks I hate and am afraid of are the ones I faced with Magdalena Niemerover years ago. I carry them around, like I carry her around, and no real-life bull shark can compete. I doubt any real-life woman could either, despite any

"There may be more than one," McQuillen says, avoiding my eyes. "Originally there were four."

"Originally?" Violet says.

"When Chris Semmel Jr. bought them."

"You mean when you told him to buy them," I say.

"Not so they would kill anyone, if that's what you're thinking. Autumn and Benjy were an accident. The bulls were never supposed to survive the first winter."

"So what was the point of them?"

"We wanted to get some video of them attacking something. A dog, or a deer. Ideally a moose. But the bulls must have been too small back then. All we got was one eating a loon."

"I'd say you got a little more than that."

"What about the bite marks?" Violet says.

McQuillen answers me instead of her. "I told you: Autumn and Benjy were an accident. It was a year later. We didn't think anything was still in the lake."

"Bite marks," I say.

He clears his throat. "It was a board. Just a two-by-four with some nails at the end of it. I only needed to modify the front of the bites to make it look like they were from *Liopleurodon ferox* instead of *Carcharhinus leucas*."

"You were the one who recovered the bodies?" I say.

"No. Of course not."

"Then how—"

I realize how.

"You're the county coroner."

He nods.

---

miraculous interlude with Violet Hurst I may or may not have had, and it's unlikely I'll get a chance to find out.

"You said they'd been killed by a boat propeller, then altered the bites to make it look like they'd been attacked by a dinosaur. Maybe that was the most you could do. Too many people had already seen the bodies for you to make it seem like they'd been through an actual accident. But at least that gave you some evidence for your hoax. And established your credentials as a skeptic at the same time."

Violet, both saddened and disgusted, says "You did all that so you could *fool* people?"

"You wouldn't understand."

"Try her," I say.

"Ford was dying. People there needed a way out. And it was my responsibility."

"In what way?" she says.

"I was their *doctor*."

"Were you Chris Jr. and Father Podominick's doctor?" I say. "Because I'm pretty sure arranging to meet your patients on a dock at midnight and then shooting them because they're your co-conspirators in a hoax that's already killed two teenagers is outside current medical guidelines. Particularly if you then use one of the patients you've just murdered to front a boat purchase."

"Chris Jr. agreed the bulls needed to be put down. We all did."

"But Chris Jr. and Father Podominick didn't want to keep the way Autumn and Benjy died a secret. Which is why you murdered them. You'd kept them quiet as long as you could."

"Chris Jr. and Father Podominick were two people in a town of two and a half thousand."

"So worth killing to save your reputation?"

"My *reputation?*" McQuillen looks up at me with what seems to be genuine anger. "I don't give a *damn* about my reputation. Everyone who knows me is either an alcoholic or a junkie. Or both. You think they'll remember me? Or thank me? And before you get any ideas, I'm not scared of prison, either. I'm seventy-eight. I probably wouldn't survive a trial."

"You seem pretty spry to me."

"*I have to be.* I'm the only doctor Ford's ever going to get. I couldn't *give* my practice away. *You're* a sorry excuse for a doctor—would *you* take it?"

It's actually kind of a thought-provoking question. Just not for this lifetime.

"You're right," I say. "I respectfully decline. Let's get out of here. How does the radio work?"

"I can figure it out," Violet says.

McQuillen says *"Wait."*

Violet swings her legs over the side of the Zodiac to go fuck with the radio.

"You're planning to turn me over to the police?" McQuillen says. "Get yourself some revenge?"

"More or less," I say.

"What about Ford?"

"Don't worry, I'm sure whoever picks us up can take us straight to Ely. We can skip Ford entirely."

"I mean *what's going to happen to it?*"

"I have no idea."

"Yes you do. You've been there. You've seen what those people are doing to themselves."

"Right…" I say.

"We can still help them."

"Bringing you in *is* helping them, McQuillen."

"Horseshit! We have the opportunity, *right now,* to make the White Lake hoax *real.* Benjy and Autumn died. That was an unintended tragedy, and the rumors it started eventually blew over. Then the Chinaman died—also unintended, and partially your fault: if you two hadn't interrupted me, I might have caught the bulls that night. But this time the rumors won't blow over. Twice now people have died here. And I know you've seen the autopsy photos of Autumn and Benjy. Together that is easily enough to turn this place into a tourist destination."

I stare at him. "That's some kind of joke, right?"

"I don't believe in humor. I've got sonar and dynamite. We can clear out the sharks *tonight.* No one will ever know they existed. After which you can do whatever the hell you want to me."

"What do you think, Dr. Hurst?" I say to Violet.

"Keep going with the lying and killing?" she says. "No thanks. But if he calls Teng Wenshu 'the Chinaman' again, I might change my mind."

35

This time Sheriff Albin drives us back to CFS himself.

On the way I tell him who I really am, and give him the names of some people who, while they might not be able to find me, will at least be able to answer questions about me that come up in the future. I figure he deserves to know. And it may come out anyway.

Even leaving aside Albin's own involvement in it, this case is going to be a mess. Missing body, missing witnesses, Teng's cause of death unclear—bullet? shark?—with no guarantee it will ever get clearer. The county prosecutor likely to give up chasing Reggie for felony murder after a while and content himself with fraud charges—which won't be easy to work with either. *Something* turned up on Reggie's tour, and his guests who brought firearms broke his clearly stated rules, and on top of that he'll never get paid. No matter what her percentage is, Palin won't certify any escrow that links her to Ford.*

So Albin's a tad stressed. He's also enough of a justice addict to blame McQuillen and not Violet and me for what's likely to be a rough year or two, and to be grateful to us for figuring McQuillen out, even if we didn't tell him we were going to do it.

He takes us down to the marina. Violet and I figure we can say goodbye to Henry and Davey and Jane and anyone else who's at the outfitters—including Bark the Dog, I suppose—on our way out. Right now we just want to get our shit and leave.

---

* Reggie's motives are a different issue. I was asked about them numerous times, and had the opportunity to discuss them with Reggie himself. What I think, for whatever that's worth, is that they weren't particularly nefarious. Reggie wanted to go live on the beach in Cambodia, and maybe even take Del and Miguel with him. But he probably could have done that with the amount of money he ended up spending on the hoax anyway—an amount he saved up in advance, managing to stay out of debt until the legal fees hit later. I believe him when he says he wanted to honor Chris Jr.'s hoax project and thought there was a chance of finding out who or what killed Autumn Semmel.

Regarding his casual lawbreaking and disregard for the potential consequences of his actions, which placed people in mortal danger in a way he should have foreseen, I consider that part of his character more than the influence of greed. I'm not a psychiatrist, but what I see in Reggie Trager is someone who, apparently since the Vietnam War, has been so consumed by feelings of shock, sadness, and unreality that the outcomes he imagined possible from his scheme—both positive and negative, both to himself and to others—seemed almost weightless. I don't think he acted out of malice. I think he's just someone who was made dangerous at a young age and stayed that way.

The lodge itself is abandoned. The deputy stationed there gets the key to our cabin, and the four of us walk over together.

The moment I crack the cabin door, though, I can tell something's wrong. I know the smell of this room pretty well, from lying in the dark and trying to smell Violet's pussy from fifteen feet away. The smell has changed.

It's cologne. And not just cologne: it's Canoe, by Dana. Every mob fuck's favorite aftershave.

Also there's a trip wire across the doorway. The door's leaning into it.

I stop short. But Violet, not realizing what's happening, and not wanting to run into me, turns sideways and slips around me. Pushes the door open a couple more inches.

I don't remember the explosion.

)∩∩∩(

I remember waking up staring at the sky. Turning to see Violet, unmoving, beside me and being unable to see Albin or his deputy at all. I remember wanting to roll over to Violet and check her for a pulse, but passing out again instead.

The next time I wake up I can't move. Or imagine how I had the energy and freedom from pain to even turn my head before. I try to talk but can't.

I also can't figure out why I'm still alive.

Leaving a bomb in our cabin—and another one in our car, I assume—is strictly Plan B material. If David Locano knows I'm near here, he'll also have a spotter watching the lodge at all times, and a hit team less than ten minutes away.

They should be here already.

What the hell's taking them so long?

EXHIBIT J

Ford, Minnesota
*One Hour Earlier**

"Cornballkowski!" the Sergeant yells. "Get your shit together!"

Dylan Arntz knows he has a weird way of berating himself. He's had it ever since he saw *Saving Private Ryan* at a friend's house as a kid.

It's even weirder than you think, though. The hard-bitten sergeant he imagines yelling at him all the time doesn't look like anyone from the movie. He looks like Dylan's dad, as far as Dylan can remember him.

"Second Lieutenant Pat Freudianism," the Sergeant would say about that. "I served with that son of a bitch in Italy."

---

* **How I know this:** See Exhibit C.

Right now the Sergeant's all in Dylan's face because Dylan's leaning against the stinking brick wall of the Highway 53 underpass on his bicycle, smoking a cigarette and thinking about how this spot used to be the crossroads of his life.

Behind him by about a mile is Walden L. Ainsworth High School. Mrs. Peters the English teacher and Mr. Terbin the history teacher and coach of the chess team. Behind him by maybe nine miles is his mother and stepfather's place. And two miles ahead of him, along Rogers Avenue, is Debbie's Diner.

The larger map has changed, though. Not because Debbie had the shit kicked out of him, although fuck knows where *that* would have gone if Caveman Doctor Cop hadn't showed up. Because she sent him to Winnipeg.

Winnipeg blew Dylan's mind. A whole city that was like some kind of fancy park, filled with people who had their shit together but weren't intimidating. Giant old bank buildings but also a river walk.

Dylan tries to picture people in Ford setting up a lake walk. "What's so funny, Clownarini?" the Sergeant wants to know.

Dylan wants to be there permanently. If not in Winnipeg, then someplace like it, in the United States or anywhere else. Every person he met in Winnipeg was nice to him, even though he was with Matt Wogum. Even fucking *Wajid,* the guy selling them the pseudoephedrine, was nice enough. He was a bit stuck up, and wouldn't let them stay overnight in his apartment, but that doesn't exactly make him Scarface.

Same thing with the girls in the bar. True, they asked

for drugs, but what they said was "Do you know where we could get some?" And they were all healthy and smiling, like what they were talking about was sunshine. Dylan has a boner just thinking about them. You could *exist* in a place like that.

You'd just have to decide how to get there. Whether to go back to Debbie—hope she sends you on the Winnipeg run again rather than kill you, ditch out on her when you get there—or finish up high school and move to Canada as a righteous citizen. Maybe even join the Canadian Army, assuming there is one.

Not the army, though, now that Dylan thinks of it. Last thing he needs is *two* sergeants.

Two paths, though. Big choice. He should discuss it with Dr. McQuillen.

Ahead of him, two black SUVs come off the highway circle and stop at the light on Rogers Avenue, one in front of the other.

Dylan notices them but doesn't really pay them any attention until the light changes and they don't go anywhere. At which point, still in the shadow of the underpass, he moves up the incline so he can see them better.

The driver of the first SUV gets out. All in black, shaved head, tattoos. Kind of like a smaller version of Dr. Neanderthal. The guy waits for the driver of the second truck to lower the window. Takes a map from him and studies it. Goes back to his own truck and turns onto Rogers Avenue.

Whatever the fuck they're up to, Dylan knows it's bad for Debbie. Which means he's got a very short time to decide what to do.

ɔ◖◖◖(

"What do you want, douchebag?" the dick who picks up the phone says.

Dylan's at the payphone outside the Pizza Grinder, the closed-down restaurant next to the highway exit. Came here a couple times when he was a kid.

"Brian, I need to speak to Debbie. Like right fuckin now."

"What's the hurry?"

"It's that if you don't put me through, when she finds out why I'm calling she's gonna have you fuckin killed for keeping her waiting."

"Sure she is."

But Brian then seems to think better of it, because five seconds later Debbie picks up.

"Dylan," she says. Softly, like she wants him to come back. To die or to go to Winnipeg, there's no way to tell.

"Debbie, I saw a bunch of guys in SUVs headed your way."

"When?"

"Just now. Coming off the highway."

"Feds?"

"I don't know. One of them had neck tattoos."

"The Sinaloans?"

"I guess."

After a pause: "Thanks, Dylan. Please come back."

"I will."

As Dylan hangs up, he hears Debbie yell *"Wake the fuck up! The Sinaloans are coming!"* in the background.

He takes his bike off the wall. Wonders why he just agreed with her that the people he saw *were* the Sinaloans.

They didn't look like any Sinaloans Dylan's seen. The Sinaloans tend to be way smaller, and always look like they've been awake for too long.

So why'd he say that's who they were?

"Eyes forward, Ambivalensky," the Sergeant warns him.

>●●●(

Biking toward Debbie's on Rogers Avenue, Dylan sees the two SUVs parked side by side in the parking lot. Then he sees a big web of cracks appear, like magic, in one of the restaurant's picture windows. As the glass sags and falls out, Dylan can suddenly hear gunfire.

He skews across the asphalt and drops into the cement half-pipe drainage ditch at the far side of the road.

After a while the shots become less frequent. It reminds Dylan of popcorn finishing popping in a micro-wave: *bangbangbangbangbang,* then only *bangbang-bang.* Longer and longer periods of silence.

When the silence lasts a full minute, Dylan runs across the road in a crouch. Looks over the sill.

Mayhem. Dead guys all over two of the booths, spill-ing out onto the floor: the men from the SUV. No Boys, alive or dead, that Dylan can see.

"Hello?" he calls through the window.

Inside, he almost gags from the hot stink of plaster dust, gun smoke, and fresh blood. When he gets control of his breathing, he counts eight bodies. A moment ago he thought there were twice that number. The carnage must be playing tricks on his mind.

Up close, sunglasses hanging off their heads, these

guys look even tougher. Some of them have guns in their hands. Dylan goes and kicks open the black Carhartt jacket of the one farthest from the tables: MP5 on a nylon strap. Next to the guy there's a menu.

What the fuck? Who comes to a place for whatever reason these guys just did—to rob or kill Debbie or just to scare her—and orders lunch first? Least that's going to happen is someone spits in your entrée.

Dylan figures out how to unhook the MP5 from the strap and moves carefully with it to the door to the kitchen. There are blood trails passing under it. Bullet holes in the aluminum.

"Whatchya doin, Dumbshitsky?" the Sergeant asks him.

"Turning off the safety," Dylan mutters.

"That's not what I—"

"Hello?" Dylan says out loud.

He opens the door with his hip, pointing the MP5.

Half a dozen Boys are on the floor around Debbie. Most of them alive, propping her up. Debbie herself unconscious or dead, with blood down one entire side of her.

The Boys all have guns out and pointed at him.

"It's me! I'm back! Don't shoot!" he thinks to say.

But his chest is suddenly jammed with static, and the room is spinning, and the floor hits him hard in one cheek.

So maybe they already have.

36

"You could have told me you were a hitman," Rec Bill says.

"No I couldn't."

"Not to mention a fugitive."

"I'm not a fugitive. I just have some assholes trying to kill me."

"I've noticed. The person they blew up instead was my paleontologist, who I hired you to protect."

What to say to that?

We're back in his all-glass office.

"I heard you saw her this morning," he says.

"That's true."

"How is she?"

"Better."

"She say anything?"

"Not much."*

"Anything about me?" Rec Bill says.

"No, but it's funny you should ask me that. Violet told me you and she had some kind of relationship, but that she didn't understand what it was."

---

* Just:

"Hello, stranger."

"How are you?"

"I feel like I've got splinters in my boobs."

"Do you, still?"

"Yeah. My surgeon says it would cause more damage to take them all out."

"Makes sense."

"You would know."

"Violet, I am so sorry."

"You didn't blow me up."

"Not directly."

"And if you hadn't stopped me from going into that cabin, it would have been a lot worse. I'm not going to say it was worth it, because I don't know what my boobs are going to look like yet. But I don't regret it."

"How could you not regret it?"

"Mostly because they haven't taken the morphine drip out of my arm. But right now, meeting you seems on balance like a good thing."

"They could at least turn the drip *down*."

"Am I ever going to see you again?"

"Probably not. I hope so."

"Then make sure it happens. You're going away?"

"Yes."

"To hide?"

"No. I'm going to try and get these assholes to stop chasing me."

He stares at me. "She *told* you that?"

"She did. I thought it was weird. I mean, I've gotten to know her pretty well, and I can't see anything that would hold *me* back."

His look turns dismissive. "Thanks for the relationship advice. Is that all you wanted to see me about?"

"No, there's one other thing. Do you smoke, Rec Bill?"

"No. Of course not."

"I didn't think so. Do you mind if other people smoke in here?"

"Yes. There's no smoking on this whole campus. Sorry."

I give it a moment. "Last time I was here you had a small ashtray on your desk."

"I don't remember that."

"You mean by killing them?"

"If that's what it takes."

"Don't. I don't want you to. I don't want you to kill anyone. Not even the people who tried to have us blown up."

"I know."

"And you *did* indirectly blow me up, so you pretty much have to do what I say."

"I know that too."

"But you won't."

"No."

"Is there anything I can say or do to change your mind?"

"No. Come on, don't cry."

"Fuck you. Why do you have to be such a dickhead all the time? Will you be careful, at least?"

"Yes."

"Good. Try to remember, for me, how shitty you are at getting yourself killed."

"It was small. Pink and gold. Tacky, like a souvenir from somewhere. It had a business card in it, facedown."

"Then someone must have given it to me. Where are you going with this? Are you asking me for an ashtray?"

"No. I don't need one. I don't know anybody whose business card catches fire."

It startles him.

He says "This might be a good time for you to leave."

"You'll want to hear this."

"I doubt it."

"Okay." I start to rise.

"Hold on," he says. "Are you *accusing* me of something?"

I sit back down.

"I'm accusing you of hiring Tom Marvell to go to White Lake with the Palin party."

"What?" he says. "*Why?*"

"Probably not to rat me out to the Mob, if Marvell's the one who did that—which he probably is, intentionally or otherwise. *Someone* found out I was there, and almost killed me and Violet because of it, and Marvell's the most likely suspect."

"And you think *I'm* the reason Marvell went to Minnesota?"

"He was here before he was there. With his souvenir Vegas ashtray—I mean, what other place still has souvenir ashtrays? And his flaming business card."

"That's a leap."

"You can waste as much of my time as you want to."

Rec Bill studies me. Eventually says "I interviewed Marvell to go check out the lake monster before I interviewed you. We didn't see eye to eye, so I went with you instead. I was as surprised as anyone else when he turned up in Ford. I'd shown him the letter and video in complete confidence."

"You're saying he went on the White Lake trip on his own?"

"As far as I know. If he'd been working for me, why wouldn't I have told you about it?"

"Why wouldn't you have told me you'd interviewed him after I sent you an e-mail saying he was there? Why wouldn't you have told Violet? For that matter, why wouldn't you have had Violet pick him up at the airport?"

"I have a lot employees. And a lot of things on my mind."

"With Violet falling into both of those categories."

Rec Bill's mouth tightens. "Finish your insinuating and get out."

"Okay. You tried to hire Marvell when he was here in this office, but it didn't work out. Either he said no or he asked for too much money and *you* said no. So you hired Michael Bennett of Desert Eagle Investigations to do the job you had asked Marvell to do—which was in fact *not* the job of checking out the lake monster. And when Violet and I busted Mr. Bennett trying to take pictures of us in what he thought was the same bed, you went crawling back to Marvell and paid him whatever he wanted. You even paid Sarah Palin to give Marvell a ride and a cover story—something that must have cost a fortune, and implies that you already knew that Palin was going to be the ref but had chosen not to share that information with me or Violet. Because if you had, we'd have known you didn't give a shit who the ref was, and therefore that you didn't give a shit whether there was a monster in White Lake or not. You were afraid of your two million dollars going to Reggie Trager, but other than that the hoax meant nothing to you. You just wanted someone to spy on Violet Hurst. While you sent her into the woods with someone so completely different from you that if she fucked me it would prove to you that she couldn't possibly be in love with you."

Rec Bill's poker face isn't bad. It's not great, though, either.

"That's insane," he says.

"It's not exactly mature, in any case. In fact it's more like the behavior of a twelve-year-old."

"Get the hell out of my office. Then get the hell off my campus."

"Stop calling it a campus. It's a fucking office park. Are you teaching French lit here somewhere?"

"Get out. And another thing. If you say a word of any of this to Violet, I will destroy you."

"Violet's my friend. I'll tell her the truth."

"So you're *blackmailing* me?"

"No. I said I'll tell her the truth. Which I will, no matter what you do or say."

He looks at me with cold eyes that gradually soften and fill with tears. If it's a performance, it's passable.

"You don't know what it's like," he finally says. "How hard it is for me to trust people."

"I'd cry you a river, but it's probably faster for you to just buy one."

"I need you to help me with her."

"No thanks. I won't try to turn her against you, but I sure as hell won't help you win her over."

"That's...fair enough." He starts to say something, then stops.

"What?"

"Did you and she...? When you went back to White Lake?"

"Oh, for fuck's sake!" I say. "*Ask* her! Ask her whatever you want. She might not answer, but at least you'll be behaving like a grown-up."

"You're right. I know. I'm sorry."

He slumps, staring down at his desk. Or at his feet. With all that glass it's hard to tell.

"Do you... want more money?" he finally says.

"No. What you owe me should be enough. What I want is help spending it."

EPILOGUE

37

Gelin, North Dakota
Eight Months Later

I'm in the armchair by the window, trying to figure out
the Image Challenge in the *New England Journal,* when
the first bullet hits the glass. The image is of two hands
with actual horns growing out of them.* Thanks to the
pressure switch under the chair, the lights are off by the
time I reach the floor.

The second shot sprays a small amount of glass into
the room, which means the sniper's using something
heavier than I expected—a Steyr .50, maybe, like Austria
sells to Iran. Since by "glass," obviously, I mean sixty-
six-millimeter Kevenex laminate mounted on shock
absorbers.

---

* I still don't know what the correct diagnosis is.

The window's doomed. Fine with me. I'm already crawling fast along the line of luminescent iron oxide tape that runs across the floor from the chair to the trapdoor. And the bullets can only come in straight-on, since what look like venetian blinds are actually steel slats anchored into the floor and the ceiling. They're meant to force snipers to use the cover spots I set up for them on the bluffs facing the house. They appear to be doing that.

I slide down through the trap and close the door, which is from a safe by Nationwide that's rated for light-aircraft impact and ten hours of chemical-fueled fire. Then I get on the sled.

The cement tunnel that Rec Bill's allegedly untraceable construction company backhoed for me is two hundred yards long: about thirty seconds of sled time. The bunker at the far end is so cramped that my poster of Geronimo stretches from the ceiling to the floor.

I close the second hatch and turn on the strip to the monitors.

Both snipers are where they should be. Six other paramilitary geeks are coming toward the house from the "shoulder" directions, to stay out of the line of their own sniper fire as long as possible. There may be more, but the companies that train these losers favor groups of eight, because that's the size of a typical Navy SEAL "boat team" and because any more than that tend to get in each other's way. And to get into fights with each other. People become hitmen for a variety of reasons—true sociopathy, military training paired with a willingness to do anything for money, a pathological need to feel like James Bond—but social skills aren't high on the list.

On the broad-spectrum monitor I can see they're wear-

ing infrared chemlights on lariats to differentiate themselves from the target.* That's okay. I've got a bucket of
chemlights next to the can of UV-reflecting spray paint I
thought they might use to mark themselves instead. Since
they didn't, I go ahead and put on my assault vest.

The best news, by far, is the helicopter. It's moving into
place right over the house, clear on the monitor, posi-
tioned to have a shot at me if I go out any of the doors.
Helicopters, and people who can fly them, are expensive.
And the house is packed with easily enough TATP to take
it down.

It's still too early for that, though. Or even for blowing
the sniper positions. The paramilitary geeks haven't
tripped any of the anti-personnel mines yet. Once they do,
I'll flip the rest of the switches with one hand, then go
outside and hunt down the stragglers. After, naturally,
frying out their night-vision goggles with the various
exotic-spectrum lamps I've put in the trees.

It's likely to be a massacre, which is unfortunate. Then
again, I didn't ask anybody to come here. All I did was
apply for a notary public license under a false name but
with my real thumbprint and this address, something fel-
ons sometimes do to get gun licenses. At the time, I worried it might be too subtle.

Are the things I'm about to do justified? Who knows?
If you count Teng, McQuillen's scheme killed five people.
My own trip to Minnesota left Dylan Arntz, four of Deb-
bie Schneke's Boys, and the eight guys sent by Locano
dead—and almost killed Violet Hurst, Sheriff Albin,
Debbie Schneke herself, and Albin's deputy. My fault,

---

* Meaning me.

yes, for getting involved, but the only way to keep something like that from happening again is to either keep running—meaning never work as a doctor under any name, stay out of public view, don't associate with anyone, and hope I get a lot luckier than last time—or fight back. Hurt the mob so badly they realize David Locano's vendetta isn't worth pursuing. Should I wait until I'm in a corner? Maybe I already am. Corners tend to be where you imagine them.

What argues *against* my doing this, I know—besides the fact that I've just spent eleven years trying *not* to kill people, mostly successfully, and to make up for having done so in the past—is how enjoyable it's likely to be. How enjoyable it already is.

The skills I'm about to unleash are things to be ashamed of, and I *am* ashamed of them. They're also fun as fuck to use, and pretending otherwise won't change what's about to happen.

I put my hand on the switches.

I mean, why lie?

APPENDIX

CANDIDATES FOR POINT OF NO RETURN ON CLIMATE CHANGE and WHAT TO DO ABOUT IT NOW

by Violet Hurst

Part I. Candidates for Point of No Return

November 2010. Americans who believe that their most pressing problem is that rich people and corporations aren't free enough to fuck them elect a Republican majority to the House of Representatives.*

In December, a month before John Boehner becomes Speaker of the House, a spokesman for him says "The Select

---

* I know: Obama had proved a massive disappointment to anyone with progressive interests, and Democrats in Congress hadn't done much to mark themselves as either honest or interested in public welfare. But that only explains *apathy*. It doesn't explain *actively voting Republican*, two

Committee on Global Warming was created by Democrats simply to provide political cover to pass their job-killing national energy tax. It is unnecessary, and taxpayers will not have to fund it in the 112th Congress." In February, Republicans introduce legislation prohibiting the Environmental Protection Agency from trying to limit greenhouse gases. Representative Darrell Issa of California, suspected car thief and arsonist and now incoming chairman of the House Oversight Committee, having already called funding for climate science "a tsunami* of opacity, waste, fraud, and abuse," promises yet another investigation of "Climategate," the fake scandal that has already been discredited by five previous investigations.† This while ocean acidity approaches the level past which shellfish won't be able to make shells.

This date is important, and it raises the perennial question of which of these assholes know full well that climate change is real and are selling out to secure whatever advantage they can get for themselves and their families before everything goes to hell, and which ones are sufficiently stupid or blinded by fear to actually not see what's going on.

But it's way too late to be a contender for the point of no return.

January 2010. The U.S. Supreme Court rules that corporations, despite never dying or doing jail time, have the same

---

years after Republicans caused the worldwide financial meltdown. Write your love of anarchistic nihilism on your Doc Martens, if you must. Shoot your own hand off. Don't vote *Republican,* for fuck's sake.

* Laugh it up.

† The bitching about "Climategate," like the Tea Party itself, was brought to us by oil billionaires Charles and David Koch. Other disinterested parties calling for further "investigation" of "Climategate" include the government of Saudi Arabia.

First Amendment rights as humans—including the right to spend unlimited amounts of money on political advertising.*

This decision destroys any balance that may have existed between people and corporations in the United States, and cripples U.S. democracy in general, but again is way too late for serious consideration.

April 2009. Failure of the Copenhagen Climate Conference, an event notable for intransigence on the part of the United States and China and for public indifference following the disclosure that professional golfer Tiger Woods had sex with women he wasn't married to.†

---

* The case is *Citizens United v. Federal Elections Commission*. Previous Supreme Court cases had addressed the concept of "corporate personhood," but this one put it over the top, and has the clearest set of fingerprints on it—particularly given that the original decision granting corporations rights (beyond the simple right to enter into a contract), *Santa Clara County v. Southern Pacific Railroad Company* (1886), may have mischaracterized the intent of the Supreme Court. Supreme Court decisions are always published with a "head note" by the court reporter that summarizes the action. In *Santa Clara,* the court reporter, who was for some reason J. C. Bancroft Davis, formerly president of the Newburgh and New York Railway, wrote that the justices had unanimously agreed that corporations should enjoy rights under the Fourteenth Amendment, which had been passed eighteen years earlier to establish the rights of former slaves. The actual opinion doesn't say this, though, and in fact Chief Justice Morrison White specifically told Bancroft that "we avoided meeting the constitutional question in the decision" in deciding *Santa Clara.* Which is why *Santa Clara*—which gave American corporations Fourteenth Amendment protections thirty-four years before American women got them—was, until *Bush v. Gore,* often called the worst Supreme Court decision of all time.

† **Guest footnote by Pietro Brnwa**: Similarly, see the June 2009 failure of the Iranian "Green Revolution" after Michael Jackson died and suddenly no one gave a shit.

Not even close, though it's nice to see golf and the people who love it* doing even more to fuck up the environment.

December 2000. After the United States elects Al Gore, the Supreme Court prohibits an accurate counting of votes from Florida, making George W. Bush president.

Republican scumbag and secretary of state of Florida Katherine Harris,† who despite being co-chair of George W. Bush's campaign in Florida is also in charge of certifying Florida's vote, provokes the case by stopping the count in the first place.

This is such a classic that people forget that prior to it there was still an operating fiction that Supreme Court justices aren't political. For example, in 1987, Republican senator Orrin Hatch said "If the [Supreme Court] judges themselves begin to base their decisions on political criteria, we will have lost the reasoning processes of the law which have served us so well to check political excesses and fervor over the last 200 years."‡

---

* Again with the John Boehner.

† 1994: Insurance company Riscorp Inc. makes an illegal $20,000 donation to Katherine Harris's campaign for state senate. 1996: Harris sponsors a bill that makes it harder for companies that aren't Riscorp to underwrite workers' compensation insurance in Florida. 2004: Harris, now a member of the U.S. Congress, tells an audience that a Middle Eastern man has been arrested for trying to bomb the electrical power grid in Indiana, although this has not actually happened. 2006: Harris loses a reelection bid after being discovered to have taken illegal contributions from defense contractor MZM, whom she subsequently helped to get federal contracts. Incidentally, Harris's grandfather Ben Hill Griffin Jr. was one of the 300 richest people in America. I'm not saying this makes her a bad person. I'm saying *What sort of lowlife who's as rich as Katherine Harris is sells out her constituents for $20,000?*

‡ Current justices Scalia and Thomas are both known to have attended the Koch brothers' annual meeting of conservative political activists, at which attendance is limited to 200.

It's also a strong contender. Al Gore's wealth, like that of George W. Bush, comes from selling political favors to oil companies,* and Gore's running mate later showed himself to be entirely aligned with corporate interests. But in reality there is very little chance Gore could have done a worse job than Bush on the environment.†

Still, choosing this option ignores things like the role of "Green" Party spoiler candidate and narcissist Ralph Nader, and ignores the fact that enough people willingly voted for Bush and Nader to make the election stealable. Write it on your tombstones, dipshits.

July 1997. Unanimous passage by the U.S. Senate (including Al Gore) of the Byrd-Hagel Resolution, which voiced opposition to ratifying the Kyoto Protocol on the grounds that China hadn't ratified.

This is a nice *"fuck y'all—including us!,"* and ratifying Kyoto would have set a precedent for international cooperation on the environment. But on its own the Kyoto Protocol was too weak to significantly slow down climate change anyway.

November 1979–January 1981. Iran takes sixty-six Americans hostage during the Carter administration, and doesn't

---

* Also tobacco. But mostly oil.

† For example, to his Council on Environmental Quality, which is the primary environmental instrument of the executive branch, George W. Bush appointed (as chairman) James L. Connaughton, who had formerly lobbied for the Aluminum Company of America and the Chemical Manufacturers Association of America, and (as chief of staff) Philip Cooney, a former lobbyist for the American Petroleum Institute. After Cooney got whistle-blown for changing the results of government global warming studies to favor the oil industry, he was hired by the public affairs department of ExxonMobil.

release them until six minutes into the Reagan administration,* thereby convincing a lot of Americans that a slick corporate tool selling sham "morning in America" optimism was somehow an improvement over a (granted) kook who, despite taking money from oil interests himself, at least *said* he wanted to reduce U.S. dependence on foreign oil. As environmentalists, Reagan's appointees—such as EPA head Anne Gorsuch, who didn't believe the federal government should *have* an environmental policy, and became the first agency director in history to be charged with contempt of Congress—were actually worse than those of George W. Bush.

This is another strong possibility. Until 9/11, the Iranian hostilities were the biggest hint Americans got of what happens when the oil industry drives politics. That their response was to flee into shortsighted denial continues to define American politics today.

Plus, as a year, 1979 has other things going for it. Like that it was the year Saudi billionaires Salem bin Laden (cousin of Osama bin Laden) and Khalid bin Mahfouz (brother-in-law of Osama bin Laden) provided startup funds for Arbusto, George W. Bush's first business venture. And that David Koch (see above) ran for vice president, an experience said to have convinced him and his brother to seek political change covertly rather than overtly.

---

* There's no evidence that the Republicans and Iranians colluded in the election of Ronald Reagan. It's just that eleven members of the Reagan administration were later convicted of illegally trading weapons to Iran (during an embargo led by the United States!) for a *different* set of hostages. Details about even *that* arms-for-hostages deal are hard to come by, though, because George Bush Sr., as one of his last official acts, pardoned everyone who had been or might be convicted in relation to it. On Christmas Eve. Tis-the-Season act of mercy, or timed so that as few people as possible would read about it in the newspaper the next day? You be the judge.

* * *

November 1962. Report commissioned by JFK from the Committee on Natural Resources of the National Academy of Sciences/National Resource Council predicts that endless clean energy from fusion will be achieved "possibly within a decade but more likely within a generation," thereby (the argument goes) convincing the Kennedy administration and subsequent administrations to ignore conservation or environmental protection.*

Serious climate nerds often choose this one, but mostly so they can identify each other at conferences. Personally I'm not that into it. If you're going to believe that anyone read this report, took it seriously, and based policy decisions on it, then you have to assume the same people read—but completely ignored—sentences in the report like this one:

> Man is altering the balance of a relatively stable system by his pollution of the atmosphere with smoke, fumes, and particles from fossil fuels, industrial chemicals, and radioactive material; by his alteration of the energy and water balance at the earth's surface by deforestation, afforestation [i.e., planting of new forests—not sure this one's turned out to be that big of a problem], cultivation of land, shading, mulching, overgrazing grasslands, reduction of evapotranspiration [i.e., the vital part of the water cycle where plants evaporate water off the tops of their leaves to produce suction, which draws nutrients up through their circulatory systems], irrigation, draining of large swamp lands, and the building of cities and highways; by his clearing forests and alterations of plant surface cover, changing the reflectivity of the earth's surface and soil structures; by his land-filling, construction of

---

* I believe the expression "renewable resource" comes from this report.

buildings and seawalls, and pollution, bringing about radical changes in the ecology of estuarine areas; by changes he effects in the biologic balance and the physical relocation of water basins through the erection of dams and channel works; and by the increasing quantities of carbon dioxide an industrial society releases to the atmosphere.

And besides, the idea that people knew this shit in 1962 and didn't do anything about it is, even for me, too depressing to dwell on.

1953. Public relations firm Hill & Knowlton, on behalf of the tobacco industry, devises the strategy of "constructing controversy," by which corporations pay crackpots to dispute scientifically proven concepts, then accuse the press of partiality if their shills aren't given equal time with people who know what they're talking about.

This is actually a very strong contender, in my opinion. The practice is in wider use than ever (the term "false equivalency" has become a popular way to describe it), and it's been modified by the understanding that—up to the point where the media won't tolerate it, which has yet to be located—the more extreme your manufactured dissent, the further you can push the "centrist" position from the truth.

1895. Henry Ford, then an executive of the Edison Illuminating Company, dedicates himself to researching gasoline engines. Alternately: 1870 (first mobile gasoline engine), 1860 (first mass-produced internal combustion engine), 1823 (first internal combustion engine to be used industrially), etc.

I don't like calling inventions and discoveries disasters. Technology's not evil; it just evolves quickly and without clear goals or ethics, requiring us to constantly defend a place for humanity in the world it makes. What causes technology to *behave* like it's evil is corporate greed. Like General Motors establishing a special unit in 1922 to buy and dismantle functioning electric public transportation systems across America. Or Congress making that kind of thing easier for GM and other companies to do by passing the Public Utility Holding Company Act of 1935.

1879–83. The War of the Pacific. This is not a cause, but it *is* a pretty egregiously missed lesson. The war was over deposits of bat and seagull shit in the Caribbean, which had been discovered to be an ideal source of fertilizer, and had enabled a boom in agricultural output—with resulting booms in population and urbanization.* Bat and seagull shit are renewable in the sense that bats and seagulls continue, where available, to shit, but the deposits in the Caribbean had taken millions of years to form and were depleted within sixty years of being found. If petroleum hadn't been discovered to replace them, there would have been a population crash *then*.†

It's a great illustration of the human tendency to quickly exhaust resources that took what paleontologists call "geologic time" to form, but there are a lot of those.‡

---

* For example: between 1819 and 1891 the population of New York City went from a hundred thousand to three million.

† Other shit, even from birds, just doesn't have the same nitrogen-phosphorus-potassium ratio.

‡ The most popular is probably Easter Island, where workers cut down all the trees to make statues honoring wealthy people's ancestors—a process that sped up as it went along, because people became more and more desperate for the spirits of wealthy people's ancestors to save them from deforestation. Eventually the military took over, 90 percent of the population died, and the survivors started toppling the statues. And that was *before* the Europeans started selling the Easter Islanders into slavery.

* * *

Fifth century BC. Consolidation of the Book of Genesis, with its claim, no doubt useful for the political demographics of the time,* that "God blessed them and said to them, 'Be fruitful and increase in number; fill the earth and subdue it....I give you every seed-bearing plant on the face of the whole earth and every tree that has fruit with seed in it. They will be yours for food.'"

Now, there are several messages you can imagine taking from this passage. One of the more obvious is that God wants us to be vegetarian. Another is that, once the earth *has* been filled and subdued, God might want us to fucking *stop over-breeding*. I mean, most people who read "lather, rinse, repeat" don't keep doing it until their scalp is a chunky mess of gore. They just can't seem to apply the same logic to the Bible.† The message they insist on seeing is that God for some reason wants us to pursue maximal reproduction until it kills off us and most of His other non-insect creatures.

Another example: we tend to think of whaling as primarily an olde-timey activity, because of *Moby Dick* and so on, but 75 percent of the world's whales were actually killed after WW2, by countries looking to use whale oil to supplement their petroleum supplies during the postwar oil shortage.

And one more: before mass human agriculture, most of the Middle East was forested. That's right: there was a time when people who used the term "the Fertile Crescent" weren't just being sarcastic.

* World population in 500 BC is unknown but is likely to have been under 200 million—less than 3 percent of what it is now.

† Or to the Constitution: the Second Amendment says "A well regulated Militia, being necessary to the security of a free State, the right of the people to keep and bear Arms, shall not be infringed," which people like to interpret as meaning that gun control is unconstitutional. But I'm pretty sure there's a "well regulated" in there somewhere.

But people will interpret *anything* in self-serving ways, so it's hard to blame what ended up being the Bible. Give people a genetics textbook, and when they read that they're going to pass on only half of their unique genes to their kids, and only a quarter to their grandkids, and only an eighth to their great-grandkids, at least some of them are going to say *"Damn—it says I need to have eight kids."*

If I had to choose, I'd go with Reagan / Carter / Iran 1979–80. It was the great turning-away from reality, and it happened the same year William R. Catton's *Overshoot: The Ecological Basis of Revolutionary Change* was published.

Because *that* was such an effective warning.

Part II: What to Do About It Now

Easy. First: plant ten billion trees. Then: Rubik's Vagina. Same pass rate as the cube, only *with* using the guidebook.

It's my idea, but you can have it for free.

SOURCES

This book is a work of fiction. While the sources mentioned below have been helpful in conceiving it, the book does not necessarily reflect those sources' findings or opinions with any accuracy. Nor is it intended to. That said, and strictly for people who care about this kind of thing:

My understanding of what it's like to be a doctor in **the cruise ship industry** owes thanks to the doctors and patients who have shared their experiences with me personally (MW in particular) and those who have seen fit to share them publicly, such as Gary Podolsky, John Bradberry, and Andrew Lucas, not all of whom perceive the industry in a negative light. For background I am indebted to *Devils on the Deep Blue Sea: The Dreams, Schemes and Showdowns That Built America's Cruise-Ship Empires*, by Kristoffer A. Garin, 2006 (including for information about the 1981 strike),* and the Cruise Lines International Association guidelines for medical facilities.

The figure of approximately $7,000 a year for some cruise ship employees is from the "Policy Guidelines Governing the Approval of ITF [International Transport Workers' Federation] Acceptable CBA's [collective-bargaining agreements] for Cruise Ships Flying Flags of Convenience," aka the ITF Miami Guidelines, 2004,† which to my knowledge have not been updated, and which *suggest* a minimum monthly basic wage for cruise ship workers of $302, rising to $608 when combined with overtime and leave. In "Sovereign Islands: A Special Report; For Cruise Ships' Workers, Much Toil, Little Protection," by Douglas Frantz, the *New York Times,* 24 Dec 1999, Frantz writes that "for laboring as long as 18 hours a day, seven days a week, most galley workers are paid $400 to $450 a month." Details on some of the expenses of cruise ship workers are from Garin, above. Note also that the flag-of-convenience registry for Liberia is run by a private company in Virginia.‡

The best piece of writing that I know of on the industry from the perspective of a passenger, even if you include *The Poseidon Adventure,* is the title essay of *A Supposedly Fun Thing I'll Never Do Again: Essays and Arguments,* by David Foster Wallace, 1997. Wallace's essay is remarkable for how much behind-the-scenes information he was able to intuit even as it was hidden from him.

As far as I know there is no cruise ship with a Nintendo Dome, but if there is I hope it's called the *Mario D'Orio.*

---

* Famously at the time, the striking workers held up a sign inviting the press—who instead mocked them from shore for being illiterate—to "COME ON BOARD AND LEARN THE TROUT."

† http://www.itfglobal.org/files/seealsodocs/884/Miami%20Guidelines%202004.pdf

‡ http://www.itfseafarers.org/files/publications/4076/globalisingsolidarity.pdf

* * *

What Violet Hurst describes as **catastrophic paleontology** is primarily the mix of sociology, anthropology, and ecology that was pioneered by William R. Catton Jr. in the 1970s, and that is sometimes called either environmental sociology or human ecology. (Catton himself is a sociologist who has concentrated on environmental issues for most of his career.) Obviously the observation that human population growth tends to check itself in unpleasant ways goes back at least to Malthus, and books like *The Forest and the Sea,* by zoologist Marston Bates,* 1960, and *Silent Spring,* by marine biologist Rachel Carson, 1962, laid immediate groundwork for Catton. But as far as I know it was Catton who first applied concepts and technical terms from wildlife management, like "carrying capacity," to human populations. His book *Overshoot: The Ecological Basis of Revolutionary Change,* 1980, remains definitive. One particularly elegant descendant of *Overshoot* is *A Short History of Progress,* by Ronald Wright, 2004, which in fact everyone on earth should read, and which has been particularly helpful to me here. I have also consulted Wright's other two books, *Stolen Continents: The "New World" Through Indian Eyes,* 1993, and *What Is America?: A Short History of the New World Order,* for information about Native American populations. (See below.)

For information on a potential **oil crash,** I am indebted to Richard Heinberg, particularly his books *The Party's Over: Oil, War and the Fate of Industrial Societies,* 2003, and *Blackout: Coal, Climate and the Last Energy Crisis,* 2009. See also

---

* Something I find particularly compelling in Bates is his observation that designed objects (and by extension designed spaces and "realities" and so on) tend to be drearier than natural ones in part simply because they have a lower level of detail—that just as we erase species from our reality, we also erase other kinds of complexity, to our detriment. See *The Forest and the Sea,* pg. 254.

the 2008 cable from the U.S. embassy in Saudi Arabia to the CIA, U.S. Treasury, and U.S. Department of Energy that says "A series of major project delays and accidents…over the last couple of years is evidence that Saudi Aramco [the Saudi national oil company] is having to run harder to stay in place—to replace the decline in existing production."* For more on **government subsidies to oil companies** see, for example, "As Oil Industry Fights a Tax, It Reaps Subsidies," by David Kocieniewski, the *New York Times*, 3 July 2010.

The idea that the **melting of the methane hydrate shelf,** by which is generally meant the East Siberian Shelf, might cause an irreversible climate change loop is to my knowledge most closely associated with the work of Natalia Shakhova, PhD, of the International Arctic Research Center of the University of Alaska, Fairbanks. See, for example, "Methane Hydrate Feedbacks," by NE Shakhova and IP Semiletov, in *Arctic Climate Feedbacks: Global Implications,* Sommerkorn and Hassol, eds., 2009.

For a **counter-argument** (granted, pre-Fukushima) **saying nuclear power *will* become a viable replacement for oil,** see *Power to Save the World: The Truth About Nuclear Energy,* by Gwyneth Cravens, 2007. For a **counter-counter argument** I recommend the chapter on Three Mile Island in *Inviting Disaster: Lessons from the Edge of Technology,* by James R. Chiles, 2002, which is a great book anyway and introduced me to Karl Weick and "cosmology episodes." For moral support and ongoing updates I am thankful to the weekly feature on nuclear power on Harry Shearer's radio broadcast, *Le Show.*

For the parts of catastrophic paleontology that are actually **paleontology,** I owe thanks to *T. Rex and the Crater of Doom: The story that waited 65 million years to be told—how a giant*

---

* Released by WikiLeaks and published online in "US embassy cables: US queries Saudi Arabia's influence over oil prices," guardian.co.uk, 8 Feb 2011.

impact killed the dinosaurs, and how the crater was discovered, by Walter Alvarez, 2008, which is readable and authoritative and also an unfortunate example of the modern tendency to put Internet search words into the titles of books. Alvarez and his father, Luis Alvarez, discovered that the climate changes that killed the dinosaurs came from a six-mile-wide asteroid plowing into the ground in Chicxulub, Mexico. Also helpful was *Bones Rock!: Everything You Need to Know to Be a Paleontologist,* by Peter Larson and Kristin Donnan, 2004.

The **pictograph of a serpentlike creature menacing a moose** exists in the Boundary Waters exactly as I have described it, but the location given for it in chapter 12 is fictional. Its actual location is Darky Lake.*

"It's a cold hard world, love, and these are cold hard times" is, obviously, a quote from "Cold Hard Times," by Lee Hazlewood.

The **100,000 golf balls on the bottom of Loch Ness** figure is from "The Burden and Boon of Lost Golf Balls," by Bill Pennington, the *New York Times,* 2 May 2010. The golf balls were located in a 2009 submersible sonar search for the monster.

For insight into **American small towns plagued by meth,** including that meth gangsters sometimes take low-level factory jobs as cover, I am particularly indebted to *Methland: The Death and Life of an American Small Town*, by Nick Reding, 2009. *Methland* is excellent and makes a particularly compelling argument about how meth appeals to the working poor by initially allowing them to work longer hours.

---

* Want to know why Darky Lake is called Darky Lake? Neither do I.

* * *

Sensei Dragonfire is of course Wendi Dragonfire of Nijmegen, in the Netherlands, 9th Dan Shuri-Ryu Karate, 2nd Dan Modern Arnis.

Successful replacement of **avulsed** (knocked-out) **teeth,** with regeneration of nerves, vasculature, and even periodontal ligaments, is indeed possible.* The difficulty of doing controlled experiments on tooth replacement in humans makes statistics hard to come by, but anecdotal evidence suggests it's worth a shot, and numerous-but-too-revolting-to-cite experiments on animals have demonstrated the validity of the principle. In "Milk as an interim storage medium for avulsed teeth," by Frank Courts, William Mueller, and Henry Tabeling, *Pediatric Dentistry* 5:3, 183, 1983, the authors show the superiority of milk as a transport medium over air, water, and the patient's saliva.

I don't remember where I read or heard that **gynecologists used to operate blind** and don't know whether it's true.

The **statistics on cranial bleeding** that Dr. McQuillen cites are from *Neurology Secrets,* by Loren A. Rolak, MD, 4th ed., or at least from my understanding of that book. Also consulted for the discussion were "Factors Associated with Cervical Spine Injury in Children After Blunt Trauma," by Julie C. Leonard et al., online version of *Annals of Emergency Medicine*, 1 Nov 2010, and "Low-risk criteria for cervical-spine radiography in blunt trauma: A prospective study," by Jerome R. Hoffman et al., *Annals of Emergency Medicine,* Volume 21, Issue 12, Dec 1992. As always, if you take any part of this or any other novel as medical advice, you are a dumb fucking idiot.

---

* For details on the biology of the various regenerative processes, see chapter 17 of *Textbook and Color Atlas of Traumatic Injuries to the Teeth,* by J. O. Andreasen, Frances M. Andreasen, and Lara Andersson, 2007.

* * *

According to *The Manga Guide to Calculus,* by H. Kojima and S. Togami, 2009, the **formula relating temperature to the frequency of cricket chirps** is Fc = 7(Tc) - 30, with Fc being the frequency of chirping and Tc the temperature in centigrade. Note that the same equation in Fahrenheit (Tf) looks unwieldy at first (Tf = 9/5[(Fc+30)/7]+32)) but reduces to Fc/0.26 + 39.71, which is usably close (particularly if crickets are less than perfectly accurate) to Tf = 4(Fc)+40, or Tf = 4(Fc+10). The metric system still rules, though. As Judith Stone says, "If God wanted us to use the metric system, he would have given us ten fingers and ten toes."*

The author of the **"Funny how it's 'Gonna give you every inch of my love…'"** pickup line has given permission for its use here but has requested to remain anonymous. He (I'll give you that much) is thanked.

Americans clearly have a strong interest in **preventative medicine,** since they spend $34 billion on unproven and unregulated health "supplements" annually,† just not in preventative medicine that actually works. American doctors, meanwhile, technically *can* bill for discussing preventative medicine with their patients, but can't actually make a living that way. The way to get paid as a doctor in the U.S. is to do as many "procedures" as possible to repair or diagnose already-existing conditions.‡ Since the doctor

---

* *Light Elements: Essays in Science from Gravity to Levity,* 1991.

† *Consumer Reports* blog for 3 Aug 2009. If corporations have rights, why can't *Consumer Reports* run for president?

‡ When I graduated from medical school the most competitive field to enter was dermatology, because it was considered a sure path to wealth through easy-to-perform (and schedule) procedures. Family practice—which is where the heroes of the medical profession are, and where, demographically, the U.S. most needs doctors—was among the least competitive. For insight on how

getting paid to do the procedure is usually the doctor deciding whether the procedure is necessary, there's an obvious potential conflict of interest. The healthcare industry (hospitals and so on) and the pharmaceutical and medical-equipment industries encourage excessive procedures as well. Opposing this, in principle, are government programs (which have odd quirks designed to lower the costs of procedures, like only paying full price for one procedure per visit*) and the private insurance industry, which profits by refusing payment for anything they can, regardless of necessity.† However, the federal government is limited in encour-

_____

hard it is to get paid as a family practitioner, see "10 billing and coding tips to boost your reimbursement," by Joel J. Heidelbaugh and Margaret Riley, *The Journal of Family Practice,* Nov 2008, Vol. 57, No. 11: 724–730.

* Notes *General Surgery News:* "A benign 1.5cm lesion of the face would be billed [to Medicare in Alabama] at $140; if you subsequently remove 3 more lesions of similar size, they would be reimbursed at $70 for a total of $350." However: "When ultrasound guidance is added to a fine-needle aspiration (FNA; CPT code 10022), the physician can bill with code 76942, which reimburses $120 for the FNA, whereas the ultrasound component reimburses $150." ("Minor Pay for Minor Procedures? Think Again: General Surgeons May Be Leaving Much on the Table By Passing on Minor Surgery," by Lucian Newman III, *GSN,* Dec 2009, 36:12.)

† A 2009 report from the Committee on Energy and Congress of the U.S. House of Representatives (which at the time was controlled by Democrats) found that insurance companies had been routinely rescinding (without refund) coverage because patients failed to inform insurance companies of pre-existing conditions they didn't know they had, because of errors in paperwork not committed by the patient, and "for discrepancies unrelated to the conditions for which patients seek medical care," as well as rescinding coverage to the dependents of rescinded patients and evaluating insurance company employees based on how much money they were able to "save" the insurance companies through rescinding policies. For a PDF of this report, go to http://democrats.energycommerce.house.gov/Press_111/20090616/rescission_supplemental.pdf.

aging preventative medicine because of the above industries (as well as the food industry) and political opposition to any sane improvement of the healthcare system. Meanwhile private insurance companies tend to operate on profit cycles (and, more important, CEO bonus cycles) shorter than things like diet and exercise are able to affect.* The role of patients in all this is complicated. On one hand, they're expected to make informed decisions to turn down unnecessary (or worse) interventions. On the other hand, they're often accused of trying to coerce doctors into prescribing and performing expensive treatments that are unlikely to work—something pretty much anyone with the life of someone they cared about on the line would do.

For information about **the Soudan Mine** and the twenty-three-story-deep **High Energy Physics Lab of the University of Minnesota** (which because of its isolation from cosmic rays is currently conducting the Cryogenic Dark Matter Search and the High Energy Main Injector Neutrino Search) I am grateful to my volunteer guides to both.

For information about **law enforcement in Lake County** I am grateful to the City of Ely Police Department, particularly Barbara A. Matthews and Chief of Police John Manning, both of whom were exceptionally kind and generous. This book is not in any way meant to be a depiction of that department or its personnel, or of actual events in or around Ely. Nor is it an accurate depiction of the Lake County Sheriff's Department, about which I know nothing except that it exists.

The chapter on **the origin of the canoe** from the perspective of Sheriff Albin is, to quote Sam Purcell, "drawn without

---

* Also, the results of poor diet and exercise habits tend to be "pre-existing conditions."

reference material."* However, the name Two Persons is an obvious reference to the work of the great Wayne Johnson, whose series of novels taking place in northern Minnesota began with *Don't Think Twice*, 2000.

The preference of (at least some) mobsters for **Canoe by Dana** cologne and aftershave is mentioned in *The Ice Man: Confessions of a Mafia Contract Killer,* by Philip Carlo, 2007. It's one of the confessions.

   Regarding **whether the medical records of dead people are confidential information,** note that the Supreme Court decision in *Office of Independent Counsel v. Favish,* 2003, was to disallow public access to photographs of the dead body of deputy White House counsel Vincent Foster, whose suicide ten years earlier continues to be a point of fascination for right-wing conspiracy nuts. (For more on the decision see "In Vincent Foster case, court upholds privacy," by Warren Richey, the *Christian Science Monitor,* 31 Mar 2004.) One reason the issue is less than clear is that Medicare pays for some autopsies, but only indirectly, as part of general hospital fees. Which kind of half-defines autopsies as healthcare procedures.

The term "spandrel" as a biological (vs. architectural) entity was coined in "The Spandrels of San Marco and the Panglossian Paradigm: A Critique of the Adaptationist Programme," by Stephen J. Gould and Richard C. Lewontin, *Proceedings of the Royal Society of London. Series B, Biological Sciences,* Vol. 205, No. 1161, 21 Sept 1979. The overall argument is that since biological traits develop within complex organisms rather than independently, they are always subject to conditions beyond that of the strict Darwinian imperative. The literal spandrels of San Marco are decorative-appearing details that are in

---

* *Sam and Max: Freelance Police,* Issue #1, 1987.

fact (the authors say) "necessary architectural by-products of mounting a dome on rounded arches." (There's even a body of literature questioning whether the *metaphor* is valid, i.e., whether architectural spandrels are really decorative or not.) The quote from Ronald Pies, MD, is from a citation in "The Evolutionary Calculus of Depression," by Jerry A. Coyne, PhD, *Psychiatric Times,* 26 May 2010.* Both Pies and Coyne are refuting claims that depression is, on its own, an evolutionary adaptation.

I attended a seminar called **"Is Female Orgasm Adaptive?"** at the University of California, Berkeley, in, I believe, 1987. As I recall, it was led by a woman and there was some arguing. I could be wrong about the date or the place, though. Or any other part of that story.

Physiologist Loren G. Martin states in a brief article in *Scientific American* (**"What is the function of the human appendix**? Did it once have a purpose that has since been lost?," 21 Oct 1999) that "We now know…that the appendix serves an important [endocrine] role in the fetus and in young adults [while a]mong adult humans, the appendix is now thought to be involved primarily in immune functions." However, others (e.g., in passing, Ahmed Alzaraa and Sunil Chaudhry in "An unusually long appendix in a child: a case report," *Cases Journal* 2009, 2: 7398) feel that the case for the immunological and endocrinological function of the appendix, though strong, remains circumstantial.

The Smurfs (originally *Les Schtroumpfs*) is a multiformat marketing and entertainment franchise created by Pierre Culli-

---

* The piece by Pies that Coyne quotes is available (without any obvious date, although it states it was written in response to an essay in the *New York Times Magazine* of 28 Feb 2010) at http://psychcentral.com/blog/archives/2010/03/01/the-myth-of-depressions-upside.

ford in Belgium in the late 1950s that, bizarrely, reimagines the 1953 Josef von Sternberg film *Anatahan* (about a woman stuck on an island with twelve men)* as a children's story, the primary difference being that where Sternberg treats aggression as innate, *The Smurfs* externalizes it onto the figures of a giant (named after Gargamelle, the giantess in Rabelais) and his pet cat Azrael (named after the Islamic and Sikh angel of death).

The principle behind **carbon dating** is that plants and animals take in but don't produce radioactive isotopes of carbon that, over time, degrade, so the amount of those isotopes still in the body shows how long it's been since a particular plant or animal interacted with its environment. It can be used on objects less than 60,000 years old (at which point the amount of radioactive carbon declines to the same as the background) and is generally accurate to +/- 40 years. Accuracy goes way up, however, for plants and animals (including humans) that have been alive since the hydrogen bomb tests of the 1950s, because of the large increase in the amount of radioactive carbon in the atmosphere. See "The Mushroom Cloud's Silver Lining," by David Grimm, *Science*, 321, 12 Sept 2008.

The verses of Matthew in which Jesus says the world will end within a generation are 16:28 and 24:34. Mark 9:1 and Luke 9:27 and 21:32 ("Truly I say to you, this generation will not pass away until all things take place") are similar.

For information about **the hit John Gotti tried to commission from the Aryan Brotherhood,** see "Former Aryan Brother

---

* And said by Ben Dattner, PhD, to have been Jim Morrison's favorite movie.

Testifies That Gang Kingpin Ordered Killings," Associated Press, 14 Apr 2006, etc.

Information about **the burn cycle of the Boundary Waters Canoe Area** is from *The Boundary Waters Wilderness Ecosystem,* by Miron Heinselman, 1996, which is by far the best book I've read on BWCA (Boundary Waters Canoe Area) history and ecology.

The use of alpha-blockers to treat PTSD symptoms is predicated on the theory that the psychological symptoms of PTSD, such as panic and nightmares, are the result rather than the cause of the physical ones, such as increased heart rate and sweating. Their efficacy continues to be debated: see, e.g., "Prazosin for the treatment of posttraumatic stress disorder sleep disturbances," by LJ Miller, *Pharmacotherapy* 28(5), May 2008 vs. "Flawed Studies Underscore Need for More Rigorous PTSD Research," by Aaron Levin, *Psychiatric News* 42(23), 7 Dec 2007. In any case it should not be confused with the use of *beta*-blockers to prevent PTSD by disrupting memory formation immediately after a trauma occurs, which looked good in rat studies but is now itself controversial. (See, e.g., "The efficacy of early propanolol administration at reducing PTSD symptoms in pediatric injury patients: a pilot study," by NR Nugent et al., *Journal of Traumatic Stress* 2010 Apr; 23(2): 282–7, and "Limited efficacy of propranolol on the reconsolidation of fear memories," by EV Muravieva and CM Alberini, *Learning Memory* 1;17(6), Jun 2010.) "Alpha" and "beta" refer to two different kinds of neuronal receptors for adrenaline and adrenaline-like substances. Though many neurons have both alpha- and beta-receptors, the two types send signals with opposite effects: for example, alpha-receptors activated by adrenaline cause blood vessels to contract, while beta-receptors activated by adrenaline cause blood vessels to dilate. This seems contradictory, but factors like the overall blood level of adrenaline favor the dominance of one type at a time.

My primary sources on **the Vietnam War** know who they are and that they have my admiration and thanks. Given how few Americans served in so-called riverine combat in Vietnam, there are surprisingly good secondary sources on the service, possibly because of interest brought about by the 2004 presidential candidacy of John Kerry (and its sabotaging), and possibly because the casualty rate was so horrendously high. My favorite and the most useful to me on the subject has been *Brown Water, Black Berets: Coastal and Riverine Warfare in Vietnam,* by Thomas J. Cutler, 2000. (Cutler is an instructor at the Naval Academy and himself a Vietnam veteran, although the book, which is excellent, is not about his personal experiences.) For a more general look at the experience of Americans serving in the South Vietnamese armed forces, I particularly like *In Pharaoh's Army: Memories of the Lost War,* by Tobias Wolff, 1995.

Note that for Reggie to be a chief radioman and an **E-4** so soon after arriving in Vietnam would not have been unusual given the hierarchy and level of incident of his posting,* and that at the time he enlisted he would have been unlikely to be drafted, since in 1967 the draft was still based on seniority, with twenty-five-year-olds going first and seventeen-year-olds last. The birthday lottery, which sent over teenagers, wasn't instituted until 1969. Ultimately 61 percent of American fatalities in Vietnam were under the age of twenty-one.†

---

* The lieutenant of Reggie's River Assault Group would have reported directly to Rear Admiral Ward, who would have reported directly to General Westmoreland, who would have reported directly to Secretary of Defense McNamara. In other words, Reggie would have been five phone calls from President Johnson.

† http://njscvva.org/vietnam_war_statistics.htm

Robert Mason says he was posted in an area of Vietnam where **thirty-one of thirty-three species of snake were poisonous** in his memoir *Chickenhawk*, 1984. Unfortunate title / great book. Mason was a helicopter pilot who quickly became disillusioned with the war.

Reggie's CPO uses the French word **"antivenin"** rather than "antivenom" because until 1981 that was standard usage (and World Health Organization policy) on the grounds that snake antivenins were invented, in 1895, by Albert Calmette, a French scientist at the Pasteur Institute. Calmette was trying to cure cobra bites occurring in what is now Vietnam.*

For information about **the abilities of various animals to survive very low temperatures** (even including freezing) I am indebted to *Winter World: The Ingenuity of Animal Survival*, by Bernd Heinrich, 2003, which is a beautiful book, along the lines of Konrad Lorenz's best work, that I would recommend to anyone with an interest in nature.

The history of **human cryogenics in the U.S.** runs from the Chatsworth scandal of 1979 to the Alcor scandal of 2003 and beyond, with defrosting and rotting the least of your worries.†

The **mammalian diving reflex** occurs when the participating mammal gets hit in the face with water 21 degrees C (70 degrees F) or colder. Even on a leopard seal, it has to be the face. (See: "Cardiovascular effects of face immersion and factors affecting diving reflex," by Y. Kawakami, B. Natelson, and A. DuBois, *Journal of Applied Physiology*, Vol. 23, No. 6, Dec 1967.)

Incidentally, according to the film version of *Goldfinger*,

---

* See *Molecular, Clinical, and Environmental Toxicology: Volume 2; Clinical Toxicology*, by Andreas Luch, 2010, pg. 250.

† Widely reported. In the case of the Alcor scandal, almost invariably with the word "chilling" in the title. See below note on shellfish.

1964, humans not only *can* breathe through their skin like reptiles and amphibians, but need to and die if they don't. Also according to *Goldfinger,* "Drinking Dom Perignon '53 above 38 degrees Fahrenheit is like listening to the Beatles without earmuffs."

Note that turtles *can* buffer their lactic acid, but only for six months or so of inactivity.

Sherlock Holmes says **"Eliminate all other factors, and the one which remains must be the truth"** in *The Sign of the Four,* 1890. He uses another version of the same phrase later in *The Sign of the Four,* as well as in "The Adventure of the Beryl Coronet," 1892, "Silver Blaze" (my favorite Holmes short story), 1893, "The Adventure of the Priory School," 1905, "The Adventure of the Bruce-Partington Plans," 1917, and "The Adventure of the Blanched Soldier," 1927. So apparently he means it. The other contender for stupidest thing said by Holmes is his report of having met the "head llama" of Tibet in "The Adventure of the Empty House," 1903, which people who have difficulty separating Holmes from reality will tell you was just a spelling error by Watson. Like they don't have llamas in Tibet!*

Although **Sarah Palin** is a real person, the events of this book, as I've said earlier, are entirely fictional. I have never met Palin, nor have any of my characters, who are themselves fictional. I know of no events involving Palin similar to the ones that transpire in Minnesota in the book, and as far as I know I have entirely fabricated the belief system Palin espouses to Pietro in the book, as well as her relationship with anyone like the (also fictional) Reverend John 3:16 Hawke. The character of Palin's young relation is fictional, too, and not meant to resemble any actual relation of Palin's, young or otherwise. Furthermore,

---

* They don't.

although I provide citations below for some references in the book that might be taken to apply to past events from the life of the actual Palin, please note that the actual Palin stands nowhere near the frontline of the anti-rationalist movement in the U.S., even among current and former politicians. For example, as I write this, the Republican frontrunner for the 2012 presidential election is Rick Perry, who as governor of Texas once proclaimed a period of three "Days of Prayer for Rain in the State of Texas,"* and who has publicly repudiated both evolution and human involvement in climate change.†

Palin's quotation of **Westbrook Pegler** in her acceptance speech as Republican candidate for vice president runs, in total, as follows: "And a writer observed, 'We grow good people in our small towns, with honesty and sincerity and dignity,' and I know just the kind of people that writer had in mind when he praised Harry Truman." The second part is particularly odd, since Pegler once called Truman "a thin-lipped hater,"‡ but may simply have to do with the fact that both the line in the speech and the "thin-lipped hater" line appear on the same page in Pat Buchanan's autobiography,§ and maybe the speech

---

* The drought continued. See "Rick Perry's Unanswered Prayers," by Timothy Egan, the *New York Times,* 11 Apr 2011, according to which he also answered a question about how he would govern as president with "I think it's time for us to just hand it over to God, and say, 'God: You're going to have to fix this.'"

† For Perry on evolution, see, e.g., "Rick Perry: evolution is 'theory' with 'gaps,'" by Catalina Camia, *USA Today,* 18 Aug 2011. For Perry on climate change, see, e.g., "Perry Tells N.H. Audience He's a Global-Warming Skeptic—with VIDEO," by Jim O'Sullivan, on website of *National Journal,* 17 Aug 2011; note that it's the article that uses video, not Perry.

‡ Although he may have meant that as a compliment.

§ *Right from the Beginning,* 1990, pg. 31. Buchanan, a turd whose frequent designation as a "paleoconservative" would make Violet Hurst

was concocted in a hurry by someone familiar, but only partly, with that book. Palin describes the writing of the speech as a "team effort" led by Matthew Scully in her memoir, *Going Rogue,* 2009.* For additional details see "The Man Behind Palin's Speech," by Massimo Calabresi, *Time,* 4 Sept 2008. Details on the tightness of the schedule leading up to the speech are from "Palin Disclosures Raise Questions on Vetting," by Elizabeth Bumiller, the *New York Times,* 1 Sept 2008. For more information on Pegler see "Dangerous Minds: William F. Buckley soft-pedals the legacy of journalist Westbrook Pegler in *The New Yorker,*" by Diane McWhorter, *Slate,* 4 Mar 2004, which is my source for the "clearly it is the bounden duty…" quote. My source for the quote about RFK is "Palin and Pegler," by Marty Peretz, the *New Republic,* 13 Sept 2008.

Video of Palin being prayed over by **Pastor Thomas Muthee,** famous for claiming to have successfully battled a witch named Mama Jane in Kenya, in which Muthee asks Jesus to "bring finances her way" and protect Palin from "witchcraft" is available on YouTube and elsewhere under the title "Sarah Palin Gets Protection from Witches."†

---

vomit, speaks of Pegler with admiration, although even he notes that "Peg did go overboard—on not a few occasions."

* Page 187. She describes Scully, a former speechwriter for George W. Bush and Dick Cheney, as "to use author Rod Dreher's term, a 'crunchy con.' A political conservative, he is a bunny-hugging vegan and gentle, green soul who I think would throw himself in the path of a semitruck to save a squirrel." I call the seat not next to that guy.

† If you watch the full 9:47 version (address below), you'll get to see Muthee call Buddhism and Islam "witchcraft and sorcery" and say "In the economic area [it is] high time that we have top Christian businessmen, businesswomen bankers, you know, who are men and women of integrity running the economics of our nations. That is what we are waiting for. That's part and parcel of transformation. If you look at the, you know, if you look at the Israelites, that's how they won, and that's how they are

Palin's mother is quoted recounting **Palin's father's fondness for ambushing seals as they surfaced** in *Trailblazer: An Intimate Biography of Sarah Palin,* by Lorenzo Benet, 2009, pg. 9.*

---

today." Address: http://www.youtube.com/watch?v=jl4HIc-yfgM&feature= player_embedded.

* Palin's own relationship to wildlife is less clear. In *Going Rogue* (pg. 250) she says that a man who had fooled her into thinking he was Nicolas Sarkozy (bear with me) "started talking about hunting, and suggested we get together and hunt from helicopters, which Alaska hunters don't do (despite circulated Photoshopped images of me drawing a bead on a wolf from the air)....*He's got to be drunk,* I thought." On the other hand, regardless of whether Alaskans shoot wolves from helicopters, during the Palin administration the Alaskan government offered $150 to anyone who could shoot a wolf from an *airplane,* and Palin approved a $400,000 "educational" program to advertise the practice. (For more on this, including Palin's false claims that killing wolves was part of a scientifically sound wildlife management program, see "Her deadly wolf program: With a disdain for science that alarms wildlife experts, Sarah Palin continues to promote Alaska's policy to gun down wolves from planes," by Mark Benjamin, *Salon,* 8 Sept 2008; also "Aerial Wolf Gunning 101: What is it, and why does vice presidential nominee Sarah Palin support the practice?," by Samantha Henig, *Slate,* 2 Sept 2008.) Also worth noting may be Palin's successful promotion of construction considered likely to be detrimental to Wasilla Lake in 1998, while she was mayor, including her saying, "I live on that lake. I would not a support a development that wasn't environmentally friendly" (Benet, ch. 7)—and her then moving to Lake Lucille, the town of Wasilla's other lake, into a house that seems to have been paid for at least in part by construction contractors. To be fair, both Wasilla Lake and Lake Lucille are now considered "dead" lakes. For questions about funding for the Lake Lucille house, see, e.g., "The Book of Sarah (Palin): Strafing the Palin Record," by Wayne Barrett, the *Village Voice,* 8 Oct 2008. For more on Lake Lucille itself, see "Sarah Palin's dead lake: By promoting runaway development in her hometown, say locals,

Palin **not knowing which three countries were in the North American Free Trade Agreement** was reported on-air by Fox News Channel reporter Carl Cameron on 5 Nov 2008. Cameron also reported that Palin didn't know until debate preparations began that Africa was a continent and not a country.* Similarly, Michael Joseph Gross in "Sarah Palin: The Sound and the Fury," *Vanity Fair,* Oct 2010, reports that at the time of her nomination Palin didn't know who Margaret Thatcher was, although this seems to have changed: Palin's Facebook page of 14 June 2010 called Thatcher "one of my heroines."

Current discussion of **Israel,** particularly in Europe, resembles in tenor and factuality the conversation that swept Europe in 1348 about whether to burn the Jews for causing the Black Death. For some reason,† and to the detriment of Palestinians

---

Palin has 'fouled her own nest'—and that goes for the lake where she lives," by David Talbot, *Salon,* 19 Sept 2008.

* Note, however, that Cameron had previously been caught attributing fake quotes to John Kerry, including, re Bush, "I'm a metrosexual—he's a cowboy." (The Associated Press article on this, by Siobahn McDonough, 2 Oct 2004, appeared in numerous publications.) In November 2008, Palin told reporters that "I think if there are allegations based on questions or comments that I made in debate prep about NAFTA or about the continent versus the country when we talk about Africa there, then those were taken out of context and that is cruel." (Widely reported, e.g., "Palin hits back at 'jerk' critics," *BBC News,* 8 Nov 2008.) In an interview in March 2011, Palin said, "Rumors like I didn't know Africa was a continent, that's still out there, that's a lie." ("Will Sarah Palin run for president and can she win?," by Jackie Long, *BBC Newsnight,* 7 Mar 2011. The interview was with Long.) Carl Cameron still works for Fox News Channel.

† Anti-Semitism.

as well as Israelis,* large numbers of people who have never, say, read a book on the subject by someone whose credentials they trust, and who might be surprised by what they'd learn if they did, now hold as their strongest political belief that Israel—not just the right-wing government that it, like most western countries (including the U.S. and U.K.), currently has, but the entire country—should be dismantled, and its civilian population, 20 percent of whom are Arab, subjected to random violence, something that gets wished on no other people in the world. For more on this phenomenon, see *A State Beyond the Pale: Europe's Problem with Israel,* by Robin Shepherd, director of international affairs at the Henry Jackson Society, 2009, or, if you can take it, Anthony Julius's magisterial *Trials of the Diaspora: A History of Anti-Semitism in England,*

---

* If you don't think western activism based on Jew-hatred rather than actual sympathy for Arabs can and does harm Palestinians, note that by 2006 Palestinians had been so severely exploited and betrayed by Yassir Arafat, the PLO, and the Palestinian Authority that, despite favoring peace with Israel by a two-to-one margin at the time (according to Palestinian demographer Khalil Shikaki; see *Dreams and Shadows: The Future of the Middle East,* by Robin Wright, 2008; note also that polls show Israeli Jews, themselves constrained by assholes at home and abroad, tend to favor a two-state solution by the same ratio), that they voted for fucking *Hamas*—a Syria-based organization that, while providing far better social services than the PLO ever did, is formally opposed to, among other things, peace or even negotiations with Israel, cooperation with non-Islamic states in general, and, evidently, ever giving Palestinians another chance to vote. That the same jackasses who lionized Arafat (in 2004, BBC's Middle East correspondent Barbara Plett said on the air that she had cried at Arafat's funeral, prompting an internal investigation of anti-Israel bias at the BBC the results of which the publicly funded network refused to release) are now lionizing Hamas does not constitute humanitarianism.

2010.* Alternately, perform the following thought experiment: imagine the largest shareholder in Rupert Murdoch's News Corporation after the Murdoch family has turned out to be the government of Israel—instead of who it really is, which is the Saudi royal family. Now picture some British people.†

For evidence-based information on modern Israel and its history, two books that are particularly short and easy to read but at the same time heavily annotated and (to my mind) convincing are *The Case for Israel,* by Alan Dershowitz of Harvard, 2003, which is organized into chapters like "Did European Jews Displace Palestinians?" and "Is Israel a Racist State?," and *The Israel-Palestine Conflict: One Hundred Years of War,* by James L. Gelvin of UCLA, 2005. Longer books I like on the history of the mess include *Palestine Betrayed,* by Efraim Karsh, professor and head of the Middle East and Mediterranean Program of King's College, London, 2010, *One Palestine, Complete: Jews and Arabs Under the British Mandate,* by Tom Segev of *Haaretz,* 2000, and *A History of Israel: From the Rise of Zionism to Our Time,* by Howard M. Sachar of George Washington University, 1985. Robin Wright's *Dreams and Shadows* from a couple of footnotes ago is a great interview-based account of the more recent history. For even less of a commitment I recommend the attempt to separately describe the history of Israel from the perspectives of Israelis, Palestinians, and Arabs generally in the first chapter of *The Missing Peace: The Inside Story of the Fight for Middle East Peace,* by Dennis Ross, chief Middle East peace talks negotiator for the

---

* My own much shorter history of the British vs. Yiddish conflict will eventually be available in some form or other. And, I'm sure, will end anti-Semitism forever.

† Source re Saudi ownership: "How Fox Betrayed Petraeus," by Frank Rich, the *New York Times,* 21 Aug 2010; also widely reported elsewhere during the News Corp scandals that began in the summer of 2011.

Clinton administration, 2005, although the whole book is good.* If you don't have the time or interest to read even that much, but feel compelled to have strong opinions about Israel anyway, that's your business. By which I mean shut the fuck up about it, at least around me.

There are fewer books in English about **Tiananmen Square** than you might think.† For the crackdown and the origins and legacy of what has come to be called in China the July 4th Movement, the sources that have been most important to me have been *Tell the World: What Happened in China and Why,* by Liu Binyan with Ruan Ming and Xu Gang, translated by Henry L. Epstein, 1989; and *Out of Mao's Shadow: The Struggle for the Soul of a New China,* by Philip P. Pan, 2008. Liu was a prominent Chinese intellectual who was investigated by the Central Disciplinary Committee (which doesn't *sound* fun) after an earlier round of student protests in 1987. Ruan was one of the actual student demonstrators. I don't really know what Xu's deal was,

---

* Historical aspects that Ross elides or glosses over for speed in this chapter, but which I would personally recommend for any longer study of the topic, include the demographics of the region prior to the twentieth century (which are contrary to what is commonly imagined) and the decision in 1921 by Great Britain, which had been "mandated" by the League of Nations to set up a homeland for Jews in the western 20 percent of Palestine and a homeland for Palestinian Arabs in the eastern 80 percent, to instead give the eastern 80 percent to the son of *Sherif* Hussein of Mecca to form first Transjordan and then Jordan. Jordan to this day has a disempowered Palestinian majority. For demographics see particularly Karsh, Segev, and Dershowitz, above. For an in-depth discussion of the history of Jordan see *Britain, the Hashemites, and Arab Rule, 1920–1925: The Sherifian solution,* by Timothy J. Paris, 2005.

† For an interesting perspective on this, see "Censors Without Borders," by Emily Parker, the *New York Times Book Review,* 6 May 2010, although things have improved slightly since then.

but his chapter in the book is good. Their book overall, though showing some of the strains of having been produced so quickly after the events, is invaluable, and its narrative of the massacre happening en route to the Square rather than within it (an element semantically exploited by the Chinese government to argue that there was no Tiananmen Square massacre) was corroborated by leaked U.S. embassy cables published by the U.K. *Telegraph* in June 2011.* Philip Pan is the former Beijing bureau chief for the *Washington Post*. His book is brilliant and will make you newly appreciate your own liberty, then make you wonder whether you would fight for it as hard as some of Pan's heroes have. Li Gang is *that* guy's father for sure. Particularly helpful was his profile of Wang Junxiu.

The number of people killed remains unknown. There were at least a million people involved in the demonstrations in Beijing. Millions more participated in over two hundred other Chinese cities. There were 120,000 arrests afterward. The Chinese Red Cross is said to have initially reported 2,600 dead during the first night of shooting in Beijing alone, but later retracted that number under pressure from the government.†

---

* Unfortunately, the manner in which the WikiLeaks cables were disclosed tended to promote the Chinese government's obfuscation of the event. For example, a 13 June 2011 article in *The Telegraph*, by Malcolm Moore, while noting that "instead, the cables show that Chinese soldiers opened fire on protesters outside the centre of Beijing, as they fought their way towards the square from the west of the city," was headlined "Wiki-Leaks: No bloodshed inside Tiananmen Square, cables show."

† Nicholas Kristoff calls the number a "rumor" in "A Reassessment of How Many Died in the Military Crackdown in Beijing," the *New York Times*, 21 June 1989, which estimates the total killed in Beijing as 400–800. Other sources, e.g., "How Many Really Died? Tiananmen Square Fatalities," *Time*, 4 June 1990, say that the Chinese Red Cross did in fact report the number 2,600 directly to reporters, and only afterward denied doing so.

The **idea that closing a coal plant in China could quickly cause noticeable changes in child development,** likely due to a reduction in exposure to polycyclic aromatic hydrocarbons that can bind to and warp DNA, comes from the research of Dr. Frederica P. Perera of the Columbia Center for Children's Environmental Health. However, its presentation here is exaggerated and not at all meant to accurately reflect Dr. Perera's actual studies or findings. For more on the dangers of ash from coal plants, see "Coal Ash Is More Radioactive than Nuclear Waste," by Mara Hvistendahl, *Scientific American,* 13 Dec 2007.*

For more on **income disparity in China,** see "China's unequal wealth-distribution map causing social problems," by Sherry Lee, ChinaPost.com.tw, 28 Jun 2010, and "Hidden trillions widen China's wealth gap: study," by Liu Zhen, Emma Graham-Harrison, and Nick Macfie, Reuters, 12 Aug 2010.

For information on **how radio stations work** I am indebted to Douglas Thompson of Minnesota Public Radio / American Public Media Engineering and to the RCA section of The Broadcast Archive (oldradio.com) maintained by Barry Mishkind.

I first came across the idea that the **"H" in Jesus H. Christ,** while probably an *eta,* might also (as "an old bio major joke") stand for "haploid," in "Why do folks say 'Jesus H. Christ'?," by Cecil Adams, *The Straight Dope,* 1986. Other sources give different definitions of the "IHS" monogram, such as "Iesus Hominem Salvator," "In hoc signo," etc. But the "IHS" entry by René Maere in *The Catholic Encyclopedia,* ed. Herbemann et al., 1910, agrees with Adams.

---

* This article, because of its title, has been controversial. However, Hvistendahl's argument is that around the world coal ash delivers much more radiation to humans than nuclear waste does, and not that, say, a kilogram of coal ash is more radioactive than a kilogram of spent plutonium.

The **biblical quote about apples** is from Song of Solomon 2:12. In the King James: "Stay me with flagons, comfort me with apples: for I am sick of love." Which to me sounds more like Shakespeare than Psalm 46 ever did.

Note that while *fresh* **fog is transparent to infrared**, so-called old fog, which has had time to equilibrate in temperature with the air, is opaque.

The **amphibious boat** that appears in the book is based on models produced by the Sealegs corporation. See sealegs.com for pictures and other information.

Promotional materials of United Poultry Concerns quote the USDA National Agricultural Statistics Service as counting 8,259,200,000 "broiler" **chickens slaughtered in the U.S.** in 2000; the 22-million-a-day figure is just that figure divided by 365. Non-broiler chickens I don't know from. Incidentally, Humanefacts .org says chickens are typically slaughtered at five weeks of age but have a natural life span of seven years.

Ronald Wright argues in *A Short History of Progress* (see section on catastrophic paleontology, above) that **technology progresses logarithmically** because every new piece of it has at least a theoretical chance of interacting with every previously existing piece. Patent law, of course, would limit this.

The controversy over whether modern, or "atypical," **antipsychotic** medications are any more effective than older and much cheaper ones* was probably inevitable in a system where the

---

* They probably aren't, but they have somewhat different side effects and may be more effective for some levels of schizophrenia and less effective for others. See "Effectiveness and cost of atypical versus typical antipsychotic treatment for schizophrenia in routine care," by T. Sargardt, S.

only thing pharmaceutical companies have to do to get a new drug approved for sale in the U.S. is show that it doesn't kill people (at least within the time frame of the study) and that it works better than a placebo. (In other words, they don't have to test it against other medications, which in addition to being cheaper could be twice as effective with half the number of side effects.) Not to mention a system in which you can spend 11.5 billion advertising dollars a year* promoting new drugs that, if they were actually better, physicians would presumably prescribe anyway.

The **quote from Karl E. Weick** is from Weick's *Making Sense of the Organization,* 2001, Vol. 1, pg. 105, but cites work by him going back to 1985. I added the italics. Many thanks to Dr. Weick for kind permission to use it.

The statistics about "New World" populations and Spanish gold are from Ronald Wright's *What Is America?,* pgs. 20–30, but **Virgil Burton's worldview** is influenced by all three of Wright's books. (Again, see section on catastrophic paleontology, above.) Note that the term "First Nations" is uncommon in the U.S., where "Native Americans" is used much more often, but since the Ojibwe lands are on both sides of the border I've taken the liberty.

There are reasons to at least wonder whether **Hitler had syphilis** besides the chapter of that name in *Mein Kampf.* By the

---

Weinbrenner, R. Busse, G. Juckel, and CA Gericke, *Journal of Mental Health Policy Economics,* Jun 2008; 11(2): 89–97.

* This figure is from the 2009 report of the nonprofit US PIRG Education Fund entitled "Health Care in Crisis: How Special Interests Could Double Costs and How We Can Stop It," by Larry McNeely and Michael Russo. Note that the only western countries in which direct-to-consumer advertising of medications is legal are the U.S. and Australia.

end of his life, Hitler had numerous symptoms consistent with late-stage neurosyphilis, such as tremors, hallucinations, digestive problems, skin lesions, and so on. The memoirs of his former confidant and press agent Ernst "Putzi" Hanfstaengl (who also claimed to have invented the *"Sig Heil"* chant, basing it on the fight song of his alma mater, Harvard) say he heard Hitler contracted syphilis at a young age in Vienna. Most sources on the topic (e.g., *Pox: Genius, Madness, and the Mysteries of Syphilis,* by Deborah Hayden, 2003, which is agnostic) make a point of not trying to use syphilis to excuse or even explain specific actions taken by Hitler, but occasionally you luck into articles like "Did Hitler unleash the Holocaust because a Jewish prostitute gave him syphilis?," by Jenny Hope, the *Daily Mail* (London), 20 June 2007. In any case, the symptoms could also have had other causes. For example, D. Doyle in the Feb 2005 issue of the *Journal of the Royal College of Edinburgh* notes that "the bizarre and unorthodox medications given to Hitler [during the last nine years of his life], often for undisclosed reasons, include topical cocaine, injected amphetamines, glucose, testosterone, estradiol…corticosteroids [and] a preparation made from a gun cleaner, a compound of strychnine and atropine, an extract of seminal vesicles, and numerous vitamins and 'tonics.'"* Doyle calls Hitler a "lifelong hypochondriac," and concludes that "it seems possible that some of Hitler's behaviour, illnesses and suffering can be attributed to his medical care." See also "Did Adolf Hitler have syphilis?," by FP Retief and A Wessels, in the Oct 2005 issue of the *South African Medical Journal,* which examines evidence that, Retief and Wessels

---

* Seminal vesicles are glands in males that produce, among other things, an ingredient of semen that has no known function and is actually spermicidal. Since it follows the sperm out, it is sometimes theorized to have developed to prevent other males from impregnating the same female. But, again, see the footnote on pp. 124–126.

conclude, "swings the balance of probability away from tertiary syphilis."

For a relatively recent discussion of **the origins of syphilis,** see "Genetic Study Bolsters Columbus Link to Syphilis," by John Noble Wilford, in the *New York Times* of 15 Jan 2008.

Despite much subsequent information coming to light, the best book about Hitler in his **bunker,** as far as I'm concerned, remains *The Last Days of Hitler,* by Hugh Trevor-Roper, originally published in 1947 but revised, God spare me, until 1995.

The one-in-four figure for diabetes among the Ojibwe/ Chippewa is for people over twenty-five years of age, and is from "Diabetes in a northern Minnesota Chippewa Tribe. Prevalence and incidence of diabetes and incidence of major complications, 1986–1988," by SJ Rith-Najarian, SE Valway, and DM Gohdes, in *Diabetes Care,* 16:1 266–70, Jan 1993.

The story of Houdini shocking Arthur Conan Doyle **by pretending to remove the end of his thumb** is in *Houdini!!!: The Career of Erich Weiss,* by Kenneth Silverman, 1997, which is definitive and a great read.*

When I talk about **the ancients linking invisibility to bad behavior,** I'm thinking most directly about the parable of the Ring of Gyges in Book II of Plato's *Republic* (which is a clear influence on Tolkien, although it's interesting that in Plato, Gyges' use of the ring, whatever moral corruption it brings, leads to lasting material success for his descendants, one of whom is Croesus), but also about the association of vision with shame (and both invisibility and sightlessness with relief from shame) in *Oedipus Rex* and so on.

---

* Note that in his autobiography, *Magician Among the Spirits* (thanks to Jason White for the gift of this book), Houdini says, pg. xiii, "I firmly believe in a Supreme Being and that there is a Hereafter."

* * *

Current **digital pocket cameras** often have a simple IR filter over the light sensor, because few of them still use IR to focus. For example, if your camera emits a series of stuttering flashes before it takes a picture in the dark, it's focusing with visible light from the flash. In which case you could theoretically remove the IR filter and (to keep the signal from being drowned out) replace it with something that filters visible light but not IR,* ending up with a functional night-vision relay.

The fake article on **bull sharks** isn't meant to be entirely scientifically sound but mostly is, because it draws heavily on two actual research papers, "Osmoregulation in elasmobranchs: A review for fish biologists, behaviourists, and ecologists," by N. Hammerschlag, *Marine and Freshwater Behaviour and Physiology,* September 2006; 39(3): 209–228 and "Osmoregulation in Elasmobranchs," by P. Pang, R. Griffith, and J. Atz, *American Zoology,* 17: 365–377 (1977).

John Boehner spokesman Michael Steel† is quoted from "House G.O.P. Eliminating Global Warming Committee," by Jennifer Steinhauer, in the Caucus blog of the *New York Times,* 1 Dec 2010. **Darrell Issa** is quoted from "12 Politicians and Execs Blocking Progress on Global Warming," by Jeff Goodell, *Rolling Stone,* 3 Feb 2011. The number of investigations debunking the **"Climategate" scam** (five) is from "British Panel Clears Scientists," by Justin Gillis, the *New York Times,* 7 Jul 2010. Note that Darrell Issa

---

* The late, great hacker Mark Hoekstra, for example, used two layers of (developed) color film negative (Geektechnique.org, 24 Oct 2005). Hoekstra credits an earlier site with some elements of his method. Note Hoekstra's warning not to shock yourself on the capacitor. Better yet, don't actually try this.

† Not to be confused with former chairman of the Republican National Committee Michael Steele.

has never to my knowledge been convicted of anything, nor has he been charged with arson. For more on his *indictment* for stealing a car (1972) and indictment for grand theft (1980), both dropped, and for details about suspicions that Issa may have been responsible for the 1982 burning of a warehouse three weeks after he more than quadrupled the fire insurance on it (as well as for details about his arrest on gun charges, and biography in general), see "Don't Look Back: Darrell Issa, the congressman about to make life more difficult for President Obama, has had some troubles of his own," by Ryan Lizza, *The New Yorker,* 24 Jan 2011.

The mention of **the impact of climate change on shellfish** was inspired by "Dissolute Behavior Up North" from *Biogeosciences,* 6, 1877 (2009) as excerpted in the Editors' Choice section of *Science* magazine, 9 Oct 2009—an article that among other things proves there's no report so grim that someone won't put a crappy pun in its title.

For more on **the Koch brothers** and the ways they've fucked you and will continue to fuck you, see "Covert Operations: The billionaire brothers who are waging a war on Obama," by Jane Mayer, *The New Yorker,* 30 Aug 2010. The Kochs' 2011 meeting was described as a "four-day, invitation-only conclave of about 200 wealthy conservative political activists" by the Associated Press, 30 Jan 2011.

Two documents that are particularly useful for understanding the damage done by right-wing activist Supreme Court justices in *Citizens United v. Federal Election Commission* are the original dissent by Stevens (joined by Breyer, Ginsburg, and Sotomayor) and Laurence H. Tribe's essay on the decision that appeared on the website of Harvard Law School on 25 Jan 2010. The disapproving reaction to the decision by 2008 Republican presidential candidate John McCain is also interesting.*

---

* E.g. as related in "McCain skeptical Supreme Court decision can be countered," by John Amick, 44 blog, washingtonpost.com, 24 Jan 2010.

The quote from **Orrin Hatch** is from the (failed) confirmation hearing of Robert Bork, whom Hatch was trying to portray as apolitical, and who subsequently wrote the apolitical-enough-sounding *Slouching Towards Gomorrah: Modern Liberalism and American Decline*.* Note that three (Scalia, Thomas, and Kennedy) of the five Supreme Court justices who gave George W. Bush the presidency are still serving. On *Citizens United,* they were joined by Roberts and Alito.

According to Armand Hammer's former personal assistant, Hammer, the CEO of Occidental Petroleum,† used to brag that he had Al Gore's father, Senator Al Gore Sr., "in my backpocket," and would then "touch his wallet and chuckle."‡ For more on **Al Gore's financial ties to the oil industry,** see "The 2000 Campaign: The Vice President; Gore Family's Ties to Oil Company Magnate Reap Big Rewards, and a Few Problems," by Douglas Frantz, the *New York Times,* 19 March 2000. You may also want to check out *The Dark Side of Power: The Real Armand Hammer,* by Carl Blumay and Henry Edwards, 1992, although it's kind of a mess.

Even leaving aside environmental issues, the amount of **corruption in the George W. Bush administration,** and the extent to which it went unnoticed, is staggering. For example, when Vice

---

* Bork also, after years of arguing for tort reform, filed a million-dollar personal injury claim against the Yale Club after he fell and bruised his leg there. If you're the kind of person who can't wait for *The Haldeman Diaries* to come out as an e-book, the actual brief is online at http://online.wsj .com/public/resources/documents/borksuit-060607.pdf.

† And interesting character for a lot of other reasons.

‡ "Mr. Clean gets his hands dirty," by Neil Lyndon, *Sunday Telegraph* (London), 1 Nov 1998, pg. 1 of the "Sunday Review Features" section. Lyndon was the personal assistant. He also says in this article that he ghost-wrote Hammer's autobiography.

President Dick Cheney shot his friend Harry Whittington in the face on 11 Feb 2006, the story was widely reported, but usually in ways that repeated the White House's line that Katherine Armstrong, who owned the ranch where the incident occurred, was an old friend of Cheney's and (in Cheney's words) "immediate past head of the Texas Wildlife and Parks Department." Both may have been true (although Armstrong had resigned from the Texas Wildlife and Parks Department, to which she had been appointed by G. W. Bush, years earlier), but Armstrong was also a registered lobbyist, including for Parsons—a company with construction and engineering contracts in Iraq—and the defense contractor Lockheed Martin.*

Regarding Katherine Harris, see, e.g., "Harris backed bill aiding Riscorp," by Diane Rado, the *St. Petersburg Times,* 25 Aug 1998; "Harris now regrets her tale of terror plot: Leaders in Carmel, Ind., contest U.S. Rep. Katherine Harris's comments

---

* For more on the sleaziness of the Cheney hunting accident, see "No End to Questions in Cheney Hunting Accident," by Anne Kornblut and Ralph Blumenthal, the *New York Times,* 14 Feb 2006. Note that the quails the party was supposed to be shooting instead of Harry Whittington had been raised in captivity and placed into bushes upside-down to confuse them and limit their mobility. (Regarding an earlier hunting trip on which Cheney personally killed 70 farm-raised ring-necked pheasants, the editor in chief of *Field & Stream* told journalist Elisabeth Bumiller ["After Cheney's Private Hunt, Others Take Their Shots," the *New York Times,* 15 Dec 2003] that "I don't see anything terribly wrong with it, but I don't think it should be confused with hunting.") This raises the question of whether Cheney—who secured five draft deferments to avoid serving in the Vietnam War, had a daughter nine months and two days after the Selective Service said it would resume drafting childless husbands (Timothy Noah, Slate.com, 18 Mar 2004), and engaged in war profiteering for much of the rest of his life—would have happily gone to Vietnam if guaranteed he would only have to fight people raised in cages and placed upside-down into bushes by lobbyists.

about an alleged plan to blow up the city's power grid," Associated Press, published in the *St. Petersburg Times,* 5 Aug 2004; "Harris Shuns Spending Requests," by Keith Epstein, the *Tampa Tribune,* 3 Mar 2006; etc. Regarding the ties to industry of James L. Connaughton and other policy-making members of the Bush administration, including the companies at which they ended up, see "Bush Environment Chief Joins Power Company," by Ned Potter, abcnews.com, 5 Mar 2009. For more on Phil Cooney specifically, see, e.g., "Ex-oil lobbyist watered down US climate research," *The Guardian* (U.K.), 9 Jun 2005; "Ex-Bush Aide Who Edited Climate Change Reports to Join ExxonMobil," by Andrew C. Revkin, the *New York Times,* 15 Jun 2005 (nice ambiguity in the title); etc.

The facts of the **Iran-Contra scandal** during the administration of Ronald Reagan are not in dispute. On 13 Nov 1986, Reagan held a press conference denying the exchange had occurred. On 4 Mar 1987, he held another one admitting that it had but denying he had known about it. On 19 Jan 1994, the independent counsel appointed at the request of the U.S. attorney general released its report finding that "the sales of arms to Iran contravened United States Government policy and may have violated the Arms Export Control Act," "the Iran operations were carried out with the knowledge of, among others, President Ronald Reagan, Vice President George Bush," et al., "large volumes of highly relevant, contemporaneously created documents were systematically and willfully withheld from investigators by several Reagan Administration officials," and "Reagan Administration officials deliberately deceived the Congress and public about the level and extent of official knowledge of and support for these operations." Source: "Excerpts from the Iran-Contra Report: A Secret Foreign Policy," the *New York Times,* 19 Jan 1994. For a Christmas Day 1988 article on George H. W. Bush's pardoning of Iran-Contra

suspects, see "Bush Pardons 6 in Iran Affair, Aborting a Wein-
berger Trial: Prosecutor Assails 'Cover-Up,'" by David John-
ston, the *New York Times,* 25 Dec 1988.

**Jimmy Carter's financial ties to the Saudis and other Gulf
states,** which have come to include tens of millions of dollars
(at least*) in donations to the Carter Center, are known to go
back to 1978, when the Bank of Credit and Commerce International (BCCI; primarily funded by Sheikh Zayed bin Sultan Al
Nahyan, the ruler of Abu Dhabi), in secret partnership with the
son of an adviser to King Khalid of Saudi Arabia, illegally
bought controlling interest in the National Bank of Georgia. At
the time, Carter owed NBG $830,000, but the bank quickly
modified his loans, including by lowering the principal.† Prior

---

* Although the "FAQs" section of the Carter Center's website says "All
donations of $1,000 or more are published in our annual reports, available
for download," the most recent annual report downloadable as of this writing (2009–2010) lists the first eleven donors in the "$100,000 or more"
category as "Anonymous," and doesn't give specific amounts for donations
even from people it does name. This report, which states the Carter Center's assets to be slightly over $475 million, is downloadable at http://cart
ercenter.org/resources/pdfs/news/annual_reports/annual-report-10.pdf.

† An article in the *Washington Post* from 1980, at which time the Saudi
involvement in the purchase of NBG was known but BCCI's was not, notes
that controlling interest in the bank changed hands on 5 Jan 1978, Carter
announced that his administration was selling sixty F15 fighter jets to Saudi
Arabia on 14 Feb 1978, and NBG changed the terms of Carter's loans on 1
May 1978—a four-month period during which, as the article puts it, "The
United States' traditional pro-Israel policy was dramatically shifted to the
Arab side at a time when President Carter's family business [which owed
even more than Carter did personally] was heavily in debt to an Arab-
controlled bank." The article also notes that Carter's personal loan, "renew-
able each year, is still outstanding." ("Of Arabs, Weapons, and Peanuts," by
Jack Anderson, the *Washington Post,* 10 July 1980.) In my opinion the clear-

to being shut down in 1991 for fraud and money laundering, BCCI donated $8 million to the Carter Center. Afterward, its founder donated an additional $1.5 million.* What Carter's sponsors, who include OPEC and the Saudi Binladin Group, have gotten for their money is not fully clear, but may be only indirectly connected to oil policy. For example, in March 2001, Carter accepted the $500,000 United Arab Emirates' Zayed [i.e., the same Zayed who funded BCCI] International Prize for

---

est description of the purchase of NBG by the BCCI / Ghaith Pharaon consortium, and of the BCCI scandal generally, is, believe it or not, *The BCCI Affair: A Report to the Committee on Foreign Relations United States Senate by Senator John Kerry and Senator Hank Brown,* Dec 1992, which is also interesting as an example of how low-key American politics, and the world generally, seem to have been in 1992. (Available as a single, continuous PDF at http://info.publicintelligence.net/The-BCCI-Affair.pdf. See particularly pages 134–138.) Note that the loans to the Carter family that BCCI took over were already ones that "Bank regulatory officials said they would characterize…as improper but not illegal" ("Lance Bank Lent Carter Business $1 Million Without Full Collateral," by Jeff Garth, the *New York Times,* 19 Nov 1978). If you really can't stop yourself, note also that Carter's brother Billy, again *during* the Carter administration, accepted $220,000 from the Libyan government and (possibly for legal cover) became a registered foreign agent for Libya. The Carter administration's response when this was publicized was to depict it as a rogue act of self-enrichment, which it may have been, but Carter subsequently tried to use Billy as a liaison to Libya during the Iranian hostage crisis. For details, see the bipartisan Senate subcommittee report "Inquiry into the Matter of Billy Carter and Libya," 2 Oct 1980, available at http://intelligence.senate.gov/pdfs_miscellaneous/961015.pdf.

* See, e.g., "Seized Bank Helped Andrew Young Firm and Carter Charities," by Ronald Smothers, the *New York Times,* 15 Jul 1991; "Carter's Arab financiers," by Rachel Ehrenfeld, the *Washington Times,* 20 Dec 2006; *The Case Against Israel's Enemies: Exposing Jimmy Carter and Others Who Stand in the Way of Peace,* by Alan Dershowitz, 2008, 33–34.

the Environment, and at the ceremony called UAE member state Dubai an "almost completely open and free society."* In September 2006, Carter legitimized the word "apartheid" in reference to Israel in *Palestine: Peace Not Apartheid,* and two months later he called Israel's treatment of Palestinians "even worse...than a place like Rwanda."† By far the most serious

---

* On 27 Nov 2009, Johann Hari, writing for the London *Independent,* called Dubai "a morally bankrupt dictatorship built by slave labour." The *U.S. State Dept Trafficking in Persons Report, June, 2009* notes that "migrant workers, who comprise more than 90 percent of the UAE's private sector workforce...are subjected to conditions indicative of forced labor, including unlawful withholding of passports, restrictions on movement, non-payment of wages, threats, or physical or sexual abuse." In Jan 2010, a British woman was arrested for illicit sex in Dubai after she reported she had been raped ("Woman raped in Dubai charged for having illegal sex," by Hugh Tomlinson, *The Times* [London], 11 Jan 2010). Etc. As of this writing Carter's acceptance speech is still available on the website of the Carter Center.

† It may be worth noting that after *Palestine: Peace Not Apartheid* came out, and fourteen members of the Carter Center's advisory board resigned in protest, including a professor of Middle Eastern history at Emory who had formerly been the Carter Center's executive director, Carter told Wolf Blitzer on 21 Jan 2007 that "I've never alleged that the framework of apartheid existed within Israel at all." On 23 Jan he told an audience at Brandeis University that he hadn't meant to equate Israel with Rwanda either. He told the same audience that "this is the first time that I've ever been called a liar and a bigot and an anti-Semite and a coward and a plagiarist," thereby airing one of the central premises of Jew-baiting, which is that criticizing Jews and Israel is somehow dangerous and brave rather than trendy and remunerative. *Peace Not Apartheid* went on to sell 365,000 copies in hardcover in the U.S. alone. For information on the Brandeis appearance, see "At Brandeis, Carter Responds to Critics," by Pam Belluck, the *New York Times,* 24 Jan 2007. For the transcript of the Blitzer interview, see http://transcripts.cnn.com/TRANSCRIPTS/0701/21/le.01

allegation against Carter, however, is that in July 2000, while serving as an adviser to Yassir Arafat, he may have advised Arafat to turn down the peace deal that included essentially everything Arafat had been asking for during the previous seven years. Carter has been asked what advice he gave Arafat but has never answered. In any case, it was eight months later that Carter accepted the Zayed prize.*

The idea that **the November 1962 report to the Kennedy administration** had a significant impact on environmental policy is from *Overshoot,* by William R. Catton Jr., 1980 (see notes for catastrophic paleontology, above). The report itself,

------

.html. The figure on sales is extrapolated from a figure reported by Nielsen BookScan (which tracks around 75 percent of book sales) of slightly over 275,000.

* The offer to Arafat was for limited return of refugees, continued custodianship of the Temple Mount in Jerusalem, 100 percent of Gaza immediately, and 73 percent, rising to 94 percent over twenty-five years, of the West Bank. Arafat's rejection of it ushered in the current age of nihilism in Arab-Israeli relations. See, including for an eyewitness account of Arafat's rejection of the deal, *The Missing Peace* (recommended above) by Dennis Ross, the negotiator for the Clinton administration. (In 2007, Jimmy Carter was caught using maps from Ross's book in *Peace Not Apartheid,* but with the borders changed to make Arafat's rejection of the peace deal look more defensible. See "Don't Play with Maps," by Ross, the *New York Times,* 9 Jan 2007.) *Peace Not Apartheid,* Carter's possible role in the collapse of the Camp David talks, and his refusal to answer questions about this, as well as other information, are discussed in *The Case Against Israel's Enemies* (see above), 17–48. To be fair, the various parties with an interest in keeping the Palestinians as perpetual hostages may have paid Arafat directly. An audit by international donors to Palestinian causes after Arafat's death discovered $800 million in his personal bank accounts. See "Where Is Arafat's Money?," by Rees, Hamad, and Klein, *Time,* 22 Nov 2004.

"Natural Resources: A Summary Report to the President of the United States by The Committee on National Resources of the National Academy of Sciences—National Research Council," NAS-NRC Publication 1000, is available on Google Books* and is worth reading. For one thing, it's a government document that's only fifty-three pages long.

The concept of **"constructing controversy,"** and its invention by Hill & Knowlton, is discussed by Alan M. Brandt in *The Cigarette Century: The Rise, Fall, and Deadly Persistence of the Product That Defined America,* 2007, which is one of the best books I've read in the past ten years.

The statistic about the **population growth of New York City** is from *Melville: His Life and Work,* by Andrew Delbanco, 2005. 1819–91 is Melville's life span. Don't pretend you knew that.

The history of **Easter Island** appears as a warning in both Ronald Wright's *A Brief History of Progress* (see above) and in various works by Jared Diamond, the earliest that I know of being "Easter Island's End," in *Discover Magazine,* Aug 1995, and the most complete being the bestselling *Collapse: How Societies Choose to Fail or Succeed,* 2005.

Regarding the decline in **whale populations in the second half of the twentieth century,** climate change may be a factor. For example, from the early to late 1990s, during which time approximately a thousand minke whales a year are believed to have been killed by whalers, the number of minkes in the Southern Ocean (which circles Antarctica) is believed to have declined from 760,000 to 380,000. Blue whales, which have been protected since 1966, may currently exist in numbers as low as 5,000, down from their pre-whaling height of 275,000. (Source: "Whale population

---

* http://books.google.com/books?id=oS0rAAAAYAAJ&lpg. Why are web addresses so fucking ugly?

devastated by warming: Retreating of Antarctic sea ice reduces numbers of minkes by 50 per cent and fuels demands to keep whaling ban," by Geoffrey Lean and Robert Mendick, *The Independent* [London], 29 July 2001.)

The **quotation from Genesis** is from the New International Version.

Note that while people do pass an average of 50 percent of their **genes** to their children, only about 1 percent of their genes are **unique** in the first place, i.e., different from those of their co-breeder. Only about 4 percent are different from those of a chimp. (See, e.g., "Genetic breakthrough that reveals the differences between humans," by Steve Connor, *The Independent* [U.K.], 23 Nov 2006.)

For information that didn't quite make it in but that I'll use in the future, thanks to James Dorsey.

The plot of this book was partly inspired, of course, by the hoax perpetrated at Loch Ness in 1933 to rescue the city of Inverness as a tourist destination after the rail line to it was closed during the Great Depression. Two aspects were particularly important to me: the role played by London gynaecologist [*Brit sic*] Robert Wilson, who agreed to say he had taken what is still the most famous photograph of the monster,* and the brazenness (and ease) with which the conspirators invented a "history" of sightings of the monster going back to the Middle Ages. By far the best book I know of about the Loch Ness Monster and its myth is *The Loch Ness Mystery: Solved,* by Ronald Binns, 1985. All false beliefs should have as thorough and

---

* And is still called "The Surgeon's Photograph," even though Christian Spurling admitted in 1993 to both taking the picture and building the fake monster that appears in it.

sympathetic an investigator as Binns. Of the many books that present themselves as believing in the monster's existence, the most famous are by Tim Dinsdale, who claimed to have personally seen the monster on several occasions.*

Another case important to the book was the 1855 hoax in Silver Lake, Wyoming County, New York.† The fact that the hoax itself, despite being celebrated in Silver Lake every July, was almost certainly a hoax—that the Walker House Hotel *did* burn down, but almost certainly no mechanical monster was found in the wreckage‡—just makes it better.

Finally, an ongoing inspiration has been the conversation I've been having with Joseph Rhinewine, PhD, for the past few decades about whether it's better to be too gullible or too cynical. While I have no reason to think the Smurfs and *Anatahan* are actually related, neither do I have proof that they aren't.

---

* My favorite "believer" book about Nessie, however, is *In Search of Lake Monsters,* by Peter Costello, 1974, because of the following sentence, pg. 14: "Having had more than its statutory nine days, the Loch Ness monster had to give way to newer sensations: the Saragossa Ghost, the talking Mongoose of Cashen's Gap, the German Occupation of the Rhineland." I could look up shit from that sentence all day.

† 1855: Seven people at Silver Lake see a giant serpent swimming through the water. Other sightings follow. 1857: The Walker House Hotel on Silver Lake burns down. In the wreckage a giant mechanical monster is discovered, made of coiled wire and waterproof canvas and capable of being propelled under water by bellows.

‡ See: "The Silver Lake Serpent: Inflated Monster, or Inflated Tale?" by Joe Nickell, *Skeptical Inquirer,* Vol. 23.2, Mar/Apr 1999.

ACKNOWLEDGMENTS

PROFESSIONAL: Terry Adams, Reagan Arthur, Rebecca Bazell, Marlena Bittner, Sabrina Callahan, everyone who's taken the time to read my books, Heather Fain, Fischer Verlage, Hachette NY, Hachette sales staff, Ellen Haller, Michael Heuer, Markus Hoffmann, Barbara Marshall, MB Agencia Literaria, Michele McGonigle, Amanda McPherson, Sarah Murphy, numerous independent bookstore workers, Robert Petkoff, Michael Pietsch, Joe Regal, Michael Strong, Txell, Betsy Uhrig, Tracy Williams, Craig Young, David Young, Jesse Zanger, Sam Zanger.

PEOPLE WHO LENT SPACES IN WHICH TO LIVE OR WORK: Ben Dattner, Ilene and Michael Gordon, Cassis and Claude Henry, Monica Martin, Joe Regal, Alison Rice.

* * *

RESEARCH-RELATED: Robert Bazell, Cassis Henry, Seth Jones of Powell's Books, John Manning, Barbara A. Matthews.

PERSONAL: Christa Assad, Bazell family, Michael Bennett, Marlena Bittner, Joseph Caston, Ben Dattner, Rae Dunn, Gordon family, Cassis Henry, Dan Hurwitz, Tamar Hurwitz, Helena Krobath, Elizabeth O'Neill, Joe Rhinewine, Lawrence Stern, David Sugar, Kiko and Maria Torrent, Txell, Jason White, Johnny Wow, Hugh Zanger, Jesse and Corrie Zanger, Sam and Kara Zanger, anyone else who turns up named Zanger.

CANINE: Lottie, Bela, and Greta.

ABOUT THE AUTHOR...

JOSH BAZELL is the author of the national bestseller *Beat the Reaper* and holds a BA in writing from Brown University and an MD from Columbia. He lives in New York.

...AND HIS PREVIOUS BOOK

If you enjoyed *Wild Thing,* don't miss Dr. Pietro Brnwa's other adventure, *Beat the Reaper.* Following is an excerpt from the novel's opening pages.

1

So I'm on my way to work and I stop to watch a pigeon fight a rat in the snow, and some fuckhead tries to mug me! Naturally there's a gun. He comes up behind me and sticks it into the base of my skull. It's cold, and it actually feels sort of good, in an acupressure kind of way. "Take it easy, Doc," he says.

Which explains that, at least. Even at five in the morning, I'm not the kind of guy you mug. I look like an Easter Island sculpture of a longshoreman. But the fuckhead can see the blue scrub pants under my overcoat, and the ventilated green plastic clogs, so he thinks I've got drugs and money on me. And maybe that I've taken some kind of oath not to kick his fuckhead ass for trying to mug me.

I barely have enough drugs and money to get me through the day. And the only oath I took, as I recall, was to *first* do no harm. I'm thinking we're past that point.

"Okay," I say, raising my hands.

The rat and the pigeon run away. Chickenshits.

I turn around, which rolls the gun off my skull and leaves my raised right hand above the fuckhead's arm. I wrap his elbow and jerk upwards, causing the ligaments to pop like champagne corks.

Let's take a moment to smell the rose known as the elbow.

The two bones of the forearm, the ulna and the radius, move independently of each other, and also rotate. You can see this by turning your hand from palm up, in which position the ulna and radius are parallel, to palm down, where they're crossed into an "X." * They therefore require a complicated anchoring system at the elbow, with the ligaments wrapping the various bone ends in spoolable and unspoolable ribbons that look like the tape on the handle of a tennis racket. It's a shame to tear these ligaments apart.

But the fuckhead and I have a worse problem right now. Namely that while my right hand has been fucking up his elbow, my left, having somehow come into position by my right ear, is now hooking toward his throat in a knife-edge.

If it hits, it will crush the fragile rings of cartilage that keep his trachea open against the vacuum of breathing in. Next time he tries, his windpipe will clench shut

---

* And you can compare this to your lower leg, where the same setup is vestigial. The two bones of the lower leg, the tibia and fibula, are locked in place. The outer one, the fibula, doesn't even support weight. In fact you can take most of it out—to use as a graft or whatever—and as long as you don't fuck up the ankle or the knee, it won't affect the patient's ability to walk.

like an anus, leaving him at ReaperTime minus maybe six minutes. Even if I ruin my Propulsatil pen trying to trache him.

So I beg and plead, and coax the trajectory of my hand upwards. Past the point where it's aiming for his chin, or even his mouth—which would have been disgusting—to where it's aiming for his nose.

Which caves in like wet clay. Wet clay with twigs in it. The fuckhead crashes to the pavement, unconscious.

I check to make sure I'm calm—I am, I'm just annoyed—before getting heavily to my knees down next to him. In this kind of work, as in every kind of work, probably, planning and composure are worth a lot more than speed.

Not that this particular situation requires much planning or composure. I roll the fuckhead onto his side so he won't choke to death, and bend the arm that isn't broken under his head to keep his face off the frozen sidewalk. Then I check to make sure he's still breathing. He is, in fact with a bubbly *joie de vivre*. Also the pulses at his wrists and ankles are reasonably strong.

So, as is usual in these situations, I imagine asking the Great One—Prof. Marmoset—whether I can leave now.

And, as is also usual in these situations, I imagine Prof. Marmoset saying *No,* and *What would you do if he was your brother?*

I sigh. I don't have a brother. But I know what he's getting at.

I put my knee into the guy's fucked-up elbow and pull the bones as far apart as the tendons feel likely to bear, then let them come slowly back together into their positions of least resistance. It makes the fuckhead groan in pain in his sleep, but whatever: they'd just do the same to him in the ER, only by then he'd be awake.

I frisk him for a cell phone. No such luck, of course, and I'm not about to use my own. If I did have a brother, would he want me getting hassled by the cops?

So instead I pick the fuckhead up and fold him over my shoulder. He's light and stinky, like a urine-logged towel.

And, before I stand, I pick up his handgun.

The gun is a real piece of shit. Two pieces of pressed sheet-metal—no grips, even—and a slightly off-center cylinder. It looks like something that began life as a starter pistol at a track meet. For a second it makes me feel better about there being 350 million handguns in the United States. Then I see the bright brass ends of the bullets and am reminded how little it takes to kill someone.

I should throw it out. Bend the barrel and drop it down a storm drain.

Instead, I slip it into the back pocket of my scrub pants. Old habits die harder than that.

In the elevator up to Medicine there's a small blond drug rep in a black party dress, with a roller bag. She's got a flat chest, and the arch of her back boosts her ass, so she's shaped like a sexy, slender kidney bean. She's twenty-six after a bit too much sun exposure,* and her nose is the kind that looks like a nose job but isn't. Freckles,

---

* Doctors always know how old you are. We use it to tell whether you're lying to us. There are various formulas for it—compare the creases of the neck to the veins on the backs of the hands and so

I shit you not. Her teeth are the cleanest things in the hospital.

"Hi," she says like she's from Oklahoma. "Do I know you?"

"Not yet, no," I say. Thinking: *Because you're new on this job, or you wouldn't have such shitty hours.*

"Are you an orderly?" she asks.

"I'm an intern in Internal Medicine."

An intern is a first-year resident, one year out of medical school, so typically about six years younger than I am. I don't know what an orderly is. It sounds like someone who works in an insane asylum, if there are still insane asylums.

"Wow," the drug rep says. "You're cute for a doctor."

If by "cute" she means brutal and stupid-looking, which in my experience most women do, she's right. My scrub shirt is so tight you can see the tattoos on my shoulders.

Snake staff on the left, Star of David on the right.*

"You're from Oklahoma?" I ask her.

"Well yes I am."

"You're twenty-two?"

"I wish. Twenty-four."

"You took a couple of years off."

"Yes, but oh my God that is a boring story."

"It's okay so far. What's your name?"

---

on—but they're not really necessary. If you met thirty people a day and asked them how old they were, you'd get good at it too.

* The tattoo on my left shoulder—winged staff, two snakes—turns out to actually be the symbol of Hermes, and therefore of commerce. The symbol of Asclepius, and therefore of medicine, is a nonwinged staff with one snake. Who knew?

"St*aaaaa*cey," she says, stepping closer with her arms behind her back.

I should say here that being chronically sleep-deprived is so demonstrably similar to being drunk that hospitals often feel like giant, ceaseless office Christmas parties. Except that at a Christmas party the schmuck standing next to you isn't about to fillet your pancreas with something called a "hot knife."

I should also maybe say that drug reps, of whom there is one for every seven physicians in the U.S., get paid to be flirtatious. Or else to actually fuck you—I've never been quite clear on that.

"What company do you work for?" I ask.

"Martin-Whiting Aldomed," she says.

"Got any Moxfane?"

Moxfane is the drug they give to bomber pilots who need to take off from Michigan, bomb Iraq, then fly back to Michigan without stopping. You can swallow it or use it to run the engine.

"Well yes I do. But what are you gonna give me in return?"

"What do you want?" I say.

She's right up under me. "What do I *want?* If I start thinking about that, I'll start crying. Don't tell me you want to see that."

"Beats going to work."

She gives me the play slap and leans over to unzip her bag. If she's wearing underwear, it's not of any technology I'm familiar with. "Anyway," she says, "it's just things like a *career.* Or not having three roommates. Or not having parents who think I should have stayed in Oklahoma. I don't know that you can help me with that."

She stands up with a sample pack of Moxfane and a pair of Dermagels, the Martin-Whiting Aldomed eighteen-dollar rubber gloves. She says, "In the meantime, I might settle for showing you our new gloves."

"I've tried them," I say.

"Have you ever tried kissing someone through them?"

"No."

"Neither have I. And I've kind of been dying to."

She hip-checks the elevator "stop" button. "Oops," she says.

She bites the cuff of one of the gloves to tear it open, and I laugh. You know that feeling where you're not sure whether you're being hustled or in the presence of an actual human being?

I love that feeling.